SIEGE AT
TIAMAT BLUFF

ALSO BY DAVID DELEE

SIEGE AT TIAMAT BLUFF

A BRICE BANNON
SEACOAST ADVENTURE

DAVID DELEE

Dark Road
PUBLISHING

COPYRIGHT

Dark Road
PUBLISHING

For more information about new releases, special events, and exclusive content only available to subscribers, sign up to get David DeLee's newsletter.

https://www.subscribepage.com/daviddelee

Thank you for purchasing this book. We hope you enjoy it.

Semper Paratus
"Always Ready"

SIEGE AT TIAMAT BLUFF

"Breathe soft, ye winds, Ye waves in silence rest."
John Gay - "An Epistle to a Lady" 1714

PROLOGUE

March 2003
Northern Iraqi Kurdistan

IT WAS GENERAL WILLIAM TECUMSEH Sherman during the Civil War who coined the phrase: War is Hell. And he was right. Right on the freakin' money. No one understands how horrific war is like a soldier does. No one possibly could. Unless they've experienced it, lived it. Died a little because of it.

The general's sentiment was probably no less true then than it is today. The sounds, the smells, the desolation of it all. But, to my way of thinking... the searing, hot, dry heat of the desert, the arid air that baked into the regions of Northern Iraq in the early months of '03 epitomized the image of Hell in my mind. Way more so than them good ole Union boys had to deal with in the southern part of these United States back in the day.

I'd been in the Sandbox almost nine months already before U.S.-led coalition forces launched their incursion into Basra Province, kicking off the 2003 invasion of Iraq, led by a Special Forces amphibious assault from the Persian

Gulf. Over the next six days, massive airstrikes bombarded the country and dropped Airborne troops from the sky. U.S., British, Australian, and Polish forces joined up to fight with the Kurdish rebels. Their objective? To secure the northern part of the country.

The opening volley of a war that would last just three months and cost me my life.

I led a small CIA paramilitary team. We were called the Special Activities Division back then. S.A.D. An appropriate acronym, as it turned out. And maybe that's why they later changed it to Special Activities Center. Our group worked alongside Army Special Forces and with Kurdistan Peshmerga fighters to plan and coordinate an attack on a Sunni Muslim insurgent group controlling the area known as Iraqi Kurdistan in the north.

They held a number of mountaintop locations. Dug in, they had advantageous positioning, defensible against ground attack, but they were wildly vulnerable to airstrikes.

Guess what we did?

That's right. We ordered a barrage of Tomahawk cruise missile strikes. Coordinated with our six-pronged ground offensive, we aimed at taking the little buggers out and securing the area for the coalition.

Not surprisingly, we were met with heavy resistance. The fighting was fierce, but we made good progress. We took out several of our objective strongholds hours earlier than we'd projected. As the insurgent's defensive positions crumbled and they began to fall back, over the course of three days, we advanced, taking town after town.

But as we moved farther north, we got bogged down. Found ourselves trapped under sustained enemy fire for hours: mortars and a fortified DShK Soviet heavy machine gun nest. The deep valleys blocked our radio signals, preventing us from coordinating more air support or calling for reinforcements. Still, we fought back. The Special Forces guys with us made excellent use of their .50 cal. sniper rifles. One team of crazy Green Berets even launched a Mk 19 grenade launcher attack from the back of a ratty, old Toyota Tacoma. A move that allowed the Peshmerga to advance and strike hard with their 82mm mortars artillery.

Loud, the sights, the sounds, the smell and feel, it was like the wrath of God reigning down.

In the end, we drove the insurgents from the last of their strongholds. Chased them into the hills, valleys, and godforsaken gorges. Like scurrying little vermin. It was there, surrounded by caves in the rock walls north of anything close to resembling civilization, where everything went south—metaphorically speaking, we were traveling eastward into the northern hills.

Overnight, we continued our pursuit of the insurgents, pushing them farther and farther into the mountains but also toward the Iranian border.

And here's where things got sticky.

In a climate where our President accused Iran, Iraq, and North Korea of being an "Axis of Evil" and the International Atomic Energy Agency (IAEA) discovered two clandestine nuclear sites under construction at Natanz and Arak—their purposes unknown at that time—relationships weren't exactly rosy between a reportedly neutral Iran and the coalition forces, we pursued the insurgents all the way to the damn Iranian border.

There, some of the insurgents were turned back. Others, as they tried to cross the border, were arrested and detained by Iranian military forces.

And yet some were taken in. Given sanctuary.

The insurgents that couldn't reach the border or were denied entry hunkered down in the surrounding foothills and caves. We spent most of the next night just maintaining our position, keeping the insurgents pinned down, preventing them from advancing or escaping. There wasn't much else we could do, not without air support.

But every time we called for assistance. We were denied.

Too close to the Iranian border, we were told. Command wouldn't risk an incident with Iran. Instead, we were told to sit tight and wait for additional orders.

They left us there like sitting ducks.

That wasn't a situation I could tolerate.

The hours dragged on.

The cold night sky was lit up with tracer fire and mortar explosions. The boom and rat-a-tat-tat of gunfire filled the air. I made a decision. We were going to advance, take out the remaining insurgents, and accomplish the mission. Bureaucratic posturing and orders to the contrary be damned.

A Green Beret sergeant named Cook helped me dismount an M2 heavy machine gun from a Humvee. Carrying the thing by hand, together with a small squad of his men, my commandos, and a handful of Peshmerga fighters, we set out on foot, picking our way through the mountainous terrain. After several hours of sporadic engagements, we managed to seize the high ground before pushing through the valley, taking out additional small pockets of enemy combatants one cave-dwelling nest at a time. Driving the rest back toward the Iranian border.

Even then, the fighting was fierce. I learned later we killed over three hundred insurgents, while only twenty-two Peshmerga lost their lives, with zero casualties for the coalition forces.

Unfortunately, we also riled the Iranian border patrols so badly they joined the fight against, well, against everyone. In the predawn light, we couldn't tell enemy combatants from Iranian nationals, coalition troops from Peshmerga fighters.

As dawn broke, an AC-130 gunship arrived. It executed a pylon turn, circling the target area overhead, and pounded the ground with its 25mm GAU-12 Equalizer cannon and 105mm howitzer rounds. We could also hear extraction choppers in the distance.

We thought we were done. We were out of there. Saved.

Two UH-60 Black Hawk helicopters arrived as the AC-130 completed its strafing run, but it was too late. The Iranians had had enough and began firing on the choppers.

The Black Hawks didn't fire back.

Not hard to understand why.

If they had, it might've sparked a war with Iran. Not something the U.S. was prepared to do.

The choppers kicked up sand and pebbles and dust as they hovered erratically, trying to land in the evac zone while avoiding incoming fire. One chopper got low enough. I ordered the Special Forces unit to retreat, and they successfully hopped on board the first Black Hawk.

It rose into the swirling dust storm its own rotor blades created, carrying the troops away.

I watched them go. Five of us were left, along with a handful of Peshmerga fighters.

The second Black Hawk moved into position.

We remained behind boulders and in gullies, waiting, trying to provide cover fire for the hovering chopper without sparking a war. The chopper was slow to drop into position.

I called over the radio, "Get us the hell out of here!"

But my transmission fell on deaf ears. We watched from the ground, helpless, as the chopper lowered, then rose, dropped again, but never got close enough to the ground for us to make a run for it.

"Come on," I muttered. "Come on."

Amid a barrage of raining rocket launcher munitions, mortar fire, and small arms tracer bullets—Like I'd said before, God's wrath—my life, our lives, depended on that chopper reaching the ground.

It never did.

We were hunkered down behind rocks and swirling sand in a godforsaken part of the world—Hell. We watched as my commanding officer onboard the Black Hawk, a full bird colonel crouched by the cabin doors, looked down on us. A grim expression on her face. She callously waved a hand in the air. Up. Up. Up.

They were retreating.

The chopper rose, wobbled as the pilot dipped and swerved to avoid getting shot out of the sky.

He got them out of range.

We watched the Black Hawk leave. Grow smaller. Become a dot in that unforgiven early morning sky. We stared as it faded away in the harsh, searing white of the sun.

Left behind to die, or worse.

We remained. Abandoned. Helpless, as we witnessed that core military oath we'd been taught, believed in, lived by and died for—leave no one behind—crumble.

We were left behind.

CHAPTER ONE

Today

A ROUND, ORANGE RACING buoy floated on the undisturbed sea. The smooth ocean surface rippled gently, reflecting brilliant flashes of twinkling sunlight under a clear, cerulean sky. The sun burned white overhead. Early January, on the New Hampshire seacoast, the air was clear and cold.

Seagulls circled near the sandy shore of Hampton Beach. Peaceful. Tranquil. Serene.

In the distance, a low hum could be heard. Grew. The sound of small outboard motors, maybe jet skis or some other small watercraft. The engine buzz grew steadily louder. Getting closer.

The orange buoy bobbed unexpectedly. Violently.

Something below disturbing it.

The water nearby bubbled like a pot of water coming to a boil. It turned white and frothy. A geyser of water sprayed ten feet into the air.

At its center, a dark, torpedo-shaped object breached the surface. Water cascaded down its gray flank, slick and gleaming along its dark slate sides as a dorsal fin and flippers appeared. The sleek body shot skyward, arched, then barrel-rolled.

What at first looked like a breaching dolphin, closer inspection made it clear it was not. Not a living one, anyway!

As its tail cleared the water, the air filled with a high-pitched whine, the sort of sound associated with the engine noise of a jet ski catching air. Forward of the dorsal fin was a polycarbonate canopy—the same used in fighter jets—and the engine hum came from a supercharged two-hundred-forty horsepower, four-stroke MerCruiser engine encased in the dolphin's hind section.

This dolphin was, in reality, a personal submersible hydrofoil watercraft.

In the dry cockpit under the clear canopy, grinning like a fool, Brice Bannon pushed one handstick forward and pulled back on the other, putting the dolphin into another barrel roll before splashing down.

Ocean water washed over the panoramic, nearly 360-degree view around him. Bannon pressed the foot pedals forward, putting the craft into a dive. The watercraft dove and zoomed northwest underwater toward the next buoy.

Over the submersible's state-of-the-art sound system, the legendary country singer Jerry Reed sang "Eastbound and Down." And like Jerry and Burt Reynolds in the *Smokey and the Bandit* movies, Bannon had a long way to go and a short time to get there.

He leveled out, keeping the craft—which he'd nicknamed Flipper—at a submerged depth of five feet. He goosed the throttle, pushing Flipper to her max underwater speed of twenty-one knots, having the time of his life.

But, if he was going to win this race, he'd have to spend more time on the surface where Flipper could reach forty knots or more. Reluctantly, he pulled the handsticks back and aimed Flipper's bottlenose bow toward the surface, which he breached once more.

From his earpiece came a gruff voice as familiar to Bannon as his own. "'Bout time you came back up for air. You in this to win it or what?"

John "Skyjack" McMurphy, Bannon's best friend and brother-in-arms over the span of their Coast Guard careers. It had been the big, ruddy Irishman who'd talked him into competing in the First Annual Hampton Beach Submersible Hydrofoil Race for Charity. Seventeen competitors raced for a ten-thousand-dollar grand prize for the charity of their choice, along with a five thousand and twenty-five hundred dollars, second and third place purse.

Bannon belly-flopped Flipper and punched the throttle. He turned to his right to see a black and white whale-patterned hydrofoil racing at top speed but a hair behind him. With his canopy open, McMurphy's red hair whipped wildly in the wind and sea spray cast off Orca.

Bannon shook his head. The man was nuts. New Hampshire winters were notorious for cold weather and a lot of snow. This season had been no exception. The air temperature hovered at a little more than freezing. A fresh two inches of snow had fallen the night before.

At least he'd put on a parka, Bannon thought.

"Unless I'm mistaken," he called out to his friend. "I'm still ahead of you."

"That's because some jerk behind me was getting too close for comfort. Almost sideswiped me once already. I lost time avoiding a collision with 'em."

Bannon twisted around to port. There, he saw a dark green hydrofoil coming up fast behind them. In Bannon's opinion, it was an ugly design patterned to look like a barracuda. Not the most attractive of sea creatures to begin with. Its painted mouth realistically represented the predator's sharp, piranha-like fangs. Its flat, black eyes were disturbing and appeared to look everywhere at once.

It was the closest of the watercraft racers to Bannon and McMurphy.

The three of them had a commanding lead over the field of fourteen who jockeyed for position well behind them. Their crafts leaping and diving, leaving a wide V of white seafoam in their collective wakes.

Bannon passed buoy three on the final leg of a four-mile, oddly-shaped pentagon course. The final one-point-one-five-mile straight away would take them shooting past the viewing stands on the beach. Stands that were overflowing with cheering spectators who'd braved the winter cold to come out and cheer the competitors on.

New Englanders were a hearty bunch.

From there, the racers were expected to make a tricky fishhook turn around buoy four, then speed through the last mile to the finish line. With a final look at the closing barracuda, Bannon told McMurphy, "Looks to me like we've got this."

McMurphy said something about not counting his chickens when Bannon glanced left again, catching a movement out of the corner of his eye. Miraculously, the barracuda had closed the gap between them. They were suddenly neck and neck.

Bannon checked his speedometer. The needle hovered at four-point-one knots. For the barracuda to catch up like that, it had to be seriously overpowered. A violation of the rules laid down by the event organizers. But that was a problem for later, Bannon thought as he squeezed his throttle. The first order of business was to win the race. They could worry about dealing with a cheater later.

Flipper surged forward, skimming smoothly over the calm ocean water. McMurphy, in Orca, raced a hair's breadth behind him on his starboard side. Still, the barracuda was coming up fast, angling closer to Bannon on the left.

Jerry Reed had turned Flipper's speakers over to Commander Cody, who sang about driving his father to drinkin' in his Hot Rod Lincoln.

"What is he doing?" Bannon said more to himself than anyone, keeping a wary eye on the ugly craft speeding closer, gaining on him.

"What?" McMurphy asked.

"Crowding me," Bannon said. There was no reason for it. No tactical advantage for such a maneuver on a long straightaway.

Bannon goosed the throttle but was already getting everything out of Flipper he was going to get.

The barracuda surged forward.

Right on top of Bannon now.

He glanced over and caught a glimpse of the pilot, distorted by sea spray and water filming the canopy. Bannon saw a man in his late fifties or early sixties with solid white hair cut short.

A military crewcut. His features were tanned, weathered, and craggy. His jawline chiseled. He glared at Bannon from behind a pair of dark-lensed Nike Tailwind sunglasses.

The barracuda suddenly swerved hard to starboard, right at Flipper.

Bannon couldn't veer out of the way without risking running into McMurphy on his starboard side.

Instead, he called out a warning to his friend. Then shoved the handsticks forward and pressed the foot pedals down, forcing Flipper into a steep dive. Like an airplane, the craft could pitch, roll, and yaw. Submerged, Bannon pulled the right handstick back and kept the left one forward, executing a roll, twisting away from the barracuda as it sped into his space overhead.

Flipper jerked violently. Her tail got clipped by the recklessly piloted watercraft above him.

Tossed violently in the cockpit, Bannon was held in his seat by the five-point canvas racing harness he wore. He rolled with the impact, twisted Flipper down and away, then pulled back on the handsticks and pedals, surging the dolphin-like craft toward the surface.

At a steep angle, Flipper breached the surface and completed a 360-degree barrel roll before splashing back down into the water, sending a cascading fan of water into the air. A maneuver that was sure to please the spectators crowding the beach.

That was the furthest concern from Bannon's mind.

Anger bubbled up inside him at the recklessness of the barracuda's pilot. He urged Flipper into a tight turn, returning her to the racecourse lane.

His intention was e was to go after the barracuda. The race be damned. But in doing so, he saw a bad situation suddenly turn worse.

In stunned silence, Bannon watched as the barracuda leaped into the air, timing its jump to match McMurphy's bounding twist, his best effort at avoiding a collision.

But without success.

In mid-air, like two battling rams, the barracuda crashed into Orca.

The crafts' flanks slammed into each other just forward of their dorsal fins. Made of lightweight Kevlar, the watercrafts' hulls shredded upon impact, making a terrible renting noise.

As designed, Orca's rear section split open and detached, jettisoning the fuel tank to avoid an explosion. What remained of Orca rolled and splashed back into the water, belly up. McMurphy's canopy still open.

With its forward hull cracked and broken, the barracuda wobbled as it sped away, veering north, far off the racecourse.

Bannon angled Flipper toward Orca's overturned cockpit section. He counted the seconds before the neutrally buoyant craft rolled, automatically righting itself.

When it did, the open, waterlogged cockpit was empty.

McMurphy was gone!

CHAPTER TWO

THE UNITED STATES SECRETARY of Homeland Security, Elizabeth Grayson, sat in the plush beige chair in the senior staff meeting room. She stared out the window of Air Force One. Located over the forward portion of the wing, she could see the ground thirty-five thousand feet below through the partial breaks in the low cloud cover. The flight, a relatively short hour and a half from Washington, D.C. to Boston's Logan Airport, hadn't been in Grayson's plans until two hours earlier.

Her Chief of Staff, James Williamson, had burst into her office, flush-faced and breathless, with an urgent, last-minute message from the Oval Office. POTUS had requested her presence on the flight to Massachusetts. Wheels up in thirty minutes.

When you serve at the pleasure of the President, a request is never simply a request. And never not to be granted. Still, it left her more than a bit annoyed, and after a half-hour into the flight, she'd still not had an audience with President David Kingsley. When she'd asked Amal Haddad, POTUS's Chief of Staff, why Kingsley wanted to see her, Amal shrugged, saying she had no idea.

Grayson believed her.

Over the last three years, the two women had formed, if not a friendship, a close professional bond. Haddad was twenty years Grayson's junior, but they viewed the world in similar ways and had worked well together since Kingsley named the Lebanese-born attorney to be his Chief of Staff.

If Haddad told her she didn't know what Kingsley wanted, it meant the President hadn't shared that information with her. A rarity.

Thus further piquing Grayson's curiosity.

She declined a drink offer from the steward and went back to gazing out the window.

Ten minutes later, Haddad tapped on the open door. She wore a rose-colored pantsuit that complimented her dark skin nicely. "He's ready for you now, Liz."

Alone, they were on a first-name basis.

Grayson got up and smoothed her skirt. "Thank you, Amal."

She followed the woman to the nose of the plane.

Located under the aircraft's flight deck and crew lounge, the office and the President's suite were in the plane's forwardmost compartments, along with a fully functional medical bay, complete with an operating theater staffed by a doctor and nurses anytime the President traveled. Further back was the dining room and galley that could prepare up to two thousand meals, then staff and secretarial quarters. The midsection held the guest quarters and, finally, in the rear of the plane, the press corps.

Grayson had noticed they were traveling unusually light, with only a minimal number of support staff and only a handful of the regular press personnel onboard.

A Secret Service agent, a large black man named Franklin Gregg, stood stoically guarding the President's office door. The Secret Service fell under the umbrella of Homeland Security and, as such, ultimately reported to Grayson.

"Good to see you again, Agent Gregg," Grayson said.

"And you, ma'am," he said with just the slightest trace of a smile.

Haddad knocked on the office door.

From inside, Kingsley's Boston Harvard voice called out, "Come."

Gregg opened the door. Haddad stepped inside, and Grayson joined her.

Agent Gregg pulled the door closed behind them.

Inside the presidential office, Haddad said, "Madam Secretary Grayson, sir."

David Kingsley sat behind his desk in a dress shirt and red power tie. His sleeves rolled up his arms. He leaned so far back in his chair as to be practically laying down, his feet propped up on the desk with his shoes off. Wearing gold toe socks. A computer tablet on his lap. This was a pose he'd never take in the Oval Office. His reverence for the office was legendary. He never came into the room wearing anything other than a business suit. Even then, rarely did he take his suit jacket off.

Kingsley looked up from the computer tablet and removed his reading glasses. "Oh, Liz. Great."

He plopped his feet to the floor and sat up.

"Would you like me to stay, Mr. President?" Haddad asked.

"No, Amal. We're good. Thanks. Get some rest before we arrive in Boston. I suspect it's going to be a long night."

"Yes, sir." She backed out of the room and closed the door behind her.

Kingsley got up and crossed the room. "Sorry to shanghai you from Washington last minute like that." At the bar, he asked, "Drink?"

"Only if you're having one, sir."

"I am."

"Then a bourbon neat."

He poured the drinks from a crystal decanter into two matching crystal glasses. Three fingers. He dropped two ice cubes in his. He handed Grayson hers neat. "Come. Sit."

He directed her to the plush brown leather sofas that lined two-thirds of the room. They sat.

"What are we drinking to?"

He shrugged, swirling his glass. The ice rattled. "I just needed a drink."

Grayson received the President's itinerary daily, so she knew he was going to Boston for a political fundraiser that was doubling as his official re-election campaign kickoff. A college professor and successful manufacturing CEO before his foray into the political arena. He'd twice served as Governor of Connecticut before his successful long-shot race for President four years earlier. Now, it was time for him to fight for a second term.

She asked, "Why am I here, David?"

He smiled. "Always right to the point. Are you sure you're not from New York?"

He knew she wasn't.

A former four-star Army General, Elizabeth Grayson, had been a one-term Senator from her home state of

Louisiana. After which, she'd been the Deputy Secretary of Defense briefly before Kingsley's predecessor tapped her to run the Department of Homeland Security. A job she'd held ever since.

Kingsley stood up and paced the small area in front of his desk. "I've made two decisions." He rattled the ice around his glass and took a sip. "One an easy one. The other one? Not so much."

He stopped pacing and faced her. "I've decided to drop Vice-President Wright from the ticket."

Grayson arched an eyebrow. "Really?"

That the two men didn't get along was well known. The previous election had been a tooth-and-nail battle between Kingsley and the one-term Democratic incumbent. Both men were considered moderates and so catered to the same broad base while pretty effectively alienating the fringe extremists of their parties. Conventional wisdom, with history as its guide, gave the advantage to the incumbent. To break that log jam, Kingsley tapped former Marine General E. Forrester Wright, a darling of the far-right, to serve as his V.P. Thus, satisfying the more conservative members of the party, the Kingsley/Wright ticket narrowly defeated the sitting president in a close election that once more fueled the electoral college debate with the outcome still questioned in many quarters.

The camaraderie between the two men ended the next day.

"Are you sure that's wise?" Grayson asked.

She'd had her time in the political barrel during her one successful run for senator of Louisiana. The power struggles, smear campaigns, and spun truths. It all left her disillusioned and angry. Though many said she navigated it well. Better than most. Perhaps. Yet, she had no patience for the politics of... politics.

"I'm not an unknown, untested neophyte this time. I have over three years of real accomplishments I can run on now," Kingsley said, justifying his decision. "The changes we've made. The good work we've done. That's a record the American people can see. That we can show them. My opposition isn't nearly as formidable as last time. I don't need Wright anymore. If his supporters don't like it...I can weather that."

Grayson sipped her drink. "Are you trying to convince me or yourself?"

He smiled. "That's why you're here, Liz. You cut through all the crap like no one I know."

"I'm not your political advisor, David." She finished her drink and stood up. "I've got a job already."

He held up a hand, stopping her. "Which brings me to my second decision. The easy one." He took her empty glass and put it alongside his on the wet bar. He turned around. "I'm smart enough to know dropping Wright is going to sting politically. There's no doubt. Enough to prevent my reelection? I don't think so. On its own, probably not."

"There's more?"

"I'm concerned about what Wright will do. What he'll say. He can be a vindictive son of a—"

Concerned soured Grayson's gut. "Does he have something on you? Something incriminating?"

"What? No." Kingsley waved his hand. "Nothing like that. But you know Wright. He's not the sort to accept my decision without—retaliating. What he says, what he does, whether truthful or not, you know that won't matter. Not in today's climate. Couple that with what I'll lose organically by dropping him."

"Double whammy."

"Exactly."

Grayson got along well with Wright. They were both military people. They agreed on a lot of the same things. They came at problems and issues the same way. Face forward and direct. They often disagreed with Kingsley together. The difference was Wright had always been a bit more hardnosed, black and white, while Grayson understood nuance. Concepts like negotiation. She could be diplomatic, while Wright lacked a certain—any—tact.

"Oh, no," she said. "You don't want me to talk to him. To be the one to tell him?"

"No. No, of course not. I can do my own dirty work." Kingsley began to pace again. "Thinking this all through. I've made up my mind. I can't work with Wright any longer. He's got to go. But I need to mitigate, reduce the fallout, downplay the attacks he'll lob against me. It'll be mud-slinging at its very worst. From a member of my own party. I'll lose a lot of his supporters, but I need to try and keep as many of them from abandoning the party as I can."

It was never just about the presidency. There were House, Senate, and gubernatorial elections to think about, too.

Kingsley stopped pacing and looked her square in the eyes. "That's why I'm asking you to run with me." He paused before formally proposing. "Elizabeth Grayson. I want you to be the next Vice-President of the United States."

CHAPTER THREE

BANNON'S HEART POUNDED IN his chest.

He moved Flipper alongside the damaged Orca.

Slamming the watercraft's canopy open, he was hit with a bracing, cold wind that he ignored. He forced down his anger and made a wide circle around the wrecked submersible. Leaning out, he searched the dark water for a shadow, bubbles, any sign of McMurphy in the water.

A forty-five-foot Coast Guard response boat assigned to patrol the water was on standby in case of an emergency. This certainly qualified, Bannon thought bitterly, catching sight of the boat speeding toward the wreck from the corner of his eye. The boat crewed with four guardsmen, and while they'd be proficient in first-aid, there'd be no medical personnel on board.

Bannon didn't wait for them.

He completed a circle around Orca and still found no sight of McMurphy.

He shut Flipper off, unsnapped his canvas harness, and dove into the icy cold water of the Atlantic without a moment's hesitation. Unlike McMurphy, Bannon didn't wear a parka. He had had no intention of opening his canopy during the race.

Diving into the water, he would have discarded it anyway. Wet, it would only serve to drag him downward, which was surely what had happened to McMurphy.

The water was a dangerous forty-one degrees Fahrenheit. Without a proper winter wetsuit, 5mm neoprene or thicker, a person would experience muscle and nerve cooling—their ability to swim and stay afloat—in as little as ten to fifteen minutes. Unconsciousness in thirty minutes.

Bannon didn't think about any of that as he dove in.

The icy water hit him, shocking his system. The cold robbed his lungs of air. He gasped. Kicking hard, he frantically twisted and turned, searching for any sign of McMurphy. Dark and murky, it was difficult to see without a facemask. He blinked and continued to search the blurry water. His lungs burned, but he dove deeper.

Then, he saw it.

In the darkness, a black and white sneaker. Its laces waving in the water like sea kelp. To his great relief, the sneaker was attached to a leg clad in blue jeans.

Bannon kicked toward it. Swimming harder.

Within arm's reach, he grabbed McMurphy's ankle and pulled. Hard.

Bannon tugged at the pant leg, pulling his large friend from the dark depths below. He clawed his way up McMurphy's leg as they both were dragged deeper. He grabbed his friend's belt and pulled harder, twisting him around. McMurphy's eyes were closed. His red hair swirled. Bannon saw a gash over his left eye. A ribbon of blood drifted around it, darkening the water.

With his lungs about to burst, Bannon snaked an arm around McMurphy's barrel chest. He tugged him upward, kicking for all he was worth, desperately clawing for the brighter water above them, holding the unconscious McMurphy in a death grip.

He prayed they'd reach the surface before his lungs gave out. Before he gasped for badly needed air only to fill his lungs with frigid, cold ocean water.

Bannon burst through the surface.

He gasped and coughed, spitting out water in a splashing frenzy, holding McMurphy around his chest. He gulped at the icy cold air, exhausted, struggling to keep his unconscious friend's face above the waterline.

The welcome sound of water lapping up against a hull greeted him. He twisted, treading water, and found himself in the shadow of the Coast Guard response boat, slipping in close to him and the hydrofoils.

"There!" A shout out from the stern of the boat. A petty officer stood leaning over the rail. He waved his dark blue Coast Guard baseball cap and pointed at Bannon and McMurphy. "There they are!"

His arm still around McMurphy's chest, Bannon swam, dragging the big man toward the side of the boat where there was an opening between the rails. The lookout petty officer was joined by two seamen. Together, they lowered a rescue basket into the water.

Bannon rolled McMurphy into it.

The men hauled him up on the deck.

Bannon shouted, "He's unconscious. Not breathing. Got a gash on his forehead."

"We've got it," the petty officer shouted back. The seamen knelt beside McMurphy, still in the basket. They started CPR.

The petty officer called out, "Captain, better get us to the EMTs."

The town had provided police and emergency medical personnel for the race. They were stationed on the beach. The Coast Guard captain stood at the bow, a worried look on his face. He pointed at Bannon. "What about him?"

"Forget me. Go!" Bannon waved for them to go.

The captain nodded and jumped into the wheelhouse. He engaged the throaty twin diesel engines as McMurphy sputtered and sprang up into a sitting position. He spit out water and coughed.

The seamen jumped back in surprise.

McMurphy shoved the one giving him mouth-to-mouth away with a powerful swipe of his arm. "What the hell you two doing? Trying to kiss me?"

Bannon laughed, a release of pent-up anger and worry and unspent adrenaline. He wiped water from his face. His friend was going to be fine.

McMurphy leaned over the side of the rescue boat. "What the hell you doing in the drink?" Cupping his hand to his forehead, it came away wet with blood. "Jesus, my head hurts. What happened?"

"Later," Bannon called out. "Let them take you in to get checked out."

McMurphy opened his mouth to protest.

"Don't argue." Bannon had already turned and began swimming back to Flipper.

"Where you going?" McMurphy asked.

"To settle a score."

By the time Bannon reached Flipper and hauled himself into her cockpit, McMurphy was yelling at the crew to quit fussing over him. The response boat's big engines rumbled loudly and bubbled up white frothy water behind the stern as the captain swung the boat in a wide, deep turn toward shore.

Once more in Flipper's cockpit, Bannon hit the ignition switch and pushed the throttle, aiming the hydrofoil toward the beach, but he wasn't returning to where the temporary bleacher stands had been set up. For him, one race was over, but another had just begun.

From the corner of his eye, he saw many of the competing hydrofoils were lined up on the wet sand of Hampton Beach already, with only a few stragglers coming in around the last buoy to finish the race. The buzz of their engines on the air. Announcements were being called out over loudspeakers to great applause.

Bannon pushed Flipper fast and straight to the right, toward the north end of the beach.

With McMurphy in good hands, he was free to go after the barracuda and its dangerous pilot. He spotted the damaged hydrofoil, beached, a mile north of where the spectators were gathered. It lay on its side in the sand, a few feet above the lapping waves of the Atlantic Ocean.

Bannon aimed Flipper in that direction. He left the canopy open. In his soaking wet clothes, the icy January wind and cold sea spray quickly chilled him to the bone. He shivered but ignored that, too. His focus was on one thing and one thing only. The barracuda and the reckless, irresponsible pilot who almost killed his friend.

In less than a minute, he beached Flipper with a jarring stop and hopped out, pausing only long enough to shut off the machine. He was down the beach from the barracuda. Its pale green belly faced him as it lay on its side. He ran toward it, getting angrier with each pounding step he took. His sneakers splashed through the surf. The waves lapped over them, washing sandy foam in and out.

Behind him, someone shouted. "Bannon! Brice! Hold up!"

He recognized the voice. Reginald Singleton. The police chief of the thirty-six member Hampton Police Department. Bannon ignored him, too.

Only when he reached the opened cockpit of the barracuda did Bannon pause. It was empty. He glanced at the damage to the front hull and frowned, then looked around at the sand, looking for footprints. Something to tell him where the pilot who'd almost killed his friend had gone.

Singleton reached him.

The cop was a big man. As tall as Bannon at six feet but wider, like a linebacker. African-American. Dark skin and completely bald, he more often than not wore a green baseball cap—as he did now—with the word Chief embroidered in yellow on it. He wore blue jeans and a forest-green parka. His badge pinned to it, winking as it reflected the sunlight.

Bannon started to shiver. "Where is he?"

"We saw what happened. But by the time my guys got here," Singleton said. "He was gone." He held his hand up to cut off Bannon's response. "We're on it. Already out looking for him. I've got men checking the cars in the lots. I've got people at the station pulling traffic cams and beach surveillance footage to see where he went. We'll get him."

"I want him charged, Chief. What he did, it was intentional."

"Seriously?"

"He looked me dead in the eye before coming straight at me. And grinned. It was a vicious, evil smile."

"Hell of a thing to do just to win a race," Singleton said.

"I'm not sure that's all it was."

"What are you saying?"

Bannon shook his head. "I don't know. Maybe I'm wrong. Overreacting. Being hotheaded."

"I know you better than that, Brice. You're the calmest, most rational man I ever met in a crisis. What are you thinking?"

Bannon took a moment to gather his thoughts. Clear his head of his anger. "If he wanted to knock me off course, it's a dirty trick, sure, but I get it. Once I dived—got out of his way—there was plenty of time for him to peel away, surge ahead. He didn't. He went out of his way to hit Skyjack."

"You think you were targeted?" Singleton asked. "Why?"

"I haven't a clue, Chief."

"You said you saw him? Do you know him?"

"No."

"Could you recognize him if you saw him again?"

"Definitely."

Singleton put a hand on Bannon's shoulder. "I'll have my guys go through the entry forms. See if we can put an ID to this numbskull. In the meantime, let's get you a coat, or inside, or both. You'll catch pneumonia out here."

Reluctantly, Bannon let Singleton steer him away from the beached hydrofoil. Singleton was a good cop. He'd put in twenty years with the NYPD before 'retiring' and trying his hand at policing the Hampton Beach seacoast community.

"We're having a thing at the Keel Haul," Bannon said as they trudged through the sand, his teeth chattering. "It was supposed to have been a victory celebration."

"And it will be," Singleton said, adding, "Just not for you or Skyjack. The charities involved made a ton of money for some really good causes. As for that idiot, don't let him spoil what was a good thing."

"You're right, Chief. Of course. And thanks."

"Speaking of Skyjack, how is the big guy anyway?"

"Banged up. Hit his head."

"Oh, that hard head of his." Singleton laughed. "Then he'll be just fine."

CHAPTER FOUR

BY MID-AFTERNOON, THE KEEL HAUL, Bannon's seacoast tavern, was in full swing.

Music played from the jukebox—country—and all the tables and booths were occupied by people, young and old. Animated conversation and laughter filled the place. A rarity off-season for a place many considered a local dive, but it held a warm and special place in Brice Bannon's heart.

Bannon was an orphan. His parents were killed before he'd reached the age of four. After that, he grew up in the system, having never known his mom and dad. He had no memory of them. He had no brothers or sisters, no next of kin. He bounced from foster home to foster home. Some good. Others, not so much. His stays were never long, and he formed no lasting bonds with any of the families with which he stayed.

At eighteen, he enlisted in the Coast Guard and served several years in the enlisted ranks before attending their officer candidate program and earning his commission. The coasties were the only family he'd ever known. One that he loved. But, fifteen years of military service never provided him with a place to call home. That was something he'd yearned for all his life.

He found it in the Keel Haul.

He'd bought it five years earlier. Bannon had lovingly renovated the gin joint to resemble the interior of the sailing ships of old he admired so much. The craftsmanship of the old frigates and galleons, the brigantines, and the clippers. Ships unlike anything constructed today.

The bar had highly polished, knotty pine walls. The ceiling had thick timber ribs. Lighted lanterns hung from the beams. Candle-like sconces glowed over the booths. Scattered throughout the bar were lashed wooden barrels, sea chests, ropes, anchors, pulleys, fishing nets, and period-appropriate coastal maps and globes. The scent of teak oil filled the air.

Above the bar was a small two-bedroom apartment where Bannon hung his hat as it were whenever he was home.

After his conversation with Chief Singleton, Bannon had gone upstairs to shower, shave, and change. Now, his mood improved and wearing a long-sleeved black polo shirt, khakis, and boat shoes, he joined the revelry downstairs.

His lead bartender, Tarakesh Sardana, hustled back and forth behind the bar, serving drinks. One of the closest people in his life, she took great pleasure in teasing him about the lack of business the Keel Haul usually did or didn't do, as the case may be. Not today.

She brushed an errant lock of jet-black hair from her forehead as she dug ice from the cooler and scooped it into drink glasses. "If I ever complain about this place being dead again, just shoot me."

"All for a good cause, Blades," he said happily, accepting a mug of beer from her. Blades, a nickname Skyjack McMurphy had given her, was far more than a simple bartender.

Raven haired with dusky skin, Tara was Egyptian by birth and nationality. A former Algerian National Navy officer, she'd trained with MARCOS, the Marine Commando Forces of the Indian Navy, their Special Forces program. They met when she rescued Bannon from a Taliban holding cell after he'd foolishly allowed himself to be captured.

The encounter had been an accidental occurrence. Fate.

She'd been in-country with a freelance mercenary group at the time. They'd gotten word from locals about the Taliban base and decided to raid it because, well, that was their stock and trade, harassing the enemy. Their only goal had been to disturb and disrupt Taliban operations. Luckily for Bannon, they did so on the day before his scheduled execution.

That was the first time she saved his life. There had been many, many times since.

Then, Bannon was in charge of a team attached to the Deployable Operations Group. The coasties' answer to the Navy's SEAL program at the time. After his rescue, Tara's group worked alongside Bannon's DOG team in an unofficial adjunct capacity. When her group disbanded—as those loosely affiliated groups often did—she continued to work with Bannon, Skyjack, and his team until the unit was decommissioned five years later.

Due to return stateside and be reassigned somewhere within the Coast Guard's domestic theater, Bannon and McMurphy decided instead to pull the pin. In doing so, they encouraged Tara to come with them to America, and she did.

Bannon sipped his beer and mingled with the crowd while from the jukebox, country legend David Frizzell sang about hiring a wino to decorate his home. Bannon paused and spoke with the locals he knew. He sought out and found the race winners and congratulated them, buying them drinks on the house. All in an attempt to put the bad events of the day behind him.

Until he heard back from Singleton, hopefully with a lead to the reckless pilot's identity, there was little more he could do.

He'd made the decision early in the day to call in his backup bartender, Ken, asking him to work. Eyeing the crowd that lined the bar and filled the tables and booths, he was glad he did. The young man rushed around the crowded room with trays of drinks while Tara kept up with the service behind the bar. There, people were stacked two deep.

The sight put a smile on Bannon's face.

Another thing that made him smile was McMurphy sitting at his customary seat at the narrow end of the bar where the service counter was flipped up. McMurphy scowled with his big hands wrapped around a beer mug. He wore a red Evinrude baseball cap. The cap covered the dressing over the cut on his forehead. He looked surly.

Bannon would describe McMurphy as warm and gregarious. Tara called him a big-hearted teddy bear. And he was unless someone angered him. When his Irish temper got the better of him, then it was Bruce Banner and the Hulk time. In those cases, what remained when he was done was usually scorched Earth.

Bannon approached him and slapped his shoulder. "How you feeling?"

"My head's ringing like a five-alarm fire bell."

"Not surprising. You cracked your skull pretty good."

The two had served in the Coast Guard for nearly fifteen years. Many of those years were spent together as part of the Deployable Operations Group until the program was decommissioned. In their mid-thirties, each retained his reserve status and officer's commissions. They continued to serve part-time in a reserve capacity.

When not serving his country, McMurphy told anyone who asked he was between opportunities. For both men, the truth was far, far different.

McMurphy didn't thank Bannon for saving his life. There was no need.

He had done it so many times over the years, and McMurphy had done the same for him. It went without saying they were grateful for each incident, every save. It was also understood either man would move Heaven and Earth, and Hell, too, if need be, to save the other. Given the nature of their real work, they knew they would save each other's lives many more times in the future. It was just a given. There was no need to dwell on it. So, they didn't.

"Who the hell was that guy?" McMurphy asked.

Bannon shrugged. "Singleton's looking into it. When he knows, we'll know."

"And then we kill him," McMurphy said.

"Maybe we don't go that far, but yeah, something like that."

"The way my head's pounding right now," he said, downing his beer even as Tara placed a full one in front of him, "don't bet on it."

She wiped the counter with a damp rag. To Bannon, she said, "Someone's here to see you."

She nodded toward the front door while Aaron Tippin sang about "Where the Stars and Stripes and the Eagles Fly."

Bannon turned.

At the door stood one of the last people on the planet he expected to see that night: Elizabeth Grayson, the Secretary of the Department of Homeland Security.

She crossed the room. Tall and thin. She wore a dark, three-quarter-length coat with a faux fur collar, her hands in the pockets. In her early sixties, she wore her naturally gray hair down and bouncy around her shoulders. It was a relaxed look as Bannon had only ever seen it up high and in a tight bun, held in place with military exactness. A handsome woman with thin, hawk-like features. She walked with practiced precision, developed from a twenty-year career in the Army where she rose to the rank of four-star general.

She cut a path through the crowd that parted like the Red Sea.

"What's Lizzy doing here?" McMurphy asked.

"No clue." Bannon put his beer on the bar and turned to greet her. "General. To what do we owe the pleasure?"

She pulled her hands from her coat pockets and tugged her black leather gloves off before shaking Bannon's hand. Her hand was soft and cool from just coming in from the cold. "Brice."

She turned to McMurphy, who started to get up. She put a hand on his shoulder, stopping him. "John, sit. I heard what happened. I trust you're okay?"

"Be better once I have my hands around that jackass' neck, and I'm done throttling him."

"I understand the sentiment," she said. "But I'd advise against homicide."

"I'll try my best, Lizzy." McMurphy's use of a casual nickname wasn't a sign of disrespect but the exact opposite. A term of endearment. Something he would only do when alone with her or within the confines of this group. She was one of the few people in the world he would go to the ends of the Earth to protect.

"Drink, ma'am?" Tara asked.

"A beer, Ms. Sardana. Anything in a bottle. And make it two." She turned to Bannon. "Would you join me for a word, Brice?"

CHAPTER FIVE

NIGHT COMES EARLY DURING the cold New Hampshire winters. Not yet five in the evening, and already the sky had darkened to a deep purple. A few stars were visible against the violet canvas overhead. The streetlamps along Ocean Boulevard illuminated the deserted main thoroughfare of Hampton Beach. A few cars were left parked along the street. Snow clung to the retaining wall and curb, browned by road and beach sand.

Bannon tossed on his dark blue parka. Together, he and Secretary Grayson strolled north along the beach. A few degrees above freezing, the wind off the water brought with it an icy chill that ruffled the fur collar on the hood of Grayson's coat and turned her thin cheeks pink. They clutched their beers in glove-covered hands. Crews from the town's park & recreation department had dismantled the bleachers used as a viewing stand for the morning's race. The iron rails and wooden boards were stacked in piles, waiting to be picked up.

Absent were the almost always present seagulls that filled the skies during the day, cawing while looking for food. The cold and night had driven them to shelter.

Bannon noted the black town car with government plates and tinted windows parked at the corner. He couldn't see him but knew at the wheel sat a U.S. Secret Service agent named Wheeler, watching. Both chauffeur and bodyguard Bannon had met him a few times. He considered Wheeler a good guy.

Grayson's job as head of the DHS wasn't a mandated protected position like the president, vice president, and their families, but the Secret Service, like the Coast Guard, operated under her ultimate command. 24/7 protection was a perk of the job.

They walked and drank their beers. Their breath clouded the cold air. Wheeler followed their progress in the car, cruising slowly northbound along the boulevard.

Grayson remained quiet and pensive. Bannon waited. They reached the New Hampshire Marine Memorial without a word exchanged between them.

The monument was a statue of a kneeling woman. Her gaze turned toward the open sea. She held a laurel wreath in her hands. It had been dedicated in 1957. Carved in the base is the inscription: *"Breathe soft, ye winds, Ye waves in silence rest."* Written by the poet John Gay in 1714. Around the statue is a semi-circular granite seat, twenty feet in circumference. Cut into the granite are the names of the two hundred forty-eight New Hampshire servicepersons lost to the sea during World War II and Vietnam.

Grayson stared at the ten columns of names and then gazed out to sea. At night, under a dark sky, the water looked cold and inhospitable. Unforgiven.

Bannon threw their empty bottles in a trash can. The rattle of glass against metal was loud in the quiet night air. He couldn't contain his curiosity any longer. "Not that I don't love seeing you, General. But what's up? Do you have an assignment for us?"

Several years earlier, after Bannon retired from the Coast Guard, Grayson had come to him—she and Bannon had first met on the battlefield in Afghanistan—with what he thought was a harebrained scheme that would never fly.

What he didn't know at the time was she'd already sold the President on it.

Frustrated by a system slow and clogged with red tape, Grayson wanted to create a small team of specially-trained, highly-skilled operatives to conduct unique, sensitive missions outside the normal preview of either Homeland Security or the Department of Defense. Or even the CIA.

"Black ops," Bannon had called it when she approached him with the idea, asking him to lead it.

"Secret, but not black ops," she said defensively. "A small, efficient, and qualified team able to respond to and investigate specific, targeted threats to the homeland. Threats that can't be effectively handled by standard operating means or normal military response."

"Sounds a lot like black ops to me," Bannon said, wanting no part of it.

"No," she insisted. "I'm talking about a single unit that's small enough and nimble enough to get the job done. One that might actually be able to make a real difference in this scary world of ours."

The general was nothing if not persuasive. She continued her pitch, laying out her plan, convincingly and with so much passion, Bannon couldn't say no. After a fair amount of negotiation, including Bannon's demands that he be allowed to choose his own people without interference or influence, that any and all Homeland Security, DoD, or any other assets deemed necessary by him be made immediately available to him without question. And finally, he wanted a direct reporting line to her and no one else.

She readily agreed to his terms.

Then, operating from a position of strength, Bannon pressed for one more demand.

He'd do it only if he and his team, whose core members were Skyjack McMurphy and Tarakesh Sardana, operated on an on-call, as-needed basis. He'd had enough of sitting around ports and on board ships twiddling his thumbs with nothing to do, waiting to be called into action. He'd spent too much downtime playing cards, doing make-work jobs, or training—not for the purpose of staying sharp, which he believed in, but to fill up the monotonous hours—between assignments when command had nothing better for them to do.

She agreed, and over the last few years, they'd run quiet, special ops for Grayson and, by extension, the President. Some of them pretty wild and hairy stuff. Bannon worried Grayson's silence now meant whatever was next would be their biggest undertaking yet, or the program was being disbanded. Decommissioned as his beloved DOG unit had been. He was wrong on both counts.

"No. No assignment." Blunt, as always, she said, "The President's asked me to be his running mate in the upcoming re-election. He wants me to be his vice president."

"Huh." Bannon had to admit he hadn't seen that coming. He guessed it had been a shock to Grayson, too. "What'd you say?"

"He just sprang it on me on the flight here. I told him I needed to think about it."

"Okay," Bannon said. Not sure what she expected him to say.

They began their stroll back down the beach.

Bannon liked and respected Grayson. She'd served a strong twenty-year military career in the Army. She'd served in and commanded combat theaters, which he respected. But, more importantly, she was one of those rare politicians who spoke her mind and not the party line. She had friends and enemies in equal measure on both sides of the aisle and enough political clout to get stuff done without compromising her position or her principles. Grayson was considered one of the five most powerful people in Washington, man or woman, and thus the world. But most importantly of all, he considered her a friend.

"Why?" he asked, breaking the silence between them and tripping over his own tongue to hastily add, "Not that you wouldn't be great. You would. I meant, what about the guy currently in the role, Wright?"

"He's dropping him from the ticket."

"Huh," Bannon said again, taking it all in as they walked on.

"I don't know much about politics," Bannon said, breaking the silence again. "Check that. I don't know a damn thing about politics, and I try to avoid it like the plague, but I thought Kingsley needed Wright to shore up his support from the party."

"He did for the first election. This time, he feels like he can run on his record." She added with a wry smile, "They don't like each other."

"That's no secret." But it wasn't the full story, and Bannon knew it. "Kingsley will never get the support he needs running on a strict centralist platform."

"Who says you don't know anything about politics?"

"You lay down with dogs…"

"Ouch."

"Present company excluded." Before he put his foot in his mouth again, Bannon said, "Kingsley thinks you can give him the same support Wright commanded."

Grayson nodded. "Enough to put him over the finish line against a weak opponent anyway. Yes."

They had walked a bit further when Bannon asked, "Makes you feel used, doesn't it? Like a pawn."

"That's not what bothers me," she said. "My entire career's been based on one guiding principle. To serve my country. The Army. The Senate. Now, this. You do what's asked of you."

"You don't have to. There are lots of ways one can do their patriotic duty. If you turn him down, do you get to remain where you are?"

She shrugged. "I serve at the pleasure of the President."

"Is he ordering you to be his running mate?"

Her negative response lacked conviction.

"Then I guess the question is," Bannon said. "What do *you* want to do?"

"Serve my country. In the best way I can."

"Then determine what that way is. You get to decide that, Liz, not Kingsley. Not anyone else." He stopped her. In the back of his mind, the question of his team and their future lingered. What happens to them if she's not Secretary of Homeland Security anymore? "You're not here to just seek my counsel, are you?"

"Yes, I am. What you think, more than most people in my life, is important to me, Brice. And I know you'll give it to me straight." She smiled. "Whether I like it or not."

"I can't tell you what you should do. Only you can do that."

"You're right. And yes, there is another reason I'm here," she admitted. "Do you have plans for the next day or two?"

"Nothing pressing. Why?"

"The President's asked me to join him on a campaign stop. I'd like you to join us."

"Stumping on the campaign trail? Shaking hands and kissing babies?" Bannon asked. "Thanks, but no thanks."

"It's at Tiamat Bluff," Grayson said.

"The city under the sea," he said. His face lit up, bright as a kid's on Christmas morning. "When do we leave?"

CHAPTER **SIX**

THE NEXT MORNING, IN a small two-bedroom brick house on a pretty, tree-lined residential street in Falls Church, Virginia, a Washington, D.C. suburb, behind a split rail fence with two cars in the driveway, the remnants of that night's snow still on the half-acre front lawn, Kate Holloway spread peanut butter and jelly on two slices of white bread. She slapped the sandwiches together and licked peanut butter off her thumb before cutting each sandwich. One diagonally and the other one straight across. She wrapped them in wax paper and shoved them into brown paper sandwich bags; one marked Kacey, and the other Karley, in black marker pen.

In the family room across from the kitchen, the TV mounted over the fireplace was on, tuned to CNN, but with the sound muted.

Kate Holloway called out, "Girls!" She added a small bag of potato chips to each sandwich bag. "Get a move on! The bus will be here any minute."

In response came the thundering sound of feet racing down the stairs. A second later, twin tornados in the form of blonde, nine-year-old girls sped through the kitchen. Backpacks were grabbed from the kitchen chairs. The sack lunches were snatched off the counter. Pleated school uniform skirts swirled under blue uniform jackets and starched white blouses.

"Bye, Mom," Karley shouted.

"Thanks, Mom," Kacey called out before their father pumped their brakes.

"Hold it right there, you two." His authoritative voice filled the hallway. Roger Holloway stood in the archway, adjusting his tie and blocking their paths. "Give your mother a proper hug and kiss goodbye."

Kate came out from around the kitchen island with a smile on her face. She bent down and hugged and kissed each of her little blonde munchkins. "I'm going to be gone for a few days, so be good for your father."

"We will," they said in chorus, enduring the hugs and squirming to escape.

"And more importantly," Kate said. "You two keep him out of trouble, too." She pointed at Roger. "He's the one we need to keep in line."

The girls giggled.

"You're funny, Mommy," Kacey said.

"Have a good trip," Karley shouted, darting around her father and running down the hallway. "Hurry, Kacey. I see the bus. Come on."

"Hurry, girls," Kate called out as Kacey charged after her older sister by seventeen minutes.

In his business suit with a mug in his hand, Roger leaned in and kissed Kate's cheek, handing her his empty coffee cup. "I'll make sure they don't miss it. Then I've got to run. I managed to arrange an early morning meeting with Senator

Strickland's staff to talk about that new Virginia highway and bridge improvement act we've been pushing."

Roger Holloway was an attorney with a lobbyist firm that advocated for cost-effective and more efficient legislation in areas of infrastructure and transportation projects.

"Bye. Have a great day," Kate called out as he was already halfway out of the house.

"Thanks. Give my regards to POTUS," he joked before the door closed.

Kate busied cleaning up the kitchen and, with a second cup of coffee in hand, went upstairs to change.

With her long blond hair gathered in a high, tight bun and wearing a dark business suit with slacks, a white shirt, and a tailored jacket, Kate opened the top drawer of her bedside table. She took out a holstered Sig Sauer P229 loaded with .357 Sig cartridges. They were designed to duplicate the performance of a 125-grain .357 Magnum load. She hooked it onto her belt, then took out the black leather case that contained her gold Secret Service badge identifying her as a special agent. Finally, she took out a small lapel pin. She pinned it to her jacket's lapel. The pin identified her as an agent to other Secret Service agents—if the severe hairstyle, dark suit, and dark Ray-Ban sunglasses, almost as much of a piece of equipment as her gun or her badge—didn't.

She thought about that scene in Men in Black. The one where Will Smith first slips on his sunglasses. Like his Agent J character, she said with playful, narcissistic pride to her reflection. "I make this look good."

Quickly, she cautioned herself. "Don't get too cocky."

But she couldn't help herself. At the moment, everything in her life was perfect. The girls were wonderful. After a brief rough patch a few years back with Roger, things between them were great and, in some ways, better than ever before. She couldn't even complain about her job. A year ago, she achieved the promotion she'd always dreamed of. Becoming the first female Secret Service agent in history to lead the President's personal protection detail.

Everything was perfect.

With a smile still on her lips, she went back downstairs.

She put the cup in the sink, grabbed her small wheeled suitcase standing by the door and scooped her keys from a pewter bowl on an antique stand in the hallway. Kate ignored the bracing cold. Not properly dressed for it, the car's heater would warm her back up quickly enough. Of greater concern was the thin layer of snow across the sidewalk. The last thing she needed was to slip and break an arm on the ice.

With her suitcase in the back seat of her silver Lexus, she slipped in behind the wheel. She backed out of the driveway and drove toward the end of the block without noticing the black sedan parked at the other end of the street. If she had, she'd have realized it wasn't a neighbor's car and how out of place it was.

But she was distracted, running late.

On the drive to Ronald Reagan Airport, Kate Holloway's thoughts were about the mission ahead.

A court trial requiring her testimony the day before had forced her to miss flying out with President Kingsley as had been scheduled. As the head of POTUS's close protection detail, she regretted not being with the President on Air Force

One. Though she'd flown on the plane hundreds of times already, the experience never grew old. Still, the chartered flight arranged for her and several others destined for Boston's Logan Airport wasn't exactly traveling in coach.

As for the day's activities in Boston, Kate's advanced team had been on site for the past two weeks. Working to vet personnel and locations for both POTUS' fundraising dinner the night before—which had gone off without a hitch—and a breakfast rally that morning.

All rather routine.

It also helped that Kate had the utmost confidence in Special Agent Franklin Gregg. A veteran agent and a very competent number two, he could act in her steed until she can join up with them later in the day. In time to supervise the President's visit to Tiamat Bluff, the so-called city under the sea.

If all went well, she'd meet up with POTUS and the rest of her detail in a few hours at Logan Airport. By then, Kingsley would be done with his breakfast rally, and Marine One would be standing by to fly them all out to a Coast Guard ship. A legend-class cutter: the *USCGC George R. Putnam.*

She'd never been on a cutter before. She smiled. So many new experiences. She whistled, looking forward to the day.

CHAPTER SEVEN

AT THE SAME TIME Special Agent Kate Holloway was driving herself to Ronald Reagan Airport, Brice Bannon stood at the pier behind the Massachusetts Bay Transportation Authority with two cups of hot coffee in his hands. The overnight temperatures had dropped into the single digits, with the pre-dawn temps only now climbing up to something close to freezing. A fresh blanket of snow had fallen, turning the Boston sidewalks and streets white again.

Thankful for his NorthEnd parka, Bannon sipped his coffee, still hearing McMurphy's whining in his ear. *Why do you get to go and not us?* Grayson's black town car rounded the corner and pulled slowly to the curb. Right on time.

Secret Service Agent Wheeler stepped out of the car, wearing his dark sunglasses, even though the overhead sky was washed-out and overcast. He looked around, gave Bannon an almost indiscernible nod, then opened the back door.

Grayson climbed out of the back seat. Her steel gray hair was once again pulled back and tight in a severe, military-style knot. "That'll be all, Tom. Give Marion my best."

"I will, ma'am. The missus is sure to appreciate the unexpected time off."

"Enjoy it," she said with a smile.

She joined Bannon. "Good morning, Brice."

He handed her the spare cup of coffee he held. The town car drove away. They watched as the brake lights flared as Tom Wheeler slowed to make the left turn at the next block.

"No bodyguard for this little excursion?" Bannon asked.

"The President will have enough Secret Service protection for both of us." She sipped her coffee, clutching it with both gloved hands. "Besides, Tom trusts you to keep me safe."

They strolled down the pier to a docked U.S. Coast Guard defender-class port security boat.

An aluminum-hulled vessel, it had a red rigid foam-filled collar with white lettering and an M240 machine gun mounted on the bow. A Coast Guard workhorse used for port security, search and rescue, and other law enforcement duties, the small boat was both quick and nimble. It had a single, midship wheelhouse and was powered by twin 225hp outboard engines capable of a cruising speed of thirty-five knots with a max. speed of forty-six. Regulations required the boat to operate with no less than a two-person crew, but the boat had the carrying capacity to accommodate up to ten people.

A seaman named Stevens, according to his name tag, dressed in the Coast Guard's standard solid dark blue ODU and a foul weather parka stood at attention on the dock. He wore a baseball-style cap embroidered with gold lettering: *US Coast Guard.* He saluted as they approached.

Grayson returned the salute.

"Morning, ma'am." He offered her his hand as she stepped through the cut-out in the gunwale to board the boat. "It'll only be a short trip out to the *Putnam*. Inside the wheelhouse would be the most comfortable place for you. Get you out of the cold, ma'am."

"Thank you, Seaman Stevens."

Stevens expertly pulled away from the dock and spun the boat in a tight circle, piloting them out to the heart of Boston Harbor. Ten minutes later, they pulled up alongside the majestic white hull—with its wide red and narrow white and blue racing stripe and Coast Guard shield on it—of the *USCGC George R. Putnam.*

They boarded from the stern and were welcomed aboard by Robert Tolliver, the ship's captain.

Bannon knew Bob Tolliver well. They'd worked together over the last couple of years as part of Bannon's regular reserve Coast Guard duties. A good man whom Bannon liked very much.

Tolliver shook his hand warmly. "I didn't know you were joining us, Commander."

"A last-minute invite by the Madam Secretary, Captain," Bannon said. "I've no official standing on this trip, so it's just Brice."

"Either way, glad to have you with us." He turned to Grayson. "We're ready to get underway whenever you are, ma'am."

"No time like the present, Captain," Grayson said. "But if I may impose. Could Commander Bannon and I join you in the pilothouse for the trip out of the Harbor?" She brushed a wind-blown lock of gray hair from her face, tossed about by a strong sea breeze. "I'd prefer that to being below deck. If that won't be too bothersome."

"Of course, ma'am," Tolliver said. "No imposition at all. Right this way."

He led them to the midship superstructure and up to the pilothouse. The room was large and comfortable. The forward section was taken up by the bridge and bridge crew, who manned five forward-facing workstations. Hot air pumped through the vents, chasing away the winter chill and dampness that even the hot coffee failed to do. Grayson crossed over to the panoramic view of the Harbor.

The Boston skyline in full view on the port side.

Tolliver said, "If you're all set, I'd like to supervise our getting underway."

"Of course. Thank you, Captain."

Bannon shook Tolliver's hand. "Good to see you again, Bob."

"You, too, Brice. Excuse me."

With the captain busy at the bridge, Bannon joined Grayson at the windows. Together, they looked out over the water, at the harbor and skyline. They watched planes land and take off at Logan Airport. The deck thrummed under their feet. The *Putnam* started to move, and the city began to slip away.

He said, "It never gets old, does it?"

"No. It doesn't."

Though Grayson served her entire military career in the Army, she grew up in New Orleans. Like Bannon and McMurphy, she'd developed a love for the water at an early age. Something she and Bannon had talked about at length over the years they've come to know each other.

Behind them, someone cleared their throat. "Excuse me, ma'am."

She and Bannon turned.

A seaman stood at attention. "Dr. Robin Larson is requesting an audience, ma'am."

"Of course," Grayson said. "Thank you, seaman."

The guardsman stepped back, turned, and retreated down the stairs, exiting the pilothouse.

A second passed before an attractive woman in her early forties stepped into the space. A dark-haired woman, Robin Larson, was casually dressed in blue jeans. They were faded, worn almost white along the thighs, and rolled up at the ankles. She had on black open-toe sandals, a loose black t-shirt tucked in at just the belt buckle, and a blue and white plaid flannel shirt unbuttoned and untucked with the sleeves rolled partway up her thin arms. On her head, she wore a wide, floppy brim, beige fedora with a black band. It appeared well used.

As she approached, she took off her oversized sunglasses.

Not a look Bannon would have expected from the youngest American female billionaire and world-renowned nautical engineer. A woman whose scientific breakthroughs and accomplishments had been lauded around the world. But then again, he guessed having achieved the level of professional and financial success she had, she could wear whatever she damn well pleased.

Her fingernails were painted bright red. A half-dozen bracelets jangled around her gold Ladies Rolex as she extended a hand toward Grayson. "When I heard you were on board, I just had to introduce myself. It's a pleasure to meet you, Madam Secretary."

They shook hands. "And you as well, doctor."

"Please, I'm just Robin."

Bannon knew, modest as she might be, she was not just Robin. Already familiar with the work being done at Tiamat Bluff, he'd done a deep dive into Larson's background after Grayson's kind invitation to bring him along.

Not yet forty, she had a net worth of over fifteen billion dollars and had graced the covers of Forbes, MIT Technology Review, and Fast Company magazine, among dozens of others. She held a doctorate in Engineering from George Washington University and had advanced degrees in Aeronautics & Astronautics and Civil & Environmental Engineering from MIT. An Advance Computer Science degree from Cambridge. She'd attended Barnard College, where she majored in Ancient Studies and minored in Greek Classics. She started her company, Aquabotics Technologies, at the age of twenty-three. They held dozens of patents for state-of-the-art advanced marine technology and underwater robotics applications. The company was employed by the private sector, several governments, and the military.

Bannon introduced himself. "Brice Bannon. Nice to meet you."

"Are you press or a government employee, Mr. Bannon?"

"Please, call me Brice," he said, avoiding her inquiry. "I'm looking forward to visiting Tiamat Bluff. I've followed its development for years."

"Is your interest professional or casual?" she asked, pursuing her unanswered question in a different way.

Bannon smiled while Grayson saved him.

"Brice is a decorated Coast Guard commander and a close friend. He's here as my guest." Grayson then changed the subject. "Let me just say, Doctor, what you've accomplished is nothing short of miraculous."

"Thank you, but I cannot take all the credit," Larson said. "It is an unprecedented joint effort between the government, private industry, and academia. I simply helped steer the project."

"You're being modest, Doctor," Bannon said. "The breakthroughs your company has made in both remote-operated and fully-automated underwater research vehicle technologies alone are nothing less than remarkable."

Grayson nodded. "It would not be an exaggeration to say you've created one of the most important modern wonders of the twenty-first century. A true city under the sea."

"Not yet." Larson seemed genuinely embarrassed by the praise. "And truth be told, there's really nothing new or all that innovative about what we've done. Not really. We've simply studied and brought together existing technologies from around the world and merged them into a single, functioning venue."

"Nonsense, Doctor," Bannon insisted. "You've built the first self-contained, self-sustaining underwater city in existence."

"When it is completed. Yes, that is the goal."

"A place that will benefit science, industry, the military, and contribute to the United States economically for decades to come," Grayson added.

"And I, for one, am interested in hearing a whole lot more about it," Bannon said.

Larson smiled. "And I'd like nothing better than to talk your ear off about it, but you'll have to wait and hear about it with the others."

"Others?" Bannon asked.

"President Kingsley's team has requested I put a presentation together for those people on board who'll be accompanying us to the Bluff. An overview of the project, if you will. Where we are and where we expect to go." She placed a hand on Bannon's shoulder. "But don't panic, Commander. It'll be short, and I promise not to bore you all to death."

"I doubt you could do that if you tried," Bannon said.

"Maybe, maybe not. Either way, they're serving lunch. I'm told there will be cocktails."

"Definite bonus points," Bannon said with a smile.

"And, Madam Secretary, I'm a big fan of yours as well. I've watched your career. Tracked your accomplishments as you've fought your way to the top. And doing so with all the grace and integrity one could ask for. I'm honored to have you join us. Now, if you'd both excuse me, I've got a few last-minute details to attend to before lunch."

"Of course, Doctor," Grayson said.

"One quick question before you go," Bannon said.

"Certainly."

"Tiamat. It's an unusual name," Bannon said. "I'm curious how you came to choose it."

"You're not familiar with ancient mythology, are you, Commander Bannon?"

"Please, call me Brice," he said, then answered, "A little."

"In the ancient Babylonian religion, Tiamat was a creation goddess. The "shining" personification of saltwater. She mated with Abzû, the god of freshwater, to create the heavens and the earth," Larson said. "The merging of salt and freshwater at the beginning of existence."

"A metaphor for the merging of the surface with the sea," Bannon said.

"What more fitting name could there be?"

"It works," Bannon said with a shrug. "As far as the legend goes."

She appeared curious. "How do you mean?"

"As I recall, Tiamat was also credited with being the monstrous embodiment of the primordial chaos. That she was described as taking on the appearance of a serpent or a dragon."

"That's true. But why?" Larson asked with a wry smile. "Do you know?"

"To war against her children. The first generation of gods. In retaliation for their murdering their father while trying to overthrow his throne. She was killed by her son, Marduk, the storm god, who sliced her dragon body in half. He used her ribs to form the vault of Heaven and Earth, her tears to form rivers, and her tail became the Milky Way."

"How gruesome," Grayson said.

"And correct. I'll admit to having cherry-picked the parts of the legend I felt appropriate," Larson smiled. "It appears there's more to you than meets the eye as well, Brice Bannon."

"You have no idea," Grayson said.

"I look forward to spending more time with you both later." She shook their hands.

Bannon nodded as Larson departed.

"Dragons sliced into pieces? Really, Brice," Grayson said. "How do you know such things?"

She knew his formal education outside of the Coast Guard ended at high school. "Sea legends, like nautical history, it's an interest of mine."

"As I recall, Ms. Sardana calls them obsessions."

An observation he didn't dispute.

But what tickled the back of Bannon's brain like an itch was another piece of the Tiamat mythos left unsaid. In her attempt to avenge her husband's death, Tiamat gave birth to eleven monsters: dragons, serpents, scorpion men, weather-beasts, and merpeople, and she set them loose upon the world.

With that cheerful thought rattling around in his head, Bannon joined Grayson to once again look out at the panoramic view the pilothouse offered of the City of Boston, now barely visible on the horizon. They stood silently watching the cityscape recede as the legend-class cutter turned and headed out for open water.

CHAPTER EIGHT

THAT AFTERNOON AT THE Keel Haul.

McMurphy sat at the bar, his fist around a thick glass mug of Coors Light, feeling restless. He wore old jeans, a plaid flannel lumberjack shirt, unbuttoned and untucked, and a navy blue t-shirt underneath. On it was a drawing of a helicopter in white with the caption: Pilots know how to stick it. A bright white bandage was taped to his forehead over his left eye.

Tara was behind the bar. Her black hair loose. It bounced around her dark face as she moved up and down the bar. She wore black leather pants and a breezy white blouse with the top buttons open, revealing a pleasant contrast between her sun-kissed dark skin and the white blouse.

The only other person in the place was Captain Floyd. An old geezer, as McMurphy called him. He'd seemingly come with the place when Bannon bought it a few years back. At barely five-foot-six, the little man sat hunched over his beer, wearing an old, gray Members Only jacket—a garment not seen in the wild since the '90—and a white captain's hat. With his two-day-old scruffy cheeks and his weathered skin, tanned and craggy. Put a black pipe in his mouth, and Captain Floyd was the spitting image of the Old Salty carved wooden nautical sea captain figurines they sell in every novelty shop and bookstore in Cape Cod.

On the TV, with the sound down, was the third leg of the World Curling Cup championship of all things: the United States against Russia.

Captain Floyd banged his empty mug on the bar. "Hey, toots. That means it's empty."

Tara strolled down the bar. She glared hard at Captain Floyd, who did not back down. She snatched the empty mug from his hand and waved it in his face.

"Do you have any idea how far up your—" The heavy front door of the Keel Haul opened and banged shut. "—I can shove this?" Tara finished.

Floyd smiled big and wide. "One can dream, sweetie. Especially if it were filled up." He arched a bushy white eyebrow at the hint. "Which would be nice."

Tara pulled the mug away and shook her head. "I have no idea why Brice puts up with you, old man." Still, she went to the tap and filled his beer.

McMurphy grinned despite the splitting headache he still had. A reminder of yesterday's hydrofoil crash and the gash it left across his forehead.

Chief Singleton strolled through the dimly lit bar, brushing snow off his shoulders and shaking it off his baseball cap. The flickering wall sconces reflected off the bald man's dark scalp.

"Hey, Reggie," McMurphy said.

"Skyjack. How's the head?" Singleton asked, noting the fresh bandage.

"Take more than that jackass to split open this old melon."

"Good to hear." Singleton plopped down on the stool next to him.

"Too early for a drink, Chief?" Tara asked.

"Is there ever such a time?" The former NYPD detective slapped a twenty down on the bar. "And back this one up, too." He indicated McMurphy and his half-filled mug. "On me."

"One Nut Brown Ale coming up," Tara said. A dark ale from the Ipswich Ale Brewery out of Massachusetts, Bannon began stocking it when he learned it was the cop's winter preference. She deposited a fresh Coors Light in front of McMurphy.

He downed his first beer and raised his second mug. "Thanks, Chief."

Singleton sipped his beer and looked at the silent jukebox. "Anything on that thing other than country?"

McMurphy crossed the bar. Scrutinizing the offerings for a minute, he made a selection. Otis Redding started singing "Sittin' on the Dock of the Bay."

McMurphy sat back down. "It was either that or Taylor Swift."

"Otis is cool," Singleton said.

"Yeah, he is." He and McMurphy clinked glasses to that. "So, what brings you around, Reg? Slow day at the cop shop?"

"I was hoping to talk to Brice. He around?"

"No." McMurphy pouted. "He ditched us. Took off to visit the city under the sea and left us behind. High and dry."

The cop furrowed his brow. "The what, where now?"

"Tiamat Bluff," Tara said. "It's a city they built under the sea."

Singleton snorted. "Yeah, and mermaids and leprechauns are real."

"Goes to show what you don't know, city boy. Mermaids *are* real," McMurphy said. "And don't be disrespecting the wee folk."

"No, seriously," Singleton said. "He's on some secret mission like you all do, and you can't tell me about it. Right?"

Until recently, Bannon and the others had successfully kept the local police chief in the dark about their extracurricular activities with the government. But, a good cop with twenty years of NYPD experience under his belt, Reginald Singleton was not some easily fooled local yokel. He'd taken note of the unusual activities circling around the bar over time. His suspicions were realized a few months back when a group of terrorists firebombed the Keel Haul, re-took a fugitive Bannon and his people were holding and killed a local Coast Guardsman in the process.

The cat was out of the bag, as they say. Afterward, he'd been pulled into helping them on a case or two, putting him on the fringe of their inner circle.

"No," McMurphy grumbled. "There really is this new, state-of-the-art city they've built on the ocean floor. It's offshore, out in the Gulf of Maine. Brice got invited to tour it. Left us here with nothing to do but twiddle our thumbs."

"Forgive Skyjack. He's a little grumpy about being left behind," Tara said.

"And my head hurts."

"And his head hurts," she said, offering him absolutely no sympathy. "Brice'll be back in a day or two. Is there something the B-team can do for you?"

"Ha. Some B-team." Singleton had seen the team in action, especially Tara, having accompanied her and Bannon onto an old derelict sub-chaser and witnessed firsthand as they savagely took out a team of enemy combatants. Especially Blades. "I wish I had you guys around when I was kicking down doors and busting heads in the Bronx. Back in the day."

Tara handed him a second beer and poured herself a gin and tonic over ice. "You held your own just fine, Chief."

"For an old guy, you mean."

She raised her hands in defense. "I didn't say that."

He smiled before turning to McMurphy. "I told Brice I'd track down that guy who did a number on you at the race."

"You found that low-down scoundrel?"

"Unfortunately, no."

McMurphy was surprised by that. From what he'd seen, Singleton was a damn good cop.

"Not from lack of trying," the cop said in his defense. "Turns out he was a last-minute entry. Paid his fees in cash. The name he used on the entry forms turned out to be bogus. Surprise. Surprise. I had my guys talk with the other racers and the organizers. Nobody knows this guy. It's like he's a ghost."

"Not the sort of behavior you'd expect from a participant in a charity event," Tara said.

"Right," the chief said. "That's what I'm thinking. Unless… "

He let the statement hang.

"Unless what?" McMurphy asked, picking up the thread and tugging.

"No. It's nothing. Probably nothing anyway."

"You've got something on your mind, Chief," Tara said.

"Spill it," McMurphy demanded.

"I'm just thinking, out loud, you know, like."

"Yeah," McMurphy said.

"Go on," Tara encouraged.

Captain Floyd jumped up and hooted. His fist punched the air. "Yeah! Take that, you Ruskies!"

The others looked at him.

"What?" He pointed at the TV. "We scored. We're winning." When no one responded, Floyd grumbled. "You put the stupid curling on the TV, not me."

He returned his focus to his beer.

"Chief," Tara said. "You were saying?"

"It's odd, is all," he said. "Traffic and surveillance cams found him getting into a dark, late-model Corolla. No tags. He used a fictitious name to enter the race. No one else knows him. I'm just wondering if it's possible, maybe, the guy was there because of you." He paused before adding, "You know your... other jobs."

The thought had crossed McMurphy's mind, but he hadn't given it any serious consideration. Neither he nor Bannon recognized the guy, so they were reasonably sure he wasn't someone from their past. They'd not heard of any new threats against them, and they were between assignments for Grayson at the moment.

"It's possible." McMurphy shrugged, outlining all the reasons why he'd dismissed the idea initially. "I just figured the guy was some idiot that wanted to win too much."

"Maybe," Singleton said. "You're probably right. Anyway, I'll get to the bottom of it. We're working on tracking down the registration and purchasing information on that ugly boat contraption he left behind. Those things aren't cheap. There's not a lot of companies that make 'em. There's gotta be a record of who bought it. If the owner's not our guy, he'll lead us to him."

He pounded down the last of his beer and stood up, leaving his change for a tip. "Gotta get going. You all have a fine day."

"You too," Tara and McMurphy said together.

He pumped a fist in the air at Floyd. "Go USA, Cap't."

Floyd waved him away.

At the door, Singleton stopped and turned. "They've actually built a city under the sea? You're not making that up."

"Building it, but yeah, hand to God, Reggie," McMurphy said.

Singleton shook his head while leaving. "Who in their right mind would wanna live underwater? The world's gone crazy."

CHAPTER NINE

BACK ON THE *PUTNAM,* the large legend-class cutter had been underway for over an hour. The seas were calm, and the sun followed high and bright in an azure sky. Crystal-clear after burning off the morning haze. A few slow-moving, white cumulus clouds followed their progress.

They cruised in an easterly direction, bisecting the Gulf of Maine. A natural, football-shaped depression bordered to the west and north by the mainland coast from Cape Cod, looping through New Hampshire and Maine and extending up to the Canadian provinces of New Brunswick and Nova Scotia. The Gulf had a surface area of thirty-six thousand square miles.

The seabed was made up of several banks or elevated seamounts. The largest of these being Georges Bank. Oval in shape, the underwater mountain range was roughly one hundred and forty-nine miles in length and seventy-five miles wide. It stretched from Cape Cod up to Cape Sable Island in Nova Scotia. The summit was three-hundred-thirty feet below the surface. The surrounding basins reached a depth of fifteen hundred feet below sea level.

Bannon knew from what he'd read—little of it available to the general public yet—Tiamat Bluff was being constructed on the leeward side of Georges Bank at a general depth of one-thousand feet. Located sixty-two miles from Boston Harbor, the *Putnam* could make the trip in two hours going all out, but they were traveling at a more leisurely pace of just twenty knots, extending their time on the *Putnam* by almost an hour.

Bannon and Grayson remained at the panoramic windows, enjoying the view and hot coffee brought to them by a seaman. Mesmerized by the calm, wide-open expanse of turquoise water, the sea stretched out to the azure skyline at the horizon, neither tired of the view.

Tolliver left his position at the bridge and joined them. "We're still a couple of hours out." He checked his watch. "If you'd like, ma'am, I could give you a tour of the *Putnam.*"

"That would be wonderful, Captain."

"Mind if I tag along?" Bannon asked.

"Hoped you would." Tolliver swept his arm toward the pilothouse door. "Grab your coats. It's cold outside."

They spent the next hour strolling the decks of the *Putnam* from bow to stern.

Named after George R. Putnam, the head of the US Bureau of Lighthouses before that agency merged with the Coast Guard in 1939. The *Putnam* was one of only a handful of ships designed and built to replace the aging Hamilton-class cutters. The legend-class vessel boasted an overall length of four-hundred-eighteen feet and a fifty-four-foot beam. With two diesel and one gas turbine engine to power the ship, they could achieve speeds of twenty-eight knots. They crewed with ninety-nine seamen and fourteen officers and could accommodate up to one hundred forty-eight personnel depending on the mission. The ship was outfitted and equipped to perform a variety of tasks, including search and rescue, port, waterways, and coastal security, conduct counter-terrorism activities, and various other law enforcement missions, as well as support a multitude of other military and naval operations.

As they stepped out from the hanger section, huddled against the January cold in their parkas, Tolliver proudly pointed out the *Putnam's* sensors and processing systems, going into great detail about its electronic warfare capability and countermeasure rapid decoy launchers. Then he told them about its combat suite, which included one bow-mounted 57mm naval gun, one midship-mounted 20mm anti-missile, an anti-aircraft gun, and six mid- and stern deck-mounted machine guns in .50 caliber and 7.62mm variations.

"Not that we anticipate needing any sort of firepower on this mission," he said, wrapping up the tour on the stern flight deck. "We also have an MH-65C Dolphin search and rescue chopper, two ScanEagle unmanned aerial and underwater surveillance drones, and," he pointed toward the rear launching ramp, "two 7-meter short-range prosecutor inflatables that can be launched from the stern ramp at speed."

"Very impressive, Captain," Grayson said.

She'd learned nothing she didn't already know from what she was shown, of course. As the Secretary of the Department of Homeland Security, which included the Coast Guard, she was fully briefed by the Commandant of the Coast Guard on all appropriations and expenditures made by the service, so she was intimately familiar with the legend-class cutters. But to experience it firsthand was certainly remarkable and not a bad way to kill time, she thought.

"How much longer before we reach the coordinates given to you by Dr. Larson, Captain?"

Toliver consulted his watch. "Less than an hour, ma'am."

"And Marine One?" she asked.

"They had a late start."

Worry lines creased her forehead.

"Nothing to be concerned about," Tolliver said. "My understanding is President Kingsley got a little... longwinded with the Daughters of the Revolution breakfast he attended earlier."

"Ah, yes," Grayson said with a smile. "He does like to pontificate."

"They should be arriving momentarily. We could wait inside if you prefer, ma'am?" Tolliver offered.

Grayson pulled a wisp of hair from her face and returned her gloved hands to the pocket of her parka. "No, Captain. I'd rather stay right here." She turned her face to the sun, warm despite the cold air, and closed her eyes. "Washington can be a bit... stuffy."

"I can imagine, ma'am. If you'd like, I can get an update on the President's progress for you."

"That won't be necessary," Bannon said. The first to spot Marine One's approach, he pointed. "Here they come now."

In the distance, a formation of dark, black specs grew larger in the sky. Three helicopters approaching.

Bannon knew, as a security measure, Marine One flew in formation with up to four additional, identically marked choppers. On route to their location, the helicopters would constantly shift, moving the aircraft that actually transported POTUS around, playing an aerial version of a shell game.

Upon approach, one of the three Sikorsky Sea King helicopters, informally called white tops because of their distinctive livery—color, graphics, and identifiers—advanced while the other two banked and peeled away to begin their journey back to Logan Airport, where they'd wait for orders to return and escort POTUS back to shore.

The remaining craft touched down on the flight deck while Bannon, Tolliver, and Grayson stood to one side, watching. Tolliver held his cap to his head against the updraft created by the main rotor blades. Bannon squinted his eyes behind the Ray-Bans he wore.

The helicopter powered down. The main and rear rotors slowed to a soft *chug-chug-chug.*

A marine in dress blues that Bannon hadn't noticed behind them marched toward the chopper. He unlocked and opened the hatch behind the cockpit and pulled it downward. The hatch formed a set of five steps. He then stood smartly at attention beside the folded stairs.

A minute passed before President David Kingsley appeared in the doorway. He paused to say something to the pilot and co-pilot, then emerged wearing a long, dark overcoat. A man approaching seventy, Kingsley was no spring chicken, but he was thin and fit. An avid runner and outdoorsman, he was an outspoken environmentalist and champion of fitness and good health. He raced every year in the Boston Marathon, refusing to give that up when he was elected to office. Much to the chagrin of his Secret Service protection detail, Bannon had heard tell.

Kingsley saluted the Marine before crossing the flight deck. He pushed his windblown white hair from his eyes. The helicopter's rotors had slowed significantly by the time he reached Grayson and the others, but the ocean breeze wasn't so accommodating. The man's coat whipped around his legs.

Tolliver snapped to attention and saluted.

Kingsley returned the salute. "Permission to come aboard, Captain?"

"Permission granted, sir." Tolliver dropped the salute and clasped Kingsley's outstretched hand. "Welcome to the *Putnam,* Mr. President."

"Thank you, Captain," Kingsley said. He nodded to Grayson. "Liz."

"Mr. President."

Kingsley turned his attention to Bannon. With a broad smile, POTUS gripped his hand in two of his, pumping it hard. "Commander Bannon. Good to see you again."

"And you, sir."

Over the breeze, Kingsley shouted, "I never got a chance to properly thank you for your work in the Oceanic Princess and Yankee Stadium attacks. Hell of a job you did. Hell of a job."

"It was a team effort, sir."

"Of course, it was," Kingsley said. "Please express my gratitude to your team, too. Of course."

"I will, sir."

POTUS released Bannon's hand and gripped his shoulder. "I just wish more people could know about your team's valiant efforts on our behalf."

"It's not an issue, sir. Frankly, we like it this way. The less fanfare, the better."

"That's a position I certainly understand, Commander," Kingsley said.

Kingsley's Chief of Staff, Amal Haddad, emerged from the helicopter wearing a dark three-quarter length coat over her pantsuit and carrying a brown leather satchel. With her was a young woman with blond hair wearing dark Ray-Ban sunglasses, like Bannon's. Even before he saw the earpiece in her right ear, her attire, her stoic demeanor, and her holstered Sig Sauer told Bannon she was Secret Service.

Haddad held a tablet in her hand. She looked at it. "Sorry to interrupt, sir," she said, "But we're behind schedule and—"

Captain Tolliver said, "Dr. Larson is expecting us in the officers' mess where lunch has been prepared."

"Excellent, Captain," Kingsley said. "Lead the way. I'm anxious to hear what the good doctor has for us."

CHAPTER TEN

"THIS WAY, SIR." TOLLIVER turned smartly. The President fell in step behind him, with the others following: Grayson, Haddad, then Bannon with the secret service agent by his side.

Bannon glanced at her and smiled.

The woman stared unflinchingly ahead. Ignoring him.

He extended his hand. "We didn't get a chance to be properly introduced. I'm Brice Bannon."

She leveled him with a hard stare. He suspected it would've been even more withering had it not been for the nearly impenetrable dark lenses of her sunglasses.

"I know who you are, Commander. We vetted every person on this ship and anyone accompanying the President to Tiamat Bluff, even last-minute add-ons."

"Didn't mean to create a fuss."

"I recommended rejecting the Secretary's request that you join us today. POTUS overruled me, Commander Bannon." She quickened her pace.

"A pleasure meeting you," he called out. "And you can call me Brice."

He didn't know if the pretty blonde with the severely pulled back hair had learned to be cold and rude at the Federal Law Enforcement Training Center in Glynco, Georgia, where the Secret Service trained their agents, or if she came by it naturally. He hoped it came from her training. If not, that would be rather sad.

They entered the superstructure. The last to step through the hatchway, Bannon pulled the watertight door closed behind them.

Tolliver led them through a narrow passageway, then down a steep flight of metal stairs. They went through two more open hatchways before they reached the Officers' mess on the main deck. Their footfalls echoed through the hollow steel corridors. Engine vibrations could be felt through the deck plates. The air was tainted with the faint, foul odor of oil. Bannon smiled. It felt like coming home.

Inside the modest cherry-paneled mess hall, a long table covered with a maroon and gold trimmed tablecloth had been set up facing the bulkhead where a white smartboard hung. Eight china place settings were arranged around the table. The white plates and cups were rimmed with a blue and thick red service mark. Centered on the plates and the sides of the teacups were the Coast Guard seal: a pair of crossed anchors superimposed by a life ring and a shield marked United State Coast Guard 1790 and their motto: *Semper Paratus*—Always Ready—surrounded by a line grommet.

Dr. Robin Larson stood with a short Asian man wearing an ill-fitting suit at the head of the table near the smartboard. He wore thick-lensed, black-rimmed glasses. As the group filed in and took their seats, she introduced her companion as Dr.

Reo Nomura. The man had advanced degrees from Japan's Hokkaido University Graduate School of Science in material science and earth and planetary dynamics. Her assistant and business partner for the past five years, she referred to him as the smart one between the two of them. He cast his eyes downward and blushed at the compliment.

Kingsley took his seat at the end of the table facing the smartboard. Amal Haddad sat down on his right. Grayson took the seat on his left. Bannon sat down beside Haddad. He knew her, of course, but they had never met. He introduced himself.

"A pleasure," she said. Cool. Professional. But neither friendly nor unfriendly.

Tolliver took his seat beside Grayson.

Kingsley indicated the chair next to Bannon. "Kate, sit. You should hear this. You're going to be down there right along with the rest of us."

"I've been fully briefed on the facility, sir," the cold Secret Service agent said. "There's no need."

"I insist."

"Then I can observe from here." The blonde pointed at the closed hatch. Clearly indicating she would remain standing.

"Don't be ridiculous. I want you to join us. Sit."

She sat down, looking quite uncomfortable doing so.

Bannon flashed her a smile. She looked away.

Dr. Nomura took one of the two remaining seats while Larson remained on her feet near the smartboard. She'd ditched her hat and sunglasses but had not changed her clothes from earlier. Still dressed in faded jeans and her plaid flannel shirt to make a presentation to the most powerful man in the free world. Her sleeves still rolled partway up her arms. While an attractive package, was it audacity or naiveté, Bannon wondered. Or did the rich and powerful just operate on a level different from everyone else?

Drinks were served and Tolliver announced lunch would be served momentarily.

"Why don't you get started, Doctor," Kingsley suggested. "I'm anxious to hear your presentation."

"Of course, sir." She clicked her remote and dimmed the lights. The white screen turned into a picture of the Earth. A blue and green and white marble slowly rotated on a field of black with bright white stars. "As most of you know, more than seventy percent of the Earth's surface is covered by water. Over fifty percent of the world's oceans are more than four kilometers deep. We have explored and learned more about the surface of the moon and Mars than we know about our own planet. The ocean remains our last great mystery, and it represents this planet's largest untapped resource. With all apologies to *Star Trek,* it is the world under the waves, not space, which is our final frontier."

She paused to take a sip of water and gazed at each person in attendance as if looking for someone to challenge her claim. No one did. "Over the next fifty years, the competition between nations to live and work at sea, and under it, will be the greatest technological rivalry to occur since America won the race to the moon.

"And it's already begun," she warned. "China is building a state-of-the-art, deep-sea platform in the South China Sea. Russia, Japan, and the French each have similar projects in various stages of completion. Underwater labs. Mining operations. Research facilities. All with the goal to claim as much of the underwater real estate and its natural resources as they can grab for themselves.

"When I learned of this, I made it my mission to ensure we do it first. And that we do it better." She aimed the remote and clicked. "Ladies and gentlemen. Mr. President. I give you Tiamat Bluff."

On the smartboard, a vivid, sloping underwater vista of bluish-purple rock and swaying vegetation appeared against blackish mountain ranges in the background. The view swept forward, racing over the bluish-green elevating expanse, rising from the lowest grade to highest—up the slope of craggy outcroppings, fanning coral, darting fish, and hydrothermal vents spewing heated water called white smokers.

The camera angle pitched and sailed around the embankment—Bannon felt like he was riding the back of an eagle but soaring underwater—until a large bluish-black dome dotted with long narrow streaks of yellow and capped with a glowing yellowish dome came into view.

Built into the graded rock were two smaller—but quite large—domes below the bigger, higher one. A long, narrow tube, half-buried in the seafloor, extended from the main structure and then forked, connecting independently to the lower two domes. Like the central dome, each had rows of long, narrow gaps of bright yellow light carved into them. Windows.

The image on the screen zoomed overhead and gave them a one-hundred-and-eighty-degree aerial view of the complex. From the main building, Bannon saw a dozen or more stubs extended outward and then capped off.

The underwater complex bathed in a reddish hue would've turned any Bond villain green with envy.

With a laser pointer, Larson identified the smaller, lower structures. "To the right is our power generation plant. Housed inside is a small nuclear reactor. We're using the same designs as the Navy's latest Columbia-class submarines. But we're also utilizing various natural resources, such as water and thermal climate methods and other experimental means, to supplement our power and energy needs. Some exciting and cutting-edge stuff. Dr. Nomura," she nodded toward the small Asian man, "is our resident expert on these matters and can give all the details you need, but basically he, and they, keep the lights on."

The red dot of her pointer circled the second building. "Over here is where our current mining operations are being done."

"Mining operations?" Bannon asked.

"Allow me to go through this, Commander. Then I'll be happy to answer any questions you have when I'm done."

"Of course." Bannon sat back and sipped his wine.

She returned her laser pointer to the screen and ran circles around the central dome.

"This is and will be the heartbeat of Tiamat Bluff. Its city center. Recreation, city administration, retail, and commercial space. Here, we have hotel accommodations, restaurants, several shopping promenades, and entertainment venues: movies, playhouses, concert halls. We even have," she aimed the pointer at the glowing top of the dome, "an 'outdoor' park." She laughed. "Not really outdoors, of course. But in my opinion, even better. Kanaloa Park lies under a large transparent dome. It has three-hundred-and-sixty-degree views of Georges Bank's magnificent vista, marine and plant life, and everything a modern city park has. A lake, a community pool with water slides, walking and bike paths, abundant green space, a gazebo, and even a bandshell with," she made air quotes, 'outdoor' seating."

Her pointer touched on the spurs Bannon had noticed earlier. "These will eventually become transportation tubes with monorail transport trains and moving pedestrian walkways that will radiate outward from the city center to our residential subdivisions. Our suburbs. All part of our future expansions, of course."

"How many residents do you expect to have?" Grayson asked, "Ultimately."

"I'm glad you asked." With a click of her remote, an overlay appeared on the screen. A gossamer bluish hue that showed dozens of transportation tubes—spokes—radiating out from the Bluff's city center in a spectacular starburst pattern, leading to dozens of smaller domes. But not only from the city center. Thinner tubes radiated out from the smaller domes to even more domes, interconnecting them. Spreading further and further away from the hub. It reminded Bannon of the molecular structure models he remembered from high school science class.

"Tiamat Bluff is in its preliminary stages. The main facility's current capacity is one thousand people. But that will grow as we complete lower levels and convert what are now various work modules into actual living spaces like the aforementioned hotels and residential apartment housing plans. The ten-year goal is for Tiamat Bluff to be home to five thousand people. Once schools, medical centers, emergency responders' services are organized and staffed, the next phase—our suburb development—will bring ten thousand more residents down to call Tiamat Bluff home."

"And right now?" Bannon asked.

"Actual homeowners? None yet. Tiamat is still classified as experimental. There are many, many hurdles: regulatory issues, safety inspections, impact statements to get through. A lot of red tape to untangle before that can be realized. But," she quickly added, "as it stands now, we have a varying population of between five hundred and one thousand personnel currently living and working in the main facility and the ancillary buildings," Larson said. "They're mostly construction workers, design engineers, miners, military personnel, researchers, and inspection workers.

"All of them away from their homes, their families, friends and other loved ones for extended periods of time. But, imagine one day, they'll be able to commute home and be with them, the way one commutes from Boston or Manhattan and other large cities today."

"I'd like to get back to my question about mining operations?" Bannon said.

"Of course." Larson smiled. Her enthusiasm for the project couldn't be ignored. She aimed the red dot along the conduits between the city center and the two lower buildings. "This facility is currently being used for private and public-funded scientific research. Primarily, the development of workable means to harvest the abundant natural resources from the ocean and beneath it. And to answer Commander Bannon's question directly. A significant function of Tiamat Bluff currently and in the future—and where a good percentage of our funding has come from—is from the private industry mining operations we support. As I said at the top of the presentation, the natural resources under the ocean available to us are…abundant."

"Underwater drilling?" Tolliver frowned.

"Yes," she admitted. "But in a new and unique way, with state-of-the-art technology and cutting-edge methods. Our top concern is to ensure we have minimal impact on the delicate ecological balance in which we are operating." She took note of Tolliver's concerned expression. "Our methods and operations have been studied and examined by every environmental impact group we could find. Our impact statements have been reviewed by numerous government and private agencies, watchdog groups, and none, not one, has found significant fault in our methods. In fact, the opposite is true. We've been praised for our methods and concern for the environment. No one is more dedicated to keeping the ocean's ecological system in balance than we are."

"That's good to hear," Tolliver said.

Bannon was relieved by this as well.

"Something else you gentlemen might be interested in. We've hosted a large number of underwater military training operations. Primarily with the SEALs, but also a number of Coast Guard training operations as well."

"Another question," Bannon said.

"Yes, Commander?"

"At what depths are we talking here?"

"I'm glad you asked. The Bluff is located sixty-two miles almost directly due east of Boston." She indicated the smartboard. The image switched to a map of the Gulf of Maine. She pointed to a lighter blue section of water beyond Cape Cod. "This elevated area here is the summit of Georges Bank. It reaches upward to around eight hundred feet below sea level. Its northern slope drops gradually to a depth here—Georges Basin—of twelve hundred feet." With a click of her remote, a side elevation view of Tiamat Bluff appeared. The domes now looked like half-buried golf balls on a gently rising slope. "The city center and recreational area have been constructed at one thousand feet below sea level. Our future expansion plans… " The starburst overlay reappeared on the screen. She pointed her red dot at the smaller domes. "Here, these are slightly above the one-thousand-foot mark. And these, of course, will be below. The power plant and mining operation are at the lowest point of the ocean floor in this area, at generally twelve thousand feet."

The screen went blank. Larson snapped off her pointer. And the lights came on. "Any more questions? I'll be happy to answer them here or once we've arrived at Tiamat Bluff. I look forward to having you all experience the many spectacular features the world's only city under the sea has to offer."

At the hatch stood two seamen. During the presentation, they'd silently wheeled in two linen-covered catering trolleys.

Larson smiled. "And it appears I finished up in the nick of time. Unless I'm mistaken, lunch is served."

CHAPTER ELEVEN

A BLACK, TORPEDO-SHAPED SHADOW loomed over the seafloor north of Georges Bank. It moved slowly out of the shadowy darkness, angling southwest as it approached the sloping seaward side of the mountain range. Traveling from New Brunswick, the vessel hugged the craggy slope of purple-blue rock, making its way predator-like toward Tiamat Bluff.

Sixty-five feet in length with a seven-foot beam, the mini-sub was powered by next-generation lithium-ion batteries. Silent and nearly undetectable by conventional radar and sonar, it cruised at a steady five knots. The engines emitted little more than a hum and a slight vibration. Inside, a pilot, co-pilot, and thirty-six men and women wearing black wetsuits and scuba gear sat in the dark, flooded compartment. A single pale red dot of light was the only illumination inside the chamber.

A mile north of Tiamat Bluff, the sub slowed to a stop. The divers inside tensed.

Though they were enclosed in a dark, windowless chamber, they knew they'd reached their target. The so-called city under the sea. A message appeared in the glass of their facemasks. The letters glowed in blood-red:

Prepare to disembark.

A soft hiss of air could be heard. The single red light overhead turned green.

The overhead hatches on either side of the crew compartment slid open. Opened by the co-pilot remotely. Because the chamber was already water-filled, the only change felt by the divers was a sudden drop in water temperature, for which they were prepared. Their wetsuits were 6/5mm thick neoprene and rated for temperatures of forty-two degrees and below. They wore full facemasks, hoods, gloves, and boots, all taped and sealed.

The scuba divers disconnected from the mini-sub's air supply. They connected their hoses to the air tanks strapped to their backs and swarmed from the vessel, emerging like bees leaving the hive.

Closed-circuit rebreathers reduced the amount of escaping air bubbles the divers produced, making their approach quieter than standard regulators, reducing the chance of detection by the skeleton crew left to oversee the Bluff's essential operations during the President's scheduled visit.

The sub hovered for several minutes before executing a slow turn to port before reversing course and departing the area.

The divers swam in formation until they reached a lockout hatch near the northwest section of the domed building. The divers hung around it as if waiting for a magic genie to say open-sesame.

The lead diver checked his dive watch. His expression one of annoyance.

A minute stretched into two. Then three.

Finally, there was a heavy thud. The hatch dialed open, like the aperture of a camera.

The divers swam two at a time through the opening into the flooded lockout trunk below. A large room that accommodated as many as forty personnel. They crowded in, adjusting their buoyancy until their finned feet touched the diamond-plated floor. Steel handrails were bolted to the walls. They clutched them as the light over the hatch turned from green to red. Overhead, the hatch dialed close. The dull, underwater sound of hydraulic pumps could be heard as the water around them bubbled and began to drain, being pumped back out into the ocean.

When the water receded to chest level, the group began to take off their regulators, facemasks, and hoods. They were a mix of ethnicities: Black, White, Hispanic, Asian, and a few women, Caucasian and of color.

The last to discard his hood, mask, and regulator was a man who most recently went by the name of Chase Lang. Over the years, he'd been known by so many names and assumed aliases; his real one was all but forgotten to him.

A commanding figure, his most prominent feature was his arctic-cold blue eyes. He ran his hand through his military-cropped steel gray hair and wiped water from his craggy, suntanned face. At first appearance, people assume he'd spent a lifetime on the water, his skin permanently tanned to a leathery brown. They were wrong. He'd spent a lifetime not on the water but on sand. In the desert. His superior fitness made pinning down his actual age difficult, over fifty for sure, but not yet sixty. Maybe or maybe not.

Like the others, while the water continued to recede, he stripped to his t-shirt and boxer briefs. Each diver opened the waterproof black bags they carried. Once the water was down to ankle depth, the warning light over the interior hatch—opposite the one they'd swam through—switched from red to green with an audible buzz that grated on Lang's nerves.

From the other side of the hatch came a metallic banging sound.

The center locking wheel spun. With a rubberized sucking sound, the seal was broken, and the door opened. Water dripped from the ceiling into the two inches of water yet to drain away.

"Let's go," Lang ordered, the first to step out of the dry lock.

In the outer chamber, a nervous-looking man with red hair stood beside the open hatch. He wore a midnight blue jumpsuit. The standard dress for the facility's maintenance staff. The Tiamat Bluff logo stitched in white over the left breast pocket. A side view of the sloping bank and dome structure. Tiamat arched over it. Bluff arched under it.

"Mr. Lang?" he said, almost wringing his hands.

"You Kilpatrick?" the man with the icy-blue eyes asked.

"Yes."

Lang glanced at the nervous little man with open disdain. "You got everything we discussed?"

"Yes, sir."

To his team, Lang said, "Get geared up."

On a nearby table were thirty-six neatly folded stacks of uniforms. Most were the same midnight blue maintenance ones like Kilpatrick wore, but there were also white jumpsuits worn by the kitchen and other service staffers, and some light blue Polo shirts with shoulder patches and dark blue slacks: security uniforms.

The strike team dressed, each knowing which uniform to wear. Each knew what their assignments were. Handpicked by Lang, they had trained for this mission relentlessly for weeks.

All nonessential operations had been suspended, and all unnecessary personnel evacuated from Tiamat Bluff, as ordered by the Secret Service, in anticipation of President Kingsley's visit. That left a skeleton crew to manage the facility, including a handful of Ops & Control center personnel, a few facility management people, some security staff, and two Secret Service agents.

Lang silently thanked the Secret Service for their assistance. It made taking over the place that much easier. And with the element of surprise on their side, he figured it'd be a piece of cake.

Lang put on a security uniform. As he dressed, he asked Kilpatrick, "No problems?"

"No, sir. But I do have a question." He steeled himself as Lang stuffed a .45 caliber Smith & Wesson police pistol, mounted with laser pointer sights, in his gun belt holster. "I haven't received my payment yet. It should've been deposited into my account by now."

Lang stared at him. His pale blue eyes were like ice. "Are you accusing me of not honoring our deal?" He added, *"Tyler."*

"No. Of course not. It's just—"

"After the facility's secure, you'll get your money. Not before." He turned his back on him, dismissing the nervous little troll.

His team, each a former member of some branch of military service from a variety of countries, had over the years found work as mercenaries far more lucrative than serving their country's war machines. Each had worked for Chase Lang at one time or another over the years. All were loyal to two things; neither of them was Lang. They cared about money and themselves and nothing else.

Because Lang understood that, he could work with it.

Once the team was dressed, most with handguns concealed on their persons and the security impostors armed with Steyr TMP 9mm machine pistols, they looked expectantly at him.

"You all know your assignments," he said. "You've studied the facility's floorplans and schematics. You've practiced your jobs. You know where to go. You know what to do."

There was a communal nod accompanied by a few grunts of acknowledgment.

"Then get to it." All but five of them filed out of the room.

Those that remained were dressed in either the blue jumpsuits of the Ops & Control personnel or as security, like Lang. One of them was a stout little man with jet-black hair and olive skin. He paced and looked at the floor, talking to himself, his lips silently moving. His anxiety rivaled Kilpatrick with his sweaty, wringing hands.

The one person in the group he'd never worked with before, Lang watched him with concern. "You good, Sucre?"

The man looked up. Nodded. "Yeah, yes." His Hispanic accent thick.

Lang stared at him. "You need to hold it together. Can you do that?"

"I said I'm fine." General Sebastian Ramos Sucre straightened his spine but still appeared to be the exact opposite of fine. He looked ready to vomit.

"Good," Lang said, not convinced. "Let's move out." He grabbed Kilpatrick by the arm. "Take us to Ops."

Kilpatrick stumbled toward the door.

He led the five men and a woman through a series of circular corridors, then up several floors in an elevator to level two, the second-highest point of the complex. He brought them to a gray sliding panel door in a turquoise wall. Beside it was a black panel. Beyond the panel lay the head and heart of the entire facility. Ops & Control.

Along the way, Kilpatrick stammered, "I know you said I'd get the money after." He held a proximity card in his hand. But rather than placing it against the pad. He turned and faced Lang. "But that wasn't exactly, I mean, that wasn't what I was promised. I'm getting paid to get you inside, get you the uniforms you asked for. I've done that."

"Are you holding me up for more money, Tyler?"

"No, I… "

Lang eyed the proximity card in his hand. "Refusing to get us inside Ops until I demonstrate proof of payment, give in to a demand for a bigger payday?"

"No. Of course not. I—"

Lang clamped a hand forcefully on his shoulder. "Good. Because that would be a big mistake on your part." He shook the man's shoulder. "Buck up, Tyler. You'll get what's coming to you. You've got my word on it."

Tyler Kilpatrick nodded, once.

"Good," Lang said. "My word. That should be enough, right? Between honorable men such as ourselves?"

"Yes. I… I suppose so."

"Great." Lang smiled and gave the shoulder a final squeeze. "Then open up that door. Let's get this party started."

Lang looked at the others. Two of his men had taken up positions on either side of the door, prepared for a military breach, handguns out. "Ready?"

They each nodded.

Lang glanced behind him. Sucre and the other two mercenaries, one male, one female, clutched their guns in two-handed grips, held low, prepared to rush through the door once Kilpatrick used his proximity key card to activate the biometric lock, then use his palm print to open the door.

There was a soft beep. The palm reader glowed red.

Kilpatrick placed his hand on it. A bright blue light scanned his palm. The palm reader turned green. The door buzzed and slid open.

Inside, facing a convex, panoramic view of Georges Bank and the aquatic underwater scenery beyond the facility's outer walls, were five rows of computerized workstations. Lights blinked, and computer screens were filled with displays of charts, graphics, pulsating bars monitoring power output, life support, and who knew what else.

The air in the room felt charged, containing a soft, constant hum. Seven men and women were working at the various stations. They wore the same blue jumpsuits as some of Lang's people. Two people stood off to one side, conversing. One was an older man with gray sideburns. He looked up from a tablet the two were concentrating on.

He called out, "Kilpatrick, this is a restricted area. Who are these people? You know better than to bring unauthorized personnel in here. Especially today."

Lang's team ignored the man and rushed into the room, spreading out to the right and the left. Guns drawn. The operators watched them, apprehension in their eyes as the gunmen advanced and spread out. They glanced at the man with gray sideburns. The man in charge.

He took a step forward, but his confidence wavered, "I demand to know what—"

"We're taking over the facility," Lang said, interrupting him.

Tyler Kilpatrick stood next to Lang. He glanced at the floor and wrung his hands. Perhaps realizing the mistake his greed had led him to.

Lang pressed the barrel of his handgun against Kilpatrick's temple.

Kilpatrick snapped his head up, looking terrified. Before he could speak, Lang pulled the trigger. The gunshot echoed in the big room. Those at their workstations recoiled and gasped. One woman screamed.

Kilpatrick fell to the floor. Dead.

Blood splatter dotted the side of his face. Lang arched an eyebrow. "Any other questions?"

CHAPTER TWELVE

AT TWO-THIRTY THAT AFTERNOON, as it did every school day, a yellow school bus pulled to the corner of the intersecting street of Kate Holloway's cul-de-sac in Falls Church. Its brakes squealed as it came to a stop. The bus's red lights began to flash. Opposite the bus driver's window, a stop sign swung outward.

On the corner stood a group of parents: waiting, chatting, huddled in winter coats and scarves. Their breath fogged the air.

The door to the bus opened with a bang. Seven little people of various ages bounded down the steps and across the street, confident the flashing red lights and extended stop sign would prevent any oncoming traffic from mowing them down. Among the children were Karley and Kacey Holloway.

Laughing and carrying on, amid backpacks thumping against legs, winter jackets half on and half off, and papers clutched in small fists rustling in the crisp breeze, the children made their way to their parents. Excited to greet their children and hear about their day.

Kacey hung back from the others. Normally shy and reserved, to begin with, she wore a worried expression on her face. She clutched the family portrait she drew in art class, wanting to show her dad. Ahead of her, Karley crossed the street, talking with Brian and his brother Ricky, whose mom met them. The bus pulled away, and the group began to walk down the street, making their way towards home.

"Karley," Kacey called out. "Wait up!"

Her sister ignored her.

Beside her, Mr. Anderson held his daughter Addie's hand. She was two years younger than the twins. He looked down, noting the girl's furrowed brow. "Is everything all right, Kacey?"

"I… our dad was supposed to meet us off the bus."

Mr. Anderson glanced around. He didn't see Roger Holloway. One of the other moms shrugged her shoulders, indicating that she hadn't seen him either.

The girls were old enough to walk from the bus home on their own. And Anderson knew it wasn't that unusual for either Kate or Roger not to be there to greet the girls. Both were very busy Washington people. Mr. Anderson smiled. "I'm sure it's fine. Maybe he got delayed at work."

"But he said he'd be here," Kacey insisted. "He promised because Mom's away."

Karley called out over her shoulder, "Don't be such a baby, Kacey." She rolled her eyes. "He's on the phone talking to someone at work like he always is. You'll see."

"Your sister's probably right, but I'll tell you what," Mr. Anderson said. "Addie and I'll walk you home. Make sure you get inside safely."

"Okay," Kacey said but continued to frown.

Karley shook her head, annoyed. She walked ahead with Ricky and Brian. They talked about the big superhero movie that was due to come out in the theater next month. Kacey didn't like them. She thought they were stupid. And she thought Karley was stupid for liking them, too.

The girls only lived a couple of houses down from the corner bus stop. As they walked, the other parents and their kids split off with a wave of hands and a round of goodbyes.

Mr. Anderson pointed. "See? Your dad's car's in the driveway. Like Karley said, he's probably talking to work and lost track of time."

Kacey brightened a little. It was true. He was on the phone all the time.

"Told ya," Karley teased. "You're such a worrywart."

She ran toward the front door.

Mr. Anderson said, "You kids can get inside? You've got keys?"

"Sure. Mr. Anderson. Thank you."

He and Addie watched them go up the sidewalk and climb the front steps. Karley had already barged through the door, leaving it to swing closed. She bellowed, "Daddy! We're home!"

Kacey climbed to the top of the steps. She grabbed the doorknob, pushed the door open and waved goodbye to Mr. Anderson. He was a nice man.

He waved back.

She slammed the door closed. The knocker banged with a heavy thud. Inside, Kacey called out. "Daddy!"

He didn't answer.

She dropped her backpack next to Karley's and went through the foyer to the kitchen, her feeling of dread gone now that she was home. Maybe Daddy had made something really good for a snack. She hoped because she was starving.

"Daddy!" She called out at the top of her voice. "I'm so hungry my stomach's eating itself."

When she reached the kitchen, she stopped in her tracks.

Daddy was sitting at the eat-in-kitchen table, but a cold fear gripped Kacey.

He sat away from the table, facing the foyer. His legs and arms and chest were taped to the chair with silver tape. duct tape, he called it. Kacey remembered seeing her dad use it once. She called it quack-quack tape. That had made Daddy laugh.

A scary-looking man in dark clothes stood next to him. He held a gun pointed at Daddy's head.

There was also a woman and another man. The woman had a scar on her cheek. The man held Karley, who was struggling in his arms. She twisted and stomped her feet, trying to escape and mumbled under the hand pressed against her mouth, but she couldn't break free. Her eyes were big and full of fear.

"Run, Kacey!" Daddy shouted. "Run!"

Kacey turned and screamed.

The woman grabbed her by the shoulder and pulled her back. She pushed Kacey toward the man with the gun. He grabbed her and picked her up. She kicked her feet out and struck his shin. He winced but held on, his grip getting tighter as he tossed her under his arm and carried her like a sack, kicking and screaming. "DADDY!"

"Don't hurt her! Please!" Tears made Daddy's eyes wet and shimmery. She'd never seen Daddy cry before. "What do you want? Take whatever it is and go. Just, please, don't hurt my children."

The woman nodded to the man holding Karley. He dragged her over to the table and pulled out a chair. This one didn't have arms on it like the one Daddy was in. The man pushed Karley down and wound the quack-quack tape around her, pinning her to the chair. The tape made a terrible ripping noise. He pulled her arms behind the back of the chair and taped them together, too.

The man holding Kacey did the same thing with her. She struggled against his efforts but was no more successful than her sister had been.

She screamed, "Daddy, make him stop! Make him stop!"

With the back of his hand, the man slapped Kacey across the face. She cried out.

So did Daddy. "Noooo!"

Stunned, Kacey stopped fighting and started to cry. The man finished taping her to the chair.

"I'll do whatever you want," Daddy said. "Just let my kids go. Please."

"Sorry," the woman said. "That's not how this is gonna work."

Taped to the chairs, the girls sobbed. The two angry men watched over them. The woman turned to the kitchen counter. On it were Daddy's keys, his cell phone, wallet, some money, and a bunch of candy mints.

For the first time, Kacey noticed her father's black eye. "Daddy," she said. "Are you okay?"

"Everything's going to be fine, Kacey. I promise. We just need to do what these people want. Then everything will be fine."

"Now, that's being smart, Mr. Holloway." The woman pushed through the wallet, the keys, the coins, and other things until her long, dark fingers landed on Daddy's cell phone. She turned around and opened it. She activated the screen. Without looking up, she said, "Passcode, please."

Daddy didn't say anything.

Without looking up, the woman pointed her gun at Karley. "Don't make me ask again."

Daddy said five numbers.

The woman tapped the surface of the phone. She swiped her finger across the screen, searching through the apps, then ticked the screen again. Her nails made a clicking noise.

"What are you looking for?" Daddy asked.

"Nothing. I found it."

The others in the room heard a ringing sound coming from the phone. It rang several long times. Then, the call connected.

From the speaker came Kate Holloway's voice. She spoke in a whispered tone. "Oh, sweetie, I can't talk now. Is everything all right?"

The woman turned the phone and faced it toward Roger, then panned it to include the girls. They could see their mother's face on the screen. The woman had video-chatted her.

She looked shocked and scared. "Roger. What the hell—"

Daddy said, "Baby, I'm so sorry. I tried to fight back but—"

The woman turned the phone back to herself.

"Who are you?" Kate asked. "What have you done?"

"You're asking the wrong questions, Agent Holloway. What you want to know is, what do I want and what am I capable of doing to get it."

"What—"

"We have your family." The woman nodded to the man standing beside Daddy. She turned the phone around again. The man slammed the bottom of his pistol across Daddy's face.

Daddy cried out and slumped to the side, spitting blood.

From the phone, yelling, "No! Stop it!"

"Listen to me very carefully, Agent Holloway," The woman said, turning the phone back around. "I'm only going to say this one. We know where you are. We know what you're doing there. You will be contacted shortly by someone who works with us. When you are, you will do everything he tells you to do. You will do it exactly as he tells you to, and you won't tell a soul about it or about us. If you deviate from your instructions in any way, attempt to tell anyone… " The woman panned the camera once more, giving her a final look at Roger, Kacey, and Karley.

"If you do anything but what you're told," the woman said, "your family will die."

CHAPTER THIRTEEN

ON THE *PUTNAM*, THE meal included New England clam chowder, Caesar salad, jumbo shrimp cocktail, a choice of grilled rainbow trout with garlic brown rice and broccoli or a fisherman's soup with whitefish, mussels, clams, and sausage in a tomato broth, and Boston cream pie and coffee for dessert. Not a cutter's typical fare, even for officers, but it wasn't every day the President of the United States dropped by for lunch.

Afterward, Tolliver escorted the group to the stern of the *Putnam* once more.

Along the way, Bannon learned a handful of press and other guests had arrived earlier. They were given a similar presentation by Dr. Nomura in the general mess hall, which explained his abrupt departure midway through lunch.

Before going back outside, a seaman handed out dark, fur-lined parkas to those who didn't have them.

Tolliver pushed the hatch door open onto the flight deck.

As they crossed the helipad, Larson turned to the group. She had a hand clamped down on her fedora to keep it from blowing away in the cold sea breeze. She'd again slipped on her dark designer sunglasses.

"Folks, this is where the adventure begins."

Bannon felt her enthusiasm and shared it.

Past Marine One, now tied down and secured, Tolliver led them to the launch ramp at the stern of the ship. Rather than housing a rigid hull inflatable rescue boat, which would've been standard for a cutter like the *Putnam*, in its place were four vessels that, to Bannon, looked like the mutated offspring of a Bell helicopter's cockpit, a hamster's exercise ball, and a Florida Glades airboat that had been fused to a pair of seaplane's pontoons.

Bannon had seen a vessel like them once before. A few years back. At the in-water Boston Boat Show.

A six-passenger submersible with space for a single pilot inside a transparent ball-like cabin. The pilot sat forward of the two-tiered rows of black leather captain's chairs. From inside the clear globe, each person would have a near three-hundred-thirty-degree unobstructed view of the underwater world around them.

From what Bannon recalled from the boat show, the submersibles had a maximum depth rating of one thousand feet. They were powered by a state-of-the-art lithium battery system. The vessel he saw had a stated mission time of eight hours, a standard speed capacity of three knots, and with six electric propulsion thrusters, it boasted superior underwater maneuverability unlike anything operating today.

According to the brochure, anyway.

McMurphy had hunted down a salesperson and spent an hour trying to talk the man into letting him take one out for a test drive. He bribed him, threatened him, and failing that, he swore to Bannon: *I'll steal one.*

Bannon leaned toward Grayson and whispered, "Now Skyjack's really going to kill us when we get back."

Near the launch ramp, Larson excused herself to take a phone call. The President stopped and conversed privately with Amal Haddad and Captain Tolliver while Bannon and Grayson strolled farther down the ramp toward the submersibles. Loitering near the top of the ramp was a man Bannon recognized. Not because he knew him, but because he filled his TV screen every evening at six o'clock.

Jerry Little, the face of WCVS News9, a local Boston news station. A talking head, in Bannon's opinion. At that moment, he spoke into a mike, facing a cameraman who was filming him. The newscaster's full head of brown hair didn't move in the brisk breeze.

Near the rear of the submersibles, four men dressed in midnight blue jumpsuits busied themselves around the four vessels. Bannon pegged them as pilots, making their final pre-launch inspections.

"What's the plan?" Bannon asked Grayson.

"We'll travel with POTUS in the lead submersible. With us will be Agent Holloway, Jerry Little, and his cameraman."

"And Dr. Larson?"

"She'll be accompanying us in the second submersible along with Dr. Nomura, Amal Haddad, and a few others."

"What about them?" Bannon indicated a small group of well-dressed men and women off to the side, waiting and watching with a large contingent of coasties there to witness the event.

"More guests," Grayson said. "Lobbyists, CEOs, political allies, and a small press contingent. They'll follow us down in the last two submersibles."

Grayson looked around. "Speaking of Agent Holloway, where is she?"

She'd been with the group when they left the officers' mess. Bannon was sure of it. But he hadn't seen her since. She must have slipped away sometime before the group came outside. That was odd, leaving the President's side that way. He did notice two men a discreet distance away wearing dark suits and dark overcoats. They wore dark sunglasses—the classic tell of a POTUS Secret Service protection detail—and earpieces with coiled wires snaking down under their collars.

Kingsley had not been left without protection.

Grayson checked her watch. "We should be getting underway."

"There she is." Bannon nodded as Agent Holloway emerged from the *Putnam's* superstructure, walking briskly across the deck. She slipped on a pair of Ray-Bans even as she dropped her cell phone into her jacket pocket.

She approached Kingsley and pulled him from his conversation with Tolliver and Haddad.

They spoke. Kingsley nodded several times, then waved to Grayson and Bannon to join them.

As they approached, Haddad brought Little and the cameraman—whose name turned out to be Malcolm Leary—into their group.

One of the pilots came over and introduced himself as Trevor Garcia. He and the other pilots worked for Tiamat Bluff, hence the matching dark blue jumpsuits. The facility's emblem stitched over their breast pockets. He gave the group a five-minute safety spiel, akin to what flight attendants do on commercial airlines, then guided them to the rolling steel ladder they'd have to climb to descend through the open hatch on the top of the submersible's bubble-like cockpit.

The President climbed in first, and the others followed. Bannon and Agent Holloway were the last to board. As they waited for the others to climb in, Bannon said, "Looking forward to our trip under the sea, Agent?"

She leveled him with a stern look. An expression he was getting used to. "It's time we boarded, Commander."

"Ladies first."

Her smooth forehead furrowed. "Don't be misogynistic."

Bannon shrugged and climbed in before her, taking the unoccupied forward seat next to the pilot, Garcia. Holloway dropped into the seat next to Kingsley behind them. A Tiamat Bluff pilot secured the acrylic bubble hatch from outside and banged on it, indicating they were good to go.

Amal Haddad stepped back from the submersible and waved. "We'll be right behind you."

After checking everyone's five-point safety harnesses, like the operator of a carnival ride, Garcia signaled a thumbs up to the seamen manning the guide ropes securing the vessel to the launch ramp. They signaled a go to the ramp operators.

"Seaview-One is good to go," he reported over the radio.

Garcia opened up the vents, filling the small round cabin with warm, canned air. With a whine from the hydraulics, the *Putnam's* ramp began to lower. White, frothy ocean water roared up the declining ramp.

Curious, Bannon watched Garcia start the battery-powered engines and manipulate the submersible's controls. With a gentle rocking motion, the vessel began to float on the bubbling white water. Bannon twisted and took in the passengers' expressions behind him.

Grayson smiled while Kingsley grinned, looking like a kid taking his first roller coaster ride. The newscaster, Little, clutched his seat tightly, white-knuckling it, while the cameraman practically bounced in his seat, twisting and turning to take it all in, filming and almost giggling.

Holloway stared out of the bubble with a blank expression, her sunglasses still concealing her eyes.

"You okay, Mr. Little?" Bannon asked, noticing the man seemed a bit green around the gills.

He forced his famous TV smile. "Just a touch of motion sickness is all. I'll be okay."

"How about you, Agent Holloway?" Bannon asked.

She glared at him. "I don't get seasick."

"Good to hear," Garcia said. "I'd prefer no one throw up in here." He maneuvered the vessel out into open water. "Things will smooth out once we're submerged. It'll just be a couple of minutes."

Bannon noticed what seemed like the entire ship's complement of coasties lined up on the stern deck to see them off, waving and clapping.

Garcia moved Seaview-One about a hundred feet astern of the *Putnam.* "Here we go."

Water bubbled up around the acrylic glass bubble.

The cameraman, Leary, gasped with excitement. Little clamped his hand over his mouth.

The bubble darkened as the submersible sank. Small, bulbous running lights along the vessel's pontoons came on. The control panel in front of Garcia glowed green, casting the cabin in an ethereal glow.

"I'll leave the cabin lights off," he said. "Give you all a better view on the way down."

"How long's the trip?" Bannon asked.

"At three knots, we'll be there in less than ten minutes." Garcia snapped a switch that turned on a spotlight under the submersible. Then, he gently pitched the vessel forward and down toward the darkness. "Sit back, relax, and enjoy the show."

CHAPTER FOURTEEN

IT WAS QUITE THE show, too.

At first, the brightness of the midday sky reflected off the surface, giving them a ceiling of shimmering white light. In the ethereal-like glow, all manner of fish swam by. A few gave them a cursory look before darting quickly away. Soon, the aptly named Seaview-One drifted slowly downward through what scientists call the Epipelagic Zone. The band of water that goes to about six hundred-fifty feet deep. This zone is the warmest and most exposed to light and thus teems with oceanic life.

Jellyfish pulsated like floating lanterns. A sea turtle swam by and gave them a curious look before continuing on. In the murky purple-blue distance, Bannon spotted a hammerhead shark in search of prey.

At one thousand feet, Tiamat Bluff lay solidly in the mesopelagic zone, often referred to as the twilight zone. The oceanic zones were measured not by depth so much as by how far light reached them. At a measured depth of twelve hundred feet, even the deepest part of the Gulf of Maine—where, according to Dr. Larson's presentation, the power plant and mining operations lay—did not extend into what is referred to as the midnight zone or the abyss.

Though the twilight zone was plenty dark.

As they furthered their descent, the natural light diminished, as did the amount of aquatic life to be seen. Here, bristlemouths, blobfish, bioluminescent jellyfish, and squid lived.

"There," Leary, the cameraman, shouted and pointed. He hoisted his camera onto his shoulder. Grayson, Little, and Kingsley leaned forward. Bannon followed the excitable young man's pointed finger.

"There she is," Garcia said.

Ahead and below them was the dark, spherical structure of Tiamat Bluff's main facility, luminous in a pale red light. The top of the dome was transparent, a white-yellow glow of light. Several layers below the dome, they could see rows of horizontal yellow windows. During the presentation, Dr. Larson informed them Tiamat Bluff contained seven levels, including Kanaloa Park.

In the darkness, Bannon could barely make out the dim glowing windows of the lower mining and training facility and power plant, smaller and deeper along the sloping terrain.

"Magnificent," Kingsley said, pulling himself forward for a better look.

"Are you getting this?" Little asked of his cameraman.

Leary leaned forward, his eye in the viewfinder of his camera. "Yeah. Yeah."

Garcia lowered his voice and gave Bannon a sideways look. "Impressive, huh?"

"It is." Bannon had no problem admitting it, either.

He'd been on ships and boats of every shape and size imaginable and had explored every one of the world's Seven Seas, under, on and above the water. He'd worked on floating islands, oil rigs, and even in submersible bathyspheres for extended periods. Nothing he'd ever experienced came close to what he was seeing at that moment.

Despite Dr. Larson's modest denials and insistence to the contrary, Tiamat Bluff was an engineering marvel. She and her team had truly built a city under the sea.

Garcia had the sleeves of his jumpsuit rolled up two turns.

"*Marina de Guerra Revolucionaria,*" Bannon said, nodding toward the tattoo he'd spotted on the man's inner forearm. It was a blue circle under an anchor and a red triangle with a star in the center of it. "Cuban Revolutionary Navy."

Garcia kept his voice low. "Before I migrated to the United States, yes. I stole an old Soviet-era patrol boat and escaped with ten others fifteen years ago. We left Varadero under the cover of night. We managed to evade the Cuban authorities but had greater trouble with the American Coast Guard."

"But you made it?"

"Not all of us. We were spotted off the coast of Key West. On the patrol boat, we had a rigid-hull inflatable. Black. We abandoned the boat as the Coast Guard was about to take us, but by doing so, we overweighed the inflatable. It capsized. We swam for it. Only four of us made it to land."

"The others?"

"The ones the Coast Guard managed to rescue." Garcia shrugged. "Returned to Cuba."

"Wet feet, dry feet," Bannon said.

That was the name given to a revision made at the time to the U.S. policy regarding Cuban refugees called the Cuban Adjustment Act. If a refugee was caught attempting to enter the U.S. while still on the water, thus wet feet, they were returned to Cuba. If they managed to reach land, achieve dry feet status, they were allowed to stay in the United States, given a chance to qualify for legal permanent residency, and eventually even U.S. citizenship.

That was no longer the case.

Garcia steered Seaview-One in a long, slow, lazy circular pattern, giving his passengers a full, three-hundred-and-sixty-degree view of the city under the sea. In doing so, Bannon noticed the second submersible descending about a hundred feet behind them.

"There's the other submersible," Bannon said.

Garcia nodded. "Oceanview-One. Right on schedule." He toggled a switch. "Tiamat Control. This is Seaview-One."

"Go for Control, Seaview-One," a voice said over the speaker system.

"We are on final approach. Requesting clearance."

"Clearance granted, Seaview-One. Moon Pool Alpha is clear and awaiting your arrival."

"Roger, control. Moon Pool Alpha it is."

"Seaview-One."

"Yes, Control?"

The voice said, "Welcome to Tiamat Bluff."

CHASE LANG STOOD IN the center of the command center of Tiamat Bluff. He held the mic in his hand while his team held Ops in quiet terror at gunpoint. He keyed the mic again and said, "Seaview-One…Welcome to Tiamat Bluff."

He returned the mic to its cradle and turned to the swarthy-skinned man beside him. Sebastian Ramos Sucre. He didn't think much of the little Hispanic man. Thought him spineless and a pain in the rear, if he had to be frank. But he needed him. The mission required him. Sucre had a role to play. So long as he could do that, maybe Lang wouldn't kill him when it was all over.

"What now?" Sucre said.

"Now, you go do your job," Lang said. "Take your team, secure the moon pool, and be ready to receive the President of the United States." Sucre stepped away but stopped at the door when Lang called out to him. "And, Sucre. Don't screw this up."

Visibly irritated, Sucre said, "You mean the way you did yesterday?"

Lang clenched his fist. "Careful, Sucre. I'm very good at improvising when missions go sideways. Don't think I haven't got a contingency plan that'll work just as well without you as our spokesperson."

Sucre opened his mouth to protest the threat but snapped it shut. He activated the door and stormed out before the door had fully opened.

Chase sent him on his way with a one-finger salute.

"Do you want me to keep an eye on him? Or I could deal with him permanently," Sasha Wilcox said, stepping forward. She wore a blue maintenance jumpsuit and clutched a machine pistol in her small hands. "It would be my pleasure."

She'd been with Lang for several years. Like his team, his loyalties ran toward himself and no one else. Certainly, it didn't extend to anyone who worked for him, but if it had, Sasha would be among that very, very small group.

Lang stared at the door, considering it. "No," he said finally. "Sucre's a spineless twit, but he wants this as much as we do. I'll let you know if that changes."

And if it did, Lang decided, he'd reserve the pleasure of doing the task himself.

CHAPTER FIFTEEN

SEAVIEW-ONE CONTINUED ITS ANGLED descent through the darkening depths of the Gulf of Maine. An excitable tenseness permeated the bubble-shaped cockpit. The main complex of Tiamat Bluff came into view as they approached. Below them, white spotlights snapped on, illuminating the terrain five feet under a tubular spur extending from the left side of the main structure. Small square lights dotted the length of the stubby offshoot. The bright white lights illuminated the area under the moon pool.

"They've turned the porch light on for us," Garcia said, adjusting course toward the spur.

Bannon glanced overhead and saw Oceanview-One hovering in line overhead. They'd cut their distance to about fifty feet.

According to Garcia, the other two submersibles were preparing to depart the *Putnam*. They'd begin their descent approximately thirty minutes after Seaview and Oceanview's arrival. The entire tour of Tiamat Bluff and photo op for the President was expected to take about four hours, after which they would return to the cutter on the surface and be back in Boston by nightfall.

Garcia expertly guided Seaview-One underneath the spur and positioned her under the open moon pool. Bannon watched, impressed, as the man manipulated the vessel's foot pedals, ballast, and controls to raise them upward in a slow, steady ascend. Everyone stared up overhead, their mouths open in astonishment while Bannon thought about all the science fiction movies he'd ever seen where the unsuspecting person was caught in a pool of light from overhead and levitated upward into an alien ship, trapped in some kind of tractor beam.

He shook the thought away. Maybe he should start watching more comedies.

Seaview-One entered the opening and soon breached the surface of the moon pool. Water bubbled and cascaded off the acrylic domed cockpit as the vessel popped like a cork into the large open pool.

Overhead, a crane was in position. Several jumpsuit-clad workers in the wet room reached out over the chipped yellow railings. They attached the cranes' straps to the vessel's cleats, ready to haul it out of the water.

Bannon noticed the room was large enough to accommodate multiple submersibles. Pallet-like platforms lined the opposite walls. Docking stations for each of the four submersibles. Garcia powered down the engines as a worker extended a gangplank. Garcia unbuckled and climbed to the rear of the cockpit.

He undogged the overhead hatch. "Welcome to Tiamat Bluff."

Kingsley started to get up, but Holloway put a hand on his shoulder. "Me first, sir."

Still smiling from experiencing the trip down, he nodded. "Of course, Kate."

She scrambled out of her seat and climbed out of Seaview-One first.

Kingsley glanced at Bannon and then each of the others. "How incredible was that? American ingenuity at its finest. Business, academia, and government working together. Brilliant."

Grayson nodded, while Jerry Little and his cameraman Malcolm Leary looked like kids coming off an amusement ride, one clamoring to go again. The other looked like he wanted to vomit.

From the hatch ladder, Garcia called out, "Agent Holloway says you're good to go, Mr. President."

Kingsley shook the pilot's hand and thanked him before climbing up the ladder and emerging through the top hatch.

"My honor, sir," Garcia said.

"Madam Secretary," Jerry Little said, waving a hand, indicating she should go first.

"No. You and Mr. Leary go ahead. We'll be right behind you." They exited.

To Bannon, Grayson said, "Glad you came along?"

Anxious to see the facility, Bannon said, "Best vacation day I've had in years."

Garcia helped Grayson climb up the ladder, where a Tiamat Bluff crewman escorted her off the gangplank. Bannon shook Garcia's hand. "Thanks for the trip down. I run a bar called the Keel Haul in New Hampshire. Next time you're in Hampton Beach, the drinks are on me."

"I'll be sure to take you up on it." Garcia winked. "But you haven't seen anything yet. Enjoy."

The last to walk down the gangplank, Bannon strolled past the men and women surrounding the President. Holloway stood by his side with a worried look on her face. Little was interviewing the workers while Leary filmed the President's interaction with them.

Grayson stood off to one side, avoiding the limelight.

Unlike any vice-presidential candidate in history, Bannon thought bemused. He joined her. They waited and watched as Seaview-One was pulled from the moon pool by the overhead crane and lowered onto one of the pallet-like platforms.

Within minutes, while they stood to the side, the procedure was repeated. This time with Oceanview-One. The operation was smooth and effective, Bannon thought, quite impressed.

Among the new arrivals were Robin Larson and Dr. Nomura. Bannon recognized Senator Jerimiah Horn from Massachusetts. And, there were two men Bannon did not recognize. One in his late fifties or early sixties. The other a kid barely out of his teens. Grayson told him one was the CEO of an electronics firm that had won a government contract to work at Tiamat Bluff. The other was a 'reporter' for an Internet news blog service. Kingsley's attempt to reach the younger generation.

As they disembarked and clamored around the President, talking excitedly, Bannon and Grayson were joined by Nomura and Robin Larson.

"I thought Ms. Haddad would be joining us," Grayson said, noting her absence as Bannon had as well.

"She had to take a phone call from Washington," Larson said. "She switched seats with the Internet reporter. Told us she'd join the next group."

"I see," Grayson said.

"Did you enjoy your trip down?"

"Immensely," Grayson said.

"Looking forward to the nickel tour," Bannon said. "I hope we don't have to wait long."

Larson smiled. "Not at all. But unfortunately, due to the strict requirements imposed upon us by the Secret Service, we're operating with a skeleton crew. All but essential functions have been shut down. Our total complement in the facility is less than fifty people at the moment."

"The safety concerns can't be taken lightly," Grayson said. "Any restrictions put into place are quite necessary, I assure you."

"Of course," Larson said. "It's just disappointing you'll not truly experience all that Tiamat Bluff has to offer. We've so many ground-breaking projects we're involved in that I'd love to have shown you them all in full operation." She smiled. "But we'll do our best to tell you about them."

"I'm sure we'll all be quite impressed, Doctor," Grayson said.

Kingsley wrapped up his photo op meet-and-greet with the moon pool operators.

With Little, Leary, and Holloway in tow, he joined the others.

"Good to see you again, doctors." He clapped his hands together. Like a little kid about to dive into a banana split dessert. "So, where do we begin?"

Before Larson could reply, the doors to the wet room opened unexpectedly. Five men in Tiamat Bluff jumpsuits and security uniforms burst in. With determined expressions, they fanned out, carrying handguns and machine pistols at the ready.

Holloway rushed at Kingsley. She seized him by the neck and forced him to the ground. "Get down, Mr. President!"

She knelt over his prone body, drawing Her service Sig Sauer. The only gun among the group.

Bannon stepped in front of them, blocking them both from the cadre of gunmen. Grayson did the same, even as Bannon angled his body to protect her as well.

"Get out of the way, Bannon!" Holloway shouted.

He called out over his shoulder. "What are you going to do? Shoot it out against seven armed men? Stand down, agent." To the armed men, he demanded, "What is this?"

Larson and Nomura stepped forward. Larson demanded of the short Hispanic man who stepped forward, carrying only a pistol, "Who are you?"

He pointed his pistol at Nomura and pulled the trigger.

The gunshot echoed loudly in the metal chamber. The bullet struck Nomura in the forehead. With a stunned expression and a trail of blood leaking from the wound, he took a step back before collapsing to the metal deck with a grunt.

Larson screamed. She covered her mouth with her hands. Her knees buckled.

Bannon grabbed her. Pulled her back. Tucked her in close behind him.

The group of workers who'd brought the submersibles up screamed. They scrambled toward the back wall. Garcia and the other pilot among them. Some dropped to the deck. Others turned to flee, but the armed gunmen had already moved into position to corral them.

The Hispanic man took another step forward. His gun aimed at Larson, Bannon, and the others. "We have taken control of this facility. I am in charge."

"Answer the lady's question," Bannon said. "Who are you?"

He stared at Bannon, sizing him up before responding. "I am General Sebastian Ramos Sucre of the Revolutionary Republic Army."

Larson clung to Bannon's arm. Nomura's blood had splattered her clothes and the side of her face. Tears streaked down her cheeks. He could feel the fear leech off her. "Who are they?"

"A South American paramilitary group," Bannon clarified.

"A terrorist group," Grayson spat out with disgust.

"The woman with the gun," Sucre called out. "You are Secret Service, yes?" He didn't wait for an answer. "Toss your weapon into the moon pool. If you do not, I will kill these two."

He indicated Bannon and Larson with his gun.

Bannon put an arm around Larson. She trembled uncontrollably.

"Where are the other Secret Service agents?" Holloway asked. "What have you done with the people working here?"

"Some are secure. Unharmed. Others, not so much."

"You killed them?" Grayson asked.

He shrugged. "Those that did not cooperate. Those that fought back."

Bannon needed to distract him. Keep him talking while he figured out a counterattack, a way to fight back without getting everyone killed. He looked around the wet room. There were plenty of things he could use as weapons if he could get his hands on them.

For now, Holloway still held onto her gun. The only real weapon in friendly hands.

But against seven armed men with machine pistols? Not good odds.

"What do you want?" Bannon asked.

"For the agent to toss her gun away. One. Two… "

Behind him, Bannon heard a splash.

And there went the only gun on their side.

"Very good," Sucre said. "My men and I have seized control of this so-called underwater city."

Out of the corner of his eye, Bannon noticed Holloway and Grayson as they helped Kingsley to his feet.

"For what purpose?" Kingsley demanded. He brushed his hands down his ruined suit, wet and dirty from laying on the wet room deck.

"Is it not obvious? To hold you hostage, Mr. President. To get your country to aid us in our struggle against the brutal regime currently governing my country. A corrupt, illegal government supported by you."

"Strange way to ask for help," Bannon said.

"You'll not receive one ounce of help from us," Kingsley said. "The United States doesn't negotiate with terrorists. We'll not do your bidding."

"I hope that is not true, Mr. President." Sucre spread his arms and turned, indicating the wet room and all of Tiamat Bluff. "Otherwise, this is where your legacy ends."

CHAPTER SIXTEEN

SUCRE ORDERED GARCIA AND the other Tiamat Bluff employees to be removed from the wet room. They were marched away to an undisclosed location at gunpoint by two armed men dressed in what passed for security uniforms: light blue Polo shirts with shoulder patches and dark blue slacks.

Then there were five, Bannon thought, liking the improved odds. But he reminded himself they were heavily armed, and he was weaponless.

Bannon assumed those remaining were Sucre's VIP hostages: POTUS, Senator Horn, Grayson, Holloway, Larson, and the three news people: Little, Leary, and the Internet kid. But why keep him around? To Sucre, he was nobody.

Sucre and his men moved them out at gunpoint.

Taken from the wet room, they were led along a windowless corridor to an elevator. They rode up to the top level of the complex. The park atrium was called Kanaloa Park. Named after the water god from ancient Hawai'i.

Even under the dire circumstances they found themselves in, Bannon couldn't help but admire their surroundings as they stepped into a large garden paradise. There was natural grass. Dozens of Japanese maples and flowering dogwoods were planted along walking paths with old-fashioned streetlamps that had flickering, candle-like lights. There were park benches and even a pond with a fountain in the middle. A water geyser shooting into the air imbued with colorful changing lights. The sound of splashing water was music to his ears.

To their left was a community-size pool with a slide and diving boards, and in the distance, a baseball diamond with a chain-link backstop and dugouts, two tennis courts, and tables with checkerboard tops.

There were even closed vendor carts and a bandshell for public concerts and events. All under an expansive dome overhead constructed of triangular-shaped, transparent acrylic panels with lattice ribs between the panels, through which the outside ocean could be seen, ablaze with red-hued light from Tiamat Bluff.

"Are those… birds chirping?" Grayson asked as they were directed toward the bandshell.

"Yes," Larson said. She'd wiped her cheeks, streaking the small flecks of blood still there. "We've brought down several commonly found North American species. Part of our attempt to create a self-sustaining closed ecological system." Her voice flat. Bannon feared she might be in shock, yet he could hear the pride in her voice as she added, "They seem to be thriving."

A gunman shoved Bannon in the back. "Keep moving."

Bannon glared at him but did as he was told.

Sucre climbed the steps to the bandshell stage. A dozen rows of seats faced the stage. Bolted to a concrete pad, Bannon noticed, dashing his impulsive thought of grabbing one and smashing as many of their captives with it as he could. He also noticed there were more armed men and women stationed throughout the park. They took up positions at several closed, sliding doors.

"Sit," Sucre ordered, holstering his gun. The others with him held their machine pistols at the ready.

"Where did you take the others?" Grayson asked, defiantly remaining on her feet.

"They are safe, Madam Secretary," Sucre said. "For now. Continue to defy me, and they won't be. Now sit!"

She did, joining the others except Kingsley. "You must realize what a mistake you're making. You haven't thought this thing through, son. You're trapped on the bottom of the sea. A legend-class Coast Guard cutter is positioned directly above you. It has roughly the same munitions and capability as a Navy destroyer. It can reign hellfire down on you like you've never seen before."

"But it will not," Sucre said with confidence. "Not so long as you are our guest, Mr. President. And I use the term guest quite loosely."

"And that's your play?" Kingsley asked. "Hold me hostage. In exchange for what? Whatever it is, you'll never get away with it."

"Let me worry about that," Sucre said. "Your only concern should be surviving the next twenty-four hours. Toward that end, allow me to demonstrate how serious we are." He pulled a radio from his back pocket. "We are ready."

A second later, the lights in the park went out, plunging them into darkness except for the red emergency exit lights over the doors leading out to the corridor that rimmed the park and soft white safety lights that lined the brick pathways like runway lights at an airport.

The exterior lights remained lit, a reddish hue.

Bannon half rose, ready to use the foolish opportunity he'd been given to strike, only to be frozen where he half-stood, the muzzle of a machine pistol pressed into his neck. And none too gently, either. He held his hands in the air.

The man holding the weapon sneered. "Sit."

Bannon sat.

"Let me be clear," Sucre said from the stage. "The only hostage I need to keep alive is David Kingsley. The rest of you. Every single one of you. Is expendable. I will end you without a moment's hesitation. Should you need convincing, watch."

He pointed over their heads to a place beyond the dome.

Collectively, the group looked up, following where he pointed. With the park lights extinguished, the underwater world beyond came to life.

First, Bannon caught sight of a moray eel swimming by. Resembling a snake with a waving fin along the length of its back. Nearly two meters long, its skin had a honeycombed pattern to it. Particles drifted in the water, visible from what light leaked out through the acrylic glass and the red hue that didn't negatively affect the sea creatures at this level. A large pinkish sea nettle, with its lacy arms and tentacles at least ten feet long, pulsated along, emitting its own glow.

But Sucre hadn't dimmed the lights to present his captured audience with an enchanted view of the ocean life outside. His true motivation came into view a moment later.

Bannon stiffened in his seat. In the distance, two small white dots of light could be seen. As they got closer. Grew larger. He recognized them for what they were. The headlights of the two remaining submersibles. Making their trip down from the *USCGC Putnam.*

Bannon's stomach soured.

The submersibles came into full view, making their circular approach to the facility the same way Garcia had earlier done for them, giving the passengers the breathtaking scope of Tiamat Bluff. Unsuspecting of the danger that awaited them upon arrival.

Sucre keyed his radio. Patched through to the communications transmission between the control center and the submersibles, he allowed the President and the others to listen to the exchange between Ops and the approaching submersibles.

"Tiamat Control," a static-filled voice said. "This is Waterview-One and Two."

"Go for Control." The same voice who'd answered Garcia on their trip down.

"We're on final approach, Control. Requesting permission to come aboard."

"Permission granted, Waterview-One and Two. Proceed to Moon Pool Alpha. We await your arrival."

"Roger, Control. Thanks."

"Don't mention it," the voice said. "And welcome to Tiamat Bluff."

Sucre broke the radio link and watched with the others as the two submersibles made their approach. A tense, anticipatory silence fell over the park. It seemed even the birds had gone silent, waiting.

Bannon kept a watchful eye on the submersibles from the corner of his eye, but his full attention was on the park. Locating the exits, identifying where the enemy combatants were positioned, gauging their level of attentiveness, looking for any weaknesses, any opportunity to fight back, to escape.

Unfortunately, none presented itself.

Each clutched a Steyr TMP 9mm machine pistol, an Austrian-manufactured, full-automatic weapon with a thirty-round box magazine capable of firing up to nine hundred rounds per minute. They wore spare magazines on their belts and a holstered 9mm Taurus PT92 semiautomatic pistol with seventeen-round magazines. The men and one woman appeared disciplined and well-trained. They didn't get distracted by the submersibles. Their attention remained solely on the hostages. Their grips firmly on their weapons.

"Watch," Sucre said, his mouth twisted into a sadistic grin. "Watch."

Bannon followed the man's gaze, returning his attention to the submersibles.

The vessels altered course, diverting to the right, continuing their angled descent toward the moon pool spur.

Why would they allow this group of passengers to arrive, Bannon wondered? More people to take prisoner, to guard over. But how many did they need? Sucre said it himself. Except for Kingsley, the hostages were expendable. Why take on more?

His thoughts were cut off by the first of two explosions.

Bannon blinked at the sudden yellow fireballs. One followed seconds later by the second.

The bright light of fire went out quickly, drowned out by the pressurized water that crushed the blackened husks. The wreckage of the two destroyed submersibles sank, dropping to the ocean floor like misshapen crumbled rocks.

Bannon leaped to his feet. "You son of a bitch!"

The lights came back on. Like the house lights after a theatrical performance.

Kingsley appeared particularly shaken. He stared wide-eyed at the column of air bubbles rising from the sinking submersibles. He reached for the back of the chair behind him before dropping heavily into the seat. He tugged at the knot of his tie.

"Dear God. Liz. Amal was on one of those vessels. Amal Haddad is dead." He turned toward Sucre. "What is wrong with you, man?" Kingsley fisted his hands in equal outrage. "Those men and women, they were—"

"Tools of your corrupt capitalistic machine," Sucre said.

"Innocent men and women," Kingsley said. "A senator and two congressmen. My...my Chief of Staff."

"And now they're dead. Their blood money and their bought votes cannot hurt anyone ever again."

"How?" Bannon asked. "Were they rigged with explosives?"

Even as he suggested it, Bannon knew that couldn't be the case. The submersibles would've been checked by the Secret Service's advanced team. Probably more than once. As had everything and everybody on board the *Putnam.*

Sucre's one-word answer sent a shiver down Bannon's spine. "Programable drone mines."

"You're a monster," Larson blurted out, more tears running down her cheeks. She would've known the pilots, had probably worked with them for years, been friends with them. Her loss was real and cut deep. If there had been any doubt, and there wasn't after the cold-blooded execution of Dr. Nomura. It was clear. Sucre would not hesitate to kill every last one of them.

"This facility is surrounded by a network of small but powerful drone mines," Sucre announced. "They're programmed to provide a random, constantly shifting net around us. Nothing larger than a dolphin can get anywhere close to us. Ops is also monitoring Tiamat Bluff's sophisticated sonar and radar systems to detect any breach attempts going forward. In addition, every means of egress: the moon pools, the locked tubes, and the cargo submarine hatches are all heavily guarded by my people who won't hesitate to kill in retaliation for any forced entry—or exit—attempt."

He walked down the steps of the stage and stood before the group of hostages.

"Cell phones do not work down here. All communication with the surface is cut off except for what we control. You see, Mr. President, while you might dismiss me as some amateur guerrilla fighter from a backwater South American country, the truth is, I have thought of everything."

"The explosions," Bannon said. "The *Putnam* will have noticed. They'll put divers in the water, come to investigate."

"No, they will not," Sucre said. "Because we will tell them not to."

"You underestimate the U.S. Coast Guard," Grayson said. "And America."

"On the contrary, Madam Secretary," Sucre said. "I do not. They will not attempt a rescue. Not because I tell them not to, but because," he pointed at David Kingsley, "he will."

"I'll do no such thing."

Sucre waved at two of his men.

They grabbed Jerry Little and his cameraman, Malcolm Leary, forcibly pulling them from where they sat. The two men protested, but neither was strong enough to put up a fight against the men. A third man approached carrying Leary's heavy TV camera. In front of the stage, Sucre forced Leary and Little to their knees. He pressed his pistol to the cameraman's forehead.

To his credit, the young man remained stoic. His jaw twitched in a tight grimace, but he stared defiantly at Sucre.

"You will appear on television, Mr. President, and inform the world of your rather unfortunate predicament. You will tell anyone who's foolish enough to attempt a rescue that I will kill all the hostages, including you if they try. You will tell them to stand down, and you will deliver my demands."

Kingsley remained unmoved.

Sucre looked at Leary. "I would prefer to have this man operate his camera. For Mr. Little to convince his network to air this breaking news story." He snapped the slide of the gun back and put the gun to Leary's head again. "But I do have contingency plans available to me." He glared at Kingsley. "If you make that necessary."

"No," Kingsley said. "No more killing. I'll deliver your damn message."

CHAPTER SEVENTEEN

SKYJACK McMURPHY SPENT THE afternoon at the Keel Haul mainly because he didn't have anything else to do. He'd exchanged the large bandage over his eye with a simple plastic strip. His skin around the cut was an angry-looking purple. When Tara asked if he wanted something to eat with his fourth beer of the day, he declined with a wave of his hand. "Naw, I'm good."

Alone in the bar for most of the day, except for a couple of twenty-somethings, McMurphy recognized them as surfer regulars from the summer. He and Tara sat, talked, and searched Facebook for funny cat videos. The two young men watched a two-man luge competition on TV. A qualifying event for next year's Winter Olympics. They drank and ate and swapped tales of derring-do while surfing the wicked waves of Hampton Beach.

At their request, Tara had silenced the jukebox so they could watch the competition in peace.

And, of course, Captain Floyd, their resident barfly, was there.

He sat midway down the bar, his sea captain's hat squashed down on his head and his old gnarled hands wrapped around a mug of beer. He glared at Tara with his bushy white eyebrows knotted so close together it looked like he had a unibrow. "Hey, Toots."

She slapped a damp rag over her shoulder. "What is it, old man?"

"Where's that boss of yours? The idiot that owns this place?"

"He's busy. Why?"

"I've got a complaint."

Tara arched her eyebrow at that. "Tread carefully, you old coot."

McMurphy smiled at the exchange. Floyd was the only person in the universe who could get away with talking to Tara like that. Not McMurphy, not even Bannon. Not that either of them was foolish enough to ever try. McMurphy hadn't nicknamed her Blades for nothing.

"These two yahoos are monopolizing the TV." He pointed a hooked thumb at the surfer.

"What've you got against luge, Captain?" McMurphy asked.

"Nothing, except I don't wanna watch it."

"What do you want to watch?" Tara asked.

"Fly fishing," he said. "It's on the outdoor channel."

McMurphy covered his face with his meaty hand. The only thing more boring to watch than that would be golf. Or maybe paint drying.

Tara said, "I'll record it for you. You can watch it when the paying customers are through."

One of the young men at the far end of the bar gave her a thumbs-up and a smile.

The bar door opened, and a cold January breeze blew in.

A young girl wearing blue jeans, brown Uggs, and a parka came in carrying a pizza box. She shook snow off her long brown hair and slid the pizza box in front of McMurphy. "Here ya go, Skyjack."

"Thanks, Cindy."

She worked at the pizzeria down the street, one of the few places, other than the bars and restaurants on the strip, that remained open year-round. He handed her a fifty. "Keep it."

She kissed his cheek. "You're a peach."

When the pizza delivery girl was gone, Tara asked, "When did you order a pizza?"

He held up his phone. "I've got an app."

"Look at you." She smiled. "How twenty-first century of you."

"How about more beer and less sass, Blades." He opened the box. Steam and the mouth-watering smell of pepperoni pizza drifted into the air. "You want some or not?"

"What's on it?"

"Half plain, just for you."

She delivered his beer and pulled out a slice. "You're a peach, Skyjack," she said, mocking the delivery girl's fawning over him.

He felt himself blush.

"Hey, dudes," one of the surfer guys called out. "You might wanna turn the volume up here."

McMurphy and Tara glanced over at them. A big red banner scrolled across the top of the flat screen. It read *Breaking News*. Tara dropped her slice of pizza back in the box and grabbed the remote. She aimed it at the TV.

A national newscaster appeared on screen. McMurphy could only remember him as Ben Something. He held several sheets of paper in his hands. A somber expression on his face.

"We've just gotten word," he said, staring straight at the camera. "The President of the United States has been taken hostage. Details are sketchy as this is a breaking news story. But inside government officials have confirmed President Kingsley is being held against his will, and we're told the White House has received a list of demands from the people responsible."

McMurphy came to his feet and walked halfway down the bar, staring at the screen. "You've got to be kidding me."

Behind Ben Something was a stock footage video of a sailing Coast Guard cutter. Not the *Putnam* but a smaller, high-endurance class ship.

"Here's what we know so far," Ben said, reading from the papers he held. "After attending a fundraiser dinner last night in downtown Boston to kick off the President's re-election campaign, Kingsley was scheduled to make an unprecedented trip with a group of handpicked VIP donors, congressional insiders, and reporters to visit Tiamat Bluff, the so-called city under the sea. Reports tell us the President departed this morning from Logan Airport to rendezvous by helicopter with a Coast Guard cutter, the *George R. Putnam*."

"Get on with it," McMurphy groused.

"According to sources, the trip progressed without incident until our local Boston station, WCVS News9, received a televised transmission from their reporter on the scene, Jerry Little. We have obtained a copy of that footage. What we are about to show is raw and uncut. Some may find the images disturbing." He looked away for a second and nodded. "We're ready to show it to you now in its entirety."

The hairs on the back of McMurphy's neck stood straight up.

The TV screen shifted to a jumpy image of a bandshell in what looked like a city park. McMurphy thought it looked eerily like Hampton Beach's own Sea Shell Stage just a few hundred feet away, but it wasn't. After a burst of static over the feed, the image went out of focus, jumbled chaotically, then refocused again.

When the image finally settled, it did so on a headshot of President David Kingsley.

His suit, dress shirt, and tie were rumpled and disheveled, the front stained brown. The knot of the tie was yanked down, his top button open. His thick white hair was mussed. He looked harried, with dark, drawn eyes.

He started, "My fellow Americans."

His eyes darted off-screen. Then he looked at the camera again. "I make this appearance today under extreme duress. During my visit today to Tiamat Bluff, the experimental and cutting-edge city under the sea, unforeseen events have taken place, and I find myself in the hands of terrorist revolutionaries."

Tara's cell phone rang. She put it to her ear without taking her eyes off the TV. "Yes, we're watching it."

President Kingsley continued speaking. "A small group and I, as well as a skeleton crew of Tiamat Bluff workers, are being held by members of the Revolutionary Republic Army. General Sucre—"

Suddenly, the screen went blank.

Ben something, in a voiceover, reminded the viewers the video was being aired uncut and uncensored. When the President appeared on screen again, he had a large welt under his right eye.

"They beat him up," one of the surfer dudes said.

"Revolutionary Republic Army and Sucre," Tara said into her phone. "You got that?"

McMurphy glanced at her.

She said, "Kayla."

He nodded.

The President had taken a tremendous risk by identifying his captor by name. And paid a steep price for the intel if the facial wound was any indication. McMurphy's admiration for the man had just jumped tenfold. He knew Kayla Clarke would run with the information. If there was anything out there to find about this General Sucre and his Revolutionary Republic Army, she'd find it.

Kingsley cleared his throat. "The RRA has delivered a list of demands in a separate communique to Vice-President Wright. Among them: a ransom demand of one billion dollars in exchange for my safe return. Also, he wants U.S. military aid and financial support for their struggle against the illegitimate regime of General Javier Aguirre and the newly formed government of South American country Boca Las Casas. He demands formal Congressional legislation or an executive order from my office to keep such aid flowing until the corrupt, dictatorial leadership is dismantled and destroyed."

The president again glanced off-screen. Whatever he was being forced to say next, it was clear he was reluctant to do so. When he again looked at the camera, his eyes shimmered with tears. "These... terrorists have already killed upward of fifteen people in front of our very eyes. Others are being held prisoner, like us. They will be executed if any attempt at rescue is made. It is with that threat imposed, with the lives of American citizens on the line, I am ordering the *USCGC George R. Putnam* to retreat to a distance of at least fifty miles from the surface area above Tiamat Bluff. I am also imposing a no-sail and no-fly zone over the immediate area of Tiamat Bluff. All ships within a fifty-mile radius are to be removed."

"Screw that," McMurphy said. "He's under duress. His orders are meaningless."

The president continued. "I am being told the RRA has the ability to monitor this activity. If the government does not comply, more hostages will die. Countermeasures have been employed to prevent any strategic approach. Any attempts to conduct a rescue will be met with armed resistance and the loss of American lives. I reiterate my order. Stand down, or people will die."

Offscreen, a voice snapped, "Say it!"

McMurphy detected a Hispanic accent. The man tried to disguise it but was unsuccessful. Had to be General Sucre.

Kingsley nodded quickly. "A time limit has been imposed in the communique delivered to Vice-President Wright. Over the next twenty-four hours, if certain benchmark conditions are not met on a timely basis—to the satisfaction of my captors—hostages will be executed."

"Turn the camera," the same offscreen voice said. "Over here."

The shaky picture swung left, blurred, then refocused on Jerry Little, the TV anchorman and personality. He was on his knees. His hands were behind his back. Tied or handcuffed. His cheeks were wet with tears. A hand extended into the frame. Dusky skin. The hand gripped a Century Arms Micro Draco AK-47 pistol. A semi-automatic with a six-inch barrel and a thirty-round banana magazine. The gun was pressed to Little's temple.

"No. Please don't," Little begged.

"To demonstrate just how serious we are," the voice said.

He pulled the trigger.

The bang caused everyone in the bar to jump. The two surfer dudes turned their heads away. Their expressions reflected the disgust they felt. On the screen, Little fell to the side amid a spray of blood and brain matter. The video feed jumbled. The audio recorded several gasps.

The voice said, "The clock is ticking."

Captain Floyd put into words what everyone was thinking. "Animals."

The screen went blank for a second before the visibly shaken Ben Something reappeared.

"To our... viewers who watched... and were... upset by that. We apologize, but—"

"Shut it off," McMurphy said.

Tara used the remote and turned the TV off. The bar remained in stunned silence. She still had her cell phone pressed to her ear. McMurphy looked at her. "You saw?"

Tara nodded. "He's there."

When the camera shifted to focus on Jerry Little, it panned past a group of people. The hostages. Among them were Secretary Grayson and Brice Bannon. They were under heavily armed guard and as helpless to act as McMurphy and Tara were standing in the Keel Haul hundreds of miles away.

"They're alive. For now." Before he could comment further, his cell phone rang.

He answered. "McMurphy... yeah, of course." He waited a minute, listening. "Yes, sir." More listening. McMurphy felt his features harden into a mask of anger and determination. "I do, Mr. Vice-President. Get us on the *Putnam*, sir. We'll take care of the rest."

CHAPTER EIGHTEEN

VICE-PRESIDENT ETHAN FORRESTER WRIGHT stood behind the Resolute Desk in the Oval Office. His suit jacket was draped over the chair behind him. He wore a white dress shirt, the collar open and his tie pulled loose. His sleeves were rolled two turns up his arm. A broad man in his fifties, his steel-gray hair was cut short to his scalp—a crew cut—the way he'd worn it since his eighteenth birthday when he was inducted into the Army in a dingy, old recruiting office on Livingston Street in Brooklyn.

He slammed the phone down in the cradle, making the bell ring.

In the Oval Office with him were the Deputy Secretary of Homeland Security, Richard Diaz, James Williamson, the DHS Chief of Staff to Diaz and Elizabeth Grayson, the DoD Secretary General, Montgomery Hall, the Secret Service Director, Clarisse Walters, the Commandant of the Coast Guard, Admiral Ray Walcott, and Abigail Flores, the Director of the FBI.

He looked at them. "McMurphy's looped in. Get him to the *Putnam*."

"We've already dispatched an HH-65 Dolphin helicopter to pick him up in New Hampshire, Admiral Walcott said. "He'll be on board in a few hours, sir."

General Hall cleared his throat.

"You've something to say, Monty?" Wright asked.

"With all due respect, sir—"

"Which means with no respect at all," Wright interrupted. "But go ahead. Let's hear it."

"We've got protocols in place for this sort of thing. This is the very reason the Hostage Recovery Fusion Cell was created."

Several years earlier, in response to an alarming increase in the number of American hostages being taken overseas, the government created a unique interagency entity responsible for coordinating and handling the recovery of U.S. hostages abroad. Made up of hostage recovery professionals from Defense, the State Department, Justice, Treasury, and the FBI, along with the intelligence community, the group operated out of FBI Headquarters in Washington, D.C.

"They've planned and trained for years for just this sort of situation. I don't think relegating the President's safety, his life, quite frankly, to a… a puddle pirate pilot is the right call." He quickly added, "Sir."

"I have to agree with the general," Abby Flores, the FBI Director, said. "We've got experienced hostage negotiation teams and rapid-response forces made up of FBI, military, and Secret Service agents, trained for this very scenario."

"Trained to storm a city one thousand feet under the ocean surface?" Admiral Walcott asked. "One we've been warned has been fortified against attack. By nutjobs who've already killed at least a dozen hostages or more, including Secret Service agents, a U.S. Senator, a congressman, and the President's Chief of Staff. Who do you have that's trained to deal with that, Abby? How do you flash-bang your way through a structure designed to withstand thirty atmospheres of water pressure?"

General Hall didn't back down. "The SEALs, sir." He looked over at Admiral Walcott, conceding a little. "Your own Coast Guard's Maritime Security Response Teams could assist."

"Quit glory-hogging, General," Richard Diaz said. "Everyone in this room is aware of just how well-trained Skyjack McMurphy is. That training you talk of? SEAL, the MSRT, Special Forces. He's had it. He was a DOG, for Christ's sake. And need I remind you. It was he and Bannon who stopped the attacks on the Oceanic Princess *and* Yankee Stadium last year. They single-handedly saved over forty thousand lives and, in all likelihood, prevented a war with Russia. And no one is more motivated to save that group of people than Skyjack McMurphy. So yeah, sending him in *is* the right call."

"But," Flores said before Wright cut her off with a raised hand.

"This is no time for this interagency bickering. Besides, correct me if I'm wrong, Abby, but wasn't it your agents, the architects of this damn hostage fusion cell, who said it had to be willing to work with anyone if it were to succeed in its mandate to get our people home? That a unified government approach was the key to success."

Flores snapped her jaw shut.

Wright went on. "McMurphy's in. End of debate. Abby. Monty. Put your teams together, draw up your plans and get your people on site. They're to check in with Captain Tolliver. I've decided to comply with Sucre's demand until we can determine if he's got the means to monitor us the way he says. The *Putnam* is standing by at the designated fifty-mile mark, waiting. For now. The SEALs will take the lead on this, but whatever they do, Skyjack McMurphy's a part of it. It's what Kingsley would want, and you all know it."

There was a unified chorus of "Understood" and "Yes, sir."

"Good. Now, Jimmy," Wright said to Williamson, Grayson's Chief of Staff. "I want you to work with State, get me everything there is to know about this Sucre character and his Revolutionary Republic Army. I want to know who they are, everything we know about them, anything that will help us fight them. Right down to what they had for breakfast this morning."

"Yes, sir. We've got some of our best people on it already."

"Good." Wright took a moment to look at each person in the room. "The priority is to get the President back safe and sound and to save American lives. But, after this is all over, there will be an internal investigation. I'm going to know how something like this could possibly happen. Secret Service. DHS. The White House. This is a catastrophic failure. Heads will roll. Mark my words."

He paused before going on. "In the meantime, we need to contain this. No talking to the press. No leaks. I want this so buttoned-up that 'need to know' looks like Wiki-leaks in comparison. Am I understood?"

They responded with a murmur of yes, sirs, and nods.

"Good. Admiral, how fast can you get me out to the *Putnam?* I need to be hands-on."

Clarisse Walters cleared her throat. "That's not happening, sir."

"Excuse me?"

"You're not going out there," the Secret Service director said. "You need to stay here. I'm even considering making you retreat to the bunker."

"Making me!" Wright exploded. He pounded his fist into the desk.

Walters didn't back down. "Yes, sir. You are the acting president. It's my job to keep you safe, even if I have to do it by force."

"If you'd done your job in the first place, we wouldn't be in this situation." That stung, and it showed. But Wright didn't let up. "A blood thirty band of terrorists waltzed right into Tiamat Bluff, a facility your advanced team supposedly cleared. They took it over without an ounce of resistance. They killed American citizens. And they're holding the President of the United States hostage. On your watch."

"That's not the issue here," she said, remaining defiant. "Your safety is. Sir."

"We're going to get to the bottom of that failure, one way or the other. Trust me."

Walters squared his shoulders. "Agreed and with my full cooperation. Once we're through this crisis and with you here, in Washington, and not on the deck of the *Putnam.*"

Wright opened his mouth to protest, but Diaz spoke first. "It only puts you in harm's way. We can coordinate everything from here. Captain Tolliver's top-notch, sir. And, of course, you'll have McMurphy on-site, too."

Wright forcefully exhaled before sitting down. "Very well. But here. The Oval Office. No bunker. The public needs that reassurance. Clear?"

Walters nodded. "For now."

Wright grunted. "Now, onto this madman's list of demands. The money, fine, we can do that."

"You're not seriously thinking of giving him what he wants?" Flores asked.

"Don't be ridiculous," Wright said. "But we're going to need to buy time. Let this clown think we're acting in good faith; string him along until we can get our act together and get Kingsley the hell out of there."

"Congress will never agree to passing a law to aid and support a terrorist organization," Diaz said. "To appear to capitulate to terrorists will ruin them politically."

"You think I give a goddamn about politics at a moment like this?" Wright demanded.

"No," Diaz said. "But they will. They won't play ball. If they pass a law like that, even temporarily, the twenty-four-hour news cycle will portray them all as giving in to the terrorists. By then, the damage to their reputations will be irrevocable."

"Then we do a run around Congress," Wright said. "Screw 'em."

"You're suggesting an executive order," Flores said, a lawyer by training before joining the FBI. "That has to come from the President. But it'd be invalid in his current situation."

"Captured and under duress," Wright said.

She nodded.

General Hall cleared his throat. "The President could be declared incapacitated… "

"You're talking about invoking the 25th Amendment," Flores said. "Are we there?"

"No," Wright said, knowing exactly where the General was going. "The President is fine."

"The president is under a terrorist's influence, capable of being coerced," Flores said. "He's already issued orders under obvious duress."

"We need a Commander in Chief who's accessible," Hall added. "One who can communicate, make decisions, issue orders, one that isn't compromised. We don't have that."

"No," Wright said again, more forcefully.

His tone softened. "Not yet. We're not there yet."

CHAPTER NINETEEN

AFTER TARA SNAPPED OFF the television at the Keel Haul, a stunned silence hung over the bar and its few occupants. It reminded Tara of that horrible day when the world stopped, shocked at watching the World Trade Center towers fall. She was in a bar in Cairo at the time, not quite twenty years old. Watching on every screen in the bar, along with everyone else, as those massive structures collapsed in a billow of black smoke.

She'd been affected by it. Of course, the entire world had been.

What she didn't know at the time was how that event would influence her life. Shape her entire future. How that same kind of cowardly terrorist act would kill her parents and set her on the path to becoming the person she was at that moment. What some have referred to as a human weapon.

Eventually, the surfer dudes quietly pushed back from the bar. Their stools scrapped the wood floor. The sound was incredibly loud in the stillness. They dug out their wallets, but Tara told them not to. They were good. They each dropped a twenty on the bar anyway, mumbled their thanks, and left. Even Captain Floyd shuffled toward the door without giving

Tara and McMurphy grief about having to leave, which he always did, even at the regular closing time.

At the door, he looked back at them. "Bannon. Get him back."

"We will, Captain," McMurphy said.

Floyd frowned as if giving the matter deep thought, then added, "Good. 'Cause breaking in a new owner's a real pain in the arse. Don't you two make me have to do that."

"Promise," McMurphy said.

Then, the old guy was gone.

Tara paced behind the bar. A caged tiger ready to tear someone's head off. "When do we leave?"

"Wright's sending a ride." McMurphy tossed back the last of his beer. The pizza was left uneaten.

He glanced at the TV. It was still shut off. He silently raged. She could feel his anger like it had a physical presence. Tara knew how he felt. She felt the same way. She tossed the countertop flap open and came out from behind the bar.

"Where are you going?" McMurphy asked.

"Get my go-bag. It's in the car."

"That won't be necessary," Kayla Clarke said, entering the bar. Letting the heavy door bang close behind her. "Not yet, anyway."

Cold, outside air swept through the bar.

An active-duty lieutenant, Kayla was officially assigned to the Coast Guard's Judge Advocate General's Office, First Division, stationed in Boston, Massachusetts, but she was also part of Brice Bannon's little strike team. More the tech and computer person, she didn't get to go out in the field as often as she'd want, but she was as good as any IT person out there at trolling the Internet and scouring databases and other information sources and coming back with gold.

"What are you talking about?" Tara asked. She and Kayla were close friends, but if she meant to stop Tara from helping rescue Bannon, the woman was treading into dangerous waters.

"You're not going to the *Putnam,*" Kayla said emphatically.

Anger bubbled over as Tara took a step toward the woman. "Who's going to stop me?"

"Orders," Kayla said, undeterred. "Straight from Diaz." The Deputy Secretary of Homeland Security, their immediate supervisor in Elizabeth Grayson's absence. "And the Vice-President." She nodded to McMurphy. "As for you. Your ride's waiting."

He crossed to the front window and pulled the shutters back.

Tara expected to see a state police car or dark government sedan from the Coast Guard's motor pool parked outside. Instead, a twin-engine HH-65 Dolphin helicopter sat on the narrow strip of beach across the street. Its single main rotor spun lazily. The cabin's side door was open, awaiting its passenger.

McMurphy looked at Tara, reluctant to leave without her.

She bit her lip, weighing her two choices: stay and follow orders, whatever they might be or defy the bureaucrats and go help save Bannon and the others. McMurphy waited. He arched a bushy red eyebrow. He'd support either decision. She knew that.

"I need you here, Tara," Kayla said. "Please."

"Blades?" McMurphy asked.

"Go," she said, making her decision but not liking it.

"You sure?"

She nodded reluctantly. "Yes. Damn it. Go. Before I change my mind."

Kayla nodded her approval.

McMurphy headed for the door.

Tara called out, stopping him. "Skyjack."

"Yeah?"

"Bring them back. All of them."

"Count on it." He pushed through the door without even pausing to grab his coat.

Tara went to the window and watched him jog across the street. He climbed into the waiting helicopter, paused to give the bar a last look before he slammed the cabin door shut. The chopper's rotors immediately picked up speed. They lifted off, creating a cyclone of sand and sea spray beneath it as it gained altitude.

Tara pushed the shutters closed and turned to Kayla. "Convince me I didn't just make a big mistake."

Kayla crossed to the bar and slapped her laptop—encased in a military-grade steel casing—onto the bar. "You didn't." She booted the computer up. "The Vice-President wants us to figure out how this could've happened. Procedure, protocol, somewhere there was a breakdown. We need to figure out what it was."

Tara returned to the server's side of the bar. "Inside information. Who got it, and who gave it to them?"

"Exactly."

"Coffee or a drink?" Tara asked.

"Put a pot of coffee on, but I'll start with booze," Kayla said. "Diaz believes the leak came from the White House's inner circle. Someone high up. We need to find him, or her, or them."

"What's that got to do with me?" Tara glanced at the closed windows, forcing down the regret churning in her gut.

"The President's trip to Tiamat Bluff wasn't a state secret, but it wasn't highly publicized either. He wanted to make a big deal of it. Make a big splash on the news tonight. Use it as the setting to launch his re-election campaign. Demonstrate what a friend he is to science, business, innovation, that sort of thing."

Tara felt her patience slipping dangerously away. "Get on with it, Kayla."

"Which means the pool of people in the know about the trip would be quite small. The White House inner circle, protocol, logistics, and travel teams, the Secret Service, high-ranking members of the Coast Guard."

"Anyone working for Tiamat Bluff," Tara added. "People who work for that company, run by that lady scientist who spearheaded this thing. What's her name?"

"Dr. Robin Larson. I've accounted for them, too, of course," Kayla said but immediately returned to her train of thought. "Diaz has given me direct access to all the White House and top agency systems: Defense, Secret Service, Justice, you name it. I've already downloaded their vetting reports, background checks, financials. Everything about anyone who was involved in arranging this trip. I also have a list of all the personnel involved in the advance teams. And anyone in government, the military, and civilian companies who had prior knowledge or information about the President's itinerary."

"Can't you just hack all that stuff?"

"I can," Kayla said, adding, "But it's so much easier when they give you permission."

"Okay, so that's great," Tara said. "It still doesn't tell me what I'm supposed to be doing. I'm not the 'pour over paperwork and spreadsheets' kind of gal." She poured two gin and tonics over rocks and handed one to Kayla. "Kicking in doors, doing enhanced interrogations, that's more my speed."

"If we're going to help Brice and the President, we need to get a handle on who's orchestrated this plan."

"I thought that was this General Sucre and his Revolutionary Republic Army?"

"Maybe, but Boca Las Casas is a small country. The RRA is a minor resistance force with minimal impact or influence."

"Until now."

"Until now," Kayla agreed. She took a healthy swallow of her drink and grimaced. Tara had been heavy-handed on the booze, figuring they both needed it. "This is a sophisticated operation. Well beyond their normal scope. Certainly, beyond the resources, they have access, too. I suspect someone's helping them, bankrolling them. Maybe even pulling the strings."

"That's where I come in," Tara said eagerly.

"That's where you come in," Kayla agreed. "We discover who's ultimately behind this…"

Tara's smile was humorless. "I get to kick ass and take names, as Skyjack might say."

"Exactly."

"Now you're talking." Tara raised her glass. They toasted and drank. "Point me to the who and where, and let's get this thing done."

CHAPTER TWENTY

THE HH-65 DOLPHIN HELICOPTER skimmed swiftly over the open ocean water, traveling due east. Its twin turboshaft engines at full throttle pushed the needle to its near max speed of two hundred miles per hour. The medivac-capable search and rescue chopper usually flew with two pilots and two crew. They were one person shy as McMurphy occupied the co-pilot seat. The craft was equipped with an M240 machine gun and one Barrett M107 12.70mm precision rifle.

McMurphy hoped they wouldn't be needed but was always happy to have that kind of firepower available. The Coast Guard's motto wasn't *Semper Paratus*—Always Ready—for nothing.

He glanced over at the pilot. A young man so fresh-faced he looked like he hadn't yet had his first shave. "What's your name, son?"

"Jamison, sir." His voice carried over the roar of the overhead rotor and the engine noise.

"How old are you, Jamison? Twelve?"

Jamison glanced over at him and grinned. "Twenty-six, sir. Don't you worry. I've got four years with the Guard and over seven hundred fifty flight hours. You're in good hands."

"Seven hundred fifty, huh? A real master then."

"Yes, sir," Jamison said proudly. "Ever thought about flying, sir?"

"Son, please. I had more time than that in the seat during my six months in the Sandbox while getting shot at," McMurphy added. "Probably while you were still in diapers."

"You're a pilot?"

McMurphy smirked. "They didn't tell you who you were picking up, did they?"

"No, sir. Just to get your ass—sorry—to the *Putnam* forthwith."

"Quit calling me sir. Makes me feel old. It's Skyjack." He stuck out his hand. "Nice to meet you, kid."

Jamison stared at him with his mouth open. "Wait. What?"

"You all right, Jamison? You look like you're seeing a ghost."

"More like a living legend. You're telling me you're Skyjack McMurphy? The Skyjack McMurphy."

"Last I checked." McMurphy couldn't help but grin. "You've heard of me?"

"Well, sure. Is it true? You actually stole the Marine One helicopter?"

"Allegedly. I can't talk about it until the statute of limitations runs out."

"Holy smokes. The guys back at the base aren't going to believe it when I tell 'em. They've told me stories about you for years."

"How about you work on landing this bird on the *Putnam* without putting us in the drink first." McMurphy pointed at the *Putnam* as they approached.

The gleaming white hull of the four-hundred-foot legend-class cutter sat majestically on the horizon of the deep turquoise sea. The prominent service mark, the angled blue and white racing stripe, and the red bar with the Coast Guard shield centered on it, and in black letters: U.S. Coast Guard under the superstructure, filled McMurphy with patriotic pride. He'd served nearly twenty years, and still, his chest swelled at sights like that.

"Unless you want me to take over," McMurphy asked.

"Appreciate the offer, si—Skyjack," Jamison said. "But I've got it."

Spoken like a true pilot. McMurphy would've been disappointed in the kid if he'd responded in any other way. As it was, even under McMurphy's watchful eye, Jamison did a fine job of gently bringing the Dolphin down in the middle of the *Putnam's* stern flight deck.

"Like a pro," McMurphy said, unhooking his five-point harness and giving Jamison a good handshake.

"Thanks. That means a lot," Jamison said. "Coming from you."

"Don't put too much stock into those old stories you hear," McMurphy said. "Most of 'em are hogwash. I ain't nothing special."

"Respectfully, I doubt that, sir."

McMurphy patted Jamison's shoulder as he climbed into the cabin in back. From there, he hopped down to the cutter's flight deck and gave the chopper crew a so-long salute. An icy wind whipped across the deck, made worse by the spinning rotor overhead. A bracing reminder McMurphy had left the Keel Haul without a coat. He jogged across the flight deck, feeling out of place on the cutter wearing civilian clothes.

And where he was greeted with his first surprise.

Amal Haddad, the President's Chief of Staff, stood off to the side, along with Captain Tolliver, waiting for him.

McMurphy threw Tolliver a salute. "Permission to come aboard, Captain."

"Permission granted," Tolliver said. He returned the salute before clasping McMurphy's hand, shaking it enthusiastically. They were old friends. "Good to see you again, Skyjack. Sorry it's like this."

"Same." McMurphy turned to Haddad. "Ms. Haddad. I was told you were among those killed in the submersible explosions. Not that I'm not glad you weren't."

"Amal, Mr. McMurphy." She cast her eyes downward. "I was called away to deal with an emergency in Washington. Rather than delay the other's departure, I told them to go ahead. That phone call saved my life."

"Lucky for you," McMurphy said. His tone left open the possibility it hadn't been luck at all.

She gave him an odd look. As did Tolliver. "A young Washington staffer took my place on that vessel, Mr. McMurphy. He died in my place."

"I didn't mean to imply anything—"

"Yes, you did," she said sharply, but then her tone softened. "And you are not wrong to do so. I was scheduled to be on one submersible that's been taken hostage, and then a second that blew up, circumstances causing me to miss both. I'd question that, too. I know your record, your reputation, Mr. McMurphy. Follow your instincts. Do your job. That's why you're here. Just try not to be disrespectful until it's justified."

"Got it." He pulled at his lumberjack flannel shirt, still wearing the 'pilots know how to stick it' t-shirt. He shivered.

"Let's get you inside before you catch a death of cold," Tolliver said. "Find you something more appropriate to wear, Chief."

He led them into the superstructure and then up the flights of metal steps to his quarters. Tolliver shut the door. Haddad took a seat on his bunk. Once inside, McMurphy could see Haddad looked exhausted. Her eyes were raw from crying.

McMurphy had never met her before but knew her to be a competent and ruthless political attack dog for the President. Fiercely loyal, this had to be a tremendous burden for her, putting her very far afield of her Pennsylvania Avenue wheelhouse.

Tolliver's quarters were small, with barely enough room to fit the single-size bunk. Still, a brown leather easy chair, a wardroom, and a desk were jammed into the compartment as well. The latter was cluttered with papers and a computer keyboard. The flat-screen monitor was embedded in the bulkhead alongside two brass-rimmed portholes.

Over the bunk was an oil painting of the *USCGC Alexander Hamilton* navigating in rough ocean waters. McMurphy knew the story. A treasury-class cutter bravely battling swirling, storm-surged waves off the Icelandic coast in 1942. It had been torpedoed by a German submarine, killing all twenty-six men on board.

"Coffee?" Tolliver asked.

A small coffee maker sat on his desk. The glass carafe full of coffee. The hot plate was on.

"Depends on what you can put in it?" McMurphy said.

He glanced over his shoulder. "On a Coast Guard cutter, Chief? Really?" He made a *tsk, tsk* sound even as he pulled a bottle of Jim Beam bourbon from a low desk drawer. He poured generous amounts of coffee and booze into two mugs he'd lined up on his desk. The mugs were white and had a blue-lined image of the *Putnam* on one side and the Coast Guard shield on the other.

"Ms. Haddad?"

"Why the hell not," she said with a sigh, accepting a mug. He filled up a third for himself.

"Okay, catch me up," McMurphy said, his broad shoulders almost as wide as the room itself.

Like players in a ping pong match, Haddad and Tolliver went back and forth, telling him everything they knew.

When they were done, Haddad said, "I need to caution you. We believe someone in the White House, maybe someone in the President's cabinet itself, may have been compromised."

"An inside job. Almost goes without saying," McMurphy said. "An operation like this took months of planning. And resources. And would require inside knowledge, information."

"This wasn't a highly publicized event," Haddad said. "The President wanted it to be a big reveal." She waved her hands like she was revealing a movie marquee. "Tiamat Bluff and his re-election campaign. It was closely controlled."

"Still, multiple agencies, including civilian organizations, had to have had 'inside information' regarding the event," McMurphy guessed.

"Of course," Haddad said.

"You're saying the mole or moles could be anyone?" Tolliver said.

"Anyone with prior or inside knowledge about the trip." He did his best not to gaze at Haddad.

"I didn't know where we were assigned to go until my orders came in this morning," Tolliver said. "Meaning you and I are in the clear."

McMurphy nodded.

"But not me," Haddad said.

McMurphy tried to sound apologetic. "Until we can vet you, yes. Your access to what we do. What we plan will be limited."

"Skyjack," Tolliver said. "She's the President's Chief of Staff, for God's sake."

"No, Captain. He's right."

"We'll clear you as soon as we can, ma'am."

"Great. How the hell do we do that?" Tolliver asked. "And who's to say whoever we get to do the vetting can be trusted?"

"It's already being taken care of," McMurphy said. "Two of the three people I trust most in the entire world are working on that even as we speak. What they give us will be solid." To dissuade any further objection, he added, "Neither of them knew anything about before the news report hit."

He turned to Tolliver. "Tell me what we know about how they destroyed the submersibles?"

"We don't." Tolliver shook his head. "Secret Service swears they checked them thoroughly before they went down, so we don't suspect planted explosives." He glanced at Haddad. "But considering what you've just said... that could be crap. One of their agents could be involved."

"Is Tiamat Bluff weaponized?" McMurphy said. "Armaments of any kind that could've destroyed those vessels?"

"Of course not," Haddad said. "It's a facility for science, peaceful research, and ultimately a community for families to live and work in."

"Just asking." Again, McMurphy addressed Tolliver. "Torpedoes? From a sub?"

"We thought about that but came up empty on radar and sonar scans. No sign of any submarine activity at all. Before the visit, we cleared the area of all surface vessels."

"NORAD reported no airborne anomalies," Haddad offered.

"The priority is to come up with a rescue plan."

"Preferably one where everyone comes out alive," Tolliver said.

"Goes without saying. What assets do we have?" McMurphy asked.

"DoD is flying a SEAL team up from Virginia," Haddad said. "With them is an FBI hostage negotiator from Quantico. They should be here within the hour."

"Does the Vice-President seriously think we can talk this Sucre guy out of there?" Tolliver asked.

"Probably not," Haddad admitted. She handed her mug to Toliver. "More coffee, if you don't mind, Captain."

As he poured the coffee, and the Jim Beam, Haddad gave them a quick rundown on the concept and background of the Hostage Recovery Fusion Cell.

"Too many cooks," McMurphy grumbled.

She accepted the refilled mug from Tolliver.

"But a negotiator might be useful in keeping Sucre distracted," McMurphy said, thinking out loud. "What do you know about the SEAL team?"

"This specific team? Nothing," Haddad said. "But the SEALs are the best of the best."

McMurphy shrugged at that. Not a point he felt like arguing at the moment. "What about you, Bob?" he asked. "Any special talent on board?"

He was hoping for a Maritime Security Response Team. They were the offshoot of the decommissioned Deployable Operations Group. When the DOG program was disbanded a number of years back, the MSRT program was born.

Still, despite being a water-down version, in McMurphy's opinion, they had some damn fine men and women among their ranks. Highly trained, competent spitfires. Teams he and Bannon had had the pleasure of working with in the past with great success.

Tolliver knew what he was getting at but shook his head. "Just your run-of-the-mill coasties, I'm afraid. But they're ready to step up and do whatever needs doing."

"I'm sure they are, Bob. And we'll keep that in mind," McMurphy said. He paced the five-foot span in the room, trying to figure out what to do next. To Haddad, he said, "When did you say this SEAL team of yours was getting here?"

CHAPTER TWENTY-ONE

BANNON BIT BACK HIS anger.

It had been several hours since Sucre publicly executed Jerry Little. Since that time, he'd left the blood-spattered body lying on the ground in front of the bandshell stage. A pool of blood, dark and shiny, had formed around his head. His eyes remained open, staring at the hostages forced to sit and look back at him. The shock the newsman had felt in those final seconds of life remained present in his expression in death.

While filming, Leary had jumped back and dropped his camera to the ground.

Bannon had rushed forward, trying to seize the opportunity to attack, but two of Sucre's people grabbed his arms from behind, arresting his charge forward. His reward was a punch in his solar plexus from Sucre.

Now, they all sat staring at the dead man. Quiet, to deal with their own private thoughts. Unable or unwilling to look away.

Sucre had left for a while, leaving the group under the watchful—and Bannon had to reluctantly admit—professional eye of the RRA terrorists stationed around the park and the concert seating area.

When the general returned, Kingsley rose to his feet.

"Sucre," Kingsley said. "Please, in the name of decency, remove the body. Have some respect for the dead."

"No," Sucre said. "He is your reminder of what we are capable of. Of what we will do if you step out of line."

"Proof of what an insane sociopath you are," Bannon offered.

"Careful, Commander Bannon, or you might find yourself with a similar hole in your head," Sucre warned.

Interesting, Bannon thought. As far as he could recall, no one had mentioned his name or who he was. And certainly, no one had referred to him by rank. Yet Sucre knew him. How?

"Now sit down," Sucre ordered, but Kingsley remained standing.

Grayson put a hand on Kingsley's arm. "David, please sit."

He let her pull him a step back and then down into the seat next to her.

Bannon sat beside Grayson on her other side.

In the row behind them, Leary stared ahead with a vacant look in his eyes. Clearly, a young man who had not experienced violence on this scale before. Most people hadn't, Bannon reminded himself. Seated beside the cameraman, Robin Larson sat, holding Leary's hands in hers. She attempted to console him while struggling to maintain her own composure. Dr. Nomura's shocking death still fresh in her mind. As were others she'd spent the last few years working side-by-side with. Many already dead. The rest? Like them, in grave danger.

Holloway sat on Kingsley's left, opposite Grayson, remaining ever vigilant.

Bannon leaned toward his bosses. He lowered his voice. Agent Holloway was still in earshot, but no one else was. "Something's not right here," he said.

"I didn't know you had a talent for understatement, Commander," Kingsley said.

"What I mean, sir, is Sucre. His story," Bannon said. "He claims he's with the RRA, yet half his men are Caucasian. Look around. The others. They're black, Hispanic, a few Asians. And women. Not exactly the Latin American hit squad you'd expect."

"Fringe sympathizers of the cause," Grayson suggested. "The way many young Americans were recruited to fight for al Qaeda and ISIL."

"Perhaps, but his demands don't make sense either," Bannon said. Something was off, but he couldn't put his finger on it. "A demand for money I get. That's basic hostage-taking 101. It's the demand for military aid and support that I can't figure out. He's got to know that's unobtainable."

"Of course, it's unobtainable," Kingsley hissed under his breath. "Everyone knows the United States doesn't negotiate with hostages."

"That's an argument for another time, Mr. President," Bannon said. "My point is this. Here's an underfunded rebel terror group, fighting against a brutal but tiny regime. Yet they have dozens of Steyr machine pistols. They're Austrian-made full-automatic weapons with thirty-round box magazines. 9mm Taurus PT92 semiautomatic pistols with seventeen-round magazines. They're not junk. They don't come cheap on the black market."

"What are you getting at, Brice?" Grayson asked.

Bannon went on as if he hadn't heard her question. "They'd need a submarine of some kind, maybe more than one, to get down here. Scuba gear and training. And they've deployed a network of explosive underwater drones. In effect, randomly shifting minefield. That level of technology, the sophistication… we're not talking fertilizer and propane tank bombs."

"I'm not following, Commander," Kingsley said, cutting to the chase.

"To do what they've done here takes a hefty bankroll. If they have access to those kinds of resources, why the demand for money?"

"War's a costly proposition, son."

"Fair enough, but here's what's really bothering me. His demand for a law or executive order to continue supporting their war efforts. Hostage takers make finite demands. Money and a getaway car or whatever. The bad guys get them, or they don't, and the situation is over, successfully or otherwise. But continual military aid and support," Bannon continued. "That's ongoing. Unless they plan on holding us hostage until the crisis in their country is resolved… "

"Something that could take months or years to achieve," Grayson said, understanding what Bannon was getting at. "If ever."

"It's an unattainable goal in this situation, even if the U.S. wanted to comply. This very act would make that impossible."

"They're idiots," Kingsley concluded, increasingly agitated. "Clueless, murdering, savage idiots."

"I disagree, sir. Everything about this operation has been methodically planned and professionally carried out."

Kingsley doubled down. "Only an idiot would think Congress wouldn't reverse the law they wrote—"

"If they could be talked into writing one in the first place," Grayson said, agreeing.

"Or that you wouldn't strike down the executive order you wrote after your release," Bannon said. "The juxtaposition is downright glaring."

"What do you think is going on, Brice?" Grayson asked.

Bannon considered the question. "I don't have it all worked out yet, but funding the RRA and overthrowing Aguirre isn't the endgame. I'm certain of it."

"What is?" Kingsley asked.

Sadly, Bannon had to admit, "I don't know. Yet." He glanced over at Little's body. "What I do know is we need to devise a plan to get out of here without getting anyone else killed."

"No argument there," Kingsley said. "I'm hoping you have something in mind."

"Working on it," Bannon said. "But that brings up another concern I have, sir."

At his hesitance, Kingsley said, "Spit it out, man."

When he had Grayson, Kingsley, and Holloway's full attention, Bannon said, "Someone helped pull this off. Someone with inside information. An insider."

"Are you accusing someone on my staff of being a... what-do-you-call-them, a mole?" He shook his head. "I categorically reject that theory."

"No, sir," Holloway said, leaning in closer. "The commander's right." She looked around at the men and women positioned at the exits, posted at the seating area, then at the stage. Sucre had returned and was in deep conversation with one of them. "Intimate details about your trip were leaked, sir. There's no question about it. No other way."

"By whom?" he demanded.

"I don't know," Holloway admitted. There was a lot of that going around.

"We have to consider the possibility, David," Grayson said as gently as she could. "Someone in our government; the Secret Service, DoD, the White House, your Cabinet, sir. Someone provided the information, paved the way to make this happen."

"The Tiamat Bluff staff," Kingsley said stubbornly.

"No doubt them, too, sir," Bannon said. "But I think we're dealing with someone with a lot more clearance and information than that. Maybe multiple someones."

Kingsley visibly stewed. A vein throbbed along his jawline. He looked like a man chewing on a hated vegetable but forced to choke it down. "Say it's true. What's it matter?" he asked. "While we're down here?"

"Because at some point," Bannon said. "We'll reestablish contact with our people on the surface. When we do, we damn well better know who we can trust. And who we can't. Otherwise, any efforts we make down here will be for naught."

"And how the hell do you expect to do that?" Kingsley asked. "Figure out who to trust?"

Bannon glanced around and lowered his voice further. "I'm confident that's already being taken care of, sir." He knew as soon as the video announcing the President's capture and Jerry Little's televised execution hit the airwaves, McMurphy, Tara, and Kayla would be working on a rescue effort and digging into what had happened, how it had happened, who was behind it, and how to execute a rescue plan that wouldn't get everyone killed.

"Bottom line, we need to figure out how to get out of here," Grayson said.

"Agreed." Bannon's expression turned grim.

"Any ideas?" she asked.

His attention was on Sucre. "A few."

"Care to share, Commander?" Kingsley asked.

"It's best I don't, sir." He looked around without elaborating. Loose lips and sunk ships and all that.

TWENTY-TWO

TARA PACED BEHIND THE bar of the Keel Haul, feeling like a caged tigress. It had been hours since McMurphy had left. She'd received a single text from him telling her he'd arrived on the *Putnam*, and he was preparing to meet with an arriving SEAL team to discuss possible rescue scenarios.

Kayla sat on her barstool, tapping on the keyboard of her laptop like crazy without saying much. Her second gin and tonic sat on a paper napkin. The glass sweating. She'd set up a second laptop at the end of the bar where McMurphy usually sat. The screen angled so both she and Tara could see it.

The more Tara listened to Kayla's incessant tapping, the more she wanted to rip the laptop away from her, smash it to the ground, and then stomp it to pieces. She should've gone with Skyjack, she told herself. She took a deep breath. Instead of indulging her violent fantasy against an undeserving Kayla Clarke and unable to mete out justice against the terrorist thugs at Tiamat Bluff, she decided to have another drink.

She grabbed the gin bottle. Had it tipped over her glass when the computer facing her beeped, the fan whirled, and the screen lit up. The established video-conference linkup caught her with the bottle of gin in her hand. On the laptop's split-screen appeared images of Deputy Director Richard Diaz and the chief of staff he and Grayson shared, James Williamson.

"You sure this is the best time for a drink, Ms. Sardana?" Diaz asked.

Tara considered telling him where she wanted to shove the bottle but refrained. She put the bottle down and tossed the ice out of her glass. Her glare at her interim boss indicated her displeasure.

James Williamson cleared his throat and jumped right in. "We've received a bit of good news we wanted to pass along. It appears Amal Haddad wasn't on her way down to Tiamat Bluff in one of the doomed submersibles like we first thought. She's safe onboard the *Putnam*."

"How'd that happened?" Tara did nothing to mask her suspicion while looking at Kayla, who shared her concern.

"A call from the White House," Diaz told them. "A last-minute emergency requiring her immediate attention."

"Huh." Tara exchanged a glance with Kayla, who shrugged. "Convenient."

Diaz continued, "Jimmy and I are in constant contact with Captain Tolliver and Ms. Haddad and will stay on top of rescue operations going on there. A SEAL team and FBI negotiator have been dispatched."

Tara knew all this. "Skyjack?" she asked.

"He's involved top to bottom," Diaz assured her. "The Vice-President insisted on it."

"Great." That all sounded good to Tara except for one thing. She was sitting in the Keel Haul, twiddling her thumbs. "What do *we* do?"

Diaz answered with a question of his own. "This Revolutionary Republic Army. What do we know about them?"

"I queried a friend of mine at State," Kayla said. "They're a relatively new group, borne from the violent struggle that separated Boca Las Casas from Venezuela. A more extreme, more violent offshoot of the South American National People's Republican Army. Smaller. But what they lacked in numbers, they more than made up for in brutality. Several years ago, they stormed a police station, kidnapped and later killed a police sergeant and his family after ransom demands were not paid. More recently, they set off a car bomb in a shopping plaza that killed twenty-one and injured sixty-seven more in protest of their government's leadership, General Javier Aguirre."

"A sentiment we can all share," Williamson said.

"But not their methods," Diaz added.

Kayla continued. "They're reportedly responsible for seizing several cargo vessels and holding them for ransom in the Caribbean Sea. More often than not, large corporations will pay the demands rather than involve law enforcement."

"Especially in that part of the world," Diaz added.

"Sounds like kidnapping for ransom is in their wheelhouse," Williamson said.

"But small-scale," Tara said. "Those attacks, while brutal, all lack the sophistication needed to pull off an operation like this. This is way out of their league."

"Their ambition may have outreached their capacity," Williamson said. "Bitten off more than they can chew, as it were."

"That might be something in our favor," Diaz said.

Tara had her doubts. There was a lot—too much—that they didn't know yet.

A silence fell among them. Tara's thoughts went to Tiamat Bluff. To Brice and Grayson, to the others. What they were up against. The horrific acts these terrorists were capable of.

"Do you have anything else for us, Deputy Director?" Kayla asked.

"Not at the moment," Diaz said. "We'll leave you two to it. I want hourly updates through the usual secured communications."

"Yes, sir," Kayla said. She closed down the connection, powered down that computer, and closed the laptop even though the screen had gone blank. She looked at Tara.

"We're not talking to them again," Tara said, making more drinks. "Insiders were involved in this. I don't know we can trust them. Or anyone. Not until we know more."

"Even if not them," Kayla said. "We can know if they speak to the wrong people. Even if not knowingly."

With a fresh drink in hand, tapping keys with one hand, Kayla said, "The RRA reportedly has, at most, fifty to a hundred members. How'd they pull something like this off?"

"They've partnered with someone with much deeper pockets. Maybe they've rejoined with the NPRA," Tara suggested. She knew from experience how these alliances formed and fell apart and reformed. Based on the constantly changing geopolitical landscapes. Today's friend was tomorrow's enemy. "Someone willing to put up the funds, resources, manpower, to make this happen."

"If that's the case," Kayla said. "Why make the demand for more money?"

"Waging war is expensive," Tara said. "Can a revolution ever have enough capital? What's interesting to me is the demand for military aid and support going forward. How do you make the U.S. do that once you've let the hostages go?"

Kayla stared at her. Tara read her expression. She didn't know the answer but feared hearing it.

"Hold the hostages indefinitely," Tara said.

"Christ."

"Or," Tara said, thinking out loud. "It's all a ploy."

"For what?" Kayla said.

"Distraction. Misdirection," Tara said.

"For what purpose?"

Tara shrugged. They had too little information. "Keep us busy with their demands, scrambling to do whatever we can to save the President while someone, somewhere else, is doing something worse."

"Worse than holding the President for ransom and killing upward of a dozen people?" Kayla asked.

It was a terrible thought, but Tara was used to terrible people doing terrible things.

"There's a twisted logic to it for sure," Kayla said, considering it. "But then, what's the end goal?"

"That is the question," Tara said, not even close to having an answer.

A knock at the Keel Haul's door interrupted them.

Kayla started to get up, but Tara waved her down. "I've got it."

She pushed open the heavy oak door, surprised to find Reginald Singleton on the other side. "Chief. Come on in."

"What're you guys doing closed in the middle of the day?"

"We'll tell you all about it over a beer," Tara said, relocking the door and returning to the bar.

"If I said that's not the best damn offer I've had all day, I'd be lying."

Tara dug out an ice-cold Nut Brown Ale and slid it to the cop as he took off his coat and shook fresh snow from it. He wore a brown baseball cap that read Chief in gold stitching. He left it on, letting the snow melt into the bill.

"You heard about what's happened to the President?" he said.

They nodded. Kayla said, "Brice is down there with them. He's one of the hostages."

"What? Damn, if you people aren't always in the thick of it. How'd that… " He held up a hand. "You probably can't say. Where's Skyjack? He was here… earlier."

"He's gone to help," Tara said.

Singleton arched an eyebrow while giving her a sideways glance. His unspoken question: why the hell aren't you there, too?

"We're doing what we can… from here," Kayla said, sparing Tara from having to explain.

"Is there something we can do for you, Chief?" Tara asked, nimbly changing the subject.

"Um, no. I mean, I just dropped by to let Skyjack know I might've tracked down his rabid hydrofoil driver. At least, I think. There's a wrinkle." He stood up and took a long swallow of beer. "But you've got your hands full with… Go do what you need to do."

"What'd you find out, Chief?" Tara asked. She glanced at Kayla, whose head was down as she tapped keys and scanned information that sped across her laptop screen. "I'm not much help at the moment."

Singleton settled back onto his barstool. He sipped his beer. "I've got a name. The joker that crashed into Skyjack. Goes by Chase Edwards. I think. Maybe."

"No offense, Chief, but you're waffling," Tara said.

"I know," he admitted without being defensive.

"Start at the beginning. How'd you come up with that name?" Kayla asked without looking up.

"Dumb luck mostly." His voice contained an undercurrent of pride. "I had one of my guys dust the interior of the hydrofoil. To tell you the truth, I figured it to be a waste of time, what with the water and salt air and all. And, I'd noticed how most of the drivers wore gloves."

"Neoprene," Kayla offered helpfully.

"Textured," Tara said. "Helps with gripping the steering wheel."

"Like racecar drivers," Kayla said.

"Well, whatever." Singleton waved all that away. "I did it mainly to give my guys some practice dusting a scene more than thinking we'd come up with anything useful. But, lo and behold, at some point, this yo-yo took his gloves off—or didn't wear any—we pulled two serviceable prints from the steering wheel and one from the dash."

"Not to rain on your parade, Chief," Tara said. "But those prints could've been left by anybody. A salesperson, a mechanic. Someone who worked on manufacturing it."

"Or my perp," Singleton said, not willing to be deterred. "I'm trying to stay positive here. But yeah, I thought the same thing, too, trying not to get my hopes up. But when my guys sent everything up to the state crime lab in Concord, again, you know, for practice, they got a hit." He pulled a paper from his coat pocket, unfolded it, and smoothed it out before handing it over to Tara. "I give you, Chase Edwards. US Army veteran."

The paper was a photocopy of an Army intake file with a description and photograph of a nineteen-year-old recruit named Chase Edwards. The enlistment papers were dated nineteen eighty-five.

"Hard to say," Tara said. "Brice and Skyjack described a man in his late fifties, early sixties." She passed the paper to Kayla.

Singleton settled back on his stool. "Which fits. This being back in eighty-five. But either way, fingerprints are fingerprints."

"That may or may not be the pilot's fingerprints," Tara insisted.

"Here's another problem, Chief," Kayla said, pausing her computer work to look up. "I just looked up Chase Edwards' service record."

Singleton raised a hand. "I know. I know. I had an old buddy of mine I worked with in the four-six back in the day—he's in the Intelligence Unit now—got me Edward's record on the QT."

Kayla said gently, "They say he was killed in action in Iraq sixteen years ago."

"Sure. I saw that, too." Singleton nodded knowingly. "So, explain to me how his fingerprints are all over the cockpit of a hydrofoil manufactured and sold less than two years ago?"

TWENTY-THREE

BANNON REMAINED WITH THE others in the two rows of seats facing the bandshell stage. They'd been forced to sit for so long his rear end ached. But he'd used the time to his advantage. He'd made up his mind there were two things he needed to do. First, he had to find a way to communicate with the surface. Get word to the *Putnam*. Warn them about the drone minefield. No more innocent lives would be lost if he could help it.

His second priority was to get the President to safety. Once POTUS was out of harm's way, then the *Putnam* would be free to act. Bannon, too.

He glanced at Little's body. Then, he thought about the lives lost in the two submersibles Sucre destroyed. Who knows how many others had been killed since the RRA General's arrival at Tiamat Bluff? Sucre needed to be held accountable. He needed to pay for the innocent lives he took.

Bannon twisted around in his seat. In the row behind him, Robin Larson sat next to Leary, the cameraman. She sat at an angle in her seat, keeping her back to Jerry Little's body still on the floor.

"You okay?" he asked, catching Larson's attention.

She forced a smile and nodded, though she was on the brink of tears. "I've never been through anything like this. You see it on the news all the time. The brutality. Murder. Violence. The utter disregard and contempt for human life. But until you experience it first-hand… "

He patted her hands, folded one over the other on her knee. They were as cold as death. "I'm going to get us out of here. All of us." He squeezed her hands. "It's going to be okay."

Bannon glanced around the park. Enclosed by a circular wall covered with a mural of blue sky, rolling grass, and a tree-filled landscape, it blended into the actual greenspace, expanding the perceived size of the park beyond its actual ten-acre footprint. The wall extended twenty feet high.

Above it, the transparent dome rose overhead. Its triangular latticework of brushed aluminum gleamed in the artificial sunlight that warmed the park, creating a simulated sunny summer afternoon.

From his position, Bannon could see four sliding doors—part of the overall mural—identifiable by a black seam and a black, square locking pad.

Two of Sucre's people were posted at each one.

Sucre remained on the stage, talking with one of his men. There were two additional armed men at either end of the stage.

"How many ways into the park?" Bannon asked Larson.

"The four sliding doors. That's it." She glanced over her shoulder at the four entrances visible from their side of the bandshell.

"And the locking pads?"

"Biometric handprint-activated, with low-priority security."

"What does that mean?" Bannon asked.

"Access to areas around the Bluff are designated low, medium, and high-security. Public areas like Kanaloa Park are accessible to anyone. A simple palm print opens or secures the door. Anyone can operate them. Guest quarters, vendor, and business-owned spaces, like restaurants and entertainment venues, are designated medium secure areas. Access is restricted to specific operators with a single-tier protocol programmed into the system."

"Only pre-assigned operators can activate the palm reader."

"Exactly." Larson went on. "Tiamat Bluff operations are accessed by a two-step process. Palm reader and ten-digit access code."

A man in blue Tiamat Bluff coveralls emerged from the backside of the stage. Impossible to tell if he was one of Sucre's people or an employee pressed into service by force. He carried a case of bottled water. Coming off the stage, he tore open the plastic and began to distribute the drinks among the prisoners.

The President refused.

Grayson urged him to take it.

"I won't accept anything from them," Kingsley said. "Not a thing."

"We don't know how long we'll be kept here."

"Drink it, Mr. President," Bannon said. "When we make a move, I can't have you passing out on me from dehydration."

Bannon accepted an offered bottle and drank it down. The water was warm but tasted good all the same.

"What if it's poisoned?" Larson asked.

"If they wanted us dead," Bannon said. "They'd have killed us already."

She nodded at the logic of that while recoiling at the brutality of the statement. She cracked open the plastic bottle and drank. As did the President and the others. Bannon watched the gunmen. Each was armed with Steyr machine pistols and Taurus 9mm semiautomatic handguns and seemed comfortable with them. Each had an Aqua Lung titanium-tipped dive knife strapped to their legs.

On the plus side, Bannon smiled wickedly. Plenty of available firepower. If he could get his hands on them.

The armed personnel appeared well-trained. Alert. They didn't slouch or get distracted despite the monotonous hours of standing around. Definitely military-trained and well-disciplined. But, if they were Latin American rebels, Bannon was Santa Claus.

He leaned over to Larson. "Give me a quick tutorial of what's where."

"What do you mean?"

"The facility's layout. Outside of the park. How do I get to Ops from here?"

She looked around. "After you get past the armed goons at the doors?"

"Yes."

"Ops is one level below us, level two. In the north section of the facility." She described the various ways in which he could get there from the park, including elevators, emergency stairwells, and even maintenance hallways built behind the bulkheads. "Once you're in the corridors, you'll find touchscreen directories every hundred feet or so. It's impossible to get lost in Tiamat Bluff."

As she spoke, he continued to watch the guards, looking for patterns, routines, habits he might be able to exploit later. Doing so, he noticed a man emerge from behind the stage. Someone he'd not seen before. He wore the light blue Polo shirt, dark blue slacks, and the dark baseball cap of the facility's security staff.

The bill of the man's cap was pulled low, covering his eyes and shadowing the lower half of his face. Bannon hadn't noticed him enter the park through the sliding doors, and he'd been watching them. Something else about him made the hairs on the back of Bannon's neck stand up.

"Is there access to the rest of the facility from the stage?" Bannon asked.

Larson nodded. "I'm sorry, I wasn't thinking. Yes. There's a suite of rooms one level below. Dressing rooms, a rehearsal hall, kitchenette, green rooms for the performers, and storage space for props and costumes," Larson said. "Oh, and there's a full woodworking and carpentry workshop down there for building sets, too. A section of the stage floor drops down, as well. It operates on hydraulics."

"Like a scissor lift?"

"Yes. Exactly."

"And from the lower complex, one could access the rest of the facility?"

"Of course. It's the central hub on level two."

Level two would put him that much closer to Ops.

Bannon kept his eye on the newcomer.

The man spoke with Sucre. Their conversation had rapidly devolved into a heated argument. The man kept his back to Bannon and the others as if he didn't want any of them to see him. The pair was too far away, their voices too low, for Bannon to hear what they were arguing over, but it was clear Sucre didn't have the iron grasp over his people that he'd presented earlier, at least not over this individual.

An interesting development, Bannon noted with a grim smile, continuing to study the man.

Caucasian. What hair was visible under the ball cap appeared to be gray and cut razor short. Though the clothes didn't fit him well, a size too large and baggy on his frame, by the way, the man held himself, moved, Bannon could tell he was fit. He demonstrated an air of quiet confidence. A man accustomed to being in charge. Though he wasn't. Not if Sucre was.

Again, Bannon thought military.

As his argument with Sucre reached its conclusion, he stormed across the stage, returning backstage, which, according to Dr. Larson, led to the complex of rooms below.

Bannon caught a fleeting look at the man's face in profile. And it stunned him.

He leaned over and whispered into Grayson's ear. "That man. The one leaving the stage... "

"What about him?" she asked.

"That's the man in the barracuda hydrofoil. From yesterday's race. The one who almost killed Skyjack."

"Are you certain?"

"I'd stake my life on it," Bannon said. There was more going on here and it was time Bannon got answers. He jumped to his feet and shouted, "Hey, you! Yeah. You!"

The man in the ballcap stopped at the far end of the stage. He turned toward Bannon and quickly turned back like a man caught on the street, not wanting to be seen. He tugged the bill of his cap lower. He hurried around a partition at the back of the bandshell and was gone.

It was enough for Bannon to get a good look. To confirm he was the pilot of the Barracuda hydrofoil. The man who tried to kill McMurphy.

But it was Grayson's reaction that caused Bannon to turn toward her. Her breath caught in her throat.

"What is it?" Bannon asked.

"That man," she said. "I know who he is. But it can't be him."

"Who is he?"

She shook her head. "It can't be who I think it is. It just can't be."

The President twisted in his seat. "Why not, Liz?"

"Because he's dead," Grayson said. "Because I killed him."

TWENTY-FOUR

SKYJACK McMURPHY STOOD ON the outer edge of the flight deck. Beside him were Tolliver and Haddad. He'd donned a Coast Guard foul weather parka given to him by Tolliver from the ship's store. He wore his dark aviator sunglasses, even though the late afternoon sky had turned gray and angry. A storm was coming up the coast from the Carolinas, but the full brunt of it wasn't expected to reach them for at least another twenty-four hours.

The cold, cloudy sky was just a harbinger of things to come, McMurphy groused. He chomped on the end of a lit Cuban, refusing to put it out when Haddad complained. He did agree to step around Tolliver and stand downwind of her. He blew a great cloud of cigar smoke into the air, trying to decide what to make of Haddad not boarding the doomed submersible at the last minute, having avoided not one but two brushes with death.

Calculated or a coincidence? A good question.

They stood in silence, watching a Navy Sikorsky MH-53E Sea Dragon approach from the stern.

It began its landing descent. A heavy-lift cargo helicopter, the Sea Dragon was identical to the CH-53E Super Stallion line built for the Marine Corp, except for the enlarged sponsons—projections that provided greater fuel storage—and the visible in-flight refueling probe.

A marvelous machine, in McMurphy's opinion.

Introduced into the fleet in the early 80s, the Sea Dragon was a durable chopper. They usually crewed with two pilots and three gunners. At an overall length of nearly one hundred feet, it had three turboshaft engines and was capable of cruising speeds of one hundred forty miles per hour and a range of six hundred twenty-one miles. Its armament included two window-mounted machine guns and a ramp-mounted weapons system.

From the way the pilot struggled to stick the landing, McMurphy could tell this beast was loaded to the gills. Carrying a SEAL team of eighteen, even with their tactical and scuba gear, that was only a fraction of the thirty-thousand-pound payload the Dragon was capable of.

What the hell did they bring along with 'em, McMurphy wondered.

The helicopter completed its landing. The engines shut down, and the rotors slowed. The side door slid open, and eighteen men in turquoise and navy blue camouflage jumpsuits clamored out of the cabin. They worked together unloading equipment and gear under the watchful eye of a platoon chief while one young man strolled confidently across the flight deck. His lieutenant bars a muted green.

He approached Tolliver but didn't salute. "Lieutenant Bradley Jones. Permission to come on board, Captain."

Tolliver stuck out his hand, and they shook. "Permission granted. Welcome to the *Putnam,* Lieutenant. Glad to have you here." He turned to Haddad. "I'm sure you know Ms. Haddad."

"Of course." He shook her hand. "A pleasure to meet you in person, ma'am."

Jones had a distinctive southern accent. McMurphy guessed his age at twenty-five, though to Skyjack, he looked like he was twelve. Kids.

"This hulking gentleman to my left," Tolliver said, "is Chief Warrant Officer John McMurphy."

Jones eyed him with a fleeting glimpse of suspicion before extending his hand. "Chief? What branch?"

They shook. Jones had a firm grip. "A Coastie like Tolliver. Call me Skyjack."

"You get called up last minute for this gig?" Jones asked, noting McMurphy's blue jeans and day-old red stubble on his face.

"Something like that. I'm here at special request of the Vice-President."

Taken aback for a second, Jones said, "Huh. Well, okay then."

"Lieutenant," Haddad said. "Perhaps it would be best if we spoke inside. Catch you up to speed."

"Sounds like a plan, ma'am." He turned toward the helicopter and called out. "Chief!"

Bent over examining the contents of a large military green container, Jones' platoon chief, an NCO named Null— Haddad had provided McMurphy with a list of the men and one woman assigned to the SEAL team—twisted around.

"Grab that feeb," Jones ordered, "and double-time it over here."

Null leaned into the open cabin and shouted.

A man in a dark suit and wearing a black overcoat poked his head out. He conversed with Null for a moment, then climbed out of the bird. Special Agent Andrew "Andy" Goodwell. He had dark, slicked-back hair and pale-skin. Skinny as a rail, McMurphy feared a good stiff wind would blow him overboard. He crossed the flight deck with Chief Petty Officer Null, jogging to keep up.

"Not to be rude, Lieutenant," Haddad said.

"Just you and the fed," McMurphy said. "Need to know only." To the chief, he said, "No offense, Null."

He looked to Jones, who nodded.

"None taken," Null said, but clearly, he was put off. He turned and strolled away.

Jones, on the other hand, narrowed his gaze as he stared at McMurphy, then abruptly turned his back to him. Here's where the interagency pissing contest began, McMurphy thought. This pissant young lieutenant vying for control of the op. And why McMurphy hated dealing with the feds and other branches. Egos bigger than the Seven Seas, all of them.

"I'd appreciate an explanation, ma'am," Jones said.

"Get over yourself, Junior," McMurphy said. "The clock's ticking. We ain't got time for that crap." He turned abruptly and started for the superstructure.

At the portal, he didn't wait for the others. Time was precious. McMurphy wasn't about to lose any of it playing politics with a swabbie wet behind the ears. Behind him, he heard the fed ask Tolliver, "Any chance I can get a good cup of joe on this rig?"

"The best in the fleet," Tolliver said proudly.

"Sounds great," Goodwell said. "'Cause the Navy's idea of coffee isn't fit for human consumption."

"Hey," Jones said, protesting.

They adjourned to the officer's mess. There, full coffee cups were passed around—without Tolliver's bourbon kicker, McMurphy thought regretfully—as they brought Jones and the hostage negotiator, FBI Andy, up to speed.

"Have we had any further communication from this Sucre fella beyond the initial contact?" Goodwell asked.

"Initial contact, you're calling that? The video he sent to all the TV news outlets?" McMurphy asked. "The one where he publicly executed a human being for the world to see?"

"Yes, Chief McMurphy, that. I studied it on the flight here." He looked at Jones. "We all did. I sympathize with your anger, but we can't let our emotions—"

McMurphy stared at Goodwell. "You don't know me, Andy—"

"Actually, I do. I studied your file on the way here, too. I am very familiar with your service record, but more importantly, your—antics—since."

McMurphy wondered how much the man really knew and how much he only thought he knew. "Antics?"

"It was why I put in a call to my superiors," Goodwell said. "To request your immediate removal from this situation. I told them you're a liability. That you're too emotionally invested—"

McMurphy pounded his big fist into the table hard enough to rattle the coffee cups set on it. "You're damn right I'm emotionally invested. My best friend, a man who's saved my life more times than years you've been alive, is trapped at the bottom of the ocean with a homicidal madman who's already shown he doesn't give two-hoots about human life. Brice may already be dead, for all I know. And if you think you or any damn Washington bureaucrat's going to stop me from rescuing him or avenging him, you've got another thing coming."

Haddad cleared her throat. "Let me ask. Agent Goodwell, how was your demand to remove Chief McMurphy received?"

The agent's face flushed red. "It was… denied. Vigorously."

"As I suspected." Haddad glanced around the table. "Now, like it or not, this is the team we've got. If any of you have a problem with that," she pointed at the door, "now's the time to remove yourselves."

No one moved.

She went on. "Good. To answer your question, Agent Goodwell, the administration did receive a private communique with a list of demands. The Vice-President is reviewing it now to determine a course of action. I am not privy to the contents in detail."

She took a sip of her coffee.

"Our job, gentlemen, is to develop a plan." She looked at Jones. "Infiltration and extraction. The safe rescue of the President is your top priority. Agent Goodwell, your job is to try and talk Sucre down, if or when we're able to reestablish contact with him. So far, all attempts to communicate have failed. If talking him down isn't an option, you're to distract him long enough to keep the President alive until Lieutenant Jones and his team successfully complete their assignment."

"Hold on a minute," McMurphy said. "We're a hell of a long way from that yet."

"Agreed," Haddad said. "We need a plan first. One we are confident will work. One that will only be implemented once the Vice-President decides we're a go."

"Hard for me to get this guy talking, keep anyone alive, with no ability to communicate with him," Goodwell said.

"We're working on that," Haddad said. "In the meantime, all we can do is hope Sucre will contact us."

"Hoping," McMurphy said. "That's not much of a strategy."

"I need a lot more to go on than what we've received so far," Jones said. "Schematics. Building plans. Visuals."

"There we can help. A little." Haddad activated the smart screen, calling up the same imagery Dr. Larson had used during her presentation. "This is Tiamat Bluff."

"From the video Sucre released," Tolliver approached the image of Tiamat Bluff on the smart screen, "we know the President, Mr. Little, and at least some of the others were being held in this large green space." He pointed at the transparent dome crowning the facility. "In the center of the park is a bandshell. They're there."

"Is there anyone on board who's been down there?" Jones asked. "Can you give me a firsthand account of the layout? I need electrical schematics. Structural materials. Means of egress."

"No," Tolliver said.

"In preparation for the President's visit," Haddad said, "The Secret Service recommended removing all non-essential personnel from the facility."

"The FBI's tracking down as many employees as we can find," Goodwell said. "Also, architects, designers, builders. Agents are speaking with them, trying to gather as much information about the place as we can get. I can put you in touch with the agent in charge."

Jones threw a pen on the table. "Christ. We've got nothing to go on? This is going to get people killed."

"Dial it down, Lieutenant," McMurphy said. "This is uncharted territory for all of us."

"You're asking me to develop a plan with nothing to work with," Jones said.

"Not nothing." Tolliver cleared his throat. "I might be able to help you out there."

He glanced over at Haddad. "Ms. Haddad, may I?"

She handed him the tablet she used to control the presentation.

He tapped in a few keystrokes. The image of Tiamat Bluff darkened then reappeared, but under a shimmer as if being seen through an actual underwater lens. When a few air bubbles drifted upward over the image, McMurphy began to get an idea of what they were looking at.

"We haven't been sitting on our hands just waiting around," Tolliver said. "Before we were ordered to move off-site, we dropped a couple of underwater surveillance drones into the water."

On-screen, the image of Tiamat Bluff grew closer.

"We've had to be very, very careful," Tolliver said. "Tiamat Bluff's equipped with very sophisticated sonar and radar capabilities. It's been a real pain, but my operators are good. Better than even I knew."

The image closed in on the park dome. Through the cross-thatched web of steel reinforcement, the inside of the dome came into focus.

"We've collected video of every square inch of that facility's exterior. My boys have hours of tape for your team to review, Lieutenant. We know there are two moon pools and several docking hatches—though no military subs match their proprietary design."

"Meaning we can't connect to them?"

"Correct," Tolliver admitted.

McMurphy shook his head. "Even if we could, we'd be spotted approaching a dozen clicks out. That will just get people killed."

"There are several trunk spurs leading from the main structure," Jones observed. "But they're capped. Sealed."

"Prep for future expansion," Tolliver explained.

"Blowing them could cause reprehensible damage to the facility," McMurphy said, short-circuiting any thoughts the gung-ho lieutenant might have of using explosives. A fool's play anyway.

"How so?"

McMurphy explained. "With P equaling fourteen point seven psi plus sixty-four thousand pounds divided by feet square with one psi equal to one pound divided by feet square pressure at one thousand feet under water is approximately six thousand four hundred fourteen point seven psi."

"What'd he say?" Goodwell asked.

"You compromise the spurs by blowing them up," Tolliver clarified, "you risk crushing the facility like an eggshell."

"We don't want that," Goodwell said.

"No," Haddad said. "We don't want that."

"We can command the surveillance drones to go anywhere," Tolliver said. "See anything you want to see, mission prior or during." He forced a grin. "I can't give you ears, but you'll have eyes, courtesy of the *USCGC Putnam.*"

"Find away inside, Lieutenant," Haddad said. "Give us a plan that doesn't include destroying Tiamat Bluff and killing everyone inside."

TWENTY-FIVE

AFTER CHIEF SINGLETON DROPPED his bombshell discovery about the mysterious Chase Edwards, Tara and Kayla were in Brice Bannon's twenty-seven-foot Sea Ray SDX-270. An open bow, sporting boat with a three hundred horsepower inboard MerCruiser engine. Built for speed, stability, and comfort, they skimmed over the dark Atlantic Ocean water, traveling south at near the craft's max speed of thirty-five knots. The ride was smooth. Kayla, like Bannon and McMurphy, had the seaman skills to handle the speedy boat over the smooth water.

Armed with Singleton's information, Kayla had done a deep dive into government records, as only she was capable of doing. While Tara and Singleton shared another drink, Kayla tapped keys, searched databases and records, and even made a few old fashion phone calls.

Finally, she glanced up. A gotcha smile on her face. "Chase Edwards was CIA. I've got the name of his caseworker. And he lives close by."

"Where?" Tara demanded.

"Cape Cod."

Tara grabbed her coat and practically raced across the bar to the door, beaming at finally having something to do. To Kayla, she said, "Let's go!"

She tossed the keys to the Keel Haul to Singleton as Kayla gathered her coat and things. "Lock up when you're done, Chief."

Tara had spent plenty of time on the water and typically would've enjoyed being out on the boat, except it was after dark in the middle of January in New England. They had to wear heavy parkas with fur-lined hoods zipped up to their throats against the weather. Their caps mashed down on their heads to keep their hair contained and their heads warm. Each wore thick winter gloves.

Tara's cheeks stung from the icy splash of sea spray. Even with her black wool cap pulled over her ears, they burned from the cold, convincing her she had frostbite and that they'd soon fall off.

Over the throaty roar of the big Merc engines, she thought about how much she loved living in America. Egyptian-born and raised, she'd fought alongside Bannon and McMurphy in Afghanistan before their time in the Coast Guard had come to an end. Having burned many bridges back home—under her real name, she was wanted for going AWOL from the Algerian National Navy, where she'd trained in the MARCOS program—the Indian Navy's Special Forces—and with no family left in Cairo, Tara had accepted Bannon's invitation to come to America, and eventually to join Secretary Grayson's strike team.

Decisions Tara hadn't regretted for an instant, except for one thing.

"Tell me again why we're here and not somewhere warm, like Florida."

Kayla laughed over the sound of the Sea Ray slapping the waves. "Winter's rough up here, I'll give you that, but it makes you appreciate summer all that much more."

Tara crossed her arms over her chest, stuck her gloved hands under her armpits, and shivered. The sun had set. The western sky, once bright orange and red, was now dark with a ribbon of purple clouds hugging the horizon. The blue sky had turned almost black. And not yet five in the evening.

"That's bull-you-know-what."

Kayla laughed again. "Yeah. You're right."

They'd cut diagonally across Cape Cod Bay, then traveled south to the canal, up a channel north of Sandwich, Massachusetts, taking them to Buzzards Bay. They passed under an elevated railroad bridge before Kayla pulled back on the throttle. From there, they circled Taylor's Point, around the Massachusetts Maritime Academy, and proceeded north again to the small, former whaling community of Bourne.

Tara clutched a military-grade, waterproof tablet in her gloved hands, a satellite image of the canal on it while she scanned the starboard shoreline. A third of the way up the peninsula, she pointed at a small concrete boat launch. "There."

Kayla expertly navigated the low water markers and pulled the Sea Ray into the docking slip that extended outward from the launch. She cut the engines as Tara leaped onto the dock and slipped the mooring lines around cleats fore and aft to secure the boat.

She looked up the embankment at a small Cape Cod-style home. Gray shingle siding with white trim and a steeply pitched roof with lighter gray asphalt shingles. White-gray smoke drifted from the central chimney. A single lamp was behind sheer curtains in what looked like a rear living room area.

Kayla joined her on the dock. "Ready?"

Tara unzipped her parka. "Ready."

They took the steps up to the lawn two at a time and strolled down the driveway past where a Dodge pickup was parked. The front of the house had a small, white-trimmed porch and an American flag. Tara pounded her fist on the frame of the metal storm door. Kayla pulled her Coast Guard credentials out, including her Investigative Services badge. Each member of Bannon's team had them, though they were not technically part of the Investigative Service. The badges were a perk of working directly for the Secretary of Homeland Security and served to give them credibility during their investigations.

The interior door opened. A man in his late sixties stood cautiously to one side of the storm door glass. Bald except for a halo of gray hair, Daniel O'Shea stared back at them with alert blue eyes. "Can I help you?"

Kayla held up her badge. "We're with the Coast Guard. We'd like to speak with you if you don't mind."

"Depends on what it's about."

"Chase Edwards."

"I don't know anyone by that name." O'Shea started to close the door.

"But you did," Tara said. "Once."

Kayla opened the storm door. "Sir, please. It's a matter of national security."

"Don't care." He continued to push the door closed.

Tara shouldered past Kayla and kicked the door in.

O'Shea stepped back, startled, but not to the point of disorientation Tara had hoped for.

He crouched and expertly drew a Colt .45 Desert Eagle he'd had concealed behind his right leg. He aimed it directly at Tara's face. His grasp rock steady.

In turn, she'd already cleared leather and pointed her Sig at him in a two-handed grip.

"Who are you?" he demanded, staring down the .45's sights.

"Coast Guard," Tara said.

"Her maybe." He indicated Kayla with a nod. "Not you. Not with a halide knife strapped to your hip, a dive knife in your boot, and if I'm not mistaken, that's a urumi you're using as a belt, isn't it? No puddle pirate I ever met carried weaponry like that."

The urumi was a sword made of a flexible, four-foot-long steel blade. Tara did indeed use the ancient weapon as a belt. The hilt worn on her left hip.

"You know your bladed weapons," Tara said, impressed.

"It's how I've stayed alive all these years. Now, I won't ask again. Who are you, and what do you want?"

Kayla stepped into the foyer. "We're here about the President's capture this morning. You're former CIA. I'm sure you'll want to help."

"Emphasis on former." He eyed Kayla thoughtfully. Then, with a twist of a smile, he lowered his gun. To Tara, he said, "You've got a hell of a fast draw, young lady."

She returned her Sig to its holster. "You're pretty spry yourself."

"For an old guy." He stepped back. "I don't know what you think I can do for you, but I'll give you five minutes."

Tara and Kayla crossed into a small living room, tastefully decorated in stereotypical nautical themes: paintings of lighthouses and ships on stormy seas, a life-ring with brained rope hung on the wall, and a wooden statue of Old Salty, a carved sea captain smoking his black pipe and wearing his blue coat and white seafaring cap on the mantel under where a fire crackled in the fireplace, filling the room with a warm, woodsy scent.

As it always did, the familiar statuette reminded Tara of Captain Floyd.

"I just put on a pot of coffee if you're interested."

The thought of hot coffee sounded like heaven to Tara as she holstered her weapon and followed the man into the kitchen. O'Shea grabbed three cups from a cabinet and filled them with steaming rich coffee.

"How do you take it?"

"Black," Tara and Kayla both responded.

He passed cups to them, then filled his own with a large helping of cream and an unhealthy heaping of sugar. He went through a glass slider and stood at the rail of the back deck.

Tara and Kayla followed him outside.

He sipped his coffee and looked out over the channel that served as his backyard. "Nice boat," he said, surveying the Sea Ray. "Yours?"

"A friend's," Kayla said.

"What's a man thirty years dead got to do with the predicament the President's gotten himself into?" O'Shea asked, dropping any pretense he didn't know him.

"We have reason to believe Chace Edwards isn't dead."

"That would be news to me," O'Shea said without turning.

Tara let Kayla do the questioning as she studied O'Shea's mannerisms. His body language, hesitations, verbal clues, looking for telltale signs of deception.

"Tell us about him," Kayla said.

"Can't." He turned. "Not that I don't want to. Can't. As his CIA Case Officer, the information I have goes way beyond your clearance levels. I may be retired, but my oath remains intact. National security, blah, blah, blah."

He waved his hand dismissively in the air.

"Beyond category two Yankee White clearance?" Kayla asked. "I don't think so."

Yankee White, the level of clearance given to personnel who work directly with the President and Vice-President in extremely sensitive positions. Clearances didn't get much higher than that.

O'Shea turned. Tara watched O'Shea's eyes in reaction to that. While his features remained stoic, he blinked in surprise. "Then I was right. You two ain't no regular puddle pirates."

"Chase Edwards," Tara said. "Lives depend on it."

"Sure. Don't they always?" He glanced at the deck's redwood flooring. Dark red and freshly treated. "Chase Edwards was a former Delta Forces operative recruited into the Agency's Special Operations Group before the second Gulf War. He was part of the Special Activities Division, the combat version of the CIA. He was embedded with the first combat troops in-country at the very start of Iraqi Freedom. Forces that were instrumental in organizing the Kurdish military and U.S.-led coalition forces in the fight against Saddam Hussein."

"What happened to him?" Kayla asked.

"Killed in action. Operation: Lightning Strike. A classified op early in the war meant to root out al-Qaeda strongholds in the northern mountain regions. Their mountaintop positions were bombarded by airstrikes. Sixty-four tomahawk cruise missiles softened up the targets for advancing ground troops. Led by Chase, Army Mountain division Special Forces and infantry regiments, along with airborne units, who'd parachuted into the area. They fought alongside Kurdish forces.

"The ground assault called for a six-prong advance. The attack from the south was met with heavy fire. The American forces were pinned down in a particularly nasty area where the deep valleys blocked radio signals and prevented them from calling in airstrikes. They persevered and fought on throughout the night. A combination of machine-gun fire, well-placed, long-range sniper fire, and artillery provided by the Kurds finally dislodged the enemy combatants, forcing them to flee further into the mountains, toward the Iranian border."

O'Shea finished his coffee and set the cup down on a nearby picnic table. As he told the story, Tara could almost hear the explosions, feel the ground tremor, smell the fear and determination of men at war. Sensations and experiences she was all too familiar with.

"The skirmish continued. The enemy tried to escape over the border into Iran. A number of them were turned back and ended up either captured or killed by the American-led forces. With al-Qaeda's forces driven back, the operation was considered an unqualified success." He sighed. "Except for a single black footnote."

He fell silent. Tara prompted him, "Go on."

"While the firefight at the border continued, extraction choppers were sent in to pull the Special Activities Division out and provide air cover for the Kurdish ground troops returning to camp. They were stopped from going in and completing their mission."

"Why?" Kayla asked. "By whom?"

"Washington. The fighting was too close to the border. The U.S. couldn't risk an incident with Iran at the time. Afraid of starting a second conflict. Against orders, they pulled out as many American soldiers as they could, but they didn't get them all. Once the Iranians started shooting back, they had to pull out."

"They left people behind?" Kayla asked.

"They had no choice," O'Shea said. "Those left behind? As is the mandate of the Agency's covert operations, they were disavowed. Publicly, the U.S. denied any knowledge of their existence."

"Chase Edwards was among those left behind?" Kayla asked.

"Yes."

"There's no proof he died there," Tara challenged. "He could've been captured, held prisoner by al-Qaeda, the Iranians… "

"Bodies were turned over afterward. DNA confirmed Chase Edwards was among the dead. He's got a damn star on the wall at CIA headquarters."

"I don't care if he's got a star on the Hollywood Walk of Fame. The DNA's wrong," Tara said. "Reports can be faked. Analysis doctored. He was in New Hampshire yesterday. He did his best to try and kill two very important people to me."

O'Shea frowned but didn't say anything.

Kayla stared at him. "You're not surprised, are you?"

He met her gaze, admitting, "I am, yes. But… there'd been rumors. Over the years. That some of them had survived. We did some checking. Looked into it. Nothing ever came of it. I never put much stock into it."

"Maybe you should have," Kayla said.

"Maybe," he conceded. "But we'd been at war for damn near twenty years then. There's a lot of missing soldiers. Rumors pop up about them still being alive, in hiding or changing sides, still fighting. Stories like that are as common as Elvis sightings and UFOs. I don't put much stock into them either."

"You're going to tell us everything you know about Chase Edwards," Tara said. "Every last damn thing."

"Fine," O'Shea said. "But what's any of that got to do with the President and what's happening at Tiamat Bluff?"

"We don't know." Kayla and Tara exchanged looks. "But maybe everything."

TWENTY-SIX

HER WORDS STILL RANG in Bannon's ears. "I killed him."

The man Elizabeth Grayson referred to had disappeared behind the bandshell. But his presence lingered. The color had drained from Grayson's face. Her posture slumped.

President Kingsley clasped her hands, trying to comfort her. Bannon twisted in his seat on the other side of her. "Tell us."

She kept her voice low. "His name is Chase Edwards."

Bannon watched as she wrestled with the questions in her head. Was it really the man she thought it was? How could he be alive? And the question he was sure they shared. What did this mysterious man have to do with the mess they were in now, and why had he tried to attack him and McMurphy at the race yesterday?

"Nearly twenty years ago, he'd been recruited into the CIA's Special Activities Division, the Special Activities Center now." She shifted in her seat. "Chase Edwards was one of the best operatives I'd ever seen, ever worked with." She looked at Bannon and forced a smile. "Until you, of course."

Bannon didn't dwell on the compliment. "What happened?"

Grayson fell silent.

"Liz, please," Bannon said. "It could be important."

"There was an op. Early in the second Iraqi war. They called it Operation: Lightning Strike. Chase and his team led a squad of Army Special Forces and other infantry troops tasked with taking out enemy forces entrenched in the mountain regions near the Iranian border. The fighting went well at first, and then it turned. Still, Chase and his people fought on, heroically pushing the retreating soldiers out of the mountains and toward the border. But there, the Iranians pushed back, refusing to allow our enemy combatants entry into their country—most of them anyway. It was a public display of their non-involvement policy at the time. The fighting was fierce. It was impossible to tell who was shooting at who. The Pentagon and the White House were nervous. A conflict with Iran then was the last thing they wanted. A Colonel at the time, I commanded an Airborne Brigade. I led the extraction effort to get them out. We brought two CH-53 Sea Stallion helicopters into the fight."

She shook her head at the memory.

"A hell of a firefight, one of the worst in my career. And then, we were ordered back."

"Before you could extract?" Bannon didn't need to ask by whom. Bureaucrats: politicians with no military experience playing war games from Washington. Playing with people's lives.

Grayson didn't need to confirm his suspicions. "So afraid we'd cause an international incident, their fear led to paralysis," she said. "I ignored the orders for as long as I could. We managed to extract the bulk of the Special Forces folks, but the fighting got too fierce. The Iranians had had enough and began shooting at us. We couldn't return fire. We couldn't let ourselves get shot down. I made the decision. I followed orders. We left... I left good men behind to die."

"You were following orders," Bannon said.

"It couldn't be helped," Kingsley said.

"I've told myself that over the years. But the truth is, I could've found another way. Today, I would have. It is and remains the biggest mistake, the biggest regret of my military career."

"If you'd stayed," Kingsley said. "If you had accidentally shot and killed an Iranian soldier. If they'd succeeded in shooting you down, capturing you, it would've started a war. Another war."

"It wasn't the wrong call," Bannon told her.

She had that million-mile stare people get. She wasn't there with them. She was on the battlefield, reliving the incident. Forced now by circumstances to second-guess her every move. Again.

A deep voice said, "It's been a long time, Colonel."

She and Bannon looked up.

The man called Chase Edwards stood facing them. His arms crossed over his chest. His blue eyes bright with intensity. His baseball cap was gone. The need for a disguise was gone.

She came to her feet, her spine ramrod straight. "It's Madam Secretary now, as you well know."

He stroked his chin. A bemused smile on his lips. Day-old stubble covered his tan features. The man's icy blue eyes were like glaciers and just as cold.

Bannon came to his feet. He got into the man's face. The stranger had a lot to answer for.

Chase Edwards took his time. Looked him up and down. Evaluating what he saw. He smirked as if thinking; *not much.* "Commander Bannon. This is a private conversation between old friends."

"That's for the lady to decide," Bannon said.

"Coming to her rescue? Ooh, chivalry." The man's mouth formed a reptilian grin. "I'm not impressed. How's your friend, Mr. McMurphy? Tougher to kill than I'd have thought."

Bannon fisted his hands. Grayson said, "No, Brice."

Kingsley came to his feet, stepping forward even as he shook off Holloway's attempt to pull him back. "Your former CIA, Edwards. Why would you throw in with… " he pointed at Sucre. "Terrorists like him?"

"Lang," he said. "I go by Lang now. Chase Lang." He shrugged. "At least that's what I'm using this week. As for you, Mr. President. Sit down before I knock you down."

Kingsley opened his mouth in shock.

Holloway tugged at his arm. "Mr. President, please."

Grayson turned. "I can handle this, David. Thank you." Reluctantly, Kingsley backed away, then sat back down. She pulled Bannon back a step. "How are you here, Chase? After all these years?"

"You mean after you left me for dead?"

"I didn't have a choice. If you were half the soldier I thought you were, you'd know that."

"Is that what being a good soldier is? Accepting when your government, your leader, your… friend leave you behind like yesterday's trash. Sacrifice you for nothing!"

"That's not fair," Grayson said.

"Isn't it? Because to me," Lang said. "That's being a goddamn pawn. Not a soldier."

"What's your deal, Lang?" Bannon asked. "What kind of game are you playing at?"

"There is so much going on, you can't even begin to comprehend it all, Commander."

"Explain it to me," Bannon said. "I'll try and keep up."

Lang barked a laugh. But he turned and looked at Sucre, who'd remained passive on the stage, watching them. "General Sucre explained it all to you already." He looked at Kingsley. "He gave your people our demands, Mr. President."

"They'll never comply," Kingsley said. "I won't allow them to."

Chase shrugged as if he didn't care one way or the other. "Then you'll die down here. Along with everyone else."

"So that's it," Grayson said. "You've become a mercenary. Sold out to the highest bidder? The man I knew would never… What happened to you?"

"You happened to me!" Lang surged forward. Bannon stepped between him and Grayson. He slammed his hand into Lang's chest, arresting the man's forward charge.

He locked his gaze on Lang's blue eyes. Even though the man was in his early sixties, Bannon had no doubt he'd prove to be a dangerous adversary. He wore a tight black t-shirt under the Tiamat Bluff Polo shirt. Physically, he matched Bannon's six-foot frame. Fit, the man remained trim. His arms were muscular and rock hard. The result of regular, strenuous weight training. Probably a carryover from his years of service. His face was craggy with lines and permanently tanned from years of exposure to the hot, burning Middle East desert sun.

Lang tilted his head, challenging him.

"You want to take a swing at me?" He held his hands out wide. An open invitation.

"The time will come. Count on it."

Chase smiled. "I look forward to it." Then, he channeled his focus on Grayson. "I spent ten years in an Iranian prison because of you, Colonel. Did you come looking for me? Did you ever try and rescue me?"

"Chase, we… I didn't know."

"Because you didn't care to know!" he shouted. "You just forgot about me!"

Grayson shrunk back. Her voice barely above a whisper. "No. I never forgot you. Not ever."

"But you never *did* anything!" Lang pushed away from Bannon and stormed toward the stage, repeating, "You left us to rot and die."

Bannon watched the man retreat to the stage. He grabbed Sucre by the arm. They again engaged in a low, heated argument. Bannon realized this was about more than kidnapping a President. More than Sucre and his so-call struggle against an oppressive dictator back home.

Lang glared over at Grayson at one point in his conversation with Sucre. The expression on his face was pure, unadulterated hatred.

And for Bannon, things began to click. Not all of it, but some things were becoming clear. This, whatever this was, was cover. A distraction. At least for Lang. For him, this was about revenge.

CHAPTER TWENTY-SEVEN

"I DON'T LIKE IT," McMURPHY said.

He stood with Tolliver and Amal Haddad on the side of the flight deck, bundled in their parkas once again, staring at the Sikorsky Sea Dragon that had brought the SEAL team to the *Putnam*. They watched as Lieutenant Jones and Chief Null supervised the unloading of what looked like two large black torpedoes.

McMurphy knew what they were. It explained the weight distribution trouble the chopper pilot experienced trying to land the bird earlier. Advanced shallow water delivery submersibles.

Submarine-like vessels. They were twenty-two feet long, had a beam of five feet, and carried a crew and passenger complement of six. They could reach speeds of six knots. With their lithium-ion battery-powered electric motors, they had a mission capacity of twelve hours, all while running silent.

There was just one problem, McMurphy thought. "Those things can't go below two hundred feet."

"You need to keep current with what's going on, old-timer," Tolliver teased. "You're thinking of the original ASDS subs. These are the next-gen Shallow Water Combat

Submersible. They've got a cutting-edge inertial navigational system, high-frequency sonar, an electro-optical periscope, wireless communication, and GPS."

"Define shallow for me," McMurphy said, returning to his original criticism. "It's in the damn name."

He shrugged. "What can I say? It's the Navy we're talking about."

"Test dives give them an approval rating to operate as deep as twelve-hundred feet," Haddad said, her shoulders hunched against the icy wind. She corralled a lock of dark hair and secured it behind her ear. Or tried to. "Plenty of room for error for this operation."

"Says the woman who's not in a wetsuit and about to climb inside one of those tin coffins." McMurphy held his fins, mask, and neoprene gloves in hand as the SEAL team efficiently set the submersibles up on the *Putnam's* ramp, preparing them to launch, refusing any assistance from the Guardsmen onboard.

So much for interagency cooperation.

In truth, McMurphy wasn't really worried about the submersibles. It was the mission that bothered him. They'd spent the last few hours cooped up in the officers' mess collecting data, dissecting it, brain-storming ideas and plans, and rejecting most of them. All of which made McMurphy a little stir-crazy.

"Well, I don't like anything about this either," Tolliver said, echoing McMurphy's thoughts. "We've got eyes on the park, but that's still a big facility down there that we can't see inside of. They could move the hostages anywhere. If they do that, we'll be blind again."

"The biggest problem still remains getting inside," McMurphy said. It had been decided the moon pools were the only viable means of breaching the facility covertly. "Junior's overconfident. Sucre's not going to leave the moon pools unguarded. Jones' men popping up through there the way he's talking, it'll be like shooting ducks in a barrel."

Especially concerning for McMurphy, he'd be one of those sitting ducks.

Earlier in the officer's mess, seated around a table with hot coffees in white Coast Guard mugs warming their hands, Jones had presented them with his plan. Two six-member teams—including McMurphy, the big Irishman was quick to remind the Navy man—would approach Tiamat Bluff in the submersibles. They would disembark a mile from the facility to avoid sonar and radar detection and swim to the facility. There, they would surreptitiously slip inside via the two moon pools. Once inside, they'd advance to the park and engage the enemy while effecting a rescue of the President and the other hostages.

McMurphy bristled at the way he added 'and the other hostages' as if they were an afterthought.

He reminded Jones Tiamat Bluff had high-tech exterior surveillance equipment, including video capabilities and who knew what else. They had no idea what the enemy could see or not see. Or hear.

Jones insisted his men were trained to slip undetected into such an environment. "It won't be a problem," he promised.

"One thing that's kept me alive over the years, Junior," McMurphy said, "is not underestimating my adversaries."

"Nor am I," Jones said, a bit defensively. "It'll take time, and the going will be slow. But trust me, Chief, we're very good at making stealth approaches like this. If you'd rather remain onboard the *Putnam* where it's safe… "

"That's enough, Lieutenant," Vice-President Wright said over the secure video feed arranged through the *Putnam's* tech people. His image, from the Oval Office, had been projected on the mess hall's wall.

"Sorry, sir. And I will admit, McMurphy's not entirely wrong on that point. Getting through the moon pools is going to be our toughest hurdle. Under normal insertion conditions, we'd cut power, which would create panic and confusion… "

"We're talking about a facility with a life support system. Heat, air," McMurphy said. "Not some drug-addled crack house. Tiamat Bluff is powered by its own self-contained, mini-nuclear power plant. Not a damn circuit breaker."

Jones ground his back teeth. "As I said, under normal conditions."

"With no other entry options available, those moon pools will be heavily guarded," McMurphy said, pleading his case. "You can bet Sucre's prepared for that. This plan, as is, will only serve to get your people cut to ribbons and the hostages killed."

"Do you have another suggestion, Chief?" Wright asked. "Or do you just want to keep poking holes in other peoples' ideas?"

McMurphy let the jab go, even if it was a low blow. Everyone was short-tempered and under pressure. "Actually, I do. Not a different one, but a supplement one."

"We're listening," Wright said.

"Jones is right in one way. We need to create a distraction. But one Sucre won't immediately think is an attack." He shot Jones a look. "Like turning out the lights."

"What kind of distraction?" Tolliver asked.

"I've thought of that, too," Jones said, still playing one-upmanship with McMurphy. "I've been wracking my brain to come up with one, but I'm drawing a blank."

"Luckily, I'm haven't." McMurphy wasn't above giving a jab or two of his own. "The Navy's old delivery vessels carried an inventory of limpet mines on board." Magnetized mines designed to be attached to the hulls of ships. Named after limpet sea snails because of how they cling to rocks and other hard surfaces. "Are these fancy new SWCS vehicles similarly stocked?"

Jones arched an eyebrow. "Yes. Each vehicle's complement is four. But if you're thinking of using them to breach, we already dismissed—"

McMurphy cut him off. "I'm not. We'd risk imploding the whole damn facility and getting everyone killed. Time fused?" he asked of the mines.

"Of course."

"What are you getting at, Skyjack?" Tolliver asked.

He ignored the question, asking instead, "The *Putnam's* got two long-range rigid-hull inflatables on board, doesn't it?"

"Sure, but… "

"We load one of the inflatables with all the combustible fuel you can spare, Captain, and we sink it near Tiamat Bluff along with—"

Tolliver looked at him with admiration.

Jones simply looked confused.

McMurphy smiled. "Timed fuses. We detonate the limpet mines on the ocean floor. It should provide a big enough bang to simulate a small but naturally occurring earthquake. Or, in this case, a seaquake."

Tolliver slapped him on the shoulder. "Splendid idea."

Haddad frowned. "I still don't see… "

But Jones caught up. "Properly timed, we can breach the moon pools while the enemy's distracted by the earth—seaquake."

Haddad seemed horrified by the idea. "What's not to say they won't think it's an attack and start killing hostages. Starting with the President?"

"Dr. Larson and her staff," McMurphy said. "They'll explain that tremors like that happen all the time, which they do. A naturally occurring phenomenon. Nothing out of the ordinary. Initially, it will rattle Sucre and his people. Distract them."

"You can't know that," Haddad said.

"And if she doesn't?" Wright asked. "Explain it away."

"Brice is down there, too, sir. He'll know what's really going on. He'll instruct her on what to say."

Wright frowned, and Haddad shook her head. Neither one seemed to like the idea. McMurphy wasn't crazy about it either, but if the Vice-President was sold on Jones' plan, it was all he could come up with at the moment to give it a halfway decent chance of success.

"Timing will be critical," McMurphy said. "We'll need to have already penetrated their surveillance and gotten into position before the blast. As soon as the seaquake's triggered—"

"Our insertion team will slip inside, use the confusion to our benefit. Secure the guards in the moon pools and move on from there undetected," Jones finished. "By the time they figure out what's going on, it'll be too late."

At least he didn't call it an assault again, McMurphy thought, still concerned at the young SEAL's overconfident zeal. Once inside, there'd be other obstacles to face. Obstacles they can't plan for. Surveillance cameras, roving patrols. No clue as to how big Sucre's force was. But, he reasoned, they were a SEAL team. Maybe he wasn't giving them enough credit. Maybe he was worrying over nothing.

"There is one more problem," Jones said. "I can't spare any of my people to go sink the inflatable and trigger the seaquake?"

Tolliver looked at McMurphy. "Should I be insulted?"

"I would be," McMurphy said. "Hell, I'm insulted for you."

"Lieutenant," Tolliver said drily. "There are fourteen officers and ninety-nine crewmembers on board this vessel. Almost every damn one of them is capable of carrying out this mission. We'll tow the loaded inflatable into position and sink it. You just do your job. Get inside that facility and get all our people out of there. Alive."

Jones held his hands up in surrender. "I didn't mean anything by that. Just trying to think of everything. Make sure nothing can or does go wrong. The stakes are too damn high."

"On that, we can all agree," Vice-President Wright said. He paused for a moment, then added, "You're a go, Lieutenant. Godspeed."

"Yes, sir." Jones stood up as the image of Wright winked out. "Let's go to work."

Now out on the flight deck, McMurphy watched the SWCSs being prepped for launch. He'd participated in formulating the plan, and though he didn't think it was a good one, he'd suited up and helped Tolliver's men load the inflatable and plot the best location for triggering their deceptive seaquake. It was the best option they had at the moment.

Still, his gut felt queasy, and it wasn't because he'd skipped lunch.

It was a sick feeling in the pit of his stomach. Familiar because he'd felt it before, like an early warning alarm. And every time he felt it, disaster followed.

Every damn time.

TWENTY-EIGHT

WITH THE *PUTNAM* STATIONED fifty miles east from Tiamat Bluff, in compliance with Sucre's orders, it would take the SWCSs—at their max speed of five knots—over ten hours to reach their target. An unacceptably long period of time. And it made a return trip impossible. The battery-powered engines only had a twelve-hour mission capability.

The Vice-President was reluctant to defy Sucre's orders and move the *Putnam* closer.

They needed an alternative way of getting the vessels within range.

Unlike the older SEAL delivery vessels that preceded them, the SWCSs couldn't be dropped from a helicopter without cracking open like an egg. A serious mission drawback in McMurphy's opinion. He shook his head. Nobody improves a thing like the Navy does.

That left them with towing the vessels into position using the two Coast Guard RHIBs. The x-factor in their plan, and why Wright wouldn't order the *Putnam* closer, was no one knew if Sucre had a means of watching the ocean surface over Tiamat Bluff as he claimed. Until they had more intel, no one was willing to risk the President's life to find out.

So, it was agreed. The RHIBs would release the submersibles five miles—or about another hour's ride—away from Tiamat Bluff. The RHIBs would go on and scuttle their explosive-laden payload at the designated coordinates and time, then return to the *Putnam.*

That was the plan, anyway.

Now, locked inside a black metal tube, flooded with freezing cold Atlantic Ocean water, even wearing a 6/5mm neoprene wetsuit with hood, boots, and gloves sealed and taped, diving to a thousand feet under the surface in the dark and feeling only the thrum of a single, nearly silent propeller while hooked up to the submersible's compressed air supply wasn't McMurphy's idea of fun. Not unless he was driving the darn thing. Which he was not.

It's a waterlogged casket, he thought, not for the first time. He focused his attention on a single red dot of light on the forward bulkhead. He sat rear-facing, though once they were underway, it was hard to tell. His sensory perception was gone. Next to him sat a young SEAL named Kowalski. They faced two others. Petty Officer Null and Bradley Jones were in the cabin at the controls.

"Nervous?" Kowalski asked.

McMurphy shot him a warning glance through his full facemask.

Kowalski snapped his gaze straight ahead, properly fearful.

The truth was, if he were honest with himself, yeah, he was a little nervous. Not because he was trapped inside a tin can descending to the ocean floor but because he wasn't at the wheel. McMurphy needed to be in control. He liked it. He thrived on it.

"Ten minutes to our dismount point," Jones' voice said over the earpiece jammed in McMurphy's left ear.

The SWCS didn't have a front window for Jones to see out of. Instead, the pilot relied entirely on a sophisticated, high-tech, and classified inertial navigational system, high-frequency sonar, radar, and GPS to direct the submersible to its target.

McMurphy glanced at his Tag Heuer Aquaracer dive watch. The dial lit in day-glow green.

Pre-arranged timing would be critical to the mission's success. Because they couldn't risk any external communication with the *Putnam* or the RHIBs being picked up by Tiamat Bluff's comm center, they had gone radio silent with the surface.

Relying on synchronized schedules, the two submersibles would settle to the sloping incline of Georges Bank, above and east of Tiamat Bluff's main complex. The submersibles would open their hatches—possible because the water-filled compartment had equal pressurization. The two SEAL teams would emerge and swim, hugging the seafloor, to their assigned positions. The two moon pools. There, they would wait for Tolliver's teams to sink the one RHIB to the ocean floor and detonate the limpet mines.

Five minutes before Jones was set to slow the submersible to a stop and let her settle to the ocean floor, an underwater explosion rocked the SWCS. If not for the seriousness of the situation, McMurphy might have joked about a premature detonation. The blast was too soon. Had something gone wrong with the RHIBs?

In the cattle car compartment, as he called it, the SEALs with him tensed.

Jones cursed through the earpiece.

"What just happened?" McMurphy asked.

"We've lost contact with Submersible Two," Jones said.

Not the RHIB then. Something else. "That was more than losing contact, damn it," McMurphy said.

A tense minute followed before Jones cursed again. "Mines."

McMurphy exchanged concerned looks in the dark with the other divers. The glow from the single red warning light. The only illumination by which he could see their faces. He read the apprehension in their expressions.

"Mines!" Jones repeated. "We've stumbled into a damn minefield. Submersible Two is down. Gone."

Before McMurphy could wrap his brain around that and formulate a response, their submersible rocked violently. They veered unexpectedly to the right. The muffled sound of another explosion followed.

McMurphy felt the vibration of the blast through his seat.

"We're hit!" Jones shouted.

A high-pitched screech pierced McMurphy's ears. From their reactions, the other SEALs heard it, too. These were tough men. Highly trained and, not to be corny about it, the best of the best. Still, McMurphy saw the fear in their eyes. They might be SEALs, but they were men first. They were scared, and they had every right to be.

Nor was that a bad thing. No one wanted to die one thousand feet underwater. It was all in how they dealt with that fear that mattered. Fight or flight kicked in. Neither one an option while they were trapped in the SWCS like they were.

"Jones. Jones!" McMurphy called but didn't get an answer.

"We need to get out of here," Kowalski said.

"Take it easy, son," McMurphy said, trying to calm him down. "We will."

The submersible rocked again. The explosion had come from the vessel's aft end. The constant engine vibration, felt through their seats up until that point, had stopped. The engine was knocked out, but they were still descending, drifting powerless to the ocean floor.

"Jones?" McMurphy said. No answer. To the others, he said, "We need to stay calm."

"We need to abandon ship," Kowalski said.

"Easy, Kowalski," the diver across from him said, reaching out to put a hand on his arm.

Kowalski shook the hand away. "We need to get out of here!"

He reached overhead and undogged the canopy release.

"Don't!" McMurphy shouted.

The young man ignored him and slid the access cover back before anyone could stop him.

With the chamber already flooded, the compartment under the same pressure as outside, opening the cover wasn't the danger. Kowalski worked at disconnecting his air supply hose from the large compression tank strapped to the SWCS's ceiling. His hands shook doing it, but he affixed the hose to the air tank strapped to his back.

"There's nowhere to go," his buddy said.

Kowalski started to drift up from his seat. "Better than being a sitting duck in here."

"Aw, crap," McMurphy said.

Kowalski spun around. Over his shoulder, a gunmetal orb the size of a softball appeared. It had several antennae sticking out of it, looking like a miniaturized version of the cold war era Sputnik. A glowing orange light beeped in the center of it.

The mine floated into the open cabin.

An antenna struck the edge of the open compartment. Another touched Kowalski, triggering the device.

The blast rocked the submersible.

Water bubbled hot around them. A violent wash of concussive energy shoved the submersible to starboard. Kowalski's dying screams filled McMurphy's head as the muffled explosion roared in his ears. Farthest from the sudden blast and shielded by Kowalski's body, McMurphy was slammed against the vessel's far bulkhead. He smashed his head against the metal, hard. The impact reopened the cut over his eye. Blood turned his vision red. A crack formed in his facemask, but it remained intact.

He survived the explosion otherwise unscathed.

That couldn't be said for the rest of the team. He checked each of them, but they were all dead. Gruesome only began to describe the carnage.

Kowalski was nowhere to be seen.

McMurphy unhooked his line from the vessel's air supply and connected his breathing apparatus to his air tank. Angry and disoriented with a headache to end all headaches blaring in his head, he swam out of the still descending submersible.

Doing so, he bumped into Kowalski's headless corpse. It floated, his arms and legs dangling. Blood and gore from his open neck clouded the water like a gory Jackson Pollock painting.

McMurphy swam toward the front of the submersible.

He made his way to the forward compartment, the one where Jones and Hull, his co-pilot, sat. The side was blown open on the starboard side. The metal peeled back like an open can, exposing the cockpit interior. Null had taken the brunt of the blast. Like Kowalski, his head was nearly gone. His chest was ripped open, ribs and organs exposed. Fish were already swimming toward the unexpected feast.

Not feeling hopeful, McMurphy grabbed at the ragged opening, holding on to check Jones. The SEAL lieutenant sat limp in his seat. His head lulled to one side. He'd sustained a deep gash through his stomach. Blood leaked from the open wetsuit.

McMurphy was about to turn away when Jones lashed out!

He seized McMurphy's wrist with a surprisingly strong grip. The young man's eyes bulged. Alive. He lunged forward and gasped for air. "Help me!"

CHAPTER TWENTY-NINE

BANNON WATCHED WITH INTEREST as Lang angrily spoke to General Sucre at the back of the stage.

Their exchange was in low, heated tones. From the confrontation, Bannon began to adjust a number of his earlier theories. First, this was definitely bigger than kidnapping the President and securing help for the RRA's struggle against General Aguirre. Secondly, it was clear to him now, Sucre wasn't the man in charge after all. He's a puppet. The public face.

Chase Lang was the one really running the show.

As Bannon mulled over that revelation, he heard a muted explosion. He felt its vibration through the platform under his feet. Those sitting in seats stood up. The armed men stationed at the park doors glanced around, their brows knotted with concern. The first break in their stoic professionalism.

Bannon glanced at Lang and Sucre. They looked around. From their alarmed expressions, he could tell this wasn't their doing.

"What the hell was that?" Kingsley asked.

Lang stepped forward on the stage. He keyed his radio. "Command! Come in. Report."

A static-filled voice reported, "A mine, sir. One apparently detonated."

"Why?" Lang demanded to know.

Grayson eased closer to Bannon. She whispered, "A rescue attempt?"

"If so, it's one that's gone wrong." The very thing Bannon had wanted to prevent. "More casualties. More dead."

Then things got worse.

The first explosion was followed quickly by two more.

"The idiots," Sucre said. More fearful than outraged. "They've launched an attack."

"Relax," Lang said. "They'll never get through the minefield. We anticipated this." He turned his attention toward Kingsley. Staring down at him from the edge of the stage. "Your people are fools, Mr. President. I'll give you one chance to get them to stand down."

"Or what?" Kingsley demanded.

"They'll die trying to rescue you, and I'll start killing hostages down here, too." Lang drew his 9mm. He aimed it at Kingsley.

Holloway rushed forward, putting herself between the President and the weapon.

"Take her," Lang ordered.

Two men in security uniforms rushed at Holloway, each grabbing an arm of the Secret Service agent. They pulled her from between Kingsley and Lang, exposing the President to the gun pointed at him once more.

Bannon took a step forward but stopped when another of Sucre's—no, Lang's—men called out. "Look!"

The cameraman, Leary, stood up and shouted, "There!"

Everyone turned toward the left quadrant of the dome. The exterior lights were still on, casting the waters with an eerie, reddish, ethereal glow. A large black object appeared overhead. Bannon's first thought was a passing sperm whale. But the front was misshapen, the rear too narrow, and it wasn't moving forward. It was dropping.

"What is that?" someone asked.

"Is it a... torpedo?'

Bannon understood their confusion. The narrow stern was equipped with two propellers. It wasn't a torpedo, but it was manmade. A minisub of some kind. Probably a large SEAL delivery vessel. Larger than the ones he was familiar with. Those crewed with only two or four divers. This one, by the look and size of it, had a crew capacity of at least six or eight personnel.

It was clear. Washington had called up a SEAL team. They'd used the *Putnam* to launch their infiltration attempt, but it had gone awry.

The delivery vessel had hit a mine.

As it drifted closer to the dome, the hole blasted through the metal nose was visible, exposing the vessel's cockpit. The glow of waterproof-encased monitors and computer screens bathed the exposed mangled bodies, still strapped to their seats, in eerie green light.

From the damage, Bannon determined a second mine had hit the vessel's flank. Had ripped the side of the crew cabin open, more than likely killing everyone inside.

The vessel continued its downward drift...

Seconds later, it crashed into the park dome.

Bannon glanced at Larson.

"It's okay." Her tone didn't instill confidence. Nor did her deep frown. "It's designed to withstand—"

Her observation was cut off by the sound of yet another explosion. This one near the tail section of the submersible and close to the paneled dome's surface. The water around it bubbled. Sections of the submersible pelted the transparent dome panels.

Bannon looked at Larson, hearing a cracking sound. He raised an eyebrow. "And now?"

"Now, we get everyone out of here." She had already started to move away from the bandshell. "Now!"

Over her words, the sound of the dome's transparent panels cracking grew louder. More cracks formed. Like in regular broken glass, irregular white lines radiated outward from the multiple points of impact. In a matter of seconds, the ocean pressure would complete the job of crushing the dome, imploding it like a squeezed egg.

"Go! Go!" Bannon waved at people to head for the exits.

The men at the doors lowered their weapons. Panicked. Their mouths gapped and their eyes wide. They looked from the quickly disintegrating dome to Sucre and Lang, their leaders, for direction.

The two men stood, staring upward. Their mouths hung open.

What happened next took just seconds but felt like an eternity to Bannon. He waved at people to run toward the closest exit to them. He pushed Kingsley and Grayson ahead of him. "Go! Go!"

Lang regained his composure first. His response to the danger was to run, to save his own hide. Sucre looked around, stunned, like a little lost boy who couldn't find his parents. Lang had abandoned him—and everyone else.

Sucre ran, disappearing behind the back of the stage.

Cowards.

The posted guards slapped at the biometric panels that controlled the large sliding doors, opening them.

Holloway pushed Kingsley forward, keeping an eye on the men but moving him quickly toward the closest exit. Bannon put his arm around Grayson's shoulders. He pulled her close as they ran, making sure Robin Larson kept up beside them.

The dome continued to crack as multiple panels failed. The crackling sound was like hundreds—thousands—of fireflies getting zapped in giant bug lamps.

"The doors," Bannon shouted. "They'll hold?"

"Yes," Larson panted. "They're designed for this. But we need to get through them and get them shut before… "

She didn't need to finish her thoughts. Bannon glanced overhead. The first panel shards began to break away.

"How much time?" Bannon asked, still running.

She stole a glance upward. "None!"

The exits were unguarded. The guards had been the first ones through the open doors. They just ran, offering no assistance to the others rushing for the opening. Bannon expected such cowardice and didn't care so long as they didn't try to prevent them from leaving the park before it was too late.

Or close the doors and seal them all inside.

Holloway reached the closest exit first. She pulled Kingsley along behind her. Bannon pushed Grayson and Larson into the corridor. Holloway caught a tripping Larson, preventing her from falling to the ground. Bannon paused at the door and helped others get out of the park.

Around the magnificent space, he saw the large doors sliding shut.

They were the last. He glanced up at the damaged dome.

The cracks stretched from the epicenter of the impact area and ran through panel after panel, racing toward the mural-painted wall surrounding the park. He watched as the transparent panels gave way. Broken pieces of panel cascading from the ceiling. With an earsplitting roar, a deluge of white frothy water poured through the imploding dome. It cascaded down like someone had opened a Niagara Falls-size spigot.

Bannon stepped through the opening, confident everyone had made it out, only to be confronted by a dark-skinned young man. He pointed his machine pistol at Bannon, barring his way into the corridor. "You stay."

Without hesitating, Bannon grabbed the barrel of the gun and shoved it back at the gunman, cutting his palms on the weapon's sight. The butt of the machine pistol jabbed the armed man's gut. He grunted. Bannon wrenched the gun from his grasp as more of the dome panels gave way behind him.

Huge cascading waterfalls splashed to the ground, uprooting trees and streetlamps. The bridge, gazebo, stage, and bandshell were crushed instantly. Splinters and debris were swept up in the torrent of relentless water, now rushing at them like a tsunami. The roar of water and destruction was beyond anything Bannon had ever heard or seen before.

Bannon held tight to his newly-acquired weapon as he spun the guard around. He landed a side-kick into the man's chest. A woof of air exploded from his lungs. The man backpedaled into the park, his eyes wide with surprise and fear as he fell and hit the ground.

Panicked, he stared up at Bannon, then over his shoulder at the crashing, sweeping torrent of water barreling toward him.

He screamed. "Noooooooo—"

Bannon leaped toward the door. Water splashed over him, soaking him to the skin.

He shouted, "Close it! Close it!"

Larson slammed her palm into the biometric reader beside the door.

The door started sliding close as the racing water roar rushed at them. Bannon's attacker was swept away. The roar of the approaching wave washed away his screams. Water splashed through the closing door with the force of a fire hose. Bannon was lifted off his feet and propelled through the door. Riding a wave of frothy water, he was thrown into the corridor wall opposite the opening.

The door slammed shut, cutting off the water that lashed against the park's perimeter, but not before the deluge of water swept through the corridor, knocking people off their feet, sputtering and splashing.

Bannon hit the floor. Soaked head to toe. He let out a relieved gasp of air. "Whoa, that was close."

Looking like drowned rats, Grayson, Holloway, and Kingsley stared back at him as they picked themselves up off the floor. Kingsley swept his wet gray hair from his face and let out a held breath. "Jesus."

Holloway shook her head, shaking water from her long blond hair that had fallen from the tight bun she wore. Wet and dark, Bannon wondered if she wore it down that way when she wasn't working. She should. It was a good look.

Grayson stepped closer to Bannon. "Brice, are you all right?"

He climbed to his feet. Cold and wet. His cut hands hurt, but he was none the worse for wear.

A gunman who'd come through the door before them started to clamor to his feet. He wore a Tiamat Bluff security uniform and held a machine pistol.

He shivered, cold and wet, and spit water. "Don't anyone move."

Bannon slammed the butt of his weapon into the man's face, breaking his nose. The man howled and collapsed to the floor. Bannon relieved him of his gun, too, strapping it across his back.

Already, he heard people rushing through the corridor towards them. Probably Lang's people. Too late for Bannon to move POTUS and the others to safety.

He squeezed Grayson's shoulder. "I've got to boogie."

She nodded, understanding.

"Where do you think you're going?" Holloway asked.

"To put an end to this." He wasn't sure how yet, but now armed with two machine pistols, this was his best opportunity.

"Not without me," she insisted.

"No. You need to stay here. With them." He indicated the others but specifically meant POTUS and Grayson. "Keep them safe. All of them."

"Go, Brice," Grayson said. "And hurry."

He nodded. "Tell 'em I didn't make it. Ultimately, they won't believe it, but it could buy me some time."

She nodded.

He ran down the corridor.

With his heart aching at leaving them behind to be recaptured, he knew he was doing the right thing. It was the only chance any of them had of surviving. But running away soured his stomach. Felt cowardly.

CHAPTER THIRTY

IN THE SUITE OF rooms under the stage, having narrowly escaped death, Chase Lang cursed. The roar—with the force of a hurricane—as a gazillion tons of ocean water came crashing down and flooded the park, turning it into a sunken wasteland, was so loud, Lang was sure the ceiling overhead wouldn't hold.

But it did.

He ordered Sucre to take as many men as he needed and gather the prisoners. Recapture them all. "Find them! Find them all!"

In the meantime, Lang burst through the door into Ops, where Sasha Wilcox, in his absence, supervised the room, now abuzz with activity. Bathed in a red warning glow, several control panels were brightly lit with cryptic messages containing the words 'critical failure' and 'containment breach,' spiking bar graphs and dials with needles hovering in red zones, muted alarms beeped additional warnings.

She turned. "You made it out." She sounded relieved. "Did everyone?"

"I have no damn idea," Lang said. "Get me the *Putnam!* Now!"

She grabbed a satellite phone from the console near her and handed it to him. He put it to his ear. She nodded to one of their men overseeing the communications console, where a Tiamat Bluff worker manipulated the controls.

An inpatient moment passed.

Wilcox switched to a video feed and pointed at it. Lang watched and frowned, waiting until the connection was made. Then, through a low crackle of static, a voice spoke. "To whom am I speaking, please?"

"The person who's going to kill the President if you try another stunt like that again."

"It'll be easier for us to talk if you tell me your name, sir. I'm Special Agent Goodwell."

"We won't be chatting, Agent Goodwell."

"I can assume this is General Sucre, then?"

"Don't worry about who I am. Worry about keeping your President alive."

"What's going on down there?" Goodwell said. His voice even. "Our equipment recorded explosions. Is everyone all right?"

"Not by a long shot. Your infiltration team is dead. You got your whole damn team killed."

"All of them?" Goodwell asked. This time, his voice was shaky.

Lang knew hostage negotiators were trained to never reveal emotion, but he could tell he'd gotten to Goodwell. "Every damn one of 'em. I warned you. Try something as stupid as that again, and all the hostages will become shark chum, too."

Lang drew a deep breath, gathering momentum before going on. "Now, tell the Vice-President he's got twelve hours to provide me with actionable assurances our demands are being addressed. If he doesn't, I start executing people one at a time until I get to POTUS. His death I will broadcast to the world. Twelve hours." He disconnected the call, missing the satisfaction one used to get from slamming an old-style phone down.

He looked around the room. "And someone, turn off those damn alarms."

The alarms fell silent.

Still in the middle of the chaos around him, as men and women, a mix of Tiamat Bluff employees, in forced alliance, and Lang's armed mercenaries supervising them, worked to monitor the strength of the reinforced park doors, ensuring the deluge of water flooding the park remained contained, and didn't threaten the rest of the facility.

Lang squeezed his hands into fists and closed his eyes. Visibly willing the rage inside him to subside. If he had a fault that he'd recognized in himself after all these years, it was his inability to control his temper. To not let his anger overwhelm him. When it did, it often resulted in him making rash, bad decisions. He couldn't afford to allow that to happen now. Not here. Too much was at stake.

With his eyes still closed, he heard the control room door open.

He turned and was greeted with the sight of Agent Kate Holloway being forcibly pulled into the room by a maintenance-clad member of his team. Lang handed the sat phone to Wilcox. Sucre came into the room behind them.

"I appreciate you joining me, Agent Holloway," Lang said, forcing himself to be calm.

"I had a choice?" Holloway asked.

Lang smiled. "No. Of course not."

"Why am I here?"

Lang said, "I've got a problem."

"I'll say. The full force of the U.S. government is about to reign down on you." She pointed at a screen displaying the now submerged park. "It started there. It'll end with you dead."

Lang glanced at the screen and dismissed it. "That? That's a hiccup. An assault was anticipated. And it was responded to. No. My problem is Commander Brice Bannon."

"I don't understand," Holloway said. "He's nobody."

"Oh, how wrong you are," Lang said. "I've known Elizabeth Grayson a long time now. Have kept tabs on her for years before embarking on this little endeavor here. Did you know Grayson ran a black ops band of stealth commandos? A team led by Commander Brice Bannon."

"I don't know what you're talking about."

"Well, she does. Bannon is her current golden boy. Thus, I anticipated he might be a problem. A problem to be dealt with before I made any move against Grayson."

Holloway remained silent.

"I tried to do that at the charity race in New Hampshire yesterday." He smiled. It was an ugly expression. "Imagine how devastating his death would've been to Grayson. I'd have so enjoyed that. But I'm forced to admit I underestimated the resilience the commander and his friends have demonstrated." He held Holloway with a stern gaze. "Then, imagine my surprise when he very unexpectedly showed up here."

Lang smashed his fist into the console shelf. Holloway jumped at the unexpected display of violence. He stared at Sucre with hateful eyes. "Now, to learn he's escaped. He's somewhere inside this damn bubble. On the loose and free to cause me even more trouble than he already has."

"He's dead," Holloway said. "We closed the door before he could make it out."

He backhanded her across the face, sending her reeling. "Liar!"

Lang tapped keys on the keyboard in front of him and replayed the video feed Wilcox had shown him as Holloway gathered herself, rubbing her hand against her bright cheek.

The screen displayed the submerged park, then switched to a new feed, one that showed Kingsley, Grayson, and the others gathered in the corridor. The recorded footage played as Bannon raced away from the group, clutching the two stolen machine pistols.

Lang looked to her for a reaction.

She said, "Looks like you underestimated him again."

Lang glared at her. "You're right. And you're here to make sure it's the last time."

"What's that supposed to mean?"

Lang waved for Wilcox to hand over the satellite phone once more. He took it and punched in a phone number. He waited, listening to the ringing of a distant telephone before he connected the call through the Ops audio system.

The phone stopped ringing. A tinny female voice answered, "Yes?"

"It's me, Lang." He tapped the phone keypad, activating the video function. "Put them on."

He held the phone out so Holloway could see the small screen. On it were her children: Kacey and Karley. Their cheeks were tear-stained. Behind them was her husband, Roger. Gagged, he had a blackened eye. Blood matted the left side of his forehead.

The girls' cried out, "Mommy! Mommy!"

Holloway stepped forward, but Lang pulled the phone back. She yelled, "Girls!"

Tears welled up in her eyes. She grabbed for the phone, but Lang kept it out of reach.

"Your family is unharmed." He stabbed the disconnect button. "For now."

"That doesn't look unharmed!"

"Roger did step out of line. Sadly, he's no action hero, I'm afraid. But good for him for trying."

"What happened? What did you do?"

"My people took corrective measures to ensure there'll be no future heroics. The girls? They're scared but untouched… for now."

"What do you want from me?"

"Bannon. Where is he?"

"I have no idea."

"You were with him last, along with Grayson and Kingsley. He killed one of my men."

"Your man was too slow," Holloway lied. "The doors closed before he got through."

Lang pointed at the frozen video on display showing Bannon running away. He knew the truth. All of it. "He must have told you where he was going. What he was planning. Where is Bannon?"

"He ran away like a scared little boy," she said. "Brice Bannon's nothing but a coward."

"Nice try." Lang backhanded her again. His gloved hand slapped her cheek, sending her reeling across the room again. He advanced on her. She straightened up and took another slap across the face. Hitting her felt good. Gave Lang a much-needed release.

She fell against a console with a grunt, using it to keep it from dropping to her knees.

Lang loomed over her. He held the satellite phone out. "A single call and your family is dead. Is that what you want?"

She didn't answer.

"Is it?" he shouted.

"No!" She pushed off the console. "Damn you, no!"

Not quite as tall as Lang, she was forced to look up at him. They squared off like that for a moment, but then Holloway sagged, emotionally and physically drained. "What do you want from me?"

"Where's Bannon?"

"I. Don't. Know."

"Bannon's no frightened little boy." Lang made a play at dialing the phone.

"No." Hollow cried out. "He ran off. You saw. But you're right. He's not frightened. Not scared. He's determined. He's armed. He's going to put an end to this. Put an end to you."

"I'm losing my patience. What is he planning?"

"I don't know. I swear. He didn't say. He doesn't trust any of us. Knows someone on the inside is feeding you information. Someone high up. He knows it's the only way you could have pulled this off. All he said was he's going to put a stop to this. Put a stop to you." She added, "And I believe him."

Lang stared at her, sizing her up, trying to determine if she had the strength, the wherewithal to continue to lie to him. He determined she didn't. She wasn't that strong. Like all people with attachments, her family came first, above duty and honor, above country.

It was her weakness. He intended to exploit it. "You're going to find him."

"What?"

"You're going to find Bannon, and you're going to bring him to me," Lang said, handing her a walkie-talkie and earpiece. He clarified, "Find Brice Bannon, or your family is dead."

CHAPTER THIRTY-ONE

TARA, KAYLA, AND O'SHEA stood on his dock, the women about to board Bannon's Sea Ray for their return trip north to New Hampshire. Daniel O'Shea, a paranoid spook if ever there was one, shared one last piece of intelligence with Tara and Kayla as they climbed into the boat.

"Either of you ever heard of Leviathan?" he asked.

"Mythical sea creature from the bible, sure," Kayla said, turning the key and starting the throaty MerCruiser engine.

"Why?" Tara asked.

"It's cropped up over the years in monitored chatter," O'Shea said, all but admitting since retirement, he's kept his ear to the ground.

"Referencing what?" Tara asked.

"I don't know." The not-so-ex-spy master paused to light a cigar. He puffed a cloud of gray smoke into the air. "Might be the name of a covert op, an operative, or an asset." He shrugged, speculating, "Codename for a place, a weapon, or a particular piece of equipment. Maybe a target."

"Maybe nothing," Tara said, frustrated.

He nodded. "Sure, or maybe the name of a group orchestrating a larger conspiracy. Something so big and widespread it's only spoken about in whispers."

"If you know something more, tell us," Tara said.

With another puff and a shrug, he said, "Just saying. Food for thought is all. But think about it. All this—kidnapping the President—it's a lot of effort for a disavowed agent to go through for revenge. Don't you think?"

He watched as Kayla backed the Sea Ray from the dock. The water behind the engine bubbled, green and frothy. He waved. "Good luck."

The Sea Ray sped through the channel, then out over the dark Atlantic Ocean waves. It's white mast, stern lights, and red and green sidelights glowing. Visible to any ships up to two miles away. With Kayla at the helm, they traveled north, roughly following the shoreline to New Hampshire. She held the boat at a steady but brisk twenty-five knots.

Overhead, the clear skies were bright with stars and a three-quarter moon. Both women had zipped their heavy parkas up to their throats. Kayla wore her dark blue Coast Guard baseball cap mashed down on her head. The brim turned to the back.

Tara had pulled her black knit cap down over the tips of her ears. Her thick black hair fluttered wildly in the wind from underneath. She placed a call and held the cell phone to her ear, cupping her hand over her other ear against the wind, the roar of the three hundred horsepower MerCruiser engine, and the slapping of the hull against the waves.

Police Chief Singleton, still at the Keel Haul, picked up.

She filled him in on what they'd learned from Daniel O'Shea about Chase Edwards. "He's tried to convince himself all these years that Edwards was dead, ignoring the rumors of an ex-American CIA operative who'd spent the last decade working for any private contractor or mercenary group he could find."

"To be fair," Singleton said. "It does sound more like the plot to a Robert Ludlum novel than real life."

Tara thought of her own very similar situation. She conceded, "Or maybe it's more common than we'd like to think. Like O'Shea said, Lang's probably not the only soldier/operative out there who's gone rogue and turned ghost over the years."

"After nearly two decades of war, sure," Singleton agreed. "You think this clown's been operating against the U.S. all these years?"

"Mostly, these guys are about the money and the thrill of what they do. I'm not sure how much ideology matters to him," she said. "But, according to O'Shea, Edwards was the sort to harbor grudges."

"Where's that leave us?" Singleton asked.

"Try to determine how Edwards fits into this whole thing. Not much more for you to do."

"You're benching me?"

"The next steps aren't really in your wheelhouse, Chief." His lack of protest told Tara he knew she was right. "We'll call if there's anything you can do."

"Fine." He sounded anything but. "What are you two going to do now?"

"We're heading back now," Tara said. "But we need to make a stop along the way."

Before they left O'Shea's house, Captain Tolliver had contacted them from the *Putnam*. He told them McMurphy was with a Navy SEAL team, having joined them on an insertion mission to Tiamat Bluff. Tolliver had admitted a shared lack of confidence in the mission plan, but considering they had no viable alternatives, the Vice-President had greenlit it, and the team was off.

Before he left, McMurphy pulled Tolliver aside and asked him to put a few wheels in motion in case this mission didn't work. He had a 'cockamamie scheme of his own,' he called it. As was typical of one of McMurphy's hare-brained ideas, he'd been skimpy on the details.

All Tolliver knew was that he wanted Tara and Kayla to make arrangements to get Flipper, Bannon's Dolphin-styled submersible hydrofoil, out to the *Putnam* as soon as possible.

"What on Earth for?" Kayla had asked.

Tolliver didn't have an answer, and Tara couldn't guess.

The marina where Flipper and McMurphy's wrecked Orca were taken after the race was on their way back to the Keel Haul. Kayla would make arrangements with the Coast Guard to fly the submersible out to the *Putnam* as soon as possible.

"Well, hurry back," Singleton said. "Otherwise, Bannon's gonna have a lot of restocking to do after I'm done here."

Tara laughed. "Have whatever you want, Chief. It's on the house. But there's no need for you to wait around."

"You sure?"

"We've got it from here, Chief," she said. "Lock up and go home."

She hung up as Kayla continued to pilot the Sea Ray north. The shoreline passed rapidly on their left. Houses dotting the seacoast. Lights on. Bright, cheery squares of glowing yellow. Civilians, warm and cuddly inside their homes, blissfully ignorant of the dark dangers out in the world. A plane flew overhead, its engines loud in the crisp night air.

Damp from sea spray and cold, Tara shivered. The cell phone still clutched in her hand. She'd gone over again in her mind what they'd learned about Edwards, and the thing Tara kept coming back to was that whatever he was up to, Chase Edwards was one dangerous man. An angry vet, mad at his country.

The phone in her hand vibrated with an incoming call.

Tara answered.

Richard Diaz was on the other end. He asked if they'd learned anything of value from Daniel O'Shea. Tara had no intention of telling him, her own natural paranoia hyped with the idea some vast conspiracy might be at work. She and Kayla had begun the day with concerns about leaky bureaucracies and planted moles. With O'Shea's talk of Leviathan fresh on her mind, a potential Washington conspiracy…

"This is not a secure line," Tara said, shutting down any further inquiry. "We'll contact you when we're back at the Keel Haul."

When Secretary Grayson first recruited Bannon for her intimate little secret ops team, she'd ensured the Keel Haul was installed with the highest electronic countersurveillance equipment available. The same measures used to protect the White House, CIA, and DoD headquarters also protected the Keel Haul.

"Fine." He seemed angry by her decision but didn't challenge it. "There's something else you need to know. A development."

"What kind of development?" She looked at Kayla. "Is everything all right?"

"No. It is decidedly not okay. I'm not sure how to tell you, know this… "

"Just say it," Tara said.

"John McMurphy, Skyjack. He joined a team of SEALs sent by the Vice-President on an insertion and extraction mission to Tiamat Bluff. A rescue mission to get the President back."

She didn't reveal she knew this from her earlier conversation with Tolliver. She didn't mention Tolliver at all. She simply said, "Go on."

"It didn't go well," he said.

With the icy brace of wind and the engine noise, Tara leaned in under the protection of the windshield. She stuck a finger in her other ear. "What do you mean, 'didn't go well'?"

"Two SEAL delivery submersibles were dispatched. Fourteen men, including McMurphy. There was a … incident." The man's voice cracked. Tara leaned in, struggling to hear. "It's all gone horribly wrong. The submersibles. They exploded. We don't have all the details. But we do know for certain… "

He said, "The team. Everyone is dead. McMurphy is dead."

THIRTY-TWO

BANNON RAN.

Behind him, he heard Sucre's—Lang's—men rounding up those he left behind. Shouts of *don't move* and *raise your hands; get on your knees* echoed in the corridor around him. He half expected to hear the clatter of machine pistol fire as the hostages, as the President and Grayson, were mowed down by hundreds of rapid-fire bullets.

To his great relief, that didn't happen.

He closed his mind to the rest, silently praying the hostages would cooperate, comply with the demands made of them. Do what was necessary to stay alive until he could figure out a way to help them. He'd wanted to stay, to fight, to protect them, but every instinct he had told him this was the right call. Get away. Remain free. Figure out a way to strike back.

The corridor was bathed in electric blue light. The curved exterior walls contained a series of transparent panels, providing observers with an almost limitless view of the dramatic ocean world outside. Red spotlights picked up schools of fish. A bioluminescent jellyfish floated by. Its vein membranes pulsed a pink strobe of color.

Any other time, Bannon could've spent hours staring out these windows just watching nature's fascinating show, like when he was a kid at the giant fish tank at the Boston Aquarium. His hands and face pressed up against the glass. Dreaming about the water, about his future.

Now, he gripped the Steyr TMP machine pistol in his hand and ran. The second weapon was strapped across his back. His mind working on a plan.

The corridor circled the park. He reached the next set of sealed doors. Doors that held the crushing ocean water filling the park at bay. Blue lights were embedded in the ceiling and ran along the carpeted floor like runway lights. They flickered and dimmed. They went out, then snapped back on before flickering again.

Bannon assumed the cause was a diversion of power. A reallocation of emergency resources.

Even though Lang's men were in control of Ops, if it had been him, he'd have kept some of the Bluff's technicians at their stations, forcing them to do their jobs at gunpoint. But even then, delays in response would be inevitable. The uneven power drains and surges were more than likely caused by the catastrophic loss of Kanaloa Park.

Depending on the amount of chaos that was being caused, it could be a perfect time for him to strike. But how best to do so, he wondered as he ran. Ops was one level down and north of his current location if he remembered the schematics Dr. Larson had shared with them on the *Putnam*.

When was that? Only this morning? It felt like a hundred years ago.

He looked for a set of stairs, reluctant to let himself get trapped in an elevator car. A thought struck him. Video surveillance. Surely, a facility like this would have cameras for the security staff to use, to monitor for unusual activity, yet he hadn't spotted any.

Concealed, maybe?

Lang would have his men monitoring those for sure. As soon as they realized Bannon had slipped away, rather than been crushed and washed away in the doomed park, they'd be using them to find him.

He cursed. Hard to avoid what you can't see.

He passed a set of interior doors and paused. From beyond the door, he heard a dull clunk. A sound so muted he almost missed it. The door was unmarked. Painted turquoise, like the surrounding walls. Bannon planted the butt of his stolen weapon against his hip and reached for the doorknob. It turned in his hand. Unlocked.

He pulled it open and stood back. Inside was a small room. The interior was dark. The blue light from the corridor cast a ghostly hue into what turned out to be a broom closet. Bannon stepped inside. Shelves lined either side. Cleaning supplies and cardboard boxes filled them. A swap bucket and mop in the corner.

Without snapping on a light, he could see a slop sink to one side in the back and an array of brooms, buckets, and long-handled dustpans propped up in the corner. The room had a musty, damp smell to it. One broom lay on the floor. As if it recently fell.

The noise he'd heard, perhaps.

Bannon moved deeper into the closet. His shadow in the pale light elongated across the floor, then rose up on the far wall. He detected a sharp intake of breath and spun to the right just as a figure abandoned their hiding spot and lunged at him. An arm raised overhead.

Bannon brought his machine pistol up but stopped short of squeezing the trigger, recognizing a wide-eyed Doctor Larson as she charged, her arms over her head.

"Doc!" he shouted. "Robin. It's me. Bannon."

He lowered the weapon and caught her raised wrist, stopping her from caving his skull in with a big, nasty-looking metal wrench. She gasped and blinked.

Their faces close, she said, "Oh, Commander. It's you."

"Yeah."

He lowered her arm and gently pulled the wrench from her clenched fist. In trying to secure a hiding place in the cramped closet. In the dark, she'd knocked the broom over.

She sucked in a deep breath and let it out again. "I, I almost brained you."

He smiled. "Not even close. Are you all right?"

"Yes. No." She shrugged, then shook her head, unsure.

He patted her arm. "I feel the same way."

The last he'd seen her was as they charged through the park door, barely escaping the crushing tsunami chasing them. "When did you sneak away?"

"Once I sealed the park door, I panicked. I didn't know what else to do. I ran. I just ran."

"You're okay. That's what counts."

"I'm a chicken. I left you all behind. I shouldn't have run away like that. I—"

He shushed her. "I'm glad you did. Back there, you're no good to anyone. This way, I can use your help."

"With what? I'm no soldier."

"I don't need you to be. You know this place. You built it. If anyone knows its ins and outs, it's you."

She shrugged. "What good is that? What can the two of us do?"

"A lot. You'll see."

He hoped he sounded more confident than he felt. Initially, his intention was to get a call to the *Putnam* and warn them about the drone mines. That was less of a priority now. With what had happened, they now knew.

"We need to get the President and Grayson to safety," he said.

"How do you propose to do that?"

"Escape vessels. Surely the facility's equipped with them?"

"Of course," she said, sounding defensive. "We've got six rescue minisubs. Each crews with a pilot and co-pilot. They can accommodate up to twenty-four passengers."

"I only need one for now," Bannon said.

"You're forgetting something."

"What's that?"

The mines. They'll keep us in as effectively as they keep everyone else out. Unless you're an expert pilot, with the skillset of—"

"I am. But it won't be me piloting the sub out of here," Bannon said, thinking on the fly. "Your submersible pilot, Garcia, will be doing that. But the mines will be out of commission long before Garcia launches."

"Oh, and who's going to do that?"

"You and I." Bannon went to the closet door and peered out, rifle in hand. "Once we've got POTUS and Grayson safely on a rescue sub, they can hover close to Tiamat Bluff until we disable the minefield."

"That means getting to Ops," she said. "There'll be dozens of armed men there, waiting for just such a move. What makes you think you can—"

He cut her off. "Because the alternative is unacceptable." He glanced out into the corridor again. The coast appeared clear. "Come on."

He grabbed her by the hand. "We need to find where they're keeping Garcia and where they'd take POTUS and the others now that the park is gone."

"I'm sure I don't have a clue."

"Think," he said, leading her down the corridor. "A large space, securable. Would take only a few people to guard?"

"Access to food, water, facilities," she said, brainstorming.

"Yeah. Sure. Close to Ops, I would guess. Keeping your people accessible."

"Neptune's Glen," she said.

"Excuse me?"

"Neptune's Glen. It's a large restaurant one level below and with direct access to Ops via a spiral staircase. It's the only restaurant to remain operational for the President's visit. The others were shut down for the duration. Only two ways in and out, equipped with a full kitchen… "

"I doubt they'll be serving seven-course meals," Bannon said.

"No, but there are dry foodstuffs, rations. Water. And restrooms."

"Close to the viper's den," Bannon said, not liking it but not surprised either.

Larson fast-walked to keep up with his long, purposeful strides. "But if you want access to whatever program they're using to control the drone mines, you can bet it's up in Ops."

"Two birds. One stone."

"Sure," she agreed. "If we can get in, rescue the prisoners, and take over Ops without getting ourselves killed."

"Let me worry about that," Bannon said, his expression hardening into a mask of determination.

"Getting you to Ops is exactly where I'll be taking you."

The voice came from around the bend ahead of them.

Bannon stopped short and shoved Larson behind him even as he raised the machine pistol, but he was too slow.

Special Agent Kate Holloway had the drop on them. Close to the interior wall of the corridor, she held a Sig Sauer P229 pointed at Bannon's forehead. "Lang wants a word with you."

"You're working for him."

Bannon lowered his weapon. Angry with himself. This was a development he hadn't anticipated.

CHAPTER THIRTY-THREE

THE WRECKED SWCS VESSEL continued its downward plunge toward the ocean floor. Air bubbles cascaded upward. The purple turquoise water around it grew darker by the second. McMurphy clung to the roll bar over the pilot's seat. He slapped away Jones' panicked, flailing hands, working to unhook the man's five-point canvas harness, ignoring the bloom of blood-tainted water from the SEAL's gashing stomach wound. He transferred Jones' air hose from the doomed vessel's air supply and hooked it to the tank strapped to his back.

"Up and at 'em, Jonesy."

McMurphy wrapped his arms around Jones in a tight bearhug and tugged him from his seat. His legs got tangled under the dashboard. His fins didn't make the job of disengaging the man any easier. Also wearing fins, McMurphy pressed his feet against the nose of the vessel.

"This is gonna hurt you more than it hurts me."

He yanked one more time.

Jones howled as he was pulled through the hole blasted into the vessel's cockpit. McMurphy held the man under one arm, carrying him like a sack of potatoes. "Sorry 'bout that, Junior."

Jones' voice spoke over McMurphy's earpiece. "Where are you... what are you doing?"

Good questions, McMurphy mused.

The two men hung in the cold darkness, hovering as if suspended in space as they watched the minisub slip away below them. The sloping grade of Georges Bank was only twenty feet away. But whether the vessel would land and settle or tumble down the embankment to the gorge below remained to be seen.

McMurphy felt a disturbance in the water before he heard the low, muted thud of more explosions. He twisted around and glanced at Tiamat Bluff fifty feet up the embankment from where their sub touched down in a cloud of blueish silt.

He watched in horror as the other submersible smashed into the Bluff's dome and exploded. Victim of yet another drone mine. The dome shattered. A billowing cloud of water blew out, then rushed in. The ocean's water pressure imploded the space, caving in the grid and transparent panels, crushing the park entirely.

Jesus.

"What's the range on these headsets?" McMurphy asked.

"Fifty feet or so. It's a closed frequency. Can't call the *Putnam* for help. But Tiamat Bluff can't hear us either." Jones clutched his gut, which was still leaking blood and coughed. "Any bright ideas?"

"You're just full of good questions."

"A couple of good answers would sure make my day."

He was alert. Was thinking clearly. That was good.

What now? Both delivery vessels were toast. As near as McMurphy could tell, he and Jones were the only survivors. That left them with three choices. Remain where they were and hope a rescue effort was mounted and arrived before their air ran out or Jones bled out. Two. Make their way to Tiamat Bluff and attempt to get inside, taking their chances they wouldn't be killed swimming through the moon pool before their air ran out or Jones bled to death. Or, three, retreat.

Head to the surface one thousand feet above them. A twelve to fourteen-hour endeavor if they were to avoid the life-threatening condition known as the bends on a couple of two-hour bottles. That meant their air would run out before they made it. *And* Jones would bleed out before them.

"Tell me you've got a plan, boss?" Jones said.

"Three, actually."

"If they're what I think they are, none of 'em are gonna work," Jones said.

"What happened to that never quit SEAL spirit?" McMurphy asked, looking hard at the man through his facemask.

"It leaked out of the hole in my gut," Jones said with a cough and a groan.

"Jokes. That's good. Well, buck up, Junior. I think I've got something that just might work."

He pressed the valves in their BCUs, releasing air, dropping them deeper in the water.

"Unless I'm mistaken," Jones said and pointed. "Up is that-a-way."

"Sometimes you've got to go down before you can go up," McMurphy said.

"How much diving have you done in your life, McMurphy?"

"A wee bit more than you, son. And being that we're in this life-and-death situation together, you should call me Skyjack."

"That's your name?"

"A nickname."

"Bet there's a story behind it."

"There is."

"Love to hear it sometime."

"Over a beer. After we're out of this mess."

"Better tell me now. Later's gonna be too late."

"Nope," McMurphy said. "Give you something to live for."

They continued their descent. Dropping, a column of cascading bubbles going up. The water around them got darker and colder, but McMurphy put that out of his mind. The neoprene suits would keep them alive, if not necessarily comfortable. At least long enough to do what he planned.

"Want to clue me in on whatever scheme you're hatching?"

Below them, the minisub came into view. Thanks to the glow-sticks McMurphy had activated that hung from their BCUs and a few passing deep-sea anglerfish whose antenna-like esca extended from its head and glowed bright blue, a means by which to attract prey. Ugly fish. With their monstrous open mouths full of irregular sharp teeth.

"Waiting at the SWCS is pointless. No one's coming for us, certainly not in time."

McMurphy nodded in silent agreement.

Jones paused, needing to catch his breath. McMurphy worried about the rate at which he sucked in the oxygen and air mix. But, he was encouraged the man had the physical strength and strength of will to keep talking, to keep fighting.

"The Bluff will be more fortified than ever, making any entry attempt damn near impossible."

"Sure," McMurphy said.

"That leaves us with making our way back topside." A cough, then, "We head straight up. The decompression sickness will kill us. If we incorporate safety stops along the way, we won't get the bends, but we'll run out of air." Jones paused to do the math in his head. "Fourteen hours. Our air supply is about two hours at best. We've got a better chance of storming the Bluff."

"No. We don't. Besides, we'll make it in twelve." McMurphy settled him on the ground near the nose of the wrecked sub, which had been stopped from tumbling further down the embankment by a boulder-sized outcropping. He set Jones' buoyancy compensator and let him sit with his back against the dark hull on the gently sloping leeward side of Georges Banks.

"Twelve what?"

"Hours," McMurphy said. "To reach the surface. Where's the tool kit?"

"You missed the part about us only having two hours of air?"

"Nope. Tool kit. This poor excuse for a submarine's got to have a tool kit on board, doesn't it?"

"Crew compartment. Overhead bin near the back. Why?"

"You'll see." He patted the man's shoulder. "Stay put."

"Where the hell would I go?"

Still joking. Good, McMurphy thought with a wry smile. Then he frowned at the grim task ahead. He swam around to where the mine had exploded midship, ripping a hole into the crew cabin.

The edges of the metal were ragged and sharp. Kowalski's headless corpse was gone. It had floated away when McMurphy pushed his way out of the doomed submersible. But, back inside the vessel once more, McMurphy couldn't avoid the remaining dead bodies still strapped in their seats. The young man who'd sat across from McMurphy, his body had taken the brunt of the explosion and had saved McMurphy's life. It was now barely recognizable as human.

He pushed his way toward the back. The young man's dead eyes seemed to follow him.

A school of small fish darted around the dead man's face mask, already curious. The way blowflies accumulated around the dead on the surface.

McMurphy found the bin Jones had mentioned. The tool kit inside had everything he needed. Along with it, McMurphy found a Desco US Navy dive knife and sheath. He strapped it to his calf and then went to work.

Twenty minutes later, he swam back to Jones. His work completed. With him, he lugged his salvaged booty from the minisub. Upon his return, he found Jones motionless and thought the worst. He shook the kid's shoulder. "Junior. Jones!"

The young lieutenant's eyes popped open. Only asleep.

"Don't do that, man," McMurphy said. "You scared me."

Jones blinked. "What's all that?"

McMurphy ignored the question. "I need you to sit forward."

Jones did so with a wince. McMurphy had a long strip of black neoprene. It was the leg of a wetsuit he'd cut off one of the corpses inside the submersible. A gruesome task. He wrapped it around Jones' waist, pulling the elastic material tight around his wound before tying it off in a knot. Not exactly a compression bandage, but the elasticity of the material would tighten. McMurphy hoped enough to stop the bleeding.

Jones winced several times during the process but never complained.

When McMurphy was done, he leaned back against the hull. His face was a sheen of sweat under his facemask. He ached to wipe it away but couldn't.

"Now, what's all that junk you're hauling around," Jones asked, eyeing the large dark tanks McMurphy had returned with.

McMurphy glanced down. "You were right. We didn't have enough air to reach the surface *and* do proper decompression stops. Now we do."

"The submersible's air tanks."

"Two of 'em anyway. Enough air to supply eight divers for twelve hours. We're only two."

"We've used up a lot getting here," Jones countered.

"Still more than enough for our needs."

He'd also cut loose one of the sub's five-point canvas straps. With it, he jury-rigged a harness so he could belt the two large air tanks to his back. They could operate off their individual tanks until they ran out of air, jettison them, then switch over to the large tanks that would take them to the surface.

He checked his dive watch. "Twelve hours from now, it'll be nothing but sunshine and clear, fresh air for us."

"It'll be the middle of the night by the time we surface."

McMurphy grinned. "Have it your way. Clear, fresh air and moonlight."

"As long as there's drinks."

"Name your poison." With the makeshift harness on, McMurphy pulled Jones into an embrace, slowly began to inflate their BCDs, and together they kicked, starting the first leg of their tedious crawl toward the surface one thousand feet away, ten feet at a time.

"You know, McMurphy," Jones said. "For a puddle pirate, you're not half bad."

"Right back at ya, swabbie." A moment of silence fell between the two men. Better to conserve their air. McMurphy continued to carefully fill their buoyancy compensator vests and held an arm tightly around Jones' chest.

"We're going to make it, Junior," McMurphy assured him. "Or we're going to die trying."

THIRTY-FOUR

BANNON STARED AT THE wrong end of the Sig Sauer P229 pointed at his face. He flicked his attention from the wide 9mm opening to the woman behind the unwavering gun: Special Agent Kate Holloway.

She'd discarded her dark pantsuit jacket. Her white blouse was damp and clung to her form, revealing the outline of a dark bra underneath. Her blond hair, previously in the tightest bun Bannon had ever seen, had fallen. It cascaded over her shoulders in bouncy, damp curls.

Without her sunglasses, he could see her clear blue eyes.

In them, he could see she meant business.

"I have to say. I didn't see this coming." Bannon shifted his stance, continuing to shield Robin Larson. She clutched his shoulders from behind. He could feel her hot, rapid breathing on his neck.

"It's not what you think," Holloway said.

"They all say that," Bannon countered. He gauged her grip. It was two-handed and steady as a rock. The Secret Service did tend to train their agents well. "Or a variation of you wouldn't understand. In the end, it comes down to one of two things: ideology or money."

"Not this time."

He ignored her protest. "Which is it, *agent?* Do you love money or hate your country?"

"You've got it all wrong."

"Oh, I get it," Bannon said, stalling while trying to figure a way out of this situation. "You love your country, but we're all misguided idiots, and you're going to fix everything. You and Lang are going to put us back on the right path."

"Shut up! You're wrong."

"Then why are you pointing a gun at us?" Larson said.

"I don't have a choice." For the first time, the gun wavered. "But you're not entirely wrong. It is about love."

"Love?" Bannon cocked his head. "You and Lang? Sucre?"

Holloway's stoic features screwed up in disgust. "God, no."

Bannon relaxed his grip on the machine pistol, letting it hang loose at his side. He could read the torture in the woman's eyes. "Then what is it, Kate. Tell us what's going on."

Larson tentatively moved out from behind his cover. Holloway looked behind her. She hesitated, then lowered her pistol and nodded, indicating they should move to the left. Bannon assumed out of camera view.

"They have my family," she said. "My husband and my little girls. They're holding them hostage."

Saying the words broke open the dam she'd erected. Tears fell down her cheeks.

"They?" Bannon said, taking a step forward. "Lang and Sucre?"

She nodded.

"How? When?"

"I don't know. After I left home this morning." She looked at her watch. "Yesterday morning. Thugs invaded my home. Armed. A woman and two men. They beat up Roger. He's taped to a chair. They sent me a video. To show me."

Afraid to ask the question, he said, "Your girls?"

"They're not hurt. Yet. Scared out of their minds."

"You said they sent you a video. How?"

"On my cell phone. When we were still on the *Putnam*. Again, just now in Ops. Lang's got a sat phone there."

"Your phone," Bannon asked. "Do you still have it?"

She nodded.

"May I see it?"

She handed Bannon her phone. He played the video, keeping the sound low. Over his shoulder, Larson gasped and covered her mouth as the video played. It lasted for just a few seconds, but with the voiceover, the threat was clear. More than enough to get the job done.

"My little girls... they're so scared. Who knows what they're doing to them."

Bannon reached out and gripped her arm reassuringly. "Nothing."

She looked at him like he was deranged.

"They won't harm them as long as they need you."

"And when they're done with me?" she said, venom in her voice. "Then what? They're dead, and I'm powerless to stop them."

"We won't let that happen," Bannon said.

Her *you're delusional* expression returned. "What can you do about it? A retired coastie. Owner of a seaside bar."

At least she didn't call it a dive bar, he thought.

"We're stuck down here on the ocean floor. You're so far out of your depth, Bannon, you're not even being rational. No pun intended."

"Listen to me. I can help. I can."

"How?" Fresh tears rolled down Holloway's face.

"I do more than own the Keel Haul. I work for Grayson. I have a team. We handle special assignments for her. Problems that crop up outside the normal purview of Homeland Security operations."

From her expression, it was clear Holloway wasn't buying it.

"Remember the incident with the *Oceanic Princess* last year?"

Publicly, the attack on the ocean liner had been reported as a catastrophic engine failure. Gas fumes trapped in the engine compartment sparked and exploded. A lie close to the truth. Tara Sardana had caused just such an explosion on the terrorist's ship. The damage to the *Oceanic Princess* had been the result of those same terrorists attacking the ocean liner in an attempt to destroy it. As the agent in charge of the President's personal protection detail, Holloway had category one Yankee White clearance, like Bannon, the highest security clearance in the nation. As such, she'd have been fully briefed on what really happened that day, but with Bannon and his team's identities redacted.

She'd know the story to be true, and the only way for Bannon to know about it in detail was if he'd been there. "The railguns? That was you?"

"With the help of some very close friends. Those same friends are out there, doing what they can to save us. I'm sure of it. They can save your family, too. If we can contact the surface."

He knew he could use an ally in his fight against Lang and Sucre, but more importantly, the last thing he needed was another foe. "What do you say?"

WHEN KINGSLEY, GRAYSON, AND the others were recaptured, they were forcibly taken to a lower level. Grayson tried to keep track of where. Definitely to the north section of the facility, but she hadn't had a chance to study the layout of Tiamat Bluff in detail—didn't think she'd need to—and now all she knew was she didn't know where she was.

Getting old, she told herself.

They arrived at a closed door. In Spanish, Sucre ordered the armed men with them to take the prisoners inside.

She, Kingsley, and the others were roughly pushed through the open door. The doors closed behind them. Locked. They found themselves inside an opulently decorated restaurant. Three-quarters of the large open space was walled by glass with a magnificent view of the ocean outside.

Two young men with olive skin and black hair were posted at the door. Like the others, they held their machine pistols at the ready and wore serious expressions.

There were two dozen more people inside, mostly sitting at curved patted dining booths or along a large bar that doubled as a brightly lit fish tank. Another fish tank served as a backsplash to the shelved bar. Among the prisoners was the pilot of Seaview-One, Trevor Garcia.

He looked up from the booth where he sat and rushed over. "Madam Secretary. Mr. President. You're safe. We've been so worried."

"Thank you," Kingsley said. He swiped his damp gray hair from his forehead. "Everyone here is okay? Unharmed?"

"Yes. They have not harmed us." Garcia glared at the men at the nearby door. Grayson noticed another guard by a wide, carpeted spiral staircase that led up to the next level.

"Come," Garcia said. "Sit. They have given us water."

Grayson and Kingsley sat down. Still wet, Grayson shivered, and Garcia ordered someone to get her a blanket. He draped it over her shoulders while another man gave them bottles of water.

"Thank you," Grayson said. "What can you tell us?"

Garcia sat down opposite them. "Not much. We have been locked up here since they took you away. From the looks of you two, I'd say you have more of a tale to tell than we do."

"The park. It's been destroyed," Grayson said.

"A rescue attempt gone wrong," Kingsley added. The responsibility he felt for the loss of life was apparent in his drawn features and slumped shoulders. A businessman and an academic before his run for the White House, he'd never experienced anything like this before.

Grayson leaned forward and lowered her voice. "Mr. Garcia, in an emergency, how would Tiamat Bluff be evacuated?"

"We have six operational midget subs, ma'am, modeled after the Navy's Deep Submergence Rescue Vehicles. The DSRVs crews with a pilot and co-pilot. They accommodate up to twenty-four passengers. If we could get to them."

Grayson looked around. "Let me worry about that."

"Liz, what do you have in mind?" Kingsley asked.

"I don't know yet," she said honestly. But she did feel an idea percolating.

She stood up and paced the room. Two ways in and out. The doorway they came through. And, across the room, a steel spiral staircase leading upward in the corner. Both were under heavy guard.

Returning to the table, she asked, "Where do those stairs lead?"

"Up to Ops," Garcia said. "It is directly above us. But even if you got past the man with the gun, the door's locked with a two-tier biometric lock. Only senior personnel have access."

She spotted a dark brown dome in the ceiling. The size of a softball. Inside it was a camera. A camera watching their every move. Her idea—too early to be called a plan—was coming into focus. But first, she needed to get to the men in charge: Sucre and Lang.

She didn't know if it would work, but she had to try. She looked at the camera and steeled herself for what she had to do next.

CHAPTER THIRTY-FIVE

"I THINK I HAVE an idea," Robin Larson said, looking from Agent Holloway to Bannon.

They remained huddled in the corridor, hugging the curved interior wall. Larson assured them it was a blind spot between cameras. Bannon questioned the lack of continuous coverage. Larson took exception to the criticism. "Tiamat Bluff's not a military installation, Commander. The cameras are in place to facilitate safety and regulate living conditions, not monitor people like they're prisoners."

"Understood," Bannon said, actually welcoming the blind spots. "Your idea?"

"Remember the rescue subs we were discussing earlier?"

"Sure." They were key to his plan for getting POTUS and Grayson to safety.

"They have independent power and communications onboard. If we can get to one, from there, we can contact the *Putnam*."

"If they're not already heavily guarded," Holloway said. "Lang's people would be all over us in seconds."

"There's a bigger problem than that," Larson added.

"Of course. Why wouldn't there be?" Holloway said.

"Access is controlled and monitored from Ops with an in-tandem locking system."

Bannon explained for Holloway's benefit. "Requires two people to gain access from remote locations. One person in Ops and the other at the hatch." To Larson, he said, "What about a power surge?"

She shook her head. "The system is EMP resistant, with redundant backups."

"Okay," Bannon thought. "Still, there would be a small window between when the power went down and the backups activated. Assuming the system is fail-safe and not fail-secure."

Electronic locks were designed to operate in one of two ways during a power failure event. Either they remained locked, called fail-secure, or they were fail-safe, meaning the locks automatically disengaged if power was lost. It made sense the sub hatches would be fail-safe, allowing personnel to escape in the event of an emergency.

"Fail-safe, of course," Larson confirmed.

One problem licked, Bannon thought.

"But," Larson said.

Because there was always a but. A however.

"The time between... we're talking seconds," Larson said. Her brow furrowed as she worked the problem in her head. "And, if there are any power disruptions, alarms sound in Ops."

"That's where she comes in," Bannon said.

"Me?" Holloway said.

"I can save your family, Agent Holloway," Bannon said. "But I need your help to do it."

"No."

Bannon blinked. "Excuse me. What do you mean no?"

Holloway's blue eyes blazed angrily. "You're talking about putting the President and others on a submarine and then contacting someone topside who may or may not be able to save my family. No. Lang will retaliate. He'll kill my family. And everyone left down here. No. I won't risk it."

"I'm staying here. I'll make sure that doesn't happen," Bannon said.

She raised her pistol. "I'll take my chances turning you over to Lang, then figure out a way to keep POTUS and my family alive from here."

An orphan growing up in the system, Bannon had no family of his own. He wondered what he'd do put in the impossible situation Holloway faced. And so, Bannon found it hard to judge her too harshly. He raised his hands. "I get it. But we're onto something. We just need to finesse the plan."

"Save my family," she said. "Then we'll talk."

"I can do that," he said with all the confidence he could muster.

"How?"

Bannon glanced over to Larson, then back to Holloway. "We get on the sub. We make the call. You keep Lang distracted."

"How do I know you won't just leave?"

She didn't know Bannon. She had no reason to trust him. Again, he got it.

"Instead of liberating the hostages first," he said, which had been his original plan. "We'll go to the sub first, make the call and get the ball rolling on saving your family."

Holloway chewed her lower lip, considering his plan. "How do I distract Lang from a massive power outage?"

Larson spoke up. "I can make it look like a series of rolling blackouts. We had to contend with them a lot when we were first up and running. Diverting power from system to system, as needed, when our output was low. The system's designed to do that."

"You think Lang's going to fall for something like that?" Holloway asked.

"He's using my people to monitor and operate the systems up there," Larson said. "They'll see it that way. No reason they wouldn't. At least in the short term."

"Enough time to get our message out," Bannon said.

Holloway lowered her gun, thinking. Finally, she stared hard into Bannon's eyes. "Okay. But there's one more thing we need to do."

"What's that?" Bannon asked.

"The cameras will have picked up our initial meet up. If I'm to convince Lang you legitimately escaped from me, I've got to sell it."

"What do you want me to do," Bannon asked. "Shoot you?"

"I was thinking something less drastic." She leaned in and jutted out her chin. "Slug me. A good one."

Bannon frowned. "I can't do that."

"Oh, for Christ's sake." Larson stepped forward and swung her fist hard and fast into Holloway's left eye.

"Oww!" The Secret Service agent staggered backward, covering her eye with her hand. She leaned over and groaned. "That hurt more than I thought it would."

With little conviction, Larson said, "Sorry."

"That's some right hook," Bannon said, impressed.

"That's what two years of kickboxing aerobics will do for you."

"Get out of here," Holloway said. Her eye was already bloodshot and swollen.

They turned to leave.

Holloway called out. "Don't mess this up, Bannon. My family's counting on you."

He nodded, and they ran, her words echoing in his ears. Silently, he promised. Her family would be fine.

"We need to stay away from the cameras," he said to Larson.

"Stay close to the interior corridor walls," she said, taking the lead. They bypassed an elevator as she directed him to a service stairwell. She unlocked it by placing her hand against the black biometric pad.

Unlocked, they slipped inside.

"The subs are docked on the lowest level." They raced down five flights of stairs.

When they reached the bottom of the stairwell, they paused at the door.

"You wait here until I've cleared the place." He clutched the machine pistol at the ready and nodded for her to open the door.

She did so.

He rushed into the corridor beyond. He swept the weapon left, then right, but there was no enemy to engage. Bannon was grateful for that, relieved at not exposing their presence via a gun battle, but concerned by the carelessness of it. Was Lang so confident he'd leave such an obvious means of escape unprotected? He didn't strike Bannon as being that foolish.

Maybe he simply didn't have enough men. Were his resources more finite than Bannon had first thought? At the moment, it didn't matter. He waved for Larson to join him.

"No one's here?" she asked, sounding as surprised as he was. Her voice low.

The corridors were dimly lit. Just a strip of icy blue running lights along the floor. This far down, there were no windows. Absent was the reddish glow from the panoramic ocean views the upper levels had. Bannon heard the low hum of engines and felt a faint vibrating under his feet.

"This way," Larson said. Bannon followed as she led him south along the corridor. "If you recall, the northernmost section of Tiamat Bluff is embedded into the sloping grade of Georges Bank. The subs are docked this way where the lowest level is still above grade."

The corridor curved toward the left.

A five-minute walk brought them to the first DSRV hatch.

Larson rushed at it, suddenly agitated. She looked through the portal. "No." She looked again as if she couldn't accept what she was seeing. "No."

She rushed to the next one. And the next. "No. No. No."

There, she stopped and turned.

By then, Bannon had glanced through the first portal and saw what had upset.

"That explains why there's no guards down here," he said.

"They're gone," she said. "They're all gone."

"All of them? Are you sure?"

She frowned, apparently frustrated with his lack of faith in her assessment. Then, as if to prove herself right, she stormed down the concave corridor, peering through each portal she came to. "Gone. Gone. Go—" She turned her mouth open in surprise. "This one! It's still here. The only one left."

"Lang must have jettisoned the others," Bannon reasoned, joining her.

"Why would he do that?"

"The only reason I can think of," Bannon said. "Lang has no intention of letting anyone escape Tiamat Bluff alive. Except himself and a small chosen few, I guess."

"What does that mean?"

Bannon said, "We stick with the original plan."

"Okay," Larson said. "Yes. Right. I can access the computer mainframe from the machine room over there." She pointed at a pair of steel doors along the interior corridor wall. "I'll start the system shutdowns away from here, in non-critical areas, before sweeping through the electronics in this section. That should allay any suspicions for a little while."

Bannon nodded. "Good."

"The runway lights will go out. That's how you'll know the power's down. You'll only have less than two seconds to open the hatch and get inside."

"Can I get back out?"

"Yes. But not without alarms going off in Ops."

"Understood. And I'll be able to power up the sub's comm system?"

"Yes. They operate completely independent of the Bluff."

He nodded. "Let's do this."

She crossed the corridor and operated the biometric pad next to the machine room's double doors. Bannon held his breath. But the door lock clicked, and she was in.

She turned. "Give me ten minutes to hack into the programs I need to access and another five to cycle through the systems."

He nodded, checking his watch.

She disappeared inside the machine room. He waited, glancing up and down the corridor, expecting a roving patrol any minute. None came. He held his hand over the hatch lever. Ready.

True to her word, fourteen minutes later, the corridor's running lights blinked and then went out. He slapped the lever down and dragged the heavy oval hatch open. Beyond it was another round hatch. He spun the center wheel until it stopped and pushed the inner hatch open, pulling the one behind him closed.

Motion-activated, the DSRV's interior lights came on.

He was in the stern section of the fifty-five-foot-long sub. The main section was an open area with fold-down seats along the bulkheads on either side. Not built for comfort, the seats were hard, molded plastic with thick canvas five-point harnesses.

Bannon crossed quickly to the cockpit and dropped down into the pilot's chair.

The dashboard gauges were lit up. Bannon quickly located the communications console and set to work to make his call. With time for just one call, he had to make it count. He listened as the sub's comm system connected to the cell phone he'd settled on.

The phone rang. And rang.

And rang.

"Pick up. Pick up," he said under his breath. This was no time to leave a voicemail.

Finally, the connection was made.

A voice, not recognizing the number of the incoming call, tentatively answered, "Yes?"

"Blades! Thank God. It's me. It's Brice."

CHAPTER THIRTY-SIX

AN HOUR AFTER GETTING Diaz's call, Tara was still shaking, reeling from the devastating news that Skyjack McMurphy was dead. The pain of that was so raw, so fresh, she struggled to find the strength to go on.

She and Kayla were still on the Sea Ray traveling north when a second, equally unexpected call came in. Her heart soared at hearing Bannon's voice, but then to have to be the one to tell him his best friend was gone. That ripped her aching heart to shreds.

She'd said the words, barely getting them to form in her dry throat.

A silence followed that lasted so long she feared the call had dropped, but then Bannon spoke. A simple and quiet response. "We'll see."

"We'll see?" she repeated, her hand covering her opposite ear against the lashing wind and engine noise. "We'll see what? They killed him, Brice. That *qiteat min alqarf—*"

Bannon interrupted her. "I've got to go. You've got your assignment."

The line went dead.

Tara lowered the phone and stared out over the dark Atlantic Ocean. Moonlight shimmered on its calm, rippling surface. *We'll see.* Had he not heard her properly? Was he in denial?

When she could find her voice again, she relayed Bannon's orders to Kayla. Then, she took the helm while Kayla planned to get a plane fueled and prepped, using her many contacts at Coast Guard Air Station Cape Cod, while Tara reversed the small craft's direction and made a beeline for Sandwich, Massachusetts.

Not long after, the wheels of the hastily readied HC-144 Ocean Sentry, one of fifteen medium-range surveillance aircraft the Coast Guard operated, touched down on a remote airstrip on the outskirts of Ronald Reagan International Airport. Though the aircraft was designed to accommodate up to nine passengers, the only ones on board were Tara and Kayla.

Wheels down, Tara unsnapped her seatbelt but remained seated.

Getting to her feet, Kayla said, "Are you all right?"

Tara stared forward without seeing anything. "No."

She blinked and stood up. "Let's go. I need to keep moving."

She brushed past Kayla and descended the fold down stairs without acknowledging the pilot who'd opened the door and flown them in from Cape Cod. Kayla offered an apologetic smile to the aviator. "It's been a bad day. Thank you."

A silver-gray and blue Virginia State Police cruiser sat on the tarmac.

There to meet them.

A tall officer, African-American, in black fatigues, stood leaning against the grille with his arms crossed over his chest. His legs were crossed at the ankles. Casual but alert. The runway was awash with the car's headlights. In addition to being a tactical SWAT team leader with the state police, Brandon Reynolds was also a petty officer second class, with the Coast Guard Police, Reserves.

He'd worked with Bannon and the others in Afghanistan before they'd left the service. Not specifically assigned to Grayson's unit, he was local to the area, and he was someone they could trust.

"Brandon, thanks for coming out," Kayla said, giving him a hug.

"Of course." He nodded to Tara. "Blades. What can you tell me about what's going on?"

"We need to move," Tara said. Stoic and all business. "We'll fill you in on the way."

She climbed into the back seat of the cruiser. Kayla and Reynolds exchanged looks. She frowned. He climbed behind the wheel and pulled out of the airport. Kayla gave him Kate Holloway's address. He plugged it into the GPS.

Reynolds glanced at the rearview mirror. His eyes on Tara. "You want to tell me what I'm driving into now?"

"A father with two young children, girls, are being held hostage," Tara said. "We need to rescue them."

"Near as we know, there are three hostiles," Kayla added. "Two males and a female."

Reynolds drove. "Why just the three of us? You insisted off-book, but… "

Tara and Kayla exchanged glances. Silently debating how much they could tell him.

Kayla said, "You're aware of what's going on at Tiamat Bluff?"

"Sure. The whole world's tuned in. This about the President?"

"And Brice," Kayla said. "He's down there, too."

"Damn it."

"It gets worse," Tara said.

Kayla said it. "Skyjack's dead, Brandon. Killed by the terrorists holding the President and Brice."

Reynolds squeezed the wheel and ground his teeth. The muscles in his jaw twitched. "Mother—

What's this hostage situation got to do with it?"

"The wife. She's a Secret Service agent," Kayla told him. "Her family's being held to force her cooperation with the terrorists holding the President."

"We save her family, she's back on our side," he surmised.

"Basically," Kayla said.

"So, no pressure then." He drove fast but without lights or sirens. "Skyjack. Jesus."

Twenty minutes later, Reynolds slowed the vehicle to a crawl. They'd entered a quiet residential neighborhood. Tree-lined, neat, well-manicured lawns. Decorative street lamps illuminated the sidewalks where an older man walked a little brown and white Pomeranian. He watched as the cruiser passed by and waved. It was that type of neighborhood, where the police were welcomed, not feared.

"The house is two blocks north of here," he said, easing the cruiser to the curb. The street curved to the left ahead of them.

"You have everything we asked for?" Tara asked.

"In the trunk." Reynolds unlocked the rear doors remotely and they got out.

He popped the trunk. Inside was a black duffle bag. He unzipped it and dug out two 9mm Sig Sauers.

"We've got our own," Tara said, even as she pulled her holstered Sig from her hip and handed it to Kayla. She repositioned the sheathed, duel-bladed haladie by slipping the weapon to the small of her back, keeping it hooked onto the bladed urumi she used as a belt.

He put the guns aside.

"In that case." Reynolds moved the duffle bag and pulled an M16 out from underneath. "Anyone want this?"

Kayla took it.

The cop was already strapped with a Sig of his own in his regulation holster. He grabbed a Benelli Supernova 12-gauge pump shotgun from the rack attached to the trunk lid. Then he fished around in the black bag again until he came out with two stun grenades. He handed Kayla one and hooked the other on his belt.

"And the rest?" Tara asked.

Reynolds moved the black duffle bag aside and pulled out a small black suitcase—the size that would fit in an airplane's overhead compartment—and passed it to Tara. It had wheels. She pulled the handle up. "It's empty."

He tossed her the duffle bag. "It's got a vest, a first aid kit, some flexicuffs and other stuff in it. Should give it enough weight to be convincing." Tara stuffed the duffle bag into the small suitcase then caught the jacket and baseball cap Reynolds tossed to her.

"Anything else?" he asked as she took off her coat and put the thinner, black jacket on and tied her black hair into a sloppy ponytail. She snaked it through the back of the ball cap. The jacket and cap each had a Southwest Airlines emblem on them. The cop handed her a clipboard with several official-looking pages clipped to them and a black felt tip pen.

"Gum," Tara said.

"Excuse me?"

"Do you have any gum?"

Reynolds dug into his pocket and came out with a pack. He tossed it to her. She took out four sticks and shoved them into her mouth. Cinnamon flavor. Chewing, she said, "Give me ten minutes."

Kayla checked her watch before slapping a loaded magazine into the M16.

"Be careful," she said.

"Always am," Tara said, walking down the sidewalk toward Holloway's house, pulling the small suitcase behind her.

"No, you're not!" Kayla called out. Then, under her breath, she added, "You're reckless as hell."

When Tara reached the house, she pulled the weighted suitcase onto the stoop of the modest Falls Church home. Reynolds had had the forethought to tie a couple of baggage claim tickets to the suitcase's handle. Tara rang the doorbell.

While she waited, Tara scribbled a note across the second page on the clipboard with the black marker.

The door opened. A tough-looking woman with Hispanic features filled the doorway. She stared out at her. "What?"

Tara sized her up while she looked at the clipboard. "Mr. Holloway?"

"I look like a mister to you?"

Tara reserved judgment on that and smiled, feigning nervousness. "I… no, of course not. My bad. It's been a long night. I meant I'm looking for Mr. Holloway."

"Why?"

"His… wife, I guess." Tara pretended to be put off by the woman's presence. She snapped her mouthful of gum. "I don't mean to assume. Her bag missed her flight this morning. We contacted her. She instructed we deliver it here rather than forward it on to Boston. She said she didn't expect her trip to last long enough to—"

The woman said, "Fine. Fine. Give me the suitcase."

Tara smiled trying to appear apologetic. Not something she had a lot of practice with. "I'm sorry, but I need to deliver it to Mr. Holloway. To Mr. Roger Holloway."

Tara glanced over the woman's shoulder and caught sight of movement in the back of the house. She guessed it was the woman's two accomplices moving their hostages out of her line of sight, and to keep them quiet.

"I'll need to see an ID and get a signature." Tara smiled insincerely. "You know how it is."

The woman stared at the Southwest insignia, no doubt trying to determine which course of action would be less problematic for her: refusing Tara's request and risk arousing suspicions, maybe causing her to talk to her supervisors about the woman's strange behavior, or get Holloway to the door and get rid of the woman straight away.

"Roger!" she called out, making her decision. "There's someone at the door for you."

There was no response.

The woman kept a watchful eye on Tara.

"He's my brother-in-law," she said, then shouted again. "Roger?"

This time, the woman turned her attention away from the front door. Tara pulled the wad of gum from her mouth and jammed the oozy mess into the door frame's strike. It would prevent the latch bolt from latching if the door were pulled closed.

Tara heard what sounded like a grunt then a voice called out, "Coming."

A man in dress slacks and a white t-shirt appeared in the hallway. He walked haltingly to the foyer from a kitchen-dining room combo. His hair was mussed, and he sported a black eye. "What's up?"

"The airline screwed up. Didn't put Kate's bag on the plane," the woman said. "You need to sign for it."

"Oh. Okay." He reached the door. The woman stepped back.

Tara noticed a dark stain on the collar of his T-shirt. Blood. As if it had soaked through an outer shirt, probably his dress shirt. He noticed her scrutiny and forced a smile. "I, um, spilled wine on my shirt. We're having a… late dinner."

Tara handed him the clipboard and a pen. She instructed, "On the bottom there. And on the second page."

Her hastily scribbled note on the second page read: *Here to help. Stay calm. Do as I say.*

She watched his eyes follow the words as he silently read the message. He looked up at her.

Tara read a mix of concern and relief in the man's eyes. She reached for the clipboard. "Thanks. I hate to ask this," she said. "And I'm not supposed to do anything like this, but could I use your bathroom? I've been out all night, and I've got five more stops to make before—"

"Of course," Holloway said quickly before the hard-looking woman could say no. "Use the one in the hallway. But please be quiet. My girls are asleep downstairs."

"I'll be quiet as a mouse." Tara danced a little. "I've really got to go."

"Just hurry," the woman said. "Our dinner's getting cold." She stepped outside and grabbed the suitcase Tara left on the stoop.

"This way," Holloway said.

Tara tried to reassure him with a smile. "Oh, you're a life saver."

THIRTY-SEVEN

TARA REACHED THE END of the short foyer. She could see the kitchen-dining room combo. Holloway's jacket and hastily removed dress shirt were in a pile on the floor. One chair was missing from the dining room table. Tara caught sight of it in the living room. A piece of duct tape still stuck to the leg.

"It's right here," Roger said, indicating the bathroom. "Next to the basement door."

Tara nodded to him. In that moment, for Tara, it was as if time slowed to a crawl.

Tactically, she determined one hostile would be downstairs with the girls, leaving the woman and second male up here, guarding Holloway and available to do random checks of the exterior and neighborhood to ensure local forces weren't amassing against them. She hoped the third hostile was in the house and not outside somewhere.

Out of the corner of her eye, a flash of movement caught her attention. She saw it reflected in a mirror over the fireplace in the living room. One hostile, a large brute of a man, hiding behind the wall adjacent to the eat-in kitchen area. He thought he was out of sight but hadn't considered the mirror. Across from the table with the missing chair were French doors leading out to a patio or deck. It was too dark for Tara to see much beyond a single brick step.

At the front door, the woman rolled the suitcase over the door saddle. The wheels rattled. Then she swung the door shut.

Next came the sound of shattering glass. The French doors. A panel smashed inward. Broken by the butt of Reynolds' 12-gauge shotgun and followed quickly by a tossed flash-bang. The grenade hit the floor, bounced, and exploded in a flash of light, quickly followed by a second smoke grenade.

"Get down!" Tara shouted, shoving a startled Holloway hard enough he fell to the floor and slid toward the kitchen island. "Stay down."

Tara unsheathed her duel-bladed haladie and paused only long enough to see—and hear—Reynolds kick in the French doors. They flew inward and smashed against the walls.

Behind her, Kayla kicked in the front door. She tossed another flash-bang through the open door. It sent the hard-looking woman scurrying into a side room. Kayla stood in the doorway, her M16 at the ready, looking every bit like a female Rambo.

Tara shouted, "One hostile's in the front room. Another's in the living room to the right. I'm going for the kids in the basement."

She tore the basement door open. Armed only with her haladie in hand, she descended the carpeted stairs to the finished basement below. The carpet kept her footfalls silent, but the open stairwell exposed her to whoever was downstairs and whatever weapons they might carry.

Before she reached the bottom step, she crouched, and her throat clutched.

The space had been turned into a bright, cheery family room. Beige walls. Curtained casement windows. A big-screen TV, gaming, and computer equipment along one wall. In the middle of the room was an arts and crafts table. Off to the side was a Barbie playhouse with all the cool things that went along with it.

A mattress had been thrown on the floor.

On it were the two little girls: Kacey and Karley. Tara didn't know which was which, but they were definitely twins.

Behind them, the man tasked with watching them held one girl in a headlock. She struggled against his grip. Her cheeks tear-stained. He pressed a pistol to her temple.

The three of them stared at Tara as she crept down the last steps. She held out her empty hand. "Take it easy. No one needs to get hurt here."

His dark eyes focused on the haladie. "Throw the knife away."

When she hesitated, he shouted, "Now!"

"Okay. Okay." She tossed it across the room. The duel-bladed knife bounced quietly on the carpeted floor.

"Take off your jacket."

She unzipped the front. He tensed.

"Take it easy," Tara warned. "It's going to be okay, girls."

Upstairs, there was a spat of gunfight.

Her guy twitched. His eyes darted to the ceiling.

"Pay attention to me," she said, opening her jacket. "I'm unarmed." She peeled the coat off her shoulders. Pulled it down her arms. She tossed it aside.

"Who are you?" he asked. "You ain't with Southwest."

"No. I'm with Homeland Security. It's over now." She closed the distance between them. The girls, frightened, remained quiet and motionless. All the better.

"The only thing over is you," the man said. He shifted his gun from the girl's head and stretched his arm out toward Tara, aiming the gun at her.

At the sound of broken glass and another boom of Reynolds' shotgun, followed by more gunfire, the terrorist tightened his grip on the gun.

Tara ducked as she seized the hilt of the urumi from around her waist and snapped it out. The blade whipped through the air and slashed across the gunman's wrist like a whip. A deep cut opened up. Blood spurted. The gun went off.

He cried out and pulled his arm back but didn't drop the gun. Blood trickled over his hand from the wound. Tara darted to the side and cracked the whip-blade again. It made a thunderclap snapping noise.

The girl pulled away from her captor's grip and dropped down onto the mattress. She clutched her sister in a tight, protective bear hug.

"Stay down, girls!" Tara shouted.

The man stepped away, squaring off with Tara. He raised his gun hand, wincing at the pain as he squeezed the trigger.

Tara snapped the blade down on his wrist again, then followed up with a quick left to right snap that caught the back of his hand, cutting yet another deep gash into his flesh. This time, he dropped the gun and tried to shake the pain from his hand.

Tara charged him, spun, and slashed the whip-blade across his gut. It cut through his shirt, drawing blood. He doubled over, clutching his middle. Tara hit him in the jaw with a punch that knocked out a tooth.

He spun away and fell to his knees.

Tara smashed her left fist into the side of his head, still clutching the urumi hilt in her hand.

On his hands and knees now, he crawled for the dropped gun, leaving bloody handprints on the carpet. He lunged for it. Tara stomped her booted heel into his hand, crushing his fingers against the hard metal grip of the gun. He screamed in pain.

Defeated, he looked up at her, his eyes pleading with her not to kill him. There was another shotgun blast upstairs. Tara punched his bloody face. He collapsed. Sprawled across the floor. The fight beaten out of him.

But that didn't stop Tara.

She flipped his semi-conscious body on to his back and rained punches down on his face. Left and right. He grunted and made a failed attempt to cover up. Blood spurted from cuts opened up under his eyes, from his nose and lips, and still, Tara didn't stop.

Her attack became feral. Out of control. Blind with rage.

Somewhere in the back of her awareness, she heard her name being called. "Tara. Tara!"

She ignored it and kept swinging. Her knuckles became bloody and raw. She ignored that, too.

"Tara. Stop. Stop!"

Something—someone—grabbed her arm, pulled her back.

She reacted by swinging. She heard a scream, almost guttural, before she realized the sounds were coming from her.

Her wildly thrown punch was blocked. Kayla stood facing her, her arms raised, blocking further punches. "Stop it!"

Breathless, Tara stepped back. She looked down at the man at her feet, bloody and beaten. Unable to tell if he was alive or dead. She staggered back and caught sight of the little girls looking at her. Karley and Kacey. The horror she saw in their eyes, aimed at her, was no different than the frightened expressions they'd had when she first came down the stairs. While in the company of a terrorist with every intention of killing them.

"Skyjack," Tara said, looking at the girls as if to explain. "They killed Skyjack."

Kayla threw her arms around her friend. She embraced her. Squeezed her as tears flowed from both their eyes. "I know."

"They need to pay for that. All of them." Numb to the embrace at first, Tara slowly raised her hands. Then, she held Kayla tightly, too. Holding on to her friend. Holding on for dear life.

"I know," Kayla said. "They will."

Tara pulled back. "Reynolds? Holloway?"

"Okay. They're both okay."

"The other two?"

"Dead."

The two girls—clutched in each others' arms—heard that. They ran for the stairs to the main floor.

Tara wanted to believe they were just anxious to be with their father. But she saw in their faces, in their eyes, the same deep-seated fear looking at her they'd had while in the presence of the terrorist. With their tiny footsteps thundering across the floor above, Tara stared at the unconscious man she'd nearly beaten to death.

"You okay?" Kayla asked.

"No. But we need to get word to Brice," she said. "Let him know the family is safe."

Kayla nodded, agreeing but realizing the problem with it. "Any suggestions on how to do that?"

Tara didn't have an answer.

THIRTY-EIGHT

ELIZABETH GRAYSON SAT AT a booth in Neptune's Glen alongside Kingsley and Garcia. Other hostages sat at different tables. Some sat on the floor, their backs to the wall. No one spoke. An occasional cough or the noise of someone shifting positions were the only sounds heard. An oppressive sense of dread hung over the room like a fog. Yet even under their dire circumstances and the somber mood, Grayson could appreciate how breathtaking the restaurant was, especially the wall of windows overlooking Georges Bank outside.

But her full attention remained on the three men guarding them. There are two at the main door. One by the spiral staircase leading up to the facility's operational center. Like Bannon earlier, she was impressed by the sense of discipline they demonstrated. A factor that only made things worse for them.

Someone had given her a bottle of water. She clutched it in her hands while she stared at the surveillance camera in the ceiling, silently daring Lang to acknowledge her.

With Bannon loose somewhere in the facility, she knew their chances of escaping this nightmare were greatly improved, but that didn't mean she'd idly sit by. She needed to talk to Lang. Reason with him. Maybe she could get him to stop this madness.

She glared at the two men guarding the door. Her patience had run out. She stood up and called out to them. "Tell your boss I want to speak to him."

Kingsley started to get up. "Liz, what are you doing?"

Grayson waved him down but otherwise ignored him.

"Your boss!" she shouted.

One of the men stepped forward.

She hurled her bottle of water at him.

He dodged it.

The bottle hit the wall behind him with a hollow thwap. It opened and splattered water everywhere.

"Now!" she demanded.

Under his breath, Kingsley hissed, "Liz. You're going to get yourself killed."

"Lang's not here for the RRA or even you, David. He's here for me. Twenty years ago, I abandoned him in the desert. Left him to die. He's here to get revenge on me." She shouted again, "Get me your boss!"

The one who'd stepped forward said, "General Sucre will not speak with you."

"I don't want to speak with Sucre. He's a puppet. A yes man for Lang. Get me Chase Lang!"

She grabbed another water bottle off the table and pitched it at the door.

That did it. The guard stormed across the room and grabbed her by the arm. He yanked her away from the booth.

Kingsley jumped to his feet. Garcia beside him.

The others in the room watched. A few of them stood up.

"Unhand her!" Kingsley demanded.

The other man at the door rushed over and backhanded Kingsley across the face. He staggered backward, banging up against the booth. Garcia caught him, arresting his fall.

"Stop this!" the pilot shouted. "Someone's going to get hurt."

"Right you are, Mr. Garcia," Lang said, suddenly appearing behind them. He waved his men back to their post. "It's all right. Settle down, everyone."

Kingsley picked himself up off the bench, using Garcia's help to steady his stance.

"I'm happy to speak with you, Colonel," Lang said. His tone void of any respect for her as he spit out her rank like a curse. Lang waved a hand toward the spiral staircase. "This way."

"Where are you taking her? I demand to know."

Lang turned toward Kingsley. "You demand nothing. Haven't you realized that yet? You're no one. A pawn. A dead man walking."

He jiggled Grayson's arm. "Come along, Colonel. You want to talk. Let's talk."

She followed him up the spiral stairs. Their footfalls rang on the metal steps. She glanced at David Kingsley and mouthed the words: *I'll be fine.*

To Garcia, she said, "Stay with him."

The pilot nodded, looking grim.

In her mind, Lang's most recent words chilled her most. *A dead man walking.* That told her Bannon had been right. There was never any intention of releasing the President, or any of them, regardless of the outcome. Taking the President hostage was just one piece of the puzzle. A much bigger play was at hand, but what was it?

At the top of the stairs, Lang held the door open, and Grayson entered Ops.

It was abuzz with muted activity. The consoles—several convex-shaped, gunmetal gray cabinets—were bright with colorful computer screen displays. Men and women seated at them, hunched over, looking frightened and defeated. Most of them wore blue Tiamat Bluff coveralls or the security staff Polo shirts, making it hard to distinguish between the legitimate workers and Lang's men.

Except for one thing…

She guessed the ones holding the guns were the bad guys.

Sucre stood with his back against a wall. As Lang let the door close, Sucre approached them, a worried expression on his face. "There's been a series of rolling power surges and failures throughout the facility."

Lang creased his forehead. "What's causing them?"

Sucre ushered over a nervous-looking woman with brown hair tied in a ponytail and wearing fashionable, dark-rimmed glasses. She cleared her throat. "Um, we saw this a lot during our early stages of operations. The system, it's AI, is designed to automatically sense service interruptions, needs, and divert—"

Lang held up his hand. "I don't need a science lesson. Do I need to be concerned about it?"

"I do not believe so," she said. "It's because of the dome's collapse, the power from the rest of the facility is being directed to reinforce—"

Lang waved, dismissing her. "Fine. Enough. Go away."

As he turned his attention back to her, Grayson said, "What happened to you, Chase?"

"Haven't we been through this already? You abandoned me. You left me and my men behind to die. Because of you, we spent a decade in Iranian captivity. Shuttled from prison to prison, one hellhole worse than the last. Tortured every day. For years. In ways that would make waterboarding seem like a spring break wet t-shirt contest. Forced to fight for our food. Abused in ways that are... quite unimaginable. And you left us there!"

"We didn't know," she said. "We thought you were dead."

"Because you abandoned us!" he shouted. "You never checked. Never tried to find us."

"That's not true," she said, but her voice was soft. Lacked the conviction she wished she could muster. Had they looked hard enough? Did they give up too easily?

"Do you know how many of us survived?" he asked. "Five of us watched you fly away in that chopper. Leave us to die. Peterson. Schwartz. Cortes. Koerner. Rijo. They're all dead now. None of 'em made it through what the Iranians did to us. Except me."

"If we'd known... "

"You have any idea what being a prisoner in Iran is like? An American prisoner? Well, Colonel, to answer your question. It broke me. What little hope I had—that I clung to—after watching you fly away? The Iranians stomped that out of me. They beat it out of me. Tortured it out of me. Abused it out of me. Left me for dead in every way possible, but physically. Left me wishing, praying, for that final release that never came. Even that was denied me. When I finally escaped, I had lost—and rejected—everything that made me weak: Love. Sympathy. Kindness. Compassion. My humanity."

"Your soul."

He smiled at that. "Yes, especially my soul."

Agent Holloway rushed through a door, interrupting them. Her hair was a mess. Her clothing in disarray. A nasty-looking bruise had begun to darken over her left eye.

"What the hell happened to you?" Lang asked.

Grayson thought she was too old, had experienced too much, to be surprised by anything. But this shook her to her core. "Kate? You're a part of this?" The accusation was laced with anger and hatred. "How could you?"

Holloway shrank from the wrath in Grayson's voice.

"No." She hesitated, searching for the words. "It's hard to explain."

"It's impossible to explain," Grayson said with disgust. "Traitor."

Lang shouted over Grayson at Holloway. "What happened?"

"Bannon," she said. "I had him. I thought I had him. But… I got careless. The woman distracted me."

Lang, with a raised eyebrow. "What woman?"

"Dr. Larson. She's with him."

Lang shot a withering look at Sucre. "You told me everyone was accounted for! You assured me!"

Sucre shrugged. "What's the difference? She's just one woman."

"The woman who built this place, who knows every damn thing there is to know about it. You idiot. Find her!"

One of Sucre's men whispered something in his ear. He turned toward a console and gave whispered instructions to the operator. Grayson didn't know if the operator was a coerced Tiamat Bluff worker or one of Sucre's men.

Lang returned his attention to Grayson and Holloway.

To Grayson, he said, "Agent Holloway's got a certain… incentive to assist me. Which she's getting back to doing right now." To the shamed Secret Service agent, he said, "Tell Sucre where this happened. Find Bannon. Find him now."

Holloway avoided Grayson's scornful glare. She moved across the room to join Sucre at a console. Grayson watched as they called up various camera angles on the monitors, tapping into the facility's video surveillance. Stepping up their search for Bannon.

"What is it you feel the need to discuss with me, colonel?"

"I wanted to talk to you about stopping this insanity. To appeal to your humanity."

Lang laughed in her face. "Well, we've already determined that's a lost cause."

"Where does it end, Chase? You're going to end up dead. Or worse."

Lang countered. "I've been through worse already. Because of you."

"You blame me," she said. "I get that. But this won't change anything."

"It'll get me what I've craved for the past eighteen years. Payback. Revenge. Retribution. That may sound petty to you, but it's what kept me going all these years. It's been the one singular driving force in my life. Gave me purpose. Something to live for."

"Then just kill me." She spread her arms. "Get your revenge. Get it over with. Don't take it out on all these people."

Lang smiled his reptilian grin.

"Oh, no. Nothing so simple as that. Death is the easy part. The release. No, Colonel, I'm going to make you suffer. I'm going to bring the country you love to its knees. Kill your President. Riddle your government with scandal and chaos. Destroy the public trust in anything American. I'm going to obliterate everything and everyone in the world you care about. And then, maybe, if I'm feeling generous, maybe then, I'll put you out of your misery."

At that moment, she knew there would be no reasoning with him. No call for his compassion, his humanity. He was right. It was gone. There was nothing left of the man she knew. The man she once…

Grayson shook the thought away. "That was why you attacked Bannon and McMurphy at Hampton Beach. To get back at me."

He didn't confirm or deny but instead glanced over at Sucre and Holloway hunched over a console. "Have you found them yet?"

To his apparent surprise and delight, they said they had.

"They're at the docking level," Sucre said. "Where the escape subs are." He paused, leveling Lang with a scornful look of his own. "Or should be."

"Then what are you waiting for? Go get them."

Sucre straightened up. "All but one of the subs have been released. They're gone."

Lang paused for a telling second before recovering. "That's not important at the moment."

To Sucre, it was. "Where'd they go? One's not enough to get us all out of here."

"And the true Chase Lang is revealed," Grayson said. If she couldn't appeal to his humanity, maybe she could turn his team against him. Sow the seeds of mistrust. "You've turned on your own people. Even they can't trust you."

Lang glared at her. "Shut up!"

The focus of the workers and their armed counterparts shifted to Lang. He waved a hand at them. "Get back to work." To Sucre, he said, "Bannon and Larson. Where are they?"

"On the last remaining sub."

"The coward's trying to escape. Get down there. Stop him!"

"The system will not allow him to launch. Not without help from someone here," Sucre said. "Where are the other subs, Lang? What have you done?"

"Get Bannon. We'll deal with the rest later."

Sucre glowered. "Yes," he vowed. "We will."

But for the moment, he grabbed Holloway's arm and pulled her toward the door. Two of his men fell in behind him, following them out.

Lang shouted, "And don't come back until you have him. Dead or alive!"

CHAPTER THIRTY-NINE

AFTER COMPLETING HIS CALL to Tara, Bannon sat in the ethereal glow of the cockpit's instrument panel, listening to the silence of the dead connection in the tubular minisub. Upon hearing Tara's words, he'd dropped heavily into the pilot seat and stared through the cockpit window. Stared out into the dark abyss of the ocean floor that lay beyond him, but he saw nothing.

Skyjack's dead?

He immediately rejected the notion. Impossible.

He'd told Tara *we'll see,* confident that if the Grim Reaper had confronted McMurphy, the tough-as-granite Irishman would've sent the Specter of Death packing, more than likely with a bloody nose. But alone in the DSRV with his thoughts, the very real possibility that he was wrong hit him hard. Someday, his stubborn old friend would take a chance too great and pay the ultimate price. They all might. Why not today?

He'd heard the explosions. Saw the devastating damage the mines had done to the SEAL delivery vessel that had crashed into the Kanaloa Park dome. If Skyjack was onboard that one, no one could've survived that.

Bannon gripped the arms of the chair and squeezed, steeling himself to reject the idea again. Until he saw a body. Until he was confronted with irrefutable proof, Bannon wouldn't believe it. He would not accept it.

"You've survived tougher scraps than that, old friend." He forced himself to his feet, repeating what he told Tara. "We'll see."

He grabbed the machine pistol he'd set down on the instrument panel when he froze. The sound of alarms, muted through the thick walls of the sub and the double hatch, reached him.

"That can't be good." Bannon made his way to the rear of the sub. By the time he reached the hatch and muscled it open, Larson was in the corridor anxiously waiting for him. With only the pale blue running lights to see by, he caught her worried expression.

"I take it that wasn't part of the plan?"

"No," she said. "They must be on to us."

"Then let's find a place to lay low until we can initiate part two of our plan."

"We have a plan?" she asked.

He took her by the hand and steered her down the corridor. Behind them came the metallic clatter of equipment. Metal buckles carelessly banging against plastic stocks. Marching footfalls. The familiar sound of approaching soldiers who didn't care about noise discipline.

Bannon pulled Larson faster in the opposite direction, only to hear the approach of more men coming from that direction as well. He stopped and handed her one machine pistol while he slipped the second off his shoulder.

She took it but said, "What am I supposed to do with this?"

"Shoot it."

"I don't know how to shoot this thing."

"See this end?" He tapped the tip of the barrel. "Point it at the bad guys and squeeze this." He pressed her finger lightly to the trigger. "Killing you is their objective. Don't be afraid to kill them back."

He knew he was asking a lot of her. She'd been through so much already, but they had little choice. It was kill or be killed. He hoped she was up to the task.

They stood back-to-back. Machine pistols at the ready.

She said, "You're going to want to pay more attention to the ones coming this way."

Over his shoulder, Bannon said, "Why?"

"Because I left a little gift in the machine room."

"Gift? What sort of gift?"

His question was answered by an explosion.

Ahead of him, a group of three armed men had just come around the bend, advancing past the machine room just as the steel doors blasted off their hinges and flew across the open space. They slammed into several of Sucre's men, knocking them to the floor before the heavy doors hurtled against the opposite wall, then crashed to the floor.

A hot, orange and red fireball roared out of the room. The men screamed in surprise and pain. Splashed with some sort of flaming accelerant, one guy's uniform caught fire. He ran chaotically in circles, screaming, trying to beat the flames down before his body was completely engulfed. He fell to the floor, immolated.

The smoky smell of burning fuel and roasted flesh permeated the air.

A wave of heat washed over Bannon. He covered his face and turned away.

The lights around them blinked out and then snapped on as emergency backup generators took over. Bannon noticed the soft hum of machinery he hadn't been aware of until it was gone, had stopped.

In the dim red glow of emergency lighting, he glanced at Larson.

She shrugged. "I had some time on my hands."

Bannon didn't waste time responding. He stepped away from the curved inner wall and opened fire at the hostiles moving forward on their position from Larson's side. With the Steyr machine pistol on full automatic, it spit out bullets at a rate of eight-hundred-fifty rounds per minute in an ear-splitting barrage of gunfire. Those not killed by the splash of flaming diesel fuel and accompanying explosion were cut down by Bannon's red tracer bullets or retreated beyond the curved corridor wall.

Bannon twisted around.

Larson struggled to hold her machine pistol down as she fired. Tracer fire stitched chaotic patterns up the walls and even into the ceiling.

Ineffective, but it was enough to keep the advancing troops back.

Bannon shouted over the reverberating echo. "Come on!"

He grabbed her by the hand and pulled her back, leading her past the crumbled, burning doors and dead bodies—some of them still aflame—at a run.

"What the hell was that?" he shouted over alarms and the hiss of fire-retardant spray.

"On the *Putnam,* I told you the facility is powered by a nuclear reactor, right?"

"Yeah."

She kept up with his long, running strides. "What I didn't go into detail about was that the reactor powers several large diesel engines that charge our lithium battery generators, which actually run this facility. A super-eco-friendly system."

"Which you rigged to explode?" Bannon concluded.

"After flooding the room with diesel fuel," Larson said, adding, "For Dr. Nomura."

Not sure whether to be scared or impressed, Bannon went with grateful.

They didn't get far before having to skid to a stop.

Three armed men filled the corridor in front of them, their machine pistols aimed and ready to fire. Behind them stood Holloway and Sucre. The rebel leader shouldered his way between his men, a pistol in his hand. He aimed it at Bannon and Larson.

Bannon pushed Larson to his rear, shielding her body with his.

"End of the line, Commander," Sucre said.

Confidently, Bannon said, "I don't think so."

"Actually, it is," Holloway said. "For you, General."

Sucre twisted around. A quizzical expression on his face.

Holloway fired.

The bullet slammed into Sucre's neck. The general grabbed his throat and fell to his knees, then keeled over.

The other terrorists, at first confused by the unexpected shooting, half-turned. Slow to react.

Holloway shot one in the chest. He staggered back with a grunt but didn't go down. No blood leaked from the hole in his coveralls.

Bannon shouted, "Vest!"

He'd started to bring the machine pistol up before. Now, he adjusted his aim higher and took out two of the gunmen with carefully plucked headshots.

Holloway fired once more and hit the armed man she'd already shot. This time, it was a bullet to the face. He got off a short burst of fire. Tracer bullets chased a line up the wall as the dying man fell back. The gun fell silent, and he hit the floor, dead.

Holloway stepped forward—over the crumbled dead— and lowered her weapon.

"We need to stop meeting this way, agent," Bannon said.

Larson followed closely behind him, clutching his hand and arm. She looked down at the gunman Holloway killed. His nose was gone. In its place was a bloody and blackened hole. Wide-open eyes stared back. She gasped and turned her face into Bannon's shoulder, doing her best to shut out the gruesomeness of it all.

Bannon turned his attention to Sucre, surprised to see the man was still alive. He dropped down to one knee beside him. Sucre clutched at the wound in his neck. Blood bubbled through his fingers. The man would bleed out in minutes. His eyes were wide with pain and the fear of facing his own mortality.

Sucre coughed. "Help me."

Bannon said, "It's too late. You're bleeding out."

Still, he lifted the man from the floor and propped him up on his bent leg. "What's Lang's real game?" Sucre's skin was clammy and sheened with perspiration.

He gasped, pleading, "Help me."

Bannon had begun to solve the puzzle, but he was missing some of the pieces. "What's Lang's endgame? Tell me."

"Lang… " Sucre said, his voice rising and falling. "Just the beginning… bring down... government. Grayson… revenge."

"Bring down the government? How?"

"Le… leviathan… "

His eyes went blank as the life slipped away from him. The bleeding in his neck stopped pumping. Sucre's limp hand slipped away from the wound and dropped to the floor. Bannon laid him gently back on the floor and closed the dead man's eyes.

Holloway asked, "What's Leviathan?"

"Other than a biblical sea monster from ancient mythology?" Bannon shook his head. "I have no idea. Whatever it is, we'll have to deal with it later. For now, we need to move."

Larson led them to a room she opened with her palm print and a keypad passcode. Inside, the motion-sensitive lights came on. A row of sinks on one side and toilet stalls on the other. A restroom. Holloway paced the length of the tile floor.

Then stopped. She looked up, confronting Bannon.

"My family?"

"I've contacted the people I needed to. They'll be safe. I need you to—"

Holloway wagged a finger in his face. "They aren't safe yet? No deal."

Bannon checked his Omega Seamaster dive watch. "You and I talked less than an hour ago. I've got people handling it. The best in the business."

"It's my family! Do you have family, Bannon? A wife? Kids?"

"No. but—"

"But, nothing. My girls, Bannon. My husband. They're my life." On the verge of tears, she said, 'I'm not doing anything more to help you until I know they're safe."

Bannon grabbed her by the arm. He shook her, gently, not threatening, but enough to catch her attention. "They'll be safe. I promise. Until then—"

"Nothing. Until then, nothing." She slapped a blue tooth device in his hand. "Take this. It can't call out, but you can reach me on it. It's set to the Secret Service frequency we're using down here. When my family is safe, you contact me. But trust me when I tell you, I'll do nothing more to jeopardize them until then."

Bannon reluctantly accepted the device. "Understood."

"Find somewhere to lay low. When you get word from the surface, word my family is okay. You contact me. Not before."

She stormed out of the restroom, slamming the door behind her. The sound reverberated in the empty space.

"What do we do now?" Larson asked.

"I'll tell you what we won't do," Bannon said. "We won't be laying low and doing nothing." He took her by the hand. "Come on."

CHAPTER FORTY

HOLLOWAY RETURNED TO OPS in response to Chase Lang's screaming through her earpiece, demanding to know what the explosion had been. At the door, she closed her eyes, took a deep breath, and uttered a silent prayer. She stared up at the camera looking down on her. Never so scared before in her life.

The door whooshed open, and she stepped inside.

Grayson remained in the room, standing off to one side. Lang paced behind a console where an operator was scrolling through video images, presumably searching for Bannon and Larson.

He turned as the door whispered shut behind her. "He slipped through your fingers. Again? How? You had them trapped. You had six armed men."

"And they're all dead. The woman. Larson. She blew up a generator or something. I barely escaped with my life."

Lang shouted, "I don't care!'

"Blame Sucre," Holloway shouted back. "If he hadn't rushed—"

"Happy to," Lang said. "Where is the little weasel?"

"He's dead, too. Survived the blast only to take one in the neck." She didn't mention it was she who'd pulled the trigger. "You think you can do better? Be my guest."

Lang fisted his hands and pounded the console shelf. The console was too solid to make the result either fear-inducing or satisfying. Grayson smirked and caught Lang's ire.

"What are you laughing at?"

A smile still on her face, Grayson said, "You. All these years of running, hiding, formulating this great plan of yours. You're sloppy. Angry. Undisciplined. Nothing like the operative you used to be. You're a broken down, pathetic version of—"

Lang turned red.

"Of the operative I trained. I created."

"Careful Colonel."

"Bannon's better than you ever were, even at your best. Which you certainly aren't now. You've met your match, and that scares you. It should. Because when Brice Bannon catches up with you—and he will—he'll end you. There's no question of that. Unless… "

Lang narrowed his eyes. "Unless what?"

"You give up now. Surrender, and there's a chance—a slim one—but a chance you survive this. Life behind bars. That's your best-case scenario."

"Locked away. To rot in yet another prison. You call that surviving?"

"You only have yourself to blame."

"That's where you're wrong. I have *you* to blame." He spun around, addressing Holloway. "You confronted Bannon.

What did he say? Did he give you any indication of where they were going, what he had planned?"

Lang raised the sat phone and waved it at her. A not-so-subtle reminder her family's safety hung in the balance. "Tell me."

"There wasn't a whole lot of conversation going on," she lied. "We were in a firefight. People were dying."

"And yet you didn't," Lang said. "The sole survivor of said firefight. Curious."

Holloway advanced on him. She fisted her own hands. "What are you suggesting?"

"Simply that being a traitor isn't easy, especially a reluctant one."

"Says a man speaking from experience," Grayson said. "Except it seems to have come very easily to you. Sell out."

Lang whirled on her. "Watch your mouth. Or have you forgotten how expendable you are, Colonel?"

Grayson bit back a retort, calculating how hard to push him. Unstable to begin with, Chase Lang was becoming unhinged right in front of her eyes.

"I wouldn't risk my family," Holloway said. "Trust me on that."

"I don't trust anyone," Lang said, adding, "And since everyone around me has proven to be so utterly inept, I'll have to take matters into my own hands." To the operator viewing the video images on screen, he said, "Open up the facility-wide comms system. I want to make sure everyone hears this. Everyone."

The operator nodded. He began to punch buttons and fiddle with dials.

Lang waited, tapping his toe and becoming increasingly irritated.

The operator said, "I've opened up communications to the entire facility. The system's ready when you are."

"Took you long enough," Lang said. "Patch this through to the *Putnam* as well. Get that FBI asshat on the line. He needs to hear this, too."

Lang again impatiently waited.

Holloway and Grayson exchanged a glance, curious as to what Lang had in mind. Nothing was said between them, but Grayson sensed in the harried woman's worried expression from a blink, and you missed it nod. Maybe the Secret Service agent was still on the side of good.

The Secretary Director received the message. Holloway hadn't gone completely over to the dark side. At least not yet.

Holloway felt a wave of relief wash over her. Perhaps by the time this was all over, she wouldn't go down as the greatest traitor in American history since Benedict Arnold. And even more importantly, that her family would survive this unharmed.

A voice, tinny and crackling, filled the ops center. "This is the *Putnam*. Agent Goodwell speaking."

"Goodwell," Lang said. "Update me. Where are we?"

"General Sucre, I'm glad you called."

"This isn't General Sucre!" he shouted. "I am Chace Lang! I'm in charge down here."

"Where's Sucre?"

"He's dead, and more people will be, too, if you don't answer my question. Where are we on our demands? They haven't changed."

Goodwell cleared his throat. "The Vice-President and select members of Congress are reviewing your demands and determining a course of action."

"You got Congress involved and you expect something to get done?"

"The law requires it, Mr. Lang. It's very specific—"

"You think I give a damn about the law?"

"No," Goodwell said. "I suspect you don't, but we do. Also, before we can act further, we require something from you."

"Are you serious? You're in no position to make demands, Goodwell."

"On the contrary, Mr. Lang. A second Coast Guard cutter and a naval destroyer are making their way here at top speed even as we speak. On board are three more SEAL and Special Forces teams."

"Send them, and they'll all die. Just like the last ones did."

Goodwell went on as if he didn't hear. "Your position will be surrounded. You will have no means of escape."

"I'll kill your President."

"And that'll seal your fate," Goodwell said calmly. "Let's work together to avoid all that, shall we? We require proof of life. Hourly."

"You're mad."

"I'm extremely angry. Yes. But that's beside the point. My instructions from Vice-President Wright and members of Congress are to secure hourly updates, verifiable video proof, that President Kingsley continues to live and is unharmed."

"If I refuse?"

Goodwell paused before answering. "I did mention cutters and destroyers and highly skilled combat operatives, didn't

I? If you do not comply, we'll have no choice but to assume Kingsley has been killed. After which, we will proceed accordingly."

"What the hell does that mean?"

"I've seen your service record, Mr. Lang. Or should I say Edwards? Either way, I know you're familiar with how this country deals with rogue nations, terrorist encampments, and enemy combatants that seek to do us harm."

"You're talking airstrikes?"

"Sea strikes might be a more appropriate term, but yes. Vice-President Wright assures me nothing is off the table."

"You're bluffing."

"If you don't wish to find out, comply with *our* demands, then we'll talk about yours."

The line went dead.

Lang stared at the speaker as if waiting for Goodwell's voice to return. It did not.

Lang turned from the console. "Wow. The *cojones* on that guy."

He sounded almost respectful as he pulled out his pistol. He swung it around the room and selected a random target, a woman. Holloway didn't know her name. She screamed and spun around in her chair, covering her face with her hands like she was playing hide-and-seek with a small child.

He fired.

The bullet went through her hand and struck her cheek. Her body slammed against the console behind her, even as she half rose, kicking the rolling chair out from under her. The workers beside her jumped from their chairs. Screaming, they ran. The woman slid off the console and fell to the floor, leaving a wet, streaky trail of blood behind.

Holloway gasped.

Grayson took a step forward. "You lunatic."

Lang turned on her. "Shut up!" He waved the gun around. "Shut up all of you!"

To the person at the communications console, he said, "Is that frequency still open? Did everyone hear that?"

"Yes. Yes." Tears streamed down her face.

Lang cleared his voice. "Listen up. This is for Commander Brice Bannon and Doctor Robin Larson, but I want everyone to hear this. I've lost my patience with the two of you. It's time for you to come in. I've just killed… " He waved his gun at the man standing next to the dead woman's body. "What was her name?"

The man stammered, "Ka… Ka… Karen."

"I've just killed," he cruelly mimicked the frightened man, "Ka… Ka… Karen here. I put a bullet in her face. That's on you, Bannon. Now. If you don't surrender to me in the next half hour, I will kill someone else. If, after that, you still don't give yourself up, if you don't think the random hostages I'm holding are worth it, then the next one I kill will be Secretary Grayson. You have thirty minutes. Starting now."

Lang indicated the transmission be cut by slashing his hand across his throat.

When the line was severed, Grayson said, "You're insane."

Lang shrugged. "Probably." He grabbed her by the arm. "Come on."

Grayson struggled against his hold. "Where are we going?"

"To give Ethan Wright what he wants. Proof of life."

He pulled her toward the spiral staircase that led down to Neptune's Glen. There, he paused and looked around the room. Lang pointed at dead Karen. "And someone, clean up that mess."

FORTY-ONE

TWO RED COAST GUARD Dolphin helicopters with their distinctive white and blue stripes around the tail boom approached the *Putnam* in the dark. Bright running lights blinking, coming in from the west. Slung in nets under each were two personal submersible hydrofoil watercrafts. One was Flipper, the submersible Bannon piloted in the Hampton Beach charity event just two days earlier. The other was similar in design but unremarkable as it wasn't painted like a sea animal. It was simply gunmetal gray.

Against explicit instructions to the contrary given to them at the start of the siege, the *Putnam* had been ordered to return to a position just five miles from Tiamat Bluff.

The SEAL's Sikorsky Sea Dragon helicopter was no longer on the flight deck. After the tragic loss of its team, the pilot was ordered to return to Boston and await further instructions. According to Haddad, Vice-President Wright was mulling over whether to send out another assault team.

Tolliver arrived on the flight deck with Haddad as the *Putnam's* deck lights snapped on. His crew scrambled in the cold to receive one, then the second, submersible. As they touched down on the flight deck in the wash of giant rotor blades, the cables were released from the belly of the large choppers. The netting fell to the deck.

Each submersible was removed and stored on the launch platform.

The first chopper peeled off and began its return flight to Boston.

The other gently touched down on the now cleared flight deck. As the roar of the engines died down and the whirl of the rotors slowed, the cabin door slid open. Tara Sardana and Lieutenant Kayla Clarke jumped down to the deck and jogged across the open space to where Tolliver and Haddad greeted them.

With a salute, Kayla shouted over the wind from the rotors. "Permission to come aboard, sir."

Captain Tolliver returned the salute. "Permission granted, Lieutenant."

He shook her hand and then Tara's. "You both know Chief of Staff Haddad."

They exchanged handshakes.

Tara knew her, of course, but they had never actually met. She left that side of their work to Bannon. He was good at dealing with the politicians, but more importantly, he kept the bureaucrats from interfering with the work they had to do, often with Grayson's immense assistance.

"I'm so sorry for your loss," Tolliver said. "Both of you. Skyjack was one of the best."

Tara brushed away the condolences. "Give us an update. What's our next move?"

Kayla exchanged an apologetic look with Tolliver.

He nodded, understanding.

He waved them toward the superstructure. "Come this way. We'll bring you up to speed and get some hot food and coffee in you."

Tara didn't tell Tolliver what she thought he could do with his food and coffee. She'd met him before. She liked and respected him. He didn't deserve an unleashing of her anger, so she remained silent and followed them inside.

In the officer's mess, a steward served two bowls of steaming hot New England clam chowder, Caesar salads, a plate of cloverleaf rolls, oyster crackers, and slices of warm apple pie. The coffee came in white Coast Guard embossed mugs and a matching coffee pot with creamer, sugar, and spoons.

As Kayla and Tara sat down, Tolliver excused the steward, holding the hatch open for him. Then, waited until they were joined by another. This was a tall man so thin as to appear sickly. He had dark hair and dark-rimmed glasses.

Tolliver introduced him. "This is FBI agent Andy Goodwell."

"The hostage negotiator assigned to the situation," Haddad added.

She and Goodwell sat down while Tolliver turned over mugs and filled them with coffee, passing them out black, allowing each to doctor them up as they wished.

Tara ignored the food and coffee. "Tell us what happened to Skyjack. How could you let him get killed like that?"

Haddad began. "The SEAL team leader came up with a plan. The Vice-President approved it. Your friend, Skyjack, willingly joined them."

As what little patience she had waned, through gritted teeth, Tara said, "Tell me what happened?"

"We've had a surveillance drone in the water since this thing started," Tolliver said. "We've video of it, if you want to see it… "

Kayla said, "Just tell us. Please."

"They went down in two SEAL delivery vessels. Fourteen men, including Skyjack. From the drone's video feed, we watched them approach Tiamat Bluff. The plan was to get close enough to dismount from the vessels and swim to the two moon pools located on the lower levels. Everything was going according to plan. That was until they were within range of the facility. One of the vessels exploded. We couldn't tell why initially. It wasn't until we re-watched. We saw… "

Tara waited for him to continue. He didn't. She prompted. "Saw what?"

"Mines," the *Putnam's* captain said.

"They piloted into a minefield?" Kayla asked, incredulous. "How incompetent—"

"Not just any minefield," Haddad said.

Tolliver explained. "Roaming explosive-laden drone mines, randomly weaving, crisscrossing, creating an impenetrable barrier around the facility. Too small to be detected by the delivery vessels' sonar and radar equipment. One vessel went down to the ocean bottom. The other crashed into the dome atop the facility, imploding it."

"And you've confirmed there are no survivors?"

"How could there be?" Haddad said.

"The dome explosion was catastrophic," Tolliver added. "The other vessel, even if anyone survived, which is almost impossible, they're trapped a thousand feet below the surface. Their only option would be to surface. Tanks hold, at best, two hours' worth of air. With compression stops, to reach the surface would take them fourteen hours."

"Without stops?" Tara asked, fearing she knew the answer.

"The bends would kill 'em before they reached the surface."

A morbid silence filled the room. Tara stared at her clam chowder, growing cold, and almost laughed. If Skyjack were there, no matter how grim the situation, he'd be noisily slurping up the creamy broth and asking if there was more.

"What do we know now?" she asked instead.

"Our drone was destroyed in one of the explosions. We're blind."

Goodwell cleared his throat.

"There's been a development." He relayed the conversation he had with Lang. "First off, it seems General Sucre is dead. The show's being run by Chase Lang now."

Tara and Kayla exchanged glances.

Earlier, they'd relayed to the *Putnam* what they'd learned about Chase Edwards from former spook, Daniel O'Shea. Which meant Haddad would have secured the man's full dossier. His military life, training, and the circumstances surrounding his capture had surely been examined and thoroughly dissected by now.

"Undoubtedly, that had always been the case," Kayla said.

"I can't speak to that one way or the other," Goodwell said. "But that crazy psychopath killed someone while I was on the call with him. Just shot a woman for no reason."

He'd looked pale coming into the wardroom. Now Tara understood why.

"Any word on the President?" Haddad asked.

"I've demanded proof of life. Lang expressed his reluctant willingness to comply. I'm waiting to hear back from him."

Kayla looked at her watch. "What can we do in the meantime?"

No one had an answer.

Tara worried about the hostages. The clock was ticking. Time was not on their side.

Tara stood up. "We need to get down there."

"Good thought," Tolliver said. "Any ideas on how?"

Haddad added, "You just heard what happened the last time we tried that."

"I did," Tara said. "And now I know why Skyjack wanted a hydrofoil brought here. He might've agreed to go along with their attack plans, but clearly, he didn't have confidence in their ability to pull it off."

With Skyjack dead, Kayla and Tara had decided to bring two hydrofoils, agreeing they would both make the trip down to Tiamat Bluff. The minefield was a new wrinkle.

"I'm sorry to say, but I'm familiar with those things," Tolliver said, meaning the hydrofoils. "They're fun toys and all, but they've got a submersible depth range of what? Five. Ten feet underwater. What good will that do us?"

"Commercial models, you're right," Kayla said. "But these were retrofitted by DARPA. Specially redesigned with Brice's and Skyjack's input for situations such as this. They've got a depth range of over one thousand feet. They'll be virtually undetectable by regular sonar and radar."

"And visually, they'll look like dolphins or big moray eels, to visual surveillance," Tara added.

"Aren't you forgetting about the drone mines? They're too small to be detected by sonar and radar."

"But not visually," Kayla said. "The hydrofoils have nearly three-hundred-sixty-degree visibility. They're versatile enough to avoid them."

"You hope," Tolliver said, doing nothing to hide his pessimism. Men had died on his watch, one a good friend. His tone was bitter and angry.

Tara conceded. "I hope."

In the silence that followed, Tara looked at each person around the table. She finally reached for the pot of coffee, overturned a fresh, empty cup, and filled it.

"Anyone have any better ideas?" she asked.

Her answer was a shrill alarm that jarred the occupants at the table. Tolliver jumped to his feet as an intercom blared. "Captain to the deck. Captain Tolliver, report to the flight deck."

He bolted from the room. The others quickly followed. They raced to the flight deck, some of them without the benefit of the heavy parkas the cold New England weather demanded.

There, several seamen and officers lined the portside railing with rifles aimed at the dark ocean surface below. Tolliver rushed over to his XO. A woman named Bridget Albright.

"What the devil's going on?"

"Radar picked up something coming up under our bow. We adjusted course—"

"I felt the adjustment down below. Wondered about it. What do we think it is?"

"No clue, sir," Albright said. "We thought torpedo, but that didn't make sense. Radar and sonar didn't pick up any indication of subs anywhere. Tiamat Bluff's not equipped with torpedoes." She spoke in a matter-of-fact way, then furrowed her forehead, adding, "Are they?"

Tara and Kayla crowded in close to Tolliver. They looked over the rail, anticipating and waiting.

Kayla said, "Slowest moving torpedoes I've ever seen."

Albright nodded. "Size and mass kind of rules that assessment out, too, ma'am."

Tara asked, guessing. "Whale?"

Albright shook her head.

"Not that big. Just big. And it stopped about ten feet below the surface for a minute."

Tolliver exchanged a glance with Kayla and Tara, but before he could utter another word, an ensign shouted, "Whatever it is, there's she blows!"

A spotlight swung over to where the ensign pointed.

Tara leaned in with the others. Metal buckles hit plastic stocks as guns were brought up to ready.

Tara squinted into the dark water. A calm sea. A clear night. Visibility was good. Moonlight sparkled over the gently lapping waves. Until the area they were staring at started to bubble white, like a boiling cauldron.

"What in the hell—"

Tolliver drew his sidearm but kept it to his side. The tension on the deck was as thick as the clam chowder they'd been served.

Suddenly, a gray metal—barrel—popped to the surface like a cork.

It settled, bobbing on the water, a loose canvas strap around the middle of it. A tense minute passed before a second similar container popped up, too. It banged into the first one and made a hollow noise before bobbing on the surface as well.

Tara noticed it was dented.

Again, she, Kayla, and Tolliver exchanged glances before the water erupted again.

This time, what shot to the surface was a man in a dark neoprene wetsuit. Guns were readied as the crew prepared to respond to an attack, but the man floated unmoving, like the containers that had preceded him. His full facemask was fogged, obscuring any visual of his face.

Immediately following the first, a second frogman popped up. This one flailing, flapping his arms. He grabbed at his facemask, similarly fogged, and ripped it off, tearing his neoprene hood off with it even as he grabbed the floating body that had come up with him.

Tara was the first to see the tangled, wet mass of red hair. She waved her arms. "Don't shoot! Don't shoot!"

McMurphy stared up at the row of guns pointed at him. He grinned as big a grin as she'd ever seen and waved. "I expected a welcoming committee, but damn, guys, you've outdone yourselves."

FORTY-TWO

TEN MINUTES LATER, AFTER a hot shower and a mug of Tolliver's specially doctored coffee, McMurphy paced in the tiny space that was the captain's wardroom. His ruddy face was flushed pink, and the skin of his fingers was so pruned he feared his hands would never return to normal. The spirited coffee burned his throat, and he was grateful for it. The chill he still felt reached down to his bones.

Tolliver, Tara, and Kayla were in the room with him. The women sat on the bed.

Tolliver had pulled out the office chair from his desk, pushed it into the corner where he could sit, and put his feet up on the edge of his bunk. His eyes were smudged from lack of sleep. McMurphy chose to keep pacing, afraid if he sat down, he'd fall into a deep sleep that would put Rip Van Winkle's twenty-year nap to shame.

After listening to what Tara and Kayla had learned from O'Shea about Lang and whatever the hell this Leviathan thing was, he decided they were right not to trust anyone. But, before he got to that, he asked, "Jones? How is he?"

"My medics stopped the bleeding and stabilized his wounds," Tolliver said. "The Dolphin airlifted him back to

Boston. He's lost a lot of blood, and he'll require surgery to address his many internal injuries. But my guys say they're confident he'll make it. Thanks to you."

McMurphy nodded. "Good to hear." Too bad the same couldn't be said for the rest of the SEAL team. McMurphy closed his eyes and shook away the image of Kowalski's headless corpse floating around the hatch of the delivery vessel. "And Brice? He's alive and on the loose, not held by this scum-sucker Lang?"

"As of twelve hours ago," Tara said. "That was the last contact we had."

"Lang didn't mention him in his last communique with Agent Goodwell," Kayla offered. "Hard to tell if that's good news or bad."

"Either way," Tolliver said. "That psychopath's put a hell of a ticking clock on this whole mess."

McMurphy tossed back the rest of his coffee. "He does. Are the submersibles prepped and ready to go?"

Tolliver nodded. "They are."

It had already been decided Kayla would remain on the *Putnam* and work with Tolliver to see if she could determine who could be trusted and who could not, going forward. Everyone was still of the mindset Haddad's last-minute absence from the doomed submersible trips was suspicious, but as a loyal cabinet member to the President for the last six years, no one was ready to throw her under the bus quite yet. Not without proof.

McMurphy nodded to Tara. "You ready?"

She stood up. "Since this whole fiasco started."

He noticed the urumi blade she wore as a belt. He pointed at it. "You missed a spot."

She looked down, seeing a faint line of dried blood still on the razor-sharp blade. She scraped it off with her fingernail. "Let's go."

She tossed the door open and left the cabin. McMurphy looked at Kayla. "She okay?"

"Sure." Kayla shrugged. "No. Probably not."

McMurphy gave her a perplexed look. "Which is it?"

"When she thought you were... she took it hard. Lost control a bit."

McMurphy got that. If he'd thought she or Brice were dead... Well, he couldn't imagine how horrible that would feel. Or what he'd do in response.

"With Brice still down there," Kayla said. "And Grayson at risk. Not knowing whether they're dead or alive... it's a lot."

McMurphy understood, wondering how much of that was about Tara Sardana and how much was about her. "Then let's go get 'em back."

From the *Putnam's* stores, McMurphy and Tara suited up in deep water 6/5mm neoprene wetsuits. They carried their fins, gloves, hoods, and facemasks as they made their way to the submersibles. The hydrofoils were dry cockpit vessels, so they hadn't worked out how they were going to get from the vessels inside Tiamat Bluff yet. The facility had docking ports, but the hydrofoils weren't equipped to connect to the hatches. Nor were the canopies constructed to open up under the extreme pressure of the ocean at that depth. Any attempt to do so would result in a crushing, imploding death.

When Tolliver and Kayla questioned him about it, McMurphy said, "We'll cross that bridge when we get to it."

They collectively shook their heads, praying he had at least a vague idea of how to accomplish such a miracle and was just being coy.

With parkas on, they crossed the open deck, shivering in the cold night air. The hydrofoils were prepped on the stern's inclined launching ramp, facing downward, the canopies open.

Like Tara, McMurphy tossed his fins, gloves, and facemask into the cockpit. Stored inside each vehicle were weight belts, a buoyancy compensator vest, and two air tanks.

McMurphy turned to Tolliver. "What about the guns?"

He'd requested two Beretta M9 pistols for each of them and an M4 carbine. McMurphy preferred the M18 Mod 1 with its shorter ten-inch barrel. It had been standard issue when they operated under the Deployable Operations Group, but after its disbandment, the weapons were in short supply around the service. The M4 would have to do.

"Loaded up and stored in the backpack like you asked." He smiled. "I tossed in a few extra goodies for you as well."

McMurphy shook his hand. "Thanks."

"Be safe and Godspeed," Tolliver said. "Both of you."

McMurphy climbed into Bannon's dolphin-motif hydrofoil, Flipper, belted in. He glanced over at Tara in her plain Jane gunmetal gray vehicle. Activating the vessel's communications panel, he asked, "Ready?"

Tara replied, "Let's just go."

She gave the launch crew a thumbs up. McMurphy followed suit.

Kayla and Tolliver backed up the ramp. The launch sequence began.

McMurphy tugged the canopy closed, watching as the water rose and bubbled up around him. Less than an hour after getting fished out of the drink, he was diving back in. The frothy water quickly swept over the canopy. McMurphy heard the tie-down clips snap away. With a jerk, the hydrofoil slid down the ramp, leaving the *Putnam* behind.

In the gloomy darkness below the surface, he located Tara's hydrofoil's lighted cockpit on his starboard side. She gave him a thumbs up. He keyed the comms. "Radio check."

"Five-by-five."

McMurphy smiled at her use of the somewhat antiquated reporting sign. Lima Charlie, for loud and clear, was in vogue in military circles nowadays, he'd been told. He still had difficulty realizing they were not part of the Coast Guard anymore, other than playing weekend warrior every once in a while.

"How far to Tiamat Bluff?" Tara asked, interrupting his thoughts.

"Twenty minutes if we book it."

Her ink-black hair tied back in a ponytail, Tara grinned at him. "Race ya!"

Her dark hydrofoil pitched downward and zoomed ahead.

McMurphy plunged his joystick forward in pursuit. While seeing Tara's playful side emerge was a good thing, he couldn't shake the feeling they were already too late to save the next hostage Lang threatened to kill.

McMurphy's stomach soured at that thought. All they could do was get there as fast as possible and hope Bannon could do something on-site in the meantime.

Before he got too morose, McMurphy figured music would lift his spirits. He activated Bannon's playlist, and the speakers exploded with old-time country singer Barbara Mandrell singing about being country when country wasn't cool.

"Oh, hell, no!" He flipped through the offerings until he found and settled on Waylon Jennings' *Ain't Living Long Like This*.

McMurphy groused. "Not exactly "Highway to Hell," but it'll have to do."

He pushed the foot pedals down and shoved the joystick forward while he sang along with Waylon about being on the wrong side of a lawman's guns, handcuffs, and steel reel racks.

Tara remained a vehicle length ahead of him until they were within sight of Tiamat Bluff.

Having been locked in the windowless tube that was the SEAL delivery vessel, McMurphy had missed the splendor that was the approach to the magnificent underwater achievement, having only caught a glimpse of it in the distance. A trivial detail during his desperate attempt to save himself and Bradley Jones from a watery grave.

The large sphere that was Tiamat Bluff was bathed in a crimson glow from the exterior lights, still operational. The red light facilitated viewing the aquatic life around the structure, which would be pitch dark otherwise. Chosen for environmental impact reasons. It was a color the deep-sea creatures didn't see. He'd read somewhere.

Only a few of the structure's long, narrow windows were lit with bright yellow light. The dark, ruined dome on top was a gut-wrenching reminder of the bad things that had gone down within the facility over the last two days.

He shut off the music and keyed the mic. "Keep an eye out for those damn mines. They're small. The size of softballs, but they pack quite the wallop."

"Roger that," Tara said. With her slightly ahead of him, he watched as her hydrofoil ducked and weaved. "I see 'em. The field's not tight, plenty of room, but they zip around fast."

"Understood," McMurphy said. "Let's just hope they don't have any homing capacity we don't know about."

As he piloted closer, he picked up several of the little buggers as they ping-ponged about. Tara was right. Their small crafts gave them plenty of room to slip between them as long as they kept an alert eye out. Nor did they seem to react or change course based on the hydrofoils' presence, remaining true to only their own chaotic pre-programmed patterns.

A rare, lucky break for them.

Minutes later, confident they'd both navigated through the minefield successfully, McMurphy aimed his hydrofoil toward Tiamat Bluff once more with a sigh of relief.

He radioed Tara again. "I'd say that puts them safely behind us."

"And brings us to that allegorical bridge you talked about with Tolliver. Are you any closer to figuring out how we cross it?"

McMurphy frowned. From the beginning, he'd had an idea, which was why he requested Flipper in the first place. He'd not said anything because he was sure Tolliver or Haddad would've tried to shut him down. Knowing Tara wouldn't like it any better, he grinned. "As a matter of fact, I do have an idea."

"Want to share with the class?"

"Nope. Just follow my lead." McMurphy pushed Flipper's joystick forward and threw the throttle full tilt. He surged past Tara, aiming the hydrofoil on a collision course with Tiamat Bluff. "This is gonna be fun."

CHAPTER **FORTY-THREE**

THEY NEEDED TO GET to Neptune's Glen. According to Holloway, it was there that Lang was holding the hostages, including POTUS and Garcia. The two people besides Grayson most important to Bannon's plans.

With time running out—should he be forced to scrap his original plan—being close to the restaurant and Lang, Bannon would be better positioned to turn himself in, which he would do to prevent another death.

Lang's loudspeaker announcement continued to ring in Bannon's ears as he and Larson made their way through the dimly lit, back maintenance tunnels and girdered stairwells deep in the central core of Tiamat Bluff. A path they'd chosen to avoid the plentiful surveillance cameras in the public access corridors.

Now ducking and racing through the facility's tunnels, shafts, and metallic stairways and ladders, Bannon glanced at his dive watch. They were short on time. "How much farther?"

His voice echoed along with the sound of their footfalls on the metal ladder rungs, climbing from one level to the next. Larson was on the ladder above him. She scrambled onto the grated catwalk with an athleticism that at first surprised

Bannon until he remembered her mentioning what an avid jogger she was.

He joined her on the platform, more winded than he wanted to let on. Tension, lack of sleep, and physical altercations were beginning to take their toll.

"We're on the south side of level two. Neptune's Glen is on level five in the north section."

"So, three more flights up."

"Yes."

Bannon again glanced at his watch. It had been twenty-two minutes since Lang killed a hostage and gave Bannon his ultimatum. Eight minutes to go before another hostage would be killed, and then Grayson was next. Knowing what he knew now, Bannon suspected that had been Lang's goal from the beginning. Revenge against the woman—and the government—that left him behind.

"This way," Larson said, snapping him from his thoughts.

She waved for him to follow as she sprinted down a catwalk, their footsteps hollow and loud.

It couldn't be helped. Time took precedence over stealth at the moment. Bannon was desperate to not have another innocent death on his hands.

They reached the far end of the chamber, a machine room. The air was thick, tainted with the smell of grease and oil. They'd reached an open flight of metal stairs—Bannon was grateful it wasn't more ladders—which led to a door.

Larson pointed at it. "That's level three."

Bannon urged her along. "Let's go."

They raced up the stairs to only get about halfway up. A hail of bullets stitched the wall and pinged off the metal rails, cutting them off. Forced to retreat down to the metal landing below, they pressed into a narrow indentation in the wall.

Breathing hard, Larson blurted, "Where did that come from?"

Bannon risked poking his head out. He was immediately brushed back by another barrage of automatic gunfire. "Below us at one o'clock. Two hostiles."

"What are we going to do?"

"You're going to make a run for that door," Bannon said. "I'm going to provide cover fire."

"Like hell! We go back. Take another way."

Bannon checked his watch. "There's no time. This is the only way."

She studied him hard. "You can keep them from killing me?"

"Yes." He hoped.

"Then what?"

"If I don't kill them." He pointed at the machine pistol she still carried. "You cover me. Give 'em all you've got."

"You saw before, right? I couldn't hit the broadside of an ocean liner."

Bannon grinned. "They don't know that. Ready?"

She nodded but said, "No."

He jumped out from behind their cover, pointed his weapon over the railing and down, and started shooting. Over the rattle of gunfire, he shouted, "Go! Go! Go!"

Larson ran up the stairs hugging the wall.

Bannon located the two men. A level below, one was behind a wall to his nine o'clock, the other crouched behind a cluster of drums. Dark and oily on the outside.

Bannon concentrated his fire on the guy behind the drums. But he wasn't shooting at him. He fired into the drums. Thick dark liquid began to pour out of the bullet holes that pierced the metal skin. He glanced up the stairs.

Larson had made it about three-quarters of the way up, running hard.

Bannon swung his aim toward the man behind the wall. He'd been getting brave and leaned forward, squeezing off a burst of fire. Bannon ducked, brushed him back, and then emptied his magazine into the drums. In the sudden silence that followed, he stared at the drums, watching, waiting, and getting disappointed. "Huh."

He started evaluating other plans in his head when his efforts were rewarded with a loud whoosh. The thick, brown liquid in the drums turned out to be flammable after all, as he'd hoped.

The drums exploded. The hostile behind them leaped away, but too late. The erupting orange and black fireball caught his pant legs which had been doused with the spilt liquid. His clothes went up like a gasoline-soaked bonfire on Hampton Beach.

He screamed.

Bannon tossed his empty machine pistol and charged up the stairwell.

Larson watched from the platform above.

She aimed the weapon at the area where the other gunman remained concealed.

Bannon made it halfway up the flight of stairs when bullets started to ping all around him. The rapid gunfire echoed in the hollow, mostly metallic chamber. He glanced down to see the threat wasn't coming from the man pinned down behind the wall.

A third shooter. Somewhere.

Bannon shouted, "Where'd that come from?"

"I don't know!"

"Well shoot back!"

"Where?"

Bannon, covering his head as he ducked and ran. "Everywhere!"

Larson swept the weapon from right to left and in circles and screamed like she was in a Rambo movie. Tracer bullets flew every which way.

Bannon ran to her. He ducked under her swinging arms before grabbing the weapon from her, twisting, and returning more effective fire. He located the third shooter hidden in a doorway at the farthest range of the machine pistol's capacity. Still, his field of fire was closer to target than Larson's attempt, and enough to keep the man from shooting back.

Bannon pushed her toward the door. "Go! Go!"

They rushed through the doorway and Bannon slammed the heavy metal door shut behind them.

He found a fire ax in a glass case. The kind that says: In Case of Emergency Break Glass.

He figured this counted.

He broke the glass with the butt of the machine pistol and pulled the ax from its securing clips. With the ax handle slipped through the hatch wheel, jamming the door shut he took Larson by the elbow, directing her away. "Come on."

If Lang was true to his word, the next hostage—whoever it might be—had less than four minutes to live. "Can we make it to the restaurant in four minutes?"

"Not even if we had rocket-powered jetpacks and could fly through walls."

That was how he had it figured, too. Bannon tapped the earpiece Holloway had given him, activating the link between himself and the agent.

"Holloway. This is Bannon. We're on our way to Neptune's Glen, but we're not going to make it in time."

He didn't expect her to respond, figuring she could be in close quarters with Lang or some of his men. To be seen talking to herself wouldn't go unnoticed.

Bannon went on, hoping at least she was listening. "I need you to stall Lang. Stop him from killing anyone. I'm on my way to surrender."

To his surprise, she answered. Her voice lower than a whisper. "Is my family safe?"

Bannon hesitated. He didn't know. There'd been no way for him to contact Tara again, to find out how the raid on Holloway's home had gone. If it had even happened yet.

Holloway hissed again. "Are they?"

Bannon opened his mouth then closed it again. What to say? What to say?

He made up his mind.

"Yes. They're fine. My people got to them. Got them out. Your husband and your girls are perfectly safe."

Larson watched him with a recriminating look. He was lying and she knew it.

Skeptical, Holloway asked, "How do you know?"

Her voice, though it was low as a butterfly's wings fluttering near his ear, he could hear the hope in it, the relief in knowing her family had been rescued. It was an almost tangible thing. And made him feel worse about the deception.

Bannon stared at Larson, then looked away. Desperate. With more lives on the line and not seeing another option, he doubled down on the lie. "Dr. Larson tapped into an old communication feed. A redundant system after upgrades were made. I spoke to my people. Your family… "

He couldn't repeat the lie again.

Holloway needed confirmation. "Is safe?"

Bannon hated himself. "Yes."

"I'll do what I can to stall him. But get here fast."

"On our way," Bannon tapped the earpiece, terminating the connection.

Larson stood facing him. "You lied to her."

"We need to keep moving."

He started past her, but she grabbed his arm and spun him to a stop. "No. Not until you explain. Why?"

"I had no choice. I need Holloway to do her job. People's lives count on it."

"At what cost? What about Holloway?"

"My people are good," he insisted. "I've counted on them time and time again. They've never let me down. This time will be no different."

"You don't know that," she said. "You can't know. How could you lie to her like that?"

"Because… because it's the only way."

"And if you're wrong? If your people didn't get them out. How do you explain *that* to her?"

He hoped it wouldn't come to that. "I'll deal with it… if it comes to that. Now, let's go."

CHAPTER FORTY-FOUR

AFTER ABRUPTLY ENDING HIS call with Agent Goodwell, Lang led Holloway and Grayson at gunpoint back down to Neptune's Glen, a level below. POTUS sat at a booth looking fatigued. His white hair unkempt. His eyes smudged from lack of sleep. His forearms resting on the table, hands cupped together.

The pilot, Garcia, stood protectively over him.

Her job, Holloway thought glumly, realizing what a mess she'd made of things.

Lang shot a short video exchange with Kingsley, having Grayson—at gunpoint—authenticate the time and date before he transmitted the file via satellite phone to Goodwell on the *Putnam.*

The next nearly thirty minutes ticked by agonizingly slowly while Lang paced the room, issuing orders and listening to updates from his search teams looking for Bannon.

Her earpiece clicked with a crackle of static heard only by her, followed by Bannon's voice. "Holloway. This is Bannon. We're on our way to Neptune's Glen, but we're not going to make it in time."

She turned away from the others, looked for something to do away from the group that wouldn't look suspicious. At the empty salad bar, she found a pile of bottled water left out for the hostages. No one was around them. She crossed the room to get one as Bannon spoke into her ear, "Stall Lang. Stop him from killing any more innocent lives. I'm on my way to surrender."

Holloway whispered, "Is my family safe?"

Bannon didn't answer.

She asked again as she picked up a bottle and cracked the cap open. "Are they?"

Finally, Bannon said, "Yes. They're fine. My people got to them. Got them out. Your husband and your girls are perfectly fine."

She closed her eyes, relieved, but remained cautious, suspicious. "How do you know?"

"Dr. Larson tapped into an old communication feed. A redundant system after upgrades were made. I spoke to my people. Your family… "

Holloway glanced over her shoulder. Lang remained on the phone with his men, his back to her. No one else paid her any mind. She asked again, "They're safe?"

"Yes."

She closed her eyes as relief washed over her. "I'll do what I can to stall him. But get here fast."

"On our way."

She heard the earpiece click off. She took a long swallow of water. Warm, it did little to refresh. It had been a long time since their meal on the *Putnam.* But the hungry growl in the pit of her stomach would have to wait. Her family was safe, she thought, grateful. But, it meant she had work to do. Her work. Her job.

She returned to the group.

Lang looked at his watch. "It's almost time."

Holloway cleared her throat. "You keep killing hostages, it'll only serve to piss Wright off. If you truly wanted America's help in your struggle against Javier Aguirre's illegitimate regime, you need to stop this."

"She's right," Kingsley interrupted. "I've already publicly voiced my support for your efforts, have implemented sanctions against Aguirre for his human rights violations. But this? This only serves to undermine what you're trying to do. Make it more difficult to help the RRA."

Lang stared at the two of them, shaking his head as a disappointed parent might with a dull child.

"Don't you see, David," Grayson said. "This was never about helping the Revolutionary Republic Army, about giving them military aid or fiscal support. That was never going to happen. We all knew that from the beginning."

Kingsley twisted in his seat. "Then what was it all for, for God's sakes?"

"To do the exact opposite," she said. "To create an international incident that would shift world sympathy away from the RRA. Your kidnapping, your death, was orchestrated to justify our retaliation against the RRA. A retaliation that would remove all who oppose Aguirre."

"Keeping him in power?" Kingsley asked. "But why?"

Lang smiled, amused they were finally piecing the puzzle together.

Grayson laid the final pieces down. "Uranium. Boca Las Casas' violent secession from Venezuela came before deposits of uranium were discovered in the Sumaria River Mines. Prior to that, half the world's uranium was produced by Canada, Australia, Niger, Kazakhstan, and Russia. The Sumaria River Mine is now third in worldwide production behind Canada and Kazakhstan.

"Uranium usage accounts for twenty percent of the U.S. electricity consumption, some twenty-five percent of the global uranium supply each year. Yet our own mining and production doesn't exceed five percent, forcing us to import over ninety percent of the uranium we need."

"So, unburdened by war and internal strife," Kingsley said. "Aguirre could put a stranglehold on the U.S. power grid. Hold us under his thumb."

"Wouldn't Aguirre be grateful to us for eliminating the RRA?" Holloway asked.

Grayson shook her head. "Aguirre's a puppet. He'll know our hands were forced. Would know who he really has to thank. Making America energy dependent not only to him, but to an enemy that's capable of," Grayson looked around, "all this."

An enemy whom we don't even know, she thought.

"We could refuse to buy the uranium from Aguirre," Holloway said.

Kingsley shook his head. "Aguirre and the U.S. are both confined by the same box. He must sell to us to fund his flailing government, and we must buy to maintain our current energy level output, though we buy as little from him as we can. In the meantime, we've publicly—and secretly—funded the rebels. Supported them in their efforts, with the hope they'll win in their struggle and establish a government—"

"Regime building at its finest," Lang said.

"That we could deal with for our energy needs. One that wouldn't leave a bad taste in our mouths," Kingsley concluded. "Until this little stunt."

"I suspect none of the participants here are even RRA," Grayson concluded. "After what happens here, the RRA is finished. Thus manipulated, we'd be forced to retaliate. Shock and awe. All but ensuring Aguirre's regime would be shored up. Afterward, we'll have no choice but to deal with an empowered Aguirre going forward."

"Putting us in bed with the devil, but really to be beholden to—" Kingsley glared at Lang "—whoever your damn benefactors are. I'll never allow such an alliance. That will never happen."

Lang smiled. "Please say over my dead body, Mr. President. Please."

"Stop the charade, Chase," Grayson said, pulling the man's attention back to her. "Stop acting like you care about any of this."

Lang leveled her with a long, hard stare. "At one point I might have. But, you're right. I don't. On the other hand, the people who hired me do."

"Who are they?" Grayson asked.

Holloway cared little about world politics, followed it only because her job demanded it. Threat assessments and the like. She realized from Grayson's revelation, the only way for this scheme to work, to swing American and world sympathies to Aguirre would be for the President to die. Nothing less would generate the justification needed to go to war against the RRA. All along there were just two goals; kill the President and pin the blame on the RRA.

It was time to act. Time for her to do her job. She stepped forward. "This insanity ends now."

Lang smiled, seemingly amused by her outburst. "Really, Agent Holloway. And what are you prepared to do?"

"Stop you," she said, full of conviction.

Grayson intervened. She placed a hand on Holloway's shoulder. "Chase, listen to reason. Sucre is dead. The Vice-President isn't going to give in to your demands. The charade is paper-thin and would never stand up to public and media scrutiny anyway. You see that, don't you?"

Lang didn't answer. Holloway wondered if Grayson was getting to him.

She pressed on. "Wright. The government. The American people. The world will see through it. We'll tell them."

"You wrongly assume any of you will get out of this alive," Lang said.

His words chilled Holloway. "The intention from the beginning… "

"That there'd be no survivors," Lang finished for her. "Myself excluded, of course." He looked around the room. "Speaking of which, it's past time." Forty minutes had passed since his declaration someone dies every thirty minutes.

"You've only delayed the inevitable, not prevented it." He clapped his hands together. "So," with a grin, he said, "Who's next?"

His gaze settled on a young Hispanic woman seated at the far end of a table. She had her hands folded over rosary beads and her lips moved in silent prayer. She looked up at him. Holloway could read the fear in the woman's eyes.

Holloway rushed forward. "Don't."

She grabbed Lang's gun arm, intent on disarming him.

Garcia, still standing behind Kingsley shoved him to the booth, pushing him under the table to protect him from stray bullets, should gunfire erupt. He covered POTUS's body with his own.

Grayson stepped forward and shouted, "Holloway! No!"

Lang pushed Holloway back with a strong shove. He swung the gun away from the praying Hispanic woman and aimed it at Holloway instead. He pulled the satellite phone from his pocket with his other hand. "Need I remind you not all the soon to be dead are in this room."

"You can't touch my family," she said defiantly. "They're free. Your plan's coming apart and you're too stupid to realize it."

She saw the crack in his confidence and almost smiled.

"Impossible. And even if it were true, how would you know?"

Holloway saw no downside to telling him.

"Bannon got word to the surface. He arranged a team to take out your people and save my family."

As she spoke, Lang dialed the phone with his thumb. After the third ring someone picked up, but no one answered.

"Sinay. Johan?" Lang shouted. "Is that you? Talk to me, damn it. Tell me what's going on?" He paused, frowning. No one spoke back. "Sinay! Talk to me!"

A male voice finally answered. "Who is this?"

Lang screamed, "Who is *this*?"

"The Virginia State Police. To whom am I speaking?"

Lang severed the connection and tossed the phone away like it was radioactive. "Damn it. How?" He looked at Holloway. "How?"

"What does it matter, Chase," Grayson said. "She's right. It's over."

"No."

Lang aimed the gun and fired.

The first bullet hit Holloway in the gut. The pain, the burning, was like a hot poker driven through her stomach. The second bullet hit higher than the first, slammed into her chest. The impact drove her back, like a punch.

She let go of Lang's arm and staggered back.

He fired a third, unnecessary shot.

Holloway gasped, fighting for breath as her lung collapsed. She fell to the floor.

Grayson dropped to her knees beside the woman. She grasped Holloway's hand, squeezed it while she pressed her hand into the gut wound that was bubbling blood. Holloway struggled to breathe, gasping for air. Her mouth filled with blood. She coughed. Blood dribbled down her chin.

"Hang in there, Kate. You're going to be fine," Grayson said. "You're going to be okay."

Holloway returned her squeeze. "Don't... you suck at lying, Madam Secretary."

Grayson forced a smile. "You're right."

Holloway gasped. "Keep POTUS safe."

Grayson nodded. "You have my word."

More coughing, a gasp.

"Tell my girls... my Roger... I'm sorry and I... I love them."

"You have nothing to be sorry for, Kate. I'll tell them. I will. I promise."

The last thing Holloway heard was Lang's voice.

"Oh, how touching." He paused, then said, "Not the hostage I would've chosen, but she'll do. Tick tock, Colonel." He tapped the face of his watch with the barrel of his gun. "Remember, It's your turn in the barrel next."

CHAPTER FORTY-FIVE

LUIS ROCHE AND PACO Molero, two of Sucre's men sat lounging in Moon Pool Alpha, smoking rolled cigarettes laced with just enough pot they didn't mind the long hours of boredom they'd endured since arriving on Tiamat Bluff. Guarding a room where nothing happened. Luis passed a small silver flask of Black Label scotch to Paco. He sipped. Their machine pistols were propped up against the hard-plastic crate they sat on. No one had been back to check on them for hours.

The two men hadn't known each other before being recruited by Sucre for this mission, so they didn't talk much. Just smoked and drank and thought about how they'd spend the money this job would pay.

Luis furrowed his thick black brow and cocked his head. Like a puppy who'd heard a high-pitched sound. "You feel that?"

"Feel what?" Paco took a long drag from his laced cigarette. "I don't feel nothing. Here." He handed the flask back, with a giggle. "This will help calm your nerves. Drink up."

"If my nerves become any calmer, I will be asleep."

Still, he accepted the booze and drank. Maybe he hadn't felt something after all. Just his imagination.

He stood up. Needed to move to stay awake. Doing so, he was sure he'd felt a vibration under his feet that he hadn't felt in all the hours they'd been there. He was sure of it.

The earlier explosions. Those they had felt and heard, of course. Afterward, General Sucre ordered that they remain in position and to stay alert. Not an easy order to follow as his eyelids drooped. He crossed the wet, diamond-plated metal floor to the low wall surrounding the moon pool. He leaned over and looked down into the dark water below.

"I think something's down there, Paco."

Paco sighed. He finished his cigarette and ground it into the sole of his boot before dropping it into a shallow puddle on the floor. It sizzled going out. Reluctantly, he got up, stretched, cracked his back, and slung his weapon over his shoulder, crossing the room to join Luis.

"Dude, you're *loco* in the head. There's nothing down there but water and fish," he insisted.

Luis cautiously peered over the wall. He squinted, not seeing anything at first. He leaned further over. He could swear the water below had become darker. Like a black cloud had crossed under the large opening.

Maybe it was a shark. Or a whale.

Pointing, about to crow about his being right, the water in the moon pool bubbled and foamed. Rather than jump out of the way, Luis bunched his eyebrows and leaned in farther for a closer look. "Look! I told you!"

Just as he said it, a large gray dolphin leaped through the opening. It arched through the air. Water streamed off its slick flank, splashing across the chipped, yellow deck. Strangely, it didn't make the trills and squeaking sound either man associated with dolphins, but instead, they heard a low humming engine noise accompanying the sea animal's incredible arrival.

The two men backpedaled away from the sight, stumbling and slipping on the wet metal floor. Their mouths hung open as they watched the dolphin's trajectory overhead.

"Whoa!" Luis said.

"*Santa mierda*," Paco shouted, crossing himself.

McMurphy threw Flipper's canopy open and tossed a hand grenade—one of Tolliver's special gifts—at the gaping men before they could raise the machine pistols they carried.

"Yipee-kai-yay, moth—oh, wait, that's somebody else's line."

The grenade hit the deck with a metal clang and rolled. The two men stared, watching it roll awkwardly towards them, as dumbfounded by the grenade as they were the sight of a man riding partially inside a dolphin. At the last second, they jumped, scrambling to get away before the munition's explosion.

McMurphy's attention was drawn from the echoing blast to the chipped and scarred yellow metal wall fast approaching the hydrofoil's blunt nose. He crisscrossed his arms over his chest and grabbed the straps of the five-point harness, all control of the fourteen-hundred-pound vessel gone. He closed his eyes, winced, and turned his head away from the impact.

For all the good that would do him.

Flipper slammed into the far wall, but not directly head-on—luckily—but at enough of an angle the craft cascaded across the wall, scraping metal against metal, an ear-splitting sound, and leaving a shower of sparks in its wake.

McMurphy slammed forward in his seat on impact.

The heavy canvas straps bit into his skin but did their job, holding him in his seat, keeping him in one piece. The hydrofoil continued its crazy ride around the room like a ball in a roulette wheel until it crashed to a stubborn stop, banging into one of the bubble-like submersibles used by the staff to ferry people back and forth.

McMurphy's neck hurt, and he felt something pop in his shoulder, but otherwise, he'd survived relatively unscathed. He thought about all the crash landings he'd endured already in his career, realizing one day the jig would be up.

But today wasn't that day.

He started to climb out of his seat, pulling the Beretta from his holster as he did so.

The two men were picking themselves up off the diamond plated floor. Their shoes slipping and squeaking on the wet surface.

One kept shaking his head. Trying to clear the ringing in his ears. He'd been too close to the grenade when it exploded. McMurphy knew the feeling. The other one stepped rather unsteadily toward Flipper, moving to the center of the room.

"I wouldn't stand there if I were you," McMurphy warned.

Defiant, but with his voice quivering, Paco raised his machine pistol. His back to the moon pool. "Don't move!"

"I'm not," McMurphy said. "But you might want to."

Before either man could react to that, the moon pool bubbled and gurgled. Water splashed over the sides as Tara's hydrofoil breached the opening and sailed through the air, following Flipper's trajectory, except…

Tara's leap had caught less air.

More line drive than pop-up, her hydrofoil came crashing down earlier than Flipper. It dipped, nose-first, short of the wall, and skidded across the wet floor. It sideswiped toward Paco, standing with his machine pistol raised. He watched, wide-eyed, as the vehicle barreled toward him. His expression comical until the hydrofoil slammed into him and carried him across the room where it crashed into Flipper's ruined flank, crushing the rebel soldier between the two vessels like a squashed bug.

McMurphy turned away to avoid most of the blood splatter and held onto the windshield to keep from being knocked out of the cockpit from the impact. Smoke billowed from the backend of Tara's hydrofoil as she popped the canopy and flung it open.

Breathless, she said, "Of all the careless, hair-brained, dangerous, stupid stunts you've ever pulled Skyjack McMurphy… This absolutely takes the cake."

McMurphy cleared his throat. "Mommy and Daddy shouldn't argue in front of the minions."

He pointed at the remaining guard as he shakenly raised his weapon. Tara glanced over her shoulder. She casually pointed her Sig and fired. Her shot hit him square in the forehead. The man went down. Dead before he hit the floor. The gunshot echoed in the chamber.

She returned her attention to McMurphy. Back on point. "And it was awesome!"

She climbed out of the hydrofoil. "I'm so glad you didn't die. Because I'd miss doing crazy stuff like that with you."

"You say the sweetest things, Blades." He joined her on the floor, carrying an Army green canvas bag over his shoulder. He surveyed the wrecked hydrofoils. "Too bad my resurrection's gonna be short-lived." He put a hand on Flipper's wrecked, light gray underbelly. He patted it. "Cause when Brice sees this, he's gonna kill me."

Tara waved her hand in a circle, indicating the space around them. "Let's make sure we all survive this first."

McMurphy opened the flap of the shoulder bag and palmed two more hand grenades. He tossed them to Tara. "Courtesy of Captain Tolliver."

She caught them and dropped them into pockets in the utility vest she wore over her black neoprene wetsuit. McMurphy did the same with the two he still had.

"Any idea how we find Brice?"

McMurphy grinned. "No, but I have a way to contact someone who can help." He tossed Tara a wireless microphone system, complete with an earbud. They started assembling them. "Remember that Secret Service agent named Gregg?"

"Franklin, sure. He's on POTUS' close protection detail.

McMurphy arched a bushy red eyebrow, repeating, "Franklin?"

"It was one date. That was it. Quit acting like a child."

He grinned. "Never. Anyway, I ran into him on the *Putnam*. He gave me these. They're programmed to the same frequency the Secret Service team down here is using."

Tara screwed the earpiece into her ear. "Meaning we can contact Holloway or her men."

McMurphy nodded. "Assuming they've got their ears on."

He played with the volume and squelch. "Agent Holloway, you out there? This is Skyjack McMurphy. I'm with the Coast Guard. Agent, can you hear me?"

A minute passed. Tara and McMurphy exchanged glances. She shrugged.

About to try again, McMurphy winced against a blast of static in his ear.

"Skyjack!" Bannon's voice, distorted but distinctive, boomed in their ears. "That you? You old walrus, you. Is that really you!"

CHAPTER FORTY-SIX

McMURPHY'S VOICE CAME OVER the earpiece in Bannon's ear. "Brice?"

Bannon grabbed Larson by the arm, halting her forward progression through the machine room. His heart swelled at hearing his old friend's voice, at realizing McMurphy was alive. His words: *We'll see,* still in his head. Not in a triumphant I told you so way but as a reaffirmation of his undying faith in McMurphy. Faith in his team.

"Where are you?" he asked.

"Moon Pool Alpha."

"Here?" Bannon blurted. "You're here? In Tiamat Bluff?" He couldn't believe it, but he broke into a wide smile all the same. "Stay put. We're coming to you."

"Negative," McMurphy said. "We made some noise and broke a few things getting here. Not sure we want to hang around for the squatters' cleanup crew to get here."

"We?" Bannon asked.

Tara said, "Later. Where do we go?"

Bannon looked to Larson, relaying what his team had told him.

"There's a small observation alcove and bar on level three. It's called Njord's Den."

Bannon repeated her instructions.

"While I like the notion of a bar," McMurphy said. "No one's given us the nickel tour yet. No clue where that is."

"Three levels up from where they are now," Larson said. "In the northwest section. They'll find directories at every stairwell and elevator."

Bannon relayed her instructions on how to get there. "Stay close to the corridor walls to avoid cameras. See you in five."

Five minutes later, Bannon and Larson burst through a teak door with frosted glass and etched porpoises leaping from crashing waves. The alcove and bar had dozens of S-shaped booths around dark, wood-stained tables, strategically positioned to take maximum advantage of the panoramic views of the red-hued ocean outside. A highly-polished teak bar ran along the east wall.

McMurphy stood with his back to them, his hands and face plastered up against the window, looking out, like a little kid visiting an aquarium for the first time. Tara was behind the bar. Hearing them come in, she looked up, grabbing the machine pistol that lay on the bar.

They were both in wetsuits and wearing battle fatigue utility vests.

Bannon raised his hands. "Easy."

She took her hand off the weapon and grinned. "Brice."

To all outward appearance, one would think they'd just seen each other five minutes ago. But in her eyes, he saw the relief she felt, similar to his own.

McMurphy was slower to respond. When he did, it was clear he was reluctant to tear himself away from the view Tiamat Bluff offered. Turning from the glass as a giant squid glided past, he said, "This place is incredible."

"I should've known you'd finagle your way down here," Bannon said with a wide grin.

McMurphy stared across the room. "Leave you alone for a minute. See the trouble you get yourself into without us?"

He clasped Bannon's hand and pulled him into a lung deflating bear hug.

"Good to see you, too, big guy," Bannon said.

McMurphy released his old friend and turned his full attention to Dr. Larson. He grasped her hand with his massive paws. "Doc, I've read... I've followed the progress you've made down here. I... I'm in awe."

Larson blushed and smiled. "Thank you."

"I'm Skyjack, by the way." He continued to hold her hand. To Bannon, he said, "Smart and beautiful, too. I like the company you're keeping down here."

Bannon shifted his attention to Tara. "Blades. Holloway's family. How are they? Were you... able... "

"Safe and sound. They're with the police. Brandon Reynolds is overseeing their protection."

Bannon nodded. "Brandon's a good man."

He exchanged a glance with Larson. Not a smug, I told you so, expression the woman probably expected. It was one of relief and of pride. He had confidence in his people, and it had paid off. This time, he thought inwardly, reminding himself that might not always be the case.

"Tell us what we're up against?" McMurphy said.

Bannon and Larson filled them in, taking turns with the narrative. They finished up by saying, "The bulk of the hostages are being held in a restaurant on level two. Neptune's Glen. Near as we know, POTUS and Grayson are there, too. Unharmed except for some bangs and bruises. So far. The rest are being held in Ops, forced to run the facility. Holloway has gone radio silent, so her status is a mystery at the moment."

He exchanged a worried glance with Larson. "I believe she's still an asset, but until we re-establish communications with her, we can't rely on any inside help from her."

"How do we proceed?" Tara asked.

"My original plan," Bannon said. "If you could call it that, was to storm Neptune's Glen, secure POTUS and Grayson, and with the help of a submersible pilot named Garcia, get them to the one rescue mini-sub that's left."

"Get them to safety, then deal with the rest," McMurphy said, approvingly.

"Simple. Direct," Tara said. "I like it."

The one hesitation Bannon had had all along, was what would Lang do if they did successfully spirit POTUS and Grayson away? How would he react? In retaliation, a man like that might start to kill off hostages. That bothered Bannon greatly. His military training, the strategist in him, said it was an acceptable risk. That was the mission. POTUS's life outweighed the value of the other hostages. He was more important in the scheme of things than the innocent men and women left behind to face the wrath of a madman.

It would be the right thing to do, any military expert would say.

Yet that stuck in Bannon's caw. In his mind, no one life should be valued above anyone else's, not even the President of the United States.

"You said original plan," Larson said, noting his hesitation.

Leave it to the scientist to notice the details, Bannon thought. "That was when it was just the two of us."

He turned to McMurphy and Tara, happy beyond words to have them by his side once more. "Skyjack, you and Dr. Larson head up to Ops. Do what you can to regain control of the facility. Dr. Larson can get you there and help with the technical stuff along the way, but not everyone you encounter is necessarily a hostile."

"What are we looking at in terms of actual enemy combatants?" Tara asked.

"I don't have a firm count. The best we could estimate was Lang came onboard with sixteen to eighteen personnel."

"Several of them are dead." Bannon mentally ticked off the casualties they knew about, included Sucre. "Probably about a dozen left."

"Minus the two we took out in the moon pool," Tara said.

McMurphy smiled. "Against the three—sorry, Doc—four of us. I like those odds."

"Heavily armed and well-trained," Bannon warned. "They're disciplined. Good. And," he emphasized, "the goal is to keep the hostages alive. All of them."

McMurphy pulled a Beretta and his two grenades from his satchel. He tossed them to Bannon. "These might help. Courtesy of Captain Tolliver."

Bannon smiled, clutching the weapons. "Guess that means I owe Bob a few rounds the next time he's in the Keel Haul."

"What'll you two be doing while the Doc and I storm the castle?" McMurphy asked, meaning Tara and Bannon.

"We'll head to Neptune's Glen. Secure POTUS and Grayson. Get as many hostages out of harm's way as we can. After that—"

"It's all mop-up," Tara said.

Bannon was about to tell them to move out when their earbuds filled with static. The three of them heard it, like someone keying a walkie-talkie on and off. It was coming over the Secret Service frequency. Bannon, McMurphy, and Tara exchanged concerned glances.

The only one without an earbud, Larson said, "What?"

Bannon shook his head to quiet her. Lang's voice crackled over the wireless frequency.

"Hope that got your attention, Commander. I know you can hear me so listen up. You have succeeded in trying my patience. That's quite the feat for someone as skilled and disciplined as I am."

Without it going out over the air, McMurphy said, "Cocky son of a dirtbag, ain't he?"

"As you might have guessed since I've taken over this line," Lang said. "Agent Holloway is no longer a factor in this little game. A pawn that's been removed from the board. With a bullet."

Tara's expression hardened into a hateful mask.

Bannon tightened his fist. He felt a muscle pulse along his jawline. Still, he remained silent.

"Her death is on your head, Bannon. As was poor Karen I-never-got-her-last-name in Ops earlier. And who else? Oh, yes, all of them. The point is, I'm going to give you one more chance to get it right. You see, I've been in contact with the surface, and it seems things aren't going as well for us as General Sucre—oh yeah, another death that I understand was by your hand—might have hoped. So, I'm here with Kingsley and the Colonel—"

Bannon couldn't remain silent any longer, he stepped forward and keyed the radio in his pocket.

"If you harm either one of them… "

"When I do, it'll be on your head, too. Two more lives you'll have to answer for."

Again offline, McMurphy said, "Don't let this guy bait you, Brice."

Bannon, his teeth gritted. "What. Do. You. Want?"

"You. I want you standing in front of me in the next fifteen minutes. At which point I will gun you down, in cold blood. Then I'll kill you precious President Kingsley all while the Colonel stands helplessly by and watches. Then I'll kill her, too. Clock's ticking. Fifteen minutes."

Bannon responded. His voice low. Cold. Intense.

"Oh, don't you worry, Lang. I'm coming. But this isn't going to end the way you think. I'm coming, and I'm going to kill you. You will pay for all the death and destruction you've caused here today. You will pay for killing Kate Holloway by laying in a puddle of your own blood and slowly bleeding out while I stand over you and watch the life seep out of your worthless, wasted body. And then—"

Bannon cut himself off. He gave McMurphy and Tara a determined nod. They nodded back. Ready to go.

Left hanging, Lang said, "And then what, Bannon? What?"

Bannon said as much to his people, his friends, as to Lang. "We end this. I end you. And Lang, don't have any misgivings. Afterward, I'll sleep like a baby."

CHAPTER FORTY-SEVEN

GRAYSON STOOD BESIDE KINGSLEY, listening to Lang taunt Bannon.

No longer even pretending anyone was ever going to get away from Tiamat Bluff alive, his arrogance had made him wire the call to his phone, putting it on speaker for all to hear. But his hubris had backfired. Now Lang shook with rage as the conversation turned against him. She recognized the signs as control slipped from his grasp. Back when she knew him, she'd warned him his cockiness would be his downfall one day.

Kingsley reached up and grasped her hand. He squeezed it.

POTUS had never been a soldier. An academic, a businessman, and a caring philanthropist, he was holding up—facing his own death—with tremendous fortitude. She'd always liked and respected David Kingsley, but never was she prouder to serve him, and possibly die for him than she was at that moment.

She squeezed his hand back. "We'll get out of this, David. I promise."

"For a former CIA spook," he said, not buying it. "You're a terrible liar."

Grim, she said, "That's twice someone's told me that today."

Lang leaned forward over the phone. His brow creased. His eyes narrowed. "And then what, Bannon? What?"

"We end this," Bannon's voice said. Cold and controlled. "I end you. And Lang, don't have any misgivings. Afterward, I'll sleep like a baby."

Lang's tanned craggy face turned three shades darker with rage. He threw the phone across the room.

Grayson couldn't resist. "You look worried, Chase."

"Shut up."

"You should be. There's a collection of corpses around the world of people who've gone up against Brice Bannon. They're all dead and he's still here."

Lang, enraged, rushed at her.

Kingsley and Garcia stepped forward, blocking his way.

"I've left bodies behind, too. More than you can imagine. More than I can remember." He pounded his chest. "And I'm still here, too!"

Quietly, calmly, Kingsley said, "For the moment."

Lang aimed his pistol at Kingsley's face. "But maybe you won't be."

Grayson stepped around the two men protecting her, stood between the gun and Kingsley.

Kingsley grabbed her shoulder. "Liz, don't."

She shook him off even as Garcia pulled him back, attempting to shield POTUS behind his own body again. A move that would make any Secret Service agent proud.

"It's over, Chase. You've never been one to fight on after the war was lost. Let this go."

"Maybe my employer's battle is lost." His gun hand never wavered. The muzzle aimed at her forehead. "But my agenda's unfolding right on schedule."

The muscles in his forearm tightened. His fingers squeezed around the grip and trigger.

This was it, Grayson thought. It's over.

Kingsley cried out. "Don't!"

It wasn't much of a distraction, but Grayson took full advantage of it.

She grabbed Lang's gun wrist, lifted his arm into the air. She stepped under it and spun. Her back to Lang now, she tossed him over her hip. The gun went off as Lang landed squarely on his back with a thud and a grunt.

Her aggressive action spurned the others in the room to react. With Lang having announced their inevitable demise, the hostages realized they had nothing to lose. They jumped from their seats at the tables and rushed at the guards positioned at the restaurant door. Two there. A smaller group charged the one posted by the spiral staircase going up to Ops. They cried out like an attacking war party.

Machine pistols were lifted.

Grayson called out, "No!"

But it was too late to stop what had begun.

The groups ran seemingly unafraid at the armed men. The first in line, their bodies jerked as they were raked with rapidly fired bullets. But that didn't stop the others. As the first line fell, the rest continued to swarm the men. Like locusts devastating a crop, they overwhelmed them with the sheer force of their numbers. They smothered them until the machine pistols went silent, then dragged them to the floor, ripping the weapons from their grasps.

Grayson, still holding Lang's wrist, twisted his arm as she stomped down on his throat.

He gagged and lost his grip on his handgun. It tumbled out of his hand and clattered to the floor.

Disarmed, Lang grabbed Grayson's ankle with his free hand and pulled her foot from his neck. He rolled into her supporting leg, knocking her off balance. She fell to the floor, chipping her elbow painfully on the base of a potted plant.

She grabbed for the gun, but Lang, gasping, savagely kicked her in the thigh. Knocked away from the weapon, she cried out.

Lang clamored to his elbows and knees, clutching his damaged throat. His voice raw, horse. "You bitch!"

Grayson lunged for the gun again. Lang caught her by the ankle and pulled her back. The gun spun out of her reach.

She twisted and kicked Lang in the forehead. That dislodged his hold on her ankle. She kicked at him again. Her heel smashed into his nose, breaking it. He howled. Free of his hold, Grayson crawled like a madwoman toward the gun. She grabbed it and rolled onto her back, firing at where Lang had been, but he was gone.

Overwhelmed by the hostages, the guards had been subdued and then beaten to death. The crowds were moving away from them, leaving the battered bodies to bleed into the carpet while they hugged and consoled those still alive. Others began the grim task of tending to the wounded and the dead.

Grayson sat up, angry, sore, and breathless. "Where'd he go? Where is Lang?"

Garcia stood protectively over a prone Kingsley face-down in the carpet. He pointed toward the kitchen area. "That way. There must be a way out the back."

Grayson kicked off her heels and stood up, her body quivering from exertion and adrenaline, but already achy. She ran for the kitchen in her stocking feet.

Behind her, Kingsley called out, "Liz. Don't!"

She glanced back to see him up on his knees, being helped to his feet by Garcia.

She didn't respond except to keep running. And she didn't stop. Not even as she heard explosions behind her and overhead in Ops. More determined than ever, she ran.

Lang was her fault, an evil of her creation. She was responsible for him, and she'd put a stop to him. One way or the other.

CHAPTER FORTY-EIGHT

McMURPHY AND LARSON LEFT the Njord's Den first. They charged down the corridor to an elevator that would take them up to the next level. From there, Larson told him, it was only a short distance to Ops.

He quizzed her along the way about the layout of the control room. How many people, means of egress in and out of the room, etc. She stood off to one side at his insistence as he hit the elevator call button. He'd picked up one of the machine pistols from the hostiles they'd encountered in the moon pool. Now McMurphy aimed it at the closed elevator doors. Waiting for it to open.

When it did, he let out a held breath. The elevator car arrived unoccupied.

Inside, he hit the button for level two.

"I guess this wasn't what you had in mind for the day's events."

"I'll say," Larson agreed. "You, Brice, and that woman. You do this sort of thing all the time?"

McMurphy watched the numbers over the door light up and then go out as the elevator rose smoothly. "I wouldn't say all the time. But... we answer the call is the best way to put it."

"And you all work for Secretary Grayson?"

"Yes," he admitted. "But we're not supposed to say that."

"I appreciate your candor. Will the Secretary disavow any knowledge of your actions if she finds out you told me?"

He laughed at the old *Mission: Impossible* reference. "Nothing that dramatic, I assure you."

The elevator pinged.

He ushered her as close to the interior wall as she could get, while he crouched and again aimed the machine pistol at the door, waiting for it to open.

A second passed.

It opened onto an empty corridor.

He signaled for her to stay put before stepping out, then nodded to her. "So far, so good."

"Only authorized personnel can gain access to Ops," she said, explaining Lang's apparent lapse in security. "Posting guards out here would be a waste of manpower for a group so lightly staffed as he seems to be."

She led McMurphy down the curved corridor, keeping them close to the wall, avoiding the numerous cameras. She stopped him a half dozen feet from Ops.

"How are your people trained to react in emergency situations like this?" he asked.

"They'll drop to the floor at their workstations, use the rows of computer consoles as barriers, then look to their supervisors for guidance."

He nodded. That was all he needed to know.

"I can open the door from that access panel," she said. "But we'll be in full view of a camera."

"How long will it take you?"

"Two, three seconds. It's a palm scan and then a five-digit code."

He didn't see any way around it. "We'll have to risk it." He pulled out two flash-bang grenades. "Once the door's open, it won't matter what they see on the surveillance system."

Larson eyed the grenades with concern.

McMurphy noticed. "These are nonlethal. Big noise, bright light."

She nodded and crossed the corridor to the access panel. Her palmprint over the black square revealed a lighted ten-digit keypad. She punched in five numbers and tapped a green checkmark.

Before she'd finished keying in the code, McMurphy charged at her from his hiding spot.

As the door slid open. He tossed the grenades.

One pitch, a perfectly executed curve. The grenade sailed through the opening door before breaking down and to the left. The other, tossed like a screwball, arced right. The flash-bangs clanged, hitting the floor then rolled before they exploded with a bang and a blinding white light.

McMurphy slipped the machine pistol down his arm and charged into the room, now full of screaming, frightened people.

Here was the hard part. Telling the good guys from the bad guys. One thing that helped was knowing the bad guys were probably the ones with the guns.

He crossed the threshold and spun left. A tall dark-skinned man in white coveralls twisted to greet him with a machine pistol in hand. McMurphy fired off a two-round burst. A red splotch bloomed across the chest of the white coveralls. The gunman dropped his weapon and fell to the floor.

McMurphy twisted to the right.

There he confronted a man wearing dark blue maintenance coveralls. Like the first one, he had a machine pistol in hand and started to fire. His rake of automatic fire went high and wide. McMurphy's didn't. The rapid-fired shooting echoed in the air. The man fell back against the wall and slid to the floor, leaving behind a thick, red streak of blood on the console.

McMurphy moved into the room, squinting through the thin veil of smoke that didn't completely fill the room, but made it hazy, considerably reducing his visibility. He stayed low, below the height of the consoles. When he reached the walkway along the right side, a woman popped up with her hands raised.

"Don't shoot!"

McMurphy kept a watchful eye on her, looking for any hostile movements.

"Move to the aisle where I can see you."

The woman sidestepped to the aisle. Later he would learn her name was Sasha Wilcox.

"Keep your hands where I can see them," he ordered.

She did. Until another man popped up like a game of whack-a-mole. McMurphy hesitated, waited a millisecond too long before he saw the gun coming up and firing. A bullet skimmed his shoulder, ripping through the thick neoprene wetsuit. It burned a hot path through his skin but ultimately was barely a flesh wound.

McMurphy returned fire, ruining the man's face with three bullets before the gunman collapsed.

In his peripheral vision, he caught sight of the woman dropping her hands as she reached behind her back. She came out with a pistol and fired.

McMurphy dove to the floor, firing two rounds into the woman's gut.

She dropped the gun and clutched her stomach. Blood pumped through her entwined fingers. Her legs gave out and she sank into a crumpled pile on the floor.

Breathing heavily, in the silence that followed, McMurphy called out, "Anyone else want a piece of this?"

He waited. No answer.

"Anyone?"

Still, no one answered.

McMurphy cautiously climbed to his feet to see three men standing with their hands interlocked behind their heads. Under his breath, he said, "Good boys."

Larson rushed into the room as people started to pick themselves up off the floor, shaken and scared. The three surrendering combatants were gathered together and circled by Tiamat Bluff employees. They glared at their former captors. Now unarmed, they were to keep at bay.

Larson came over to McMurphy. "You've been shot."

She picked at the neoprene hole, examining the wound.

"It's nothing. A scratch."

"That was incredible."

McMurphy deflected. "Let's just hope Brice makes out as well."

BANNON KNEW THE WAY to Neptune's Den. He ran at a fast clip with Tara close beside him. Earlier, she had started to express her concerns over the potential Leviathan conspiracy she and Kayla had uncovered. First brought to light by O'Shea and later mentioned by Sucre, his dying word. Bannon told her they'd need to table that conversation until after POTUS, Grayson, and the others were safe.

And Chase Lang was dealt with once and for all, he added silently.

Bannon wasn't a blood-thirsty man by nature, he didn't think. But Lang, this whole operation, the execution of Kate Holloway… it had gone beyond the pale.

They reached Neptune's Den.

The doors were closed and locked.

Bannon and Tara had no access code to get through them. With a wry smile, he thought. I've got something better.

He and Tara stood back. They each pulled a pin from the hand grenades McMurphy had given him.

They rolled them across the corridor floor toward the door. The devices wobbled awkwardly because of the lug and fuse on top. And while they'd never bowl a three-hundred game with the little explosive devices, they only needed to get close.

The munitions reached the door and exploded.

The twin blasts knocked the doors inward, off their tracks.

He and Tara raced across the corridor and shouldered their way into Neptune's Den.

Bent and twisted, the doors bounced inward.

He and Tara clamored over them and stumbled to a stop, stunned by what greeted them.

There were two dead men in security uniforms on the floor. One was shot dead. The other appeared to have been bludgeoned to death. Along with them were two dead civilians.

The surviving hostages, bloodied and disheveled, sat on the cushioned seats, being attended to by others.

Bannon saw no living hostiles. And no Lang.

If he was reading the room right, in his absence, the hostages had raised up, fought back, and freed themselves. His gaze fell on President Kingsley. Alive and in reasonably good appearance considering what he'd been through. The pilot, Garcia, sat in the booth beside him.

Tara moved away from the doors, moved deeper into Neptune's Den, desperate to find an enemy to fight. She stopped and stared down at a body on the ground. A woman. She slid her machine pistol up onto her shoulder and knelt.

When Bannon stepped up beside her, she asked, "Is this Agent Holloway?"

But it was Kingsley, joining them, who said, "Yes. She gave her life for her country. A true American hero."

Tara's throat tightened. "Her husband. Their children. Damn."

Bannon gave Holloway a respectful minute. It was all he could afford. There would be time for proper mourning later. He looked around. "Lang. Where is he?"

Kingsley pointed at the kitchen area. "He ran off. That way."

"And where's Secretary Grayson?"

"She… she went after him."

CHAPTER FORTY-NINE

BEHIND THE REAR PARTITION, Lang had disappeared through what was a full-service, commercial-grade kitchen, filled with stainless steel counters, pots and pans, and black cast iron cooktops, industrial size refrigeration units, and stoves. Grayson ran past all that, having seen the door at the far end of the room swinging closed.

Lang wasn't interested in hiding. His focus was on escaping.

It had been years since she was in the field, but as she reached the door, catching it before it swung shut, old instincts kicked in. She pushed through the door and swept the stairwell with her pistol. Her muscle memory guided her movements. Comfortably. Instinctively. She cleared the stairwell and ran stocking footed down to the next level as if no time had passed at all since her last mission.

Lang had forsaken stealth for speed. She could hear his boots on the stairs.

She followed quickly downward, stealing an occasional glance over the railing. Lang reached the bottom level, five flights of stairs, and ran through the door without a second look back. No doubt confident no one was after him.

Grayson had gained on him and reached the exit door seconds later.

She pulled it open, and with the pistol in a two-handed grip, let the door fall against her back as she swung her weapon from right to left. The lowest level of the facility. The lights in this section of corridor were off but for a faint radiant glow of pale orange-red lambent light from floor-embedded emergency lights.

Her eyes teared. She put the back of her hand against her nose to ward off an awful stench. Faintly of cabbage and something coppery and acrid. A smell as familiar to an old field agent as it was disgusting. Death. Violent, burning death.

Cautiously, she moved forward.

She found Lang climbing over a pair of buckled and wrecked metal doors. They were scorched black and coated in a white fire-retardant film. The smell of a burnt accelerant still heavy in the air. A few small fires still burning.

"Chase! Stop!"

He froze, perhaps surprised to hear she'd followed him. He twisted.

"Back off, Colonel. You've managed to escape my retribution today. Don't push your luck."

He resumed climbing the awkwardly angled doors and scrambled over a dead body. Burned and still smoldering.

"To look over my shoulder for the rest of my life?" she asked. "To wonder and worry about what atrocity you might commit next? Atrocities I'll be responsible for if I let you escape."

He leaped to the other side of the door and faced her.

"Let me escape? Ha. You can't stop me. But yeah, there's a certain sort of delicious satisfaction in the torture you'll endure, constantly wondering if—no—when I'll strike again."

The gun in her hand still trained on him. She pulled the trigger. Her eyes were bleary. The shot was a hair off and Lang ducked to the side. Always an excellent shot, even though her eyesight wasn't what it used to be, she wondered, how had she missed him? Had it been intentional? A last-second flinch as she hoped against hope she could still reason with him, still reach him? Even after all this time. After all this chaos.

He was out of her line of sight, crouched behind the burning door.

"Chase. Chase?"

He popped up suddenly armed with a machine pistol. He fired off a long burst. Tracer bullets lit up the darkened hallway. They pinged off the curved walls, sparked brightly.

Grayson flattened herself against a door. The bend in the corridor provided her with some protection.

When the shooting stopped, and the echo of gunfire faded, she risked another look.

Lang had reached, and now stood, at the open door of the last remaining rescue sub.

She squeezed the trigger of her handgun. Bullets pinged harmlessly off metal walls until the gun clicked dry.

Safely behind the heavy metal hatch, when he'd heard her gun dryfire, Lang stepped back out. He paused long enough to give her a taunting wave. "Like I said. Can't stop me. Until next time, Colonel. When we meet again. *Wadaeaan al 'an.*"

"Goodbye for now."

He was going to get away and she was too far away to stop him.

Behind her a voice. "Liz. Here."

Bannon.

She turned in time to see him toss her a grenade.

She dropped her now useless pistol, caught the hand grenade, and without hesitation threw it at Lang. Her aim was pitch-perfect. The grenade sailed through the open hatch, past him, bounced around inside…

Lang glared into the DSRV. His expression first one of annoyance and then of concern.

The grenade exploded.

The blast blew him cartwheeling out of the hatch opening. He hit the corridor floor several feet away.

Grayson scrambled over the wrecked doors. The metal hot on her stocking feet. The retardant slippery.

Bannon caught up behind her. He grabbed her hand to steady her as she navigated the rumble.

"Careful." His concern was as much about the fact she was weaponless, and Lang might not be dead as it was for her not injuring herself climbing over the wreckage.

He joined her on the other side of the debris. The interior of the mini-sub was aflame. The fire crackling. It brightened the corridor with a dancing yellow luminescence.

Lang laid on his back. His stolen Tiamat Bluff clothes and face were darkened with black soot and burned flesh. His white eyes and twisted burned lips made his face look like a truly wicked Halloween mask.

Bannon aimed his machine pistol at him. His expression made it clear, one false move…

Grayson dropped to her knees.

Lang reached a burnt hand up to her face, patted her skin.

"Chase," she said. "You should have come in. We could've... I could've helped. It didn't have to end this way."

Lang, his voice weak. "You shouldn't have left me, Liz."

His hand moved from her cheek and quickly seized her throat. She gasped and grabbed for his wrist. His skin, his clothes, were hot from the blast. She struggled, pulling at his arm, desperate to break his death grip.

"Chase! No! Please!"

Standing over her, Bannon fired a single bullet into Chase Lang's face.

Lang died instantly.

His limp arm dropped away from her neck as she gasped and let go, jolted back by the sound of the gun going off so close to her. She sat back on the floor and covered her ear. The gunshot's echo rang inside her head. On the verge of tears, she moaned, "No. No. No."

Bannon laid his pistol down and gently urged Grayson to her feet.

"I had no choice." He pulled her into him, hugged her, comforted her. "I know he was your friend. But that person was gone. Has been for a long, long time. That wasn't the man you knew." He indicated the dead body at their feet. "That's not the man you remember."

"No. No, he wasn't." She pushed back from Bannon, sniffled, and wiped her nose with the back of her hand. "But when we... when I abandoned him, we were more than colleagues. More than friends. We were involved, Brice. Engaged to be married and I... I left him in the desert to die."

CHAPTER FIFTY

BANNON RADIOED TARA AND McMurphy, told them he and Grayson were okay, and that Lang was dead. McMurphy confirmed he'd retaken Ops. The facility was once again under Robin Larson's control. Tara informed him that with the help of Trevor Garcia, the submersible pilot and former Cuban Revolutionary Navy man, and a handful of Tiamat employees, they'd tracked down the rest of Lang's men. They'd given up without a fight and were being held in a conference room under armed guard.

While he gave Grayson the time she needed to grieve, and to compose herself, during which she said little, Bannon took a minute to examine Lang's body. He searched his pockets, searching for papers, anything that might be a clue to the greater conspiracy Tara and Kayla believed had orchestrated this whole thing. Hopefully a lead to who Chase Lang had been working for.

He didn't find anything. But neither did he expect to. Chase Lang was too well-trained, too experienced to be that careless, even in death.

About to give up, something did catch Bannon's eye.

He squatted and pulled Lang's charred and torn sleeve up his right arm. On the underside of his wrist, Bannon found a small, bluish-black dragon tattoo. But something about it struck Bannon as curious. It wasn't simply a dragon, but a dragon surrounded by seaweed and waves. More than a sea dragon. Or even a sea monster. It brought to mind one thing: a leviathan.

He stood up, leaving the dead undisturbed.

He gathered Grayson without mentioning the tattoo or Tara's and Kayla's suspicions. There would be time for that later. For now, the two of them silently returned to Neptune's Glen.

Retracing Grayson's steps, they slowly shuffled out from behind the partition separating the kitchen from the restaurant's seating area. Bannon had his arm around Grayson's shoulders and was holding her hand. It was ice cold. He heard the chatter of those still there, felt the excited euphoria the hostages experienced having just been freed, primarily by their own hands. The place was abuzz with activity, and not just by Tiamat Bluff survivors.

The wounded were either seated at booths and tables around the restaurant or laid on makeshift stretchers. Those still alive were being attended to by Coast Guard medics.

How had they arrived so quickly? Bannon wondered.

Among the new arrivals, Bannon noticed Captain Tolliver in the corner conversing with McMurphy and Larson. Tara stood over where Kate Holloway's body lay, now mercifully covered with a blue sheet.

Bannon would later learn the *USCGC Gordon Lewis*, a three-hundred-seventy-eight-foot Hamilton-class cutter, had joined the *Putnam* on the surface above them. She brought with her two mystic-class DSRVs. Subs capable of accommodating twenty-four personnel each. The rescue subs were being used to ferry guardsmen down and transport injured hostages and prisoner's topside to the two cutters.

Medics hovered over Kingsley, who was physically battered but unhurt. Intently watching over him were a fresh cadre of Secret Service agents, including Franklin Gregg.

He was the first to see Bannon and Grayson emerge from the kitchen. "Madam Secretary!"

The whole place stopped and stared. Kingsley came to his feet, waving away a medic but accepting Gregg's hold on his elbow, steadying him. He beamed. "Liz!"

McMurphy rushed across the room with Tolliver and Larson in tow. Tara came over as well, surrounding Bannon and Grayson. All of them happy and curious as to their ordeal below.

McMurphy slapped him on the back with a big grin. "Glad you made it."

Tolliver took his hand and shook it. "Bang-up job, Brice. Bang-up."

"Thanks to you and your little gifts, Captain."

"Just glad I could lend a hand."

Grayson disengaged her arm from Bannon's, giving him a brave but weak smile. She moved off toward Kingsley.

Larson gave Bannon a kiss on his cheek. "I'm so glad you're okay."

"Thanks to you, Doctor." Bannon looked at Tolliver, McMurphy, and Tara. "Thanks to all of you." He glanced across the room to where Kingsley and Grayson embraced in a hug. "We saved a lot of lives today."

Tara looked at the bodies still on the floor, draped in blue sheets. Her gaze fell lastly on Kate Holloway. "And lost too many."

Quietly, respectfully, Bannon agreed. "Yes, we did." He reached out and squeezed her arm. Then he turned to Tolliver. "Bob, can I assume you've got this? I'd like to get my people—"

Tolliver raised his hand, stopping him. "Say no more, Commander. We've got this. You heroes go get some rest. You've earned it."

"No offense, Doctor Larson," Bannon said, reaching out to shake her hand. "But I've had enough of Tiamat Bluff for the time being."

"None taken," she said. "Under the circumstances, I could use a break from here myself."

To Tara and McMurphy, Bannon said, "Ready?"

They nodded in silent agreement. He swept an arm toward the doors cleared away from the opening that led out of Neptune's Glen. McMurphy and Tara moved in that direction. Bannon caught Grayson's eye and nodded. She forced another smile and nodded back.

To his people, Bannon said, "Let's go home."

CHAPTER FIFTY-ONE

THREE DAYS LATER, THE Keel Haul was closed to the public. Bannon hung a sign on the door that read: closed for a private gathering. The adverse effect on business would be minimal. A seaside bar operating in January in New Hampshire wasn't exactly the hottest of hot spots.

As for this event, it was part memorial repast for those who'd died at the Siege of Tiamat Bluff—as the media had dubbed it—and part celebration for the heroic efforts of so many who saved the President and everyone else targeted for death by Sucre and Lang.

Bannon and the others had spent the last three days in Boston, then Washington, D.C. Their time spent in debriefs with just about every alphabet soup agency known to exist and dragged before enough congressional subcommittees to give them their fill of government, politics, and politicians for a long time to come.

Prior to, Bannon had instructed his team to minimize any mention of the potential conspiracy Tara and Kayla had dug up. The Leviathan thing, as McMurphy called it. During the debriefs, they focused their testimonies strictly on the context of POTUS' kidnapping and the events directly involved with that singular event.

Bannon knew this wasn't the end. It was the beginning.

Eventually, they'd have to deal with Leviathan, but for now, and until they could figure out who could or couldn't be trusted, they would keep what they knew to themselves. They would watch and listen and wait. And be ready to take action when the time came.

But for now, their time was spent honoring the Navy SEALs killed in action. Then it was on to Falls Church. There, they attended the funeral of Agent Kate Holloway, a fallen American hero.

Tara found the service particularly difficult despite having never met Kate Holloway in life. It had been the traumatic rescue of the woman's family that made the event especially hard. Feeling as if she'd let the family down by not saving the agent's life, though Holloway had been killed before Tara had even reached Tiamat Bluff.

The dark Egyptian beauty was one of the toughest, bravest, strongest people Bannon had ever known. She would face a battalion of enemy combatants with only her haladie in hand and never hesitate. But seeing Roger and the girls, Kacey and Karley. The girls were dressed in black. Their blond hair pulled back in severe ponytails—like their mother when she was on duty—she told Bannon she had to leave, ready to flee the cemetery.

"How can I face them? What the girls saw... how they saw me that day."

"We do it together." Bannon took her by the hand. Together, they approached Roger Holloway. Tara introduced Bannon. The men shook hands.

"Thank you for believing in my wife, Commander Bannon," he said. "I heard what the… they put her through, the impossible position they put her in. And I've been told, through it all, you never bought into it. Thank you for that." He turned to Tara. "My family. We owe you our lives. Thank you."

The girls moved from their father's side and wrapped their arms around Tara's legs, hugging her tightly. Tears flowed from her green eyes as she got down on her knees and hugged them back.

"I am so, so very sorry," she said.

BACK AT THE KEEL Haul, from behind the bar, Bannon raised a mug of beer. "To Kate Holloway."

He looked out over a small sea of raised glasses, grateful for every single person in the room.

McMurphy sat in his usual spot at the end of the bar, deep in conversation with Robin Larson.

Tara, on the customer's side of the bar for a change, sat next to Captain Floyd, of all people.

"Glad you didn't die, toots. Ain't got it in me to train yet another floozie behind the bar."

Tara smiled.

They clinked glasses and silently sipped their drinks.

Chief Singleton stood speaking with Kayla, Grayson, and Captain Tolliver.

Elizabeth Grayson excused herself and drifted over to the bar. She ordered one more drink for the road. Agent Wheeler would serve as her designated driver. "I'm heading back to Washington tonight. Tom's waiting for me outside."

"You okay?" Bannon asked.

She nodded and forced a smile. "I will be."

"None of this is your fault," Bannon said. "It's all on Lang."

"Isn't it?"

"You were following orders."

"Said every Nazi soldier ever."

"You're being too hard on yourself, Liz. Lang was dealt a crappy hand. No doubt about it, but how he played it, that was up to him."

"Easy for us to say. We didn't go through what he did." She forced another smile as she pushed away from the bar. "We'll have to agree to disagree on this one, Brice."

Bannon changed the subject. "Have you decided what you're going to do about Kingsley's offer?"

"I have."

"Gonna tell me?"

This time, her smile was genuine. "After I tell him."

Bannon returned the smile. "Way to build suspense."

"Keeping secrets. It's what a good spy does." She reached across the bar and grasped his hand. The warmth had returned to her skin. "Thank you for what you did down there. All of it."

"Just doing my job."

"For once, graciously accept the gratitude of a grateful nation, a grateful President. And a very grateful old woman who is standing here with you, because of you."

Bannon raised a glass.

They toasted, and she finished her drink. "An old biddy who's still sore as hell three days later."

She lowered her voice. "As for that other thing." The night before, Bannon had brought her up to speed on everything they knew—which wasn't much—about Leviathan, including the tattoo he'd found on Chase Lang's wrist. "Look into it, but discreetly. Not that it needs to be said, but report only to me."

"As always." Bannon nodded. "Safe travels, General."

Once she left, Bannon refilled McMurphy's empty beer mug.

"What was that all about?" the big Irishman asked.

"Nothing we need to worry about just yet." To Larson, he said, "Can I get you another?"

"No. I don't think so. John and I have to get going."

Bannon looked at McMurphy. He raised an eyebrow. "John?"

McMurphy's ruddy complexion deepened three shades of red. Larson noticed and smiled.

"Where might you and *John* be going?" Bannon said. "If I may ask?"

McMurphy downed the last of his beer and stood up. "I promised to help Robin and her team begin repairs on Tiamat Bluff. I figured it's the least I could do, considering the mess we made of it down there."

"All for a good cause," Larson said, hooking her arm in the crook of McMurphy's arm.

"Yes," Bannon said. "It's the least you can do."

"Anything comes up in the meantime," McMurphy said. "You know how to reach me."

"I do." Bannon smiled. "Have a good time."

"It's work," McMurphy said. "Strictly work."

Bannon smiled. "I'm sure it will be."

As they started to leave, Larson stopped and turned. "Oh, I almost forgot."

She dug around in her shoulder bag as Kayla, Tara, and some of the others drifted over to say their goodbyes. She rummaged around until she extracted an item from her bag and handed it to Bannon. It was a rather large snow globe, but rather than containing snow, the clear water inside had tiny gold starfish and other aquatic animals floating around as Bannon shook it.

Also, there was a replica of Tiamat Bluff, built into the sloping ocean grade of Georges Bank, as it was in real life. The craftsmanship was superb, down to the tiny details of small rectangular lights and a glowing replica of the domed park on top of Tiamat Bluff.

"It's from our gift shop," she said.

Bannon held the globe out, noticing a star and long crack in the glass shell. "Not that I'm complaining, but it's damaged."

"Yes. I thought that rather appropriate, actually."

Bannon nodded. "Yeah. Me, too. Thank you."

He set the sea globe on the shelf over the register, then watched them head out into the night. A gentle snow had started to fall. The flakes fluttered softly in the outside streetlamp lights. Once the door closed, Bannon turned to those who remained. "Captain, I believe I owe you a drink."

"You don't," Tolliver said. "But I'll graciously accept one anyway."

"With my gratitude, name your poison."

The Coast Guard captain rattled the almost empty tumbler he held with a little bit of ice left. "Another of these would work just fine."

Bannon went to work on making the gin and tonic. As he busied himself behind the bar, he called out to Singleton. "Ah, Chief. I've noticed

I'm running a little low on Nut Brown Ale since I was here last. Anything we need to discuss? Like maybe starting a tab."

Singleton furrowed his forehead. "Tab?" He pointed at Tara. "She said, 'Have whatever you like. It's on the house.'"

"She don't own the joint," Bannon said it with a smile on his face, making it clear he was giving the old cop a hard time. "But I've learned long ago, whatever she says, goes."

Relieved, Singleton settled onto a barstool. "In that case, I'll take another one."

EPILOGUE

CIA Headquarters
Langley, Virginia

THE FOLLOWING MORNING, ELIZABETH Grayson stood facing the CIA's Memorial Wall.

The white Alabama marble gleamed in its brightness. Five rows of stars carved into the marble represented the men and women of the CIA who'd made the ultimate sacrifice for the Agency and their country. Framing the display are the United States stars and stripes and a flag bearing the CIA seal. Under the stars, in a steel frame jutting out from the wall and encased in thick glass, is the Book of Honor, listing by name some, but not all, of the fallen agents. The unnamed stars remained secret, even in death.

One of those unnamed stars belonged to Chase Edwards. That would only be the case until the next CIA employee was killed in action. Then Edwards would be removed. Dishonored. Disavowed.

Elizabeth Grayson didn't know when that would be or who, but she wasn't naive enough to think that it would never happen. Wars, cold and otherwise, were an ongoing reality in the world. And in war, good people died.

She thought Chase Edwards had been one of those people. At one time, he had been. But no longer. When the next agent fell, the last honorable vestige of Chase Edwards would fall, too.

She bore that responsibility no matter how many others said she didn't. Her greatest military regret had become an even worse cross to bear than ever before.

She hoped she could live with it.

David Kingsley came up behind her. His footsteps whispered over the polished lobby floor. Alone, except for the two Secret Service agents watching but well out of earshot, she said, "Hello, David."

"I was told I'd find you here."

She'd last seen him at Agent Holloway's funeral service. He'd given the eulogy. It had been quite moving. "You're looking good, David."

And it was true. Hair spray held his white hair in place. His skin had regained its color and complexion. He smiled, flashing his trademark sparkling white teeth, as bright as a toothpaste ad. Up close, she could see the concealer that had been applied to the worst of his bruises. The black and blue color had faded to an ugly eggplant color underneath.

"I was about to say the same of you."

She might have succeeded in putting herself together enough to be presentable, but she was achy, sore, and had slept poorly over the last few nights. Her sleep interrupted by horrific nightmares. All of it left her drained and tired. And that said nothing about the guilt and crushing weight of responsibility she felt. The last three days—especially during her debriefings—her self-doubt mounted. She felt like it would break her.

But now was the time to put things right.

"I'm glad you're here, actually." She glanced behind them, ensuring his Secret Service detail remained out of eavesdropping range. "I wanted to tell you, as much as it means to me, I have to decline your offer to take the VP job. Respectfully, sir. I believe I can better serve you and the country by doing what I do now. If, of course, you'll still have me."

Kingsley stood with his hands clasped behind his back, staring at the wall. He gently rocked on the balls of his feet. "I expected you might say that. And the truth is, I came here to withdraw that offer. Had you not declined. After seeing you over these last few days. Down there," he explained, "I realized having you as my Veep would be a terrible waste of your ability and talents, not to mention an unconscionable disservice to a country that needs you."

"Thank you for understanding, sir. There is something else we need to discuss."

His interest piqued, Kingsley said, "That is?"

Grayson leaned forward. "The person or persons responsible for all this."

"Chase Lang? What about him?"

"Not him. You heard Chase—he was a hired gun. He had manipulated the circumstances to serve his own agenda. But make no mistake. He was working for someone else. My team's discovered evidence of a greater threat."

"What sort of threat?"

"A conspiracy. A group working at some as yet unknown purpose. But one I'm sure isn't in this country's best interest."

"Who?" Kingsley got angry.

"I can't answer that. Yet. All I can say for sure is General Javier Aguirre is an important part of it. There are those in the political spectrum that believe we need to have a more... positive working relationship with Aguirre than you've allowed."

"Because of our dependence on his damn uranium." Kingsley shook his head in disgust. "Despite the man being a brutal mass murderer and butcher."

"Money and power trump moral compasses far too easily," Grayson said.

"Too true, unfortunately."

"We don't know how big or how deep into the halls of government this might go. How international it might be. All we've got to go on is a single reference. The name Leviathan."

"What does it mean?"

"We don't know, sir."

"Find out. Dig all the way to the bottom of this. No stone left unturned, and Liz... "

"Yes, sir?"

"Stop it before anyone else gets hurt."

"We're already on it."

"Bannon and his team?" Kingsley guessed.

"Yes, sir," Grayson said.

"Excellent. Tell me what you need, and it's yours."

"For now, I think it best we let them do their work without interference. Keep it strictly clandestine. Off the books. Need to know, just you and I, sir. Until Brice has more to tell us."

"Agreed. Keep me apprised."

"There's one more thing," she said. "Ethan Wright? Are you still considering removing him from the ticket?"

"In light of recent events, I don't think that would even be possible. He's publicly credited with saving my—our—lives." Part of the public spin put out to keep the role Bannon and his people played in the shadows. "Rather poor taste to fire the man after that, don't you think?"

Grayson agreed.

One of the Secret Service agents cleared his throat and approached. "Excuse me, sir. Vice-President Wright is here, requesting a word."

In unison, Kingsley and Grayson turned. Ethan Wright stood beside the other Secret Service agent, a discreet distance away. He carried several file folders by his side.

Kingsley summoned him over. "Morning, Ethan."

"Good morning, Mr. President." He nodded toward Grayson. "Elizabeth. How are you? After your horrible ordeal?"

Wright and Grayson exchanged a polite hug. She'd known and worked with Wright over the years during her military career. "I'm fine, thank you, Ethan. Thanks to you and the work you did up here."

"I'm just relieved everyone's all right."

"Not everyone," Kingsley reminded him. He'd spent a good part of the last three days writing condolence letters, meeting with family members and attending memorial services for the American civilians killed at Tiamat Bluff.

"Of course, sir, I meant present company only."

Kingsley clasped his shoulder. "I know. What can I do for you, Ethan?"

Wright handed over the files he carried.

"The after-action reports you requested, including the debriefs from DoD, Secret Service, the FBI. Justice." He nodded toward Grayson. "Homeland Security and Coast Guard. I've taken the liberty of adding my recommendations on who should be part of the internal investigation to tease out what happened and how we can prevent it from happening going forward."

Kingsley accepted the files. "Thank you, Ethan." He extended his hand to shake. "I believe we've got time scheduled to get together later in the day. To talk. At length."

"Looking forward to it, sir."

They shook hands. Wright again nodded to Grayson. "Elizabeth."

He backed away and retreated past the two stoic secret service agents.

As he crossed the rotunda, Vice-President Ethan Forester Wright tugged at the sleeves of his dress shirt where they'd ridden up under his suit jacket. The crisp white cuff again covered the small, bluish-black tattoo on the inside of his wrist. A sea dragon surrounded by seaweed and waves. But not simply a sea dragon. A winged sea monster.

A raising Leviathan!

Thank you for purchasing this book. We hope you enjoyed it.

If you'd like to stay informed about new releases, special events, and exclusive content only available to subscribers, sign up to get David DeLee's newsletter

https://www.subscribepage.com/daviddelee

BY DAVID DELEE

Grace deHaviland Bounty Hunter series
Fatal Destiny
Pin Money
With Intent to Deceive
Takedown
Stare at the Moon
Too Far

Brice Bannon Seacoast Adventures
Facing the Storm
The Oceanic Princess
Strike of the Stingray
The Yakuza Gambit
Siege at Tiamat Bluff
Crimson Storm

Nick Lafferty Crime Thrillers
Crystal White
Out of the Game
Cold Cases

Flynn & Levy Police Thrillers
Moral Misconduct
While the City Burns
Between Truth and Lies

ABOUT THE AUTHOR

David DeLee is the author of the Grace deHaviland Bounty Hunter series, including the novels *Fatal Destiny, Pin Money, With Intent to Deceive, Takedown.* And *Too Far*. David's also written many short stories featuring Grace, most notably *Bling, Bling*, which appeared in the anthology *The Rich and the Dead* edited by Nelson DeMille.

David's other work includes the novel *Crystal White,* which SUSPENSE MAGAZINE called "…a dark portrayal of the evil that men—and women—can do." The second novel in the Nick Lafferty thriller series, *Out of The Game*, and *Moral Misconduct,* his Flynn & Levy police procedurals, and his Brice Bannon Seacoast Adventures.

A member of the Mystery Writers of America and the International Thriller Writers organization and a former licensed private investigator, David also holds a Master's Degree in Criminal Justice. He makes his home in New Hampshire.

For more information, check out David's website:
www.daviddelee-author.co

www.ingramcontent.com/pod-product-compliance
Lightning Source LLC
Chambersburg PA
CBHW072258020726
47501CB00002B/307